The Pitman's Daughter

OTHER BOOKS BY MARJORIE DELUCA:

The Savage Instinct
Lilah
A Proper Lady

FOR YOUNG ADULTS:

The Forever Ones
The Parasites
Chasing A Thrill
Doll's Eyes and Other Stories

The Pitman's Daughter

Marjorie DeLuca

The Pitman's Daughter
Copyright © 2013 by Marjorie DeLuca

All Rights Reserved. No part of this book may be reproduced in any form or by any electronic or mechanical means, including information storage and retrieval systems, without written permission from the publisher or author, except in the case of a reviewer, who may quote brief passages embodied in critical articles or in a review.

This is a work of fiction. Any similarity to persons living or dead is coincidental and not intended by the author.

Book design by Maureen Cutajar
www.gopublished.com

Cover Photographs:
Back Street Hetton: Image Copyright M. McDonald.
Mine: Image Copyright Hayley Green.
The Smithy: Image Copyright Alexander P Kapp.

These works are licensed under the Creative Commons Attribution-Share Alike 2.0 Generic License. http://creativecommons.org/licenses/by-sa/2.0/ or Creative Commons, 171 Second Street, Suite 300, San Francisco, California, 94105, USA.

ISBN-13: 978-1492162063

To Bob and Betty and to Fausto, Mike and Laura

With memory set smarting like a reopened wound, a man's past is not simply a dead history, an outworn preparation of the present: it is not a repented error shaken loose from the life: it is a still quivering part of himself, bringing shudders and bitter flavors and the tinglings of a merited shame.

—George Eliot

1988

1

They put her house into a museum.

Pulled down the whole of Crag Street, brick by brick, wall by wall, coal shed by coal shed. Carted it miles across Durham County and built it up again. Preserving the miners' heritage, they said. Saving a little piece of their past for posterity. Pay eight pounds a head but you'll never see the North East of England as it really was. Knee deep in coal dust, its sons breaking their backs and blackening their lungs in the foul underground tunnels of the coalmines.

When Rita held the invitation in her hand she felt the pull of the street, though she hadn't set foot on it in years. She'd travelled four thousand miles to Vancouver to escape it, and now invisible hands from the past summoned her back to the north-east of England, where they would unveil her childhood home in a new outdoor museum.

Should she go? Did she really give a damn about a row of ramshackle hovels? Not her, she told herself. Not Rita Hawkins, named by her dotty mam after Rita Hayworth. Rita the spoiled bairn that grew into the good-time girl. The street gossips used to call her *Lady Muck*. Twenty-five years ago when the morning sun crept over the pit heap at the top of the street, she'd stumble out of strange men's cars at daybreak, with tousled hair and wrinkled clothes. "Brazen madam," the neighbours whispered through lace curtains.

In 1959 when she was fourteen, her grandma told her, "Marry a miner. It was good enough for your mother and it's good enough for you."

"Like hell I will!" Rita said. Not for her a lifetime of swollen bellies, a squad of snot-nosed children running barefoot in the dirt and a black eye every time she looked at her man the wrong way. That's what Maggie endured for twenty five years.

Before she could change her mind, she picked up the phone and booked the flight, her hand trembling as she took down the details. She would go. Rita, the pitman's daughter, who'd clawed her way over all obstacles, triumphed in the business world and was now set to return in style and watch *him* officially open the museum. *Him*. George Nelson, legendary union leader, respected and revered by all members past, present and future. George, the hero who'd climbed out of the coal mine, wiped every last speck of dust from the soles of his shoes, then buggered off into the sunset. As the most honoured guest he'd make a polite speech, cut the ribbon and declare the museum officially open.

Now, after a grueling transatlantic flight, she stood at King's Cross Station, woozy and jet-lagged, surrounded by suitcases. A lot had changed in a decade. Crowds were bigger and clothes greyer – not a canary yellow leisure suit or Hawaiian shirt in sight.

She opened her tan carry-on bag to check that the invitation was still in the front pocket, then headed towards the platform, her mind wandering again. She and George had both wanted out of Crag Street. He flew out on the wings of his high-minded ideals but she used good, hard cash. Made more money than *he'd* ever see in a month of Sundays. Enough to keep her in mink coats and Pimms for the rest of her life. She kept them *all* talking but she still looked after her Mam and Dad, even though her Da told her "yer ower big for yer byuts"[1] and swore he wouldn't take a penny from a 'painted whore.' But he ate his words in the end when she got the business going.

---

[1] too arrogant

On the journey north she pressed her cheek against the window of the first-class carriage. Cool glass streaked with mud. Fields swished by. Dry, grass shimmering in a southern heat wave. She longed for a tall glass of iced water – the type produced promptly by trim waiters in spotless Vancouver restaurants. Her head throbbed and she drifted into restless sleep as the train rushed on past villages, churches, sheep in fields, and dusty stations filled with faceless people sipping tea in anonymous waiting rooms.

Later she woke with hot tears streaming down her cheeks. Failure seemed inescapable now. A grinding heel on tender skin. Everything in her life had been a poor imitation, her marriage a pale and drab excuse for a relationship. No children, no joy, lots of money and a few laughs. At forty-three years old passion was buried somewhere deep in her past – until lately. Little pieces of it had sprouted, bursting like vines into her night times, filling her dreams with fragments of old stories that played themselves over and over until she woke wild-eyed and breathless in the gilded suites of anonymous hotels in Chicago, Toronto or Seattle.

In her dreams it was always night on Crag Street. Like the old days when the street lamps shone through her bedroom curtains dappling the wall with white flakes of light. The moon silvered her painted face as she dabbed cheap perfume on her wrists. Then leaning against the windowsill, she lit an untipped cigarette. The thrill of anticipation felt like fingers stroking her thighs as she waited for the swish of car tires through sooty puddles and the possibility of another man who'd carry her away.

In her dreams it was always drizzling outside and the smell of coal in the air was like the bite of a newly struck match. The car door creaked open and, as she leaned in towards the man, the smell of leather seats and Brylcreem made her retch. The man turned to look at her but she fell to the wet cobblestones, crying. *He's not George – again.* She sat hugging her knees as the car drove away.

2

The train pulled into Durham station, gliding silently past the castle and the ancient Norman cathedral. With its ghostly stone turrets illuminated by grey-blue floodlights, the cathedral appeared other-worldly, projected onto the black backdrop of night sky. A world away from Camden wine bars and the whole London thing, and two worlds away from Vancouver's twentieth century, pristine luxury.

George always said he loved this place. Said every time he set foot inside the cathedral he sensed the ghosts of St. Cuthbert, the Venerable Bede and all the other early Christians. Rita never had time for religion. Her days were crammed with appointments, meetings, and endless business trips. Her television rental business took almost ten years to build up, but once everyone started buying their own TV's, she and her ex-husband, Mark, moved to Vancouver, diversified the business and moved into video rentals. Lending Hollywood dreams to ease life's monotony. So much for spirituality, but then she never was one to let guilt spoil her fun.

The taxi took the Chester-le-Street exit and drove towards the Langley Castle Hotel. She needed to be pampered and catered to. Somewhere to lick her fresh wounds. Mark, her husband, walked out of her life less than two weeks ago.

The Pitman's Daughter

That day she'd been settling down to read the paper after a last minute Japanese takeout. All the empty cartons were still scattered across the coffee table. They'd eaten in front of the telly as usual with the carved mahogany chopsticks Mark picked up in Chinatown. Some History Channel documentary about the North-West Passage was droning in the background but Rita's mind was at work. *The financial projections for the next fiscal year had to be ready by Friday, so tomorrow's lunch meeting with the accountants would have to be rescheduled, and then there was the tax audit she had to prepare for.* She hadn't noticed how quiet Mark was that night and when she finally glanced across at him, his eyes could have burned holes into the side of her cheek. The rice began to stick in her throat. After the meal he stood up and said, "News is in three minutes," then marched into the bedroom. Precisely three minutes later he burst through the door with two suitcases and set them down in the foyer, his face blank and reproachful like one of those white mime masks.

"*You're just a frigid bitch, – the worst type of Northerner,*" he said, throwing the parting comment at her like he was flinging a live cigarette butt. That was when he tossed the platinum wedding band onto the key table in the foyer and walked out of her life forever.

When the door closed on him she sat for a few minutes as the room spun around, then staggered into the bedroom. There she made a large pile of all the unisex jockey underwear he'd bought her and loaded it in a large box. Looking at the neutral black and white interlock cotton, she was reminded of draughty school gymnasiums and thick-legged gym teachers with faint moustaches, brisk voices and heavily bolstered bosoms.

As soon as the underwear was safely stowed, she took the invitation and slept with it under her pillow, and the childhood images flooded back, bringing the faint but bittersweet scent of coal into her dreams.

The Langley Castle lobby was a cavernous oak-beamed space hung with gilt framed replicas of old masters, and antique wrought iron chandeliers. She stood at the front desk trying to smooth the wrinkles from her beige linen trouser suit. Linen was the worst fabric to wear for travelling. Her mam would say, "*Yer look like a sack of choppy*" and though nobody had ever explained exactly what *choppy* was, she guessed it was something the rag and bone man would pick up from your back door.

The after dinner crowd filtered out of the restaurant in couples or foursomes. No room for a woman alone unless she was looking for action. A fire blazed in the wood-panelled hearth and a piano played below the buzz of conversation. Rita's eyelids felt scratchy and her tongue stuck to the roof of her mouth. She could have murdered a tall gin and tonic in front of that fire.

The porter rolled her suitcases towards the stairs. She told the receptionist she was a restorer of ancient paintings. "Sent to revive a small mural in Durham Cathedral." Lying was a diversion. A new identity would keep reality at bay until she was strong enough to face it head on. She wasn't ready to see anyone yet. Not even her Mam and Dad, now living comfortably in a cosy seaside bungalow thanks to her generosity.

She was saving herself for the big occasion. To make a grand entrance and knock George's socks off. Subtlety had never come naturally to her, but money had gradually refined her tastes in food and clothing and she no longer overheard whispered comments after business meetings like, "She's got a good head on her shoulders but she's common as muck."

The hotel room was sumptuous. Carefully co-ordinated in muted shades of cream, sage and cinnamon. A gold rimmed porcelain vase of white daisies stood on the night table by a four-poster bed draped in floral chintz. Two matching cream towelling bathrobes lay in two soft rolls on the bed. *His and hers – but what the hell, at least she'd get a good night's sleep.*

At the far side of the room a wall of leaded windows looked onto the sweep of hills. It was dusk, the sky lit by a buzz of orange lights lining the High Streets of Sunderland, Belton, Whittington and all those other communities. Each small neighbourhood composed of row upon row of terraced brick houses, punctuated here and there with fish and chip shops, banks, bus stations, pubs, newsagents and hairdressers. The landscape unchanged and so familiar even after ten years away.

Later, inside the white marble glare of the bathroom, she scrutinized her face. Tried to imagine what George would see. *Any old lady chin hairs like her grammar school Chemistry teacher? Nope! She'd tweezed her chin bald. Skin still good – only a few crows' feet that showed if she laughed too much.* Her eyes were a clear green and definitely her main claim to beauty, her brows sharply defined and her hair grazed her shoulders in natural chestnut waves. She'd worn it that way all her life except for a brief period when she dyed it blonde at the age of fifteen. *Everyone was blonde then. Marilyn Monroe, Jayne Mansfield, Diana Dors and Rita Hawkins.*

Turning away from the sudden memory of her platinum phase, she ran the cold tap and splashed icy water on her eyes and forehead. Being home made her dizzy. The smell of Pears Transparent soap or the way a passing car threw a bluish lacework of light across the wall, dredged up a flood of memories. Up till now she'd protected herself with money but now the old childhood demons returned, together with a detailed catalogue of all her stupid decisions. *George had really asked her to stay, hadn't he?*

Back in the room she phoned the front desk, ordered a small Greek salad and a large gin and tonic with three slices of lime. Then she showered, wrapped herself in the comfy bathrobe, and settled down on the bed to watch Coronation Street just as room service appeared in the shape of a red faced boy, uncomfortable in his black bow tie and pin-striped waistcoat. She had to rummage in her handbag for a tip.

Never could organize her handbag. Mark always rolled his eyes when he saw the jumble of gum wrappers, Visa receipts, business cards, pen tops, un-capped lipsticks and crumpled up reminder notes. A five pound note was the smallest change she could find and when she pressed it into the lad's sweaty hand, he gasped and scuttled off down the deserted hallway before she could ask for anything else. *Hey big spender,* she sang as she tilted the glass and heard the comforting clink of ice cubes.

Later, bolstered by the gin, she phoned the front desk again and ordered a taxi to pick her up at dawn. Then with eyes fixed on a portrait of Lord Lambton, and a pillow clutched against her chest, she fell into a deep sleep.

3

Next morning the taxi driver jammed the car into second gear and laboured up Whittington Hill, which at five o'clock was bathed in warm, orange light. At the top, just by the Colliers' Arms, Rita tapped his shoulder and asked him to stop.

The morning wind chilled her ears, so she pulled her sheepskin collar up to her chin and stood on the edge of the crag overhanging Belton valley. It lay below her, spread out like a thousand green tablecloths stitched together neatly with stone or wood fencing; a panorama of smooth, rolling fields spreading from Durham to the south and Hanshaw to the north.

How green and clean it looked now! This land that was once soiled with slag piles and gouged with machines that cut deep shafts into the earth so the coal could be torn out. Now no trace remained of the coal mining days. Grass and greenery had grown over the old scars and those black years were nothing more than a bad dream – two hundred years or more that might never have happened.

For years people had walked from Crag Street to the top of this hill looking for clean air, fresh green grass and flowers – away from the dirt of the colliery houses. All those people she left behind were frozen in time and suspended somewhere deep in her memory. She'd have to see the old street to remember them – maybe then she'd understand how they had shifted the pattern of her own life like ripples change the surface of water.

The smell of cigarettes reminded her that the taxi driver was waiting. He leaned against the car, smoking.

"I need to see Crag Street," she said, pulling her scarf tighter.

He ground the cigarette butt with the heel of his cowboy boots. Must be a country and western fan she thought. He shrugged. "Nowt there anymore, hinny. Just a few bits of brick and stone *strewn ower an ard*[2] field."

But they still drove down the other side of the hill, past the old glass factory, the Six Bells pub, the leek hut, and the sleeping council estate where the milkman had just finished his daily delivery.

Two hundred yards more and she saw it. The skeleton of Crag Street. Humps of rough grey turf among piles of brick and rubble – as if they'd gouged out the houses from the mud and clay. Her head throbbed. *Why wasn't she here when they pulled the houses down?*

She stumbled out of the taxi and found the remains of the curved brick wall that marked the bottom of Crag Street. Touching the rough brick, she willed herself to let it come back, let her see it just as it used to be. Almost at once the pictures came flooding back – a tidal wave of images like an old super 8 home movie.

Brick terraced houses wind upwards in two straight rows towards flaming red sky at the pit end of the street. A giant black wheel cranks the winding gear that sends the cages of men underground. Smoke from the morning coal fires hangs in a greyish haze while down on the street a ragged toddler pulls up her skirt and tries to piddle against the wall like a boy.

Children run barefoot or in dog-eared boots, poking sticks in puddles or following the clank of the milkman's cart. Kettles sing and steam on hobs and mantel clocks tick away the hours. Ella Danby, with hair net covering last week's cold perm, wipes wet hands on her pinny and leans over the wooden gate to gossip until the washing flaps itself dry.

Old man Barker checks the timing of the men on their way to the morning shift. He coughs and checks his pocket watch. "Buggers are late again," he says, shaking his head and spitting out a gob of black phlegm.

---

[2] over an old

Then she sees her own house – Da pottering around his pigeon coops. Gently, gently he strokes their fluttering throats, making kissing noises as they coo – coo softly. Mam throws open the bedroom window and shakes out the clean, white bed sheet into the gritty air.

Toilets were outside here. Netties, they called them. Little brick houses in the back yard with a good supply of newspaper for wiping yourself and it was tough if you had to go when the rain was slashing across your face as you ran from the back door. Next to that was the coal shed. Coal man came around once a week to dump the coal in a big pile ready for shoveling. And the coal dust was everywhere, settling like a black web into every crevice of your insides till you could almost piss black sludge. Coal dust, coal dust everywhere and you could sweep till you were blue in the face but you wouldn't budge a speck of it.

In a sudden panic she worried about the opening ceremony. What would she do when she saw George shaking a thousand hands and exchanging bland pleasantries? It'd all be second nature to him, like taking a bath or blowing his nose. He'd be clean-shaven, his fair hair smooth and groomed. His body unchanged – well clothed in a good navy suit, a stiff white collar chafing his neck – and Rita, she'd clasp her handbag tightly and wear her dignity and money like armour. But first she had to remember. All of it.

She closed her eyes and listened for the whispers of the street gossips. Those tongues that never stopped, and the eyes always watching every move from behind fences, gates and lace curtains. She wondered, when the houses were moved, if the memories were dismantled along with the bricks or maybe they were still there waiting for darkness to fall? She shivered as she sensed them, felt them settle around her like the dry sweep of a moth's wing. The stories shaped from years of telling, the gossip that spawned legends. Invisible threads that bound the street together.

1943

4

Jesse Nelson trudged along the railway tracks under a coral streaked morning sky, clasping the moist hand of her three-year-old son George. He trotted along beside her, his breath blowing out in a cloud. She looked down at the frayed collar of his coat that cradled his glowing curls.

Eeh, she thought, *he's a beauty, this bairn of mine.* With a bloom that would take her breath away when she gazed at him in his moments of play, eager to take in every comely movement. When he looked up at her with those wide, blue eyes and his rosy lips curved into a dimpled smile, she'd sweep him up into her arms, and cover his face with smacking kisses until he screamed with joy.

At mealtimes she'd sit, not touching a bite herself, and watch him play with his food. She'd tap the shell of his soft-boiled egg and say "Chuck, chuck," then spoon the golden yolk into his waiting mouth. Careful not to let his dad see, she saved all the extra morsels for George and she'd often go without.

"Spoiling him like a bit lass." Archie would say if he found out.

He was her last boy. Three of them were already gone. Consumption had torn through her family like a scavenging beast.

What was the song, she wondered – the song that played itself over and over in her head? *Ladybird, ladybird, fly away home. Your house is on fire, your children are gone.* She'd come across it in George's book of nursery rhymes and when she tried to read the words she'd felt tears burning down her cheeks.

Her boots crunched across the gravel embankment – his hobnail ones too big – the toes curled up and hard but the sole still good. But they'd last him another winter.

After a steep climb they reached the top and looked across to Hanshaw where the black monument was framed by the crimson dawn sky that blazed as if the heavens were on fire.

She breathed deeply, drinking in the pure, cold air, and in one swift movement she lifted up the little boy and held him high on her shoulders, then waited for the sun to rise and praise this child, her greatest treasure.

"Breathe deep, my lad, for it's this that will make your lungs grow strong.

"When is the sun coming Mammy?" he called down to her.

"Just wait, flower, and you'll see him peeping up over Hanshaw Hill."

Down there in the valley, row upon row of chimneys spewed out smoke from early morning fires. Down there you breathed the stink of burning coal until the fine black dust coated your lungs.

Well he wouldn't be like the others. Every day she recited this vow. Every day she mourned her lost sons: Jimmy, eighteen, a pitman for six years and courting a lass from Ecclesdon Street. Jimmy the comedian who coughed up blood on his handkerchief and never laughed again.

Then there was Robert, with his carroty hair and pale, freckled skin. Down the pit at twelve and a year later coughing and hawking like an old man: and Peter, a frail thin child of seven who never strayed further than the front step, where he'd sit by her side wrapped in her old blue shawl.

At the end, each one lay there clasping her hand, staring hungrily into her eyes, willing themselves not to lose sight of her. And each time she'd run out into the street sobbing and wailing – falling to her knees and clawing the dirt like a madwoman until the neighbours came and carried her back to the empty house.

No, George wouldn't be like the others. She'd take him up there every day to fill his lungs with clean air and somehow she'd see to it that he'd never go down the mine. Never burrow underground in the filth like some blinded animal, breathing in stinking black air. Her heart blazed with such fury she could have torn wild beasts apart with her bare hands to protect him.

Lost in terrifying thought, she was jolted into the present by small hands tugging at her hair.

"Mammy, mammy – it's here," the voice shrilled.

And she looked up to see the sun as it crept over the horizon, its crimson rays blazing into the sky and bathing the head of her child with gold. Then, grasping her son by the haunches she held him up to the heavens. Her heart swelled as she defied The Almighty, The Creator, Jehovah, The All Powerful, and The All Merciful.

"Enough – I've paid with my blood and tears and three of them are gone. George is my last bairn, my lovely golden lad, and you'll not take this one away from me."

Then she lowered her arms and clasped him tightly, feeling the warmth of the sun creep into her bones.

5

*L*ife had dealt a cruel blow to Ella Danby. As a child her mind had run wild with stories of wizards, princesses and buried treasure. She'd dreamed of adventures in Arabian deserts and tropical islands with dashing cavaliers who recited speeches in posh Shakespearean language. But the reality of her newly married adult state could be summed up in two words: Jack Danby.

Drawn to him by his soft cheeks, clean collars and meek grin, she'd married him after a four-week courtship. Besides she was already twenty-eight and had grey hair at her temples, so a lonely spinsterhood was a poor alternative.

"Yer ower ard ter be choosy," her mam declared as she buttoned Ella's blooming bosom into a tight satin wedding dress, and Ella had to agree.

But it had taken only four days for her to realize what kind of future yawned ahead of her. Jack was a well-meaning man of scant conversation: "Ay lass, nay lass," was all he could muster. But most of the time his face would simply crack open in a wide grin that exposed at least an inch of gums and a quarter inch of gleaming, childish teeth, then his head would nod mechanically in accompaniment. At supper he'd sit at the table with fork and knife pointed up to the ceiling while Ella laid out the supper. Then after five minutes of moist chomping sounds, he sucked his teeth, pushed the plate away and beamed at Ella. If her nerves weren't already on edge she'd be almost shaking when he started picking meat out from between his teeth. Later he drifted over to his fireside chair, filled his pipe and started smoking it with little *pfft pfft* sounds.

"I swear, he was *born* a pensioner," Ella complained to her knife-lipped mother.

"Dinna fess yersel' – he's clean – not like some o' those other dirty buggers on the street," her mother said.

"But he – he's got *habits* mother," and went on to describe the after-supper rituals.

"By you're a dumb cluck, Ella. That's nowt compared to the filthy arses some poor wives are married to – with great big hands all ower them as soon as they walk in the door and demandin' all manner of *animal satisfaction*. Your Jack's harmless, so count yer blessings."

Lately Ella had taken to leaving the house as soon as the breakfast dishes were cleared off the table and she'd sent Jack off to work, happily swinging his bait[3] bag. At first she'd gone shopping at Belton Downs but lately she'd started climbing up Whittington Hill. At the top, she'd lean on the wooden fence overlooking the valley and gaze south, her eyes like binoculars as she strained to pick out the grey ribbon of the Great North Road. The road that could take you north to the busy streets and grand castles of Edinburgh or south to the glamour and excitement of London.

On this sunny day in June, Jack had dawdled so much trying to pump up his bicycle tires to the right degree of firmness, that Ella was almost squirming with impatience and the anticipation of a day spent at the top of the hill, daydreaming and reading the Women's Weekly.

"Hadaway with yer," she chided as he fussed with his bicycle clips. "Or the foreman'll be dockin' yer pay."

Then finally she was away from the street, striding uphill past the leek hut and the Six Bells pub. She swung the grey string bag that held

---

[3] lunch

the magazine, the red flask she'd bought from Woolworth's and a packet of fig rolls. She even waved at the milkman riding by on his cart and felt the blood pump through her solid legs as they carried her up – up towards the road that led away from the endless streets of grey houses, grey people and the monotony of a day spent washing the step, dusting the wall plaques and picking up Jack's dirty underwear from the bedroom floor.

The lure of the open road at the top of the hill drove her onwards until she was almost running, her chiffon scarf streaming out behind her like a turquoise flag, and as she ran her body felt as light as if she were seventeen and bubbling over with ideas and imaginings. *But what was she thinking – she was still only twenty-eight and she'd heard that sometimes those Yankee or Canadian soldiers went drinking at the Collier's Arms.* All it would take was one question – one invitation – and she'd be gone. Gone with anyone that would take her – *and bugger Jack and all the rest of the gormless fools on Crag Street.*

She'd drive down the motorway in one of those fancy army cars. They'd go as far as it would take to find a ship that would carry her across the sea. Ella knew she was born to ride wild mustangs or ski down snowy mountain slopes or dive from the top board at one of those shiny Hollywood swimming pools. Dooley, the postman, skimmed past on his rusty bike. "Runnin' away from the ard man then," he shouted, his voice swallowed up by the wind.

Ella laughed louder than usual and did a few little skipping steps. When her mother saw her skip last week on the way to the spiritualist meeting she told her to, "Act your bloody age, or I'll bust yer mouth for yer." Ella always had to take her mother to the séances so the old lady could keep asking for a sign from her late husband Derek, Ella's showy father, who'd passed away five years ago. She felt a cold hand on her heart when she remembered how he'd suffocated to death after being trapped down the mine in a dust-filled crawlspace for twelve hours, when an explosion backfired.

They'd always take the same personal items of his to the spiritualist meeting: the paisley silk scarf with the scent of sandalwood still lingering on it, the lambskin gloves that Ella held to her cheek the night after the funeral and the wallet with the picture of the Empire State Building stamped on the front in silver.

In his younger days he'd worked one year for the Canadian Pacific Railway, then traveled the length and breadth of North America, collecting postcards along the way. Postcards that he'd spread across the kitchen table and, with a light in his eyes that burned brighter than the fire on a Saturday night, he told Ella stories about the big cities and wide open spaces he'd loved. Ella knew he didn't answer them at the spiritualist meeting because he was away – far away somewhere in the sky above the prairies or the mountains or even the skyscrapers.

Ella rooted in the fig roll packet and picked out one to chew while she climbed the last few yards, but a dry ball of biscuit stuck in her throat when she reached the crest of the hill. Across the fence and right at the edge of the valley a blonde girl – *it had to be Maggie Harris, the forward little slut* – was brazenly holding hands with a soldier. Her face was level with his *broad shoulders and it looked like he was wearing a Yankee uniform too*. Ella dropped the string bag and heard a sharp crack. *Damn the new flask.* She kicked the bundle under the fence and ripped the pages of The Women's Weekly. Maggie was such a little slip of a thing with her white hair and those *googoo baby blue eyes – fluttering her eyelashes like a plastic doll.*

Ella's fingers touched the metal clip that held her straight hair back from her forehead and looked down at her thick legs in their lisle stockings above the laced-up brown walking shoes her mother had found for her at the Co-op. Ella had wanted the navy peep-toe shoes with the ankle strap and three-inch heels.

"Where do yer think yer'd be gannin' in them then, Lady Muck?" Her mother snapped, snatching them from Ella's hands. "Standin' on the corner of Fence Street?"

"*Mother*, they're dancing shoes."

"Aye, for dancin' right into some backstreet like a drunken street girl."

As usual Ella gave in to her mother's demands and, but when she watched the retreating shape of her mother's stout behind, she marveled that her father hadn't ever run away from her. Netta, Ella's older sister, had left at the age of sixteen; got into trouble with a lad from Fence

Row, had to get married before the baby showed and spoiled everything for Ella.

Now spots danced in front of her eyes and her head ached. Maggie and the soldier turned to glance at her then they laughed and ran down the hill towards the bus stop. *Towards Durham. Maggie Harris was running away with a soldier boy —with a soldier boy.* The words echoed in her brain like the chorus of a song. Suddenly the sun was too hot and Ella's stomach felt so queasy she vomited all her breakfast up, right there at the side of the road. Somehow she had to get back to the peace and quiet of her own bedroom. A lie-down and a strong cup of tea would put everything right again.

Ella's whole body felt cold and clammy as she turned the corner at the bottom of Crag Street. The butcher's van was parked up on the kerb two doors away from her house and a small queue of women stood by, gossiping and waiting to haggle with Arkley, the sly butcher who often slid heavy lumps of fat under the meat before weighing it. By now Ella felt a bit perkier. *Must be one of them women's moods that got me all flustered.* The moods that made some women run away with gypsies or fiddle around with the neighbour's husband or something.

She ran right into Iris Hawkins, who was carrying three brown paper packages of meat and trying to stop her two bairns, Lenny and Bill, from poking each other's eyes out with a pair of sticks. The lads were fencing like two little soldiers.

"I'll brae yer backsides for yer," Iris nagged, tugging at Lenny's arm.

Ella's hand reached out and swiped Bill's stick. "By yer a pair of little tigers, you two." She clipped him on the behind with it.

"Oh, ta Ella," said Iris. "These two little rascals'll run me into the ground."

"Got yersel a nice piece of meat then?" said Ella nodding at the packages.

"Walter likes his beef on Sunday, oxtails on Monday and a few pork sausages with his chips on Tuesdays."

They walked towards Iris's house and the boys ran ahead, stopping every now and again to poke the sticks down drains or trace shapes in the gravel.

"I just had a nice walk up Whittington Hill," said Ella, burning to spread the new gossip about Maggie.

"Lovely up there this time of year," said Iris. "I've been meaning to take the lads there for a picnic but I canna get Walter off his arse. Once he gets in the house he has his supper, smokes his pipe and then puts on the wireless and then yer canna get a word out of him."

"I saw Maggie Harris up there."

"Oh aye, I hear Jordy Willis is courtin' her."

"Why that's queer – she was up there with a fella."

"What – a different fella?"

"Aye – and one in a uniform. A Yankee. They were runnin' down the hill holdin' hands."

"Eeh – brazen madam," Iris said, her slippers slapping across the cobblestones, as she tried to keep up with Lenny and Bill. Ella followed close behind.

When they reached Iris's gate the boys ran back into the street and chased Neddy Barker's nervous wire-haired fox terrier round and round. Ella gasped when she felt a sharp pain jab across the fleshy area just below her stomach. Like red-hot wires were scraping at her insides.

"Are yer all right hinny?" said Iris.

The pain went away and Ella breathed easy again. "Too much runnin' uphill I think. I'd better have a rest – a cup of tea and a hot water bottle does wonders."

"You do that, flower."

They were about to go their own ways when they saw a small grey haired woman dressed in a pinny, the grizzled curls of her perm caught in a brown hairnet. It was Hannah Willis, Jordy's mother, who'd just finished washing the step and was squeezing out the mop. Ella looked at Iris and then back at Hannah's grinning toothless gums. An unfamiliar feeling of excitement fizzed like little bubbles racing through her veins. *Who said yer had to run away to find enjoyment? There was plenty here for the taking.*

"I'll just have a word with Hannah," she said, without looking at Iris.

The boys had climbed into the coal shed and were painting their faces with black stripes. "Are yer sure Ella – it might cause a bit too much trouble yer na's, " said Iris.

Ella didn't wait to hear any more. Her eyes were fixed on the beaming moon of Hannah Willis's face.

"Hannah," Ella called as she crossed the street, sidestepping the back end of Arkley's van. "Hannah, are yer makin' a cup of tea now?" The old lady nodded and beckoned Ella inside as she carried the mop and bucket into the kitchen. "Let's have a little natter then."

6

Maggie Harris lay naked on the faded flannel sheets of the upstairs back room at the Old Mill Pub eating square after square of dark chocolate. The soldier, his pockets full of pound notes and heavy silver, had gone downstairs to buy bottles of Newcastle Brown as well as crisps and peanuts. She held the sweet, bitter squares on her tongue for as long as she could until they dissolved into wafers, then rolled onto her back and raised her stocking covered leg into the air. Chuck, the soldier from Wisconsin, told her they were silk direct from France and the chocolate was Swiss.

She hadn't set out to get picked up by a Yankee soldier. She'd gone for a walk – her last Saturday walk alone, since tomorrow Jordy Willis was taking her out for the first time and from then on she and Jordy would walk together. *Together* despite the fact her cousin, Mary said his family were nothing but a pack of tinkers: "Drinkin' and fightin' and nowt but trouble."

She closed her eyes and let the morning sun warm her half-closed lids. She could see red – the colour of last night's sky when German planes had flown over Sunderland docks for the second of two night raids.

Jordy cut such a figure when he walked up to her on Belton High Street with his glossy black hair, husky shoulders and gap-toothed smile.

His face was smudged with soot. "I just come from Sunderland," he said, taking the string bag of potatoes from her and placing a guiding hand across her shoulder. "Cleanin' up after the Gerries bombed the station." Jordy was in the firemen's reserve. She had just finished her shift at the infirmary where she was a ward cleaner. "Yer catchin' the 83?"

Though Maggie felt light headed and breathless – her cousin's warnings lurked in the back of her mind: *"Dinna tek a bite there – they piss on the rhubarb and empty the chamber pots near the taty patch – and the house is like a midden"*

"Me Dad's getting' back from his shift at four o'clock – the taties are for supper," swallowed Maggie as they walked towards the bus stop.

"Why I could've given yer some from me Dad's back garden," said Jordy squeezing her shoulder. "Good crop this year."

"Next time," Maggie said faintly.

He followed her along the busy high street, past the library and into the bus shelter. "Yer should've seen the mess – station clock was stopped at one o'clock – minute hand blown clean off and a set of iron wheels from one of the train carriages stickin' out from the roof of Jacob's tea shop next door." When Jordy laughed his whole body shook and Maggie felt the thrill again, but it was the kind of excitement she'd felt as a child when she went on the Big Dipper at Seaburn for the first time or jumped off a tall tree branch into the river. She let him kiss her outstretched hand when she got onto the bus and wouldn't listen to a word of warning when her cousin told her again to watch out because the Willis's bred like rabbits and were the toughest buggers on Crag Street.

Today she'd climbed to the top of Whittington Hill and the soldier sauntered out from The Colliers' Arms. When he stretched out a broad, tanned hand towards Maggie the sun came out from behind a cloud. Perhaps it was a trick of the light, but he seemed to be made entirely of sunshine from his gleaming wheat coloured hair to the slate blue of his eyes that reflected the June sky.

"Where are you from?" she gulped.

"I walked here – all the way from Milwaukee, Wisconsin."

She shook his hand, which felt warm and dry.

"Truth is –I'm not a city boy."

"Why would you come to this midden of a place?"

"In hopes of running into a jewel like you right smack in the middle of the coalmines."

Maggie felt her cheeks flush: "I've heard about you Yanks from some of the other girls – charmin' them with chocolates and nylons and what have you."

"As a matter of fact I have a bar of the best chocolate you can get – if you wanna share some with me."

His name was Chuck. "Do you have a steady?" He asked.

Maggie hesitated. "N-not yet." She felt a brief flicker of guilt when she thought of Jordy's face and then her mother's voice saying, "Yer a bloody doormat, Maggie – easily led."

"That means you're looking for one."

"Maybe."

"Come to the Rialto Dance Hall tonight." Chuck jumped up and held his hands out to her. "We'll waltz the night away. Bring a girl-friend."

Maggie looked up and felt suddenly carefree as the wind blew her hair back. *If only she'd worn her daisy-print cotton dress with the matching lavender ribbon. They could've waltzed right down the hill together.* She grasped his hands and allowed him to pull her upwards. With his back to the sun he looked like part of a dream. You don't belong in this filthy place," Maggie blurted, "and I wish you could take me now – across the sea."

"I'd dive right in with you – then we'd come to the surface like two wet seals, shake off the water and bake ourselves brown up on the ship's deck." He laughed and caught her hands in his. "I haven't even asked your name."

"Maggie – Maggie Harris of fourteen Crag Street, Belton, County Durham."

She looked down at her scuffed black shoes. She'd tried to black in the worn parts and now they'd gone a dull blue.

He pulled at her hand. Maggie looked over her shoulders at the grey rows of houses at the far side of the hill, then back at Chuck's shining face.

"How fast can you run to that bus stop at the bottom of the hill?" She said, feeling so happy the top of her head could have whirled right off. "Race you."

They ran, fingertips touching, towards the Durham road but at the bottom of Whittington Hill they passed the Old Mill Pub and he suggested they get a drink first in the privacy of one of the guest rooms.

She whispered yes, her stomach turning somersaults, and they'd told a lie at the reception desk. Chuck gave her a small gold ring from his pocket and said they were newlyweds. Then she felt her heart fluttering when he almost backed into the doorpost on the way up. He'd settled her in the small room that looked out over the fields and said, "I'll be back with beer, honey. Don't go anywhere."

Left to her own devices, Maggie took off her dress and the old cotton bra with the safety pin on one strap and the navy blue knickers. She sluiced herself down quickly in the old sink, then lay watching the door willing him to come back. It took about fifteen minutes before he burst in and dropped everything on the floor when he saw her lying there with her arms crossed behind her head.

The army uniform had so many buttons and its rough fibres scratched her skin to the point that she was almost ripping off the jacket. And then his warm, silky body covered hers and his mouth licked and kissed every part of her.

The sky grew dark outside as rain clouds billowed over the horizon and by three o'clock in the afternoon they lay across each other, sleeping like corpses.

Chuck woke at four and scrambled back into his clothes.

"You're a lovely lady," he said, smoothing down his hair. "But I have to report to barracks by five and then I'm shipping out to Normandy tomorrow." He slipped her a photograph. "That's me outside my daddy's fishing lodge. Caught a ten pound catfish."

She held the picture tightly.

"There's an address on the back," he said, kissing her forehead. "Write to me."

It was ten past five when the bus pulled up at the end of Crag Street and Maggie climbed down the steps trying to fight back the tears.

She walked briskly, nodding at the few people who were out gossiping. There was nothing to worry about – she was just a girl coming back from a walk – but when she saw her mother standing on the step, her arms tightly folded across her bosom, her heart sank.

The gate crashed against the posts and she could see how white the knuckles of her mother's hands looked pressed into the crook of her elbow.

"And where the bloody hell do yer think yer've been?" she said, lifting up her arm and slamming her hand across Maggie's face. Blue and silver stars exploded in front of Maggie's eyes. "Who've yer bin with – some bloody soldier boy? The whole street knows about it."

"How – who said?" was all she could stutter.

"That nosey bugger Ella Danby – the bloody tattle-tale – and she's lost her baby with the strain of it all."

"What," gasped Maggie as her Mam pushed her inside.

"Bleedin' like a stuck pig she was and who would guess Jack Danby had the balls to mek her pregnant anyway."

Her mam grasped her left ear and pulled her towards the scullery. "You'll come inside now and get yersel' cleaned up because tonight yer gannin' out wi' Jordy Willis if he's still willin' ter make an honest woman of yer. Play yer cards right and he'll marry yer afore there's any trouble."

Maggie dragged her feet across the doorstep and the door closed with a final bang behind her.

1952

7

Rita's family was well off by Crag Street standards, and small. There was only Rita, two brothers, Lenny and Bill, her dad Walter, a foreman at the pit and her mother, Iris. They'd recently come into some extra money from an aunt who died childless, and the widow of a well-to-do shopkeeper, so Rita was doted on, dressed up and turned out onto the street with fresh white ribbons tied into her ringletted hair. Shunned by other children for being snooty and toffee-nosed, she began to read, and soon lapsed into a fictional world of princesses and ballerinas, and girls named Veronica and Faith, who went to boarding schools, had midnight suppers of crackers and tinned sardines and used words like 'ripping' and 'jolly decent.'

But Rita also loved to listen to the street gossip – crouching so low in the back corner of her yard that Ella and all the other blabbermouths had no idea she was even there – ears straining, heart beating, afraid to breathe or swallow for fear of being found out.

Ella Danby told Mrs Barker that Rita's mam had her nose *ower far in the air*. "Look at her all dressed up to the nines with the silver earrings and mohair coat."

"Why she looked quite smart," said Mrs Barker.

"Tek a second look. She comes into my house and her eyes are all ower the place. Smokes a cigarette in one of them fancy holders – and her coming from nothing. I knew her mother – part Irish – feisty little bugger, that one – she could sup whisky through a sweaty stocking and on Sundays she'd get the big mending basket out and all the sons would have to help darn the socks. She'd even have them turning the mangle or possing the clothes on Mondays. Not natural, I tell you. Comes from a queer family that one – a queer family."

The two women saw Hannah Willis and drifted across the street still nattering. Rita stood up, checked her dress hem for stains, stretched her cramped legs and decided to ask her mam for more details about her grandma's drinking habits.

Beattie Webb's sweet shop was just across the street from Rita's house. On Saturdays her mam always told her to "Gan over to Beattie's and get yersel' some sherbet." Then she'd run fast across the street, afraid to look at the dirty children who poked sticks into gutter puddles or cut up worms and cockroaches into tin cans to make witches' brew.

You went through Beatties's gate and round the side of her coal shed and climbed a step to see in the window. From there you could see barley sugar sticks, sherbet fountains, liquorice pipes, tall jars of sugared almonds, buttered brazils and chocolate éclairs, all laid out in front of a faded black curtain. But if you stayed too long looking, the curtain would part and Beattie's pointed, white face would loom out of the shadows. Her mouth, a thin knife slash across her face, barked comments like "Haway wi' yer" or "Ger'a move on" and even the bravest child raced in, croaked an order, then, grasped the brown paper bag and ran out of the shop without looking back.

Some folks said the body of her late father had been mummified and was kept in the front parlour. Others said his ashes had been put in a huge brass urn that stood in the middle of the kitchen table as a reminder that he was still watching Beattie and her sister from the spirit world.

"The father *ordered* them to carry on with the shop," Ella said to Rita's mam. "There's no other explanation why a sour faced ard[4] wife like her should be selling sweeties."

Beattie lived together with her widowed sister Ida, but as far as anyone on the street knew, the two hadn't spoken in ten years. Apparently Ida had done something terrible to cause the death of her three-year old daughter, Bertha's cherished niece. Rita also overheard Ella Danby telling Olive Coombes it was something to do with the delivery man who put his dirty hands on Ida and made her forget to watch the little girl. That day the poor bairn was knocked over by the ice cream van. Beattie never forgave her and Ida went strange afterwards.

Rita often imagined the sisters swishing by each other like two shadows in the narrow hallways of the house or sitting quietly at meals with only the sound of their chewing and the ticking grandfather clock breaking the silence.

One Saturday when Rita's mother had another one of her headaches and needed to lie in bed for a while, she fished into her beaded purse and handed Rita a whole shilling. "Go and buy yersel summat at Beattie's, hinny – I need to put me head down for a while – yer Da's not due back from the football game for another hour. Hadaway now and keep yersel' out of trouble."

It was a warm day in May and Rita, hair set into tight chestnut ringlets and wearing her favourite yellow gingham smocked dress with the white collar, carried her best doll, Wendy (named after Wendy in Peter Pan) through the gate and across the street to Beattie's. She always walked with her eyes down once she was away from the safety of her gate. To meet the eyes of the common bairns might mean a torn dress or pulled hair or a string of nasty, filthy words she didn't understand.

She'd almost reached Beattie's when she heard a rush of feet clattering across the damp cobblestones behind her. Carol Parker and two other girls screeched into her ear and pushed her so hard against the wall she dropped Wendy into a puddle.

---

[4] old

Marjorie DeLuca

Carol pushed her dirty face into Rita's and jeered, "Rita Hawkins likes to kiss boys' bare bums. Everybody knows." The smell of piss and greasy hair made Rita cover her face with her hands and she sobbed as they circled around her, screaming words like *fuck* and *shit* and *arse* other words that Rita's mam had slapped Lenny and Bill for saying. The Parkers were a filthy family. Everyone knew their house smelled of pee. At school the children said the Parkers peed in the bathwater and Ella said they never emptied their chamber pots outside – just tipped them down the scullery sink, splashing piss all over the house. Olive said Mrs Parker wouldn't know what a floor mop was if it hit her over the head.

Now Rita sobbed harder and wished for someone magical to pluck her away and tell her that she didn't belong on this street but was really the long-lost daughter of a rich Count.

Carol had just grabbed Wendy and was poking at her eyes with a lollipop stick when Rita heard a boy's voice say, "Get yer mucky hands off the doll." She looked through the spaces between her fingers and saw a boy of about eleven or twelve – it was George Nelson. Carol scowled and thrust the doll towards Rita, shouted "Haway" to her friends and ran off kicking and slapping them.

George lived opposite Rita, and his family were "nice but shabby" as her mother said – "but they keep themselves to themselves and the lad is always scrubbed clean and well turned out."

Today his hair was wet and combed tidily to the side. He had dark blue eyes and was carrying a book.

"Here's your dolly back," he said, holding Wendy towards her. She grabbed its legs. "Where you gannin' anyway?"

"To the sweet shop," Rita replied, feeling like a princess rescued from the mouth of a dragon.

"I'll tek you over there," he said, crossing the street.

Rita was over the moon with happiness and skipped along beside him, "What's your book?" she asked wiping her damp cheeks with a hanky; the lace one she kept tucked into her little silver charm bracelet. She noticed George sneaking a sideways look at it.

"The poetry of Robert Burns," he said.

"I just read Peter Pan," said Rita.

The Pitman's Daughter

"Smashing," he said.

They stood at Beattie's window.

"I've got a shilling, I'll buy you summat," said Rita.

"All right – cinder toffee – anyway where did you get so much money from? Did you steal it?"

"No me mam gave it to me."

"I heard you were rich."

"Well we are – and we're only living here temporarily – until our rich grandfather sends for us," Rita announced.

The black curtain parted but instead of Beattie's mask-like face, the pale circle of Ida's face peered out, her eyes magnified by thick, cloudy spectacles. Rita jumped back.

"They always take you by surprise," he said.

"She's the mad one. Me mam told me," said Rita.

"She's harmless though," said George

Ida was waving them inside, her eyes wide and frantic. Puzzled, they glanced at each other then stepped down and entered the brown gloom. Only one naked light bulb hung from the rafters and a heavy black curtain separated the shop from the rest of the house. Beyond that, Rita supposed, was the mummy or the big urn or, worse still, Beattie lurking around a dark corner.

"By you're a pair of bonnie bairns," said Ida. "It's not often Beattie lets me serve but I'm happy I did today." She wiped her hands on a flour-covered apron. Her lank, brown hair was pinned back with a diamante hair clip.

"Er – a threepenny packet of cinder toffee," said George, standing close to the door.

"And sixpennorth of dolly mixture," said Rita.

"And aren't you a real dolly," said Ida, eyes fixed on Rita. "Just a little smasher."

"Where's Beattie?" George asked.

"Gone into Sunderland. She's left me in charge." Ida continued to stare at Rita.

"The toffee," said George impatiently, chewing at his nails.

Rita glared at Ida. Who did she think she was? This plain old lady with the crooked glasses and the silly hair clip – gawking at her with a mouth so wide she could catch a fly like the old woman in the song.

"And I'll have the dolly mixture," repeated Rita, knitting her brow into a frown and scowling.

"Oh – the sweeties – yes, but first I want you bairns to come and try the coconut macaroons I've made. If you don't mind spending a minute with a poor, lonely old soul."

Of course, thought Rita, witches always used cakes and sweets to entice little children into their dens. She looked up at George who appeared to think for a moment. He reminded her of Dickon in *The Secret Garden* with his kind, freckled face, his shiny, blond hair and the smell of fresh air about him. If he went through that curtain then she would too.

"Just for a minute then," he said, "I have to help me mam in the garden."

When the heavy curtain swished back down behind them they stood in a room that smelled of mothballs and contained many ticking clocks. A large brass urn stood in the centre of the kitchen table. Rita's hands felt sweaty. She wiped them on her dress. "What's that?" she asked, pointing.

"That contraption there – that's a samovar. Belonged to my great-grandma. She was a lovely woman – came from Russia, yer na's. It's a big tea urn."

"Oh," sighed Rita with relief.

"Now," said Ida, ushering them in, "George you sit over in the da's chair." She gestured to a large red brocade armchair by the fireplace. "And you Rita, you take Mam's chair. Mam was a very delicate woman – very refined. Nervous temperament though – come from the Russian blood."

Rita sat on the edge of a small green velvet chair.

"Now make yerselves comfortable and – oh I'll get the cakes and a drink."

She disappeared behind the curtain again and Rita looked over at George who was perched silently on the other chair.

"She's cuckoo," said Rita. "What if she tries to poison us?"

"Don't eat anything," he replied.

Ida reappeared with a bottle of orange pop and a plate of cakes. "Beattie'd clout me if she knew I was helping mesel to the pop but she'll never know will she? We'll keep it a secret." She carefully poured the pop and stuck straws into each glass. "One for each of us," she said, handing them round.

Rita sat back in the chair sucking at the straw and began to look around the room.

"There's a lot of photos here," she said.

"Do you see that one?" said Ida, pointing at a picture of a young, dark-haired woman, with thick wavy hair, cupid's-bow lips and a fur wrap. "That's me. I was a real beauty. Just like you Rita. Me mam always loved to dress me up and all the young men came to call – I had me pick. But my heart belonged to Eric, a dashing young soldier from the Durham Light Infantry. He was clean-cut and handsome like you, George, but both of his legs were crushed in an explosion at Ypres and he died of gangrene poisoning. Oh the agony of his death – it was horrible – but before he passed away he left me this clip. Bought it in Paris. They sent it afterwards with his last letter." She fingered the diamante clip, her eyes fixed in some faraway dream.

Rita giggled and looked over at George who was blushing a hot beetroot red and had spilled some pop over his shirt – which was clean and white but darned and patched on the collar and sleeves.

"Aye, looking at you two pretty children makes me think of how my life should have turned out. George, I'm sure you'd like to marry a perfect little lady like Rita – eh?"

"Oh – yes," he stumbled.

"She's so bonny isn't she and, Rita – George is quiet and well mannered – not like the other horrible, dirty boys on the street."

"Yes," said Rita, thinking that he really was nice and good-looking too.

"If you two were married, you know," said Ida, "you'd sit by the fire and Rita would sew and you, George would smoke your pipe and talk about your business dealings."

"But I'm going to live in a big house with servants," said Rita. "I really don't belong here."

"Well you live here now," said George.

"George, read us something from your poetry book – something lovely and romantic," said Ida wiping her glasses. Her eyes looked teary and unfocused without them.

"Why don't you stand up and read to Rita."

George chewed at his lip and took a long time to get to his feet. Rita swung her legs and felt important that this older boy was giving her such attention. He finally stood up and flicked through the pages, moistening his lips with his tongue as he looked.

"George is a nice, serious boy, isn't he Rita – well brought up too. You can always tell."

George looked sad as he read the poem, while Ida sniffled and pressed a hanky to her nose. Rita watched them her brows knit. *What was all the fuss about?* She didn't really understand the poem but managed to catch some lovely words about love and roses and dying.

When he finished, Ida clapped her hands and waved the hanky high. George smiled and said thank you.

"And now George, you must kneel down and kiss Rita's hand like a gallant young gentleman. That's what they did in the old days."

Rita held out her hand hardly daring to believe this was really happening and feeling like Cinderella and every other fairy-tale princess she'd ever read about. Incredibly George knelt down and with some hesitation took her hand and held it. His hand felt cool and smooth and she nodded her head like any royal person would, permitting him to continue. A nervous giggle tickled deep inside her throat but she fought it as George solemnly put his lips to her hand. Thank goodness she'd used lavender hand cream that morning and his lips felt warm and tickly but nice.

"Lovely," said Ida, "Lovely. But yer'd best hadaway before Beattie gets back or she'll have me hide. She's a hard woman – no feelings in that cold heart of hers."

George jumped up quickly his face suddenly flushed.

"Come back again," said Ida. "Beattie goes out every second Saturday and I love the company. I'll get yer sweeties for you."

"Oh yes," said Rita.

Once outside George rushed on ahead.

"Wait," said Rita "will you walk me across the street?"

"All right," said George.

"You liked it – don't pretend you didn't," said Rita, as they crossed the cobbled courtyard. "That's why you read that soppy poem about love."

"So what if I did – just because you're too young to understand it," he said when they reached the gate.

"What's it like being really poor?" asked Rita.

"It's horrible but I'm not going to be poor forever you know," he said, "Me mam's saving for me to go to university so I can be a great lawyer or doctor. That's when I'll leave this street."

"And I'm going to marry someone famous or royal," said Rita, smoothing out her curls and enjoying the way he looked at her pretty, shiny ringlets.

"How? Famous royal people don't come to this street."

"Then I'll go out and find them," said Rita. "Now will you take me to Ida's again?"

"Aye – it's worth the free pop to spend half an hour with a loony old woman and a bairn."

"Don't bother then," said Rita seeing her mother looking anxiously through the window.

"All right – I'll take you," he said. "In two weeks."

1954

8

The last time Rita went to Ida's and played the game with George, was a horrible day. It started off badly when her dad smashed one of her mam's best china teacups and called her a lazy bloody cow. "Lie on the couch and drink yer bloody tea," he said. "I'm gannin' to the club for a few pints – I'm as dry as a wooden god."

Every two weeks for the last two and a half years Rita had spent thirteen days waiting until she almost burst for Saturday afternoon to arrive. Then, for one brief hour she'd put on her prettiest dress and slip into a world of make-believe and glittering possibilities with Ida and George. George was her prince, her knight – a dashing young hero who would rescue her from Crag Street, and for two and a half years he'd willingly taken part in Rita and Ida's fantasies.

They'd meet every second Saturday – except for Christmas and holidays – outside of Beattie's gate. George was always quiet and polite but didn't smile much – as if he was doing Rita a great favour coming along, since he was fourteen and she was ten and still in awe of him. She took care to wear something new and pretty each time they met. A bright hair ribbon or a fresh pair of white socks or a shiny brooch or necklace – because he'd always notice. His eyes were drawn to nice things. When she'd bought him a pencil from Woolworths or a small notebook, or bookmark, he'd blush, nod his head and quickly put it away in his pocket. Once or twice he brought something for her – a small carved wooden box made in his woodwork class or a clay pot or a homemade butterfly cake. He never had any of his own money and so he'd offer the gift, mumbling, "I made it" or "me mam made it." She'd catch his blue eyes for a moment and then he'd march ahead towards Beattie's shop. Rita accepted the gifts like a princess, and she always placed them on her shelf beside the framed photo of Freddie Bartholomew as Little Lord Fauntleroy and her red and gold bound copy of *The Secret Garden*.

George wouldn't speak much at first. But once he was settled in front of Ida's blazing fire, his face softened by the reddish glow of the coals, Rita knew he was just pretending to hate being there. Ida made him bring a different book every time. She was greedy for stories and poems about men and women and love. Stories about lovely, polite people with soft hands and posh voices. People who lived in beautiful houses with views of the sea or in far-off exotic places. People who promised undying love to each other, who adored each other, who'd die for each other. People, who never swore, burped, farted, picked their nose or crammed their food down greedily like Rita's dad.

Over the years Rita began to understand the poetry: *Shall I compare thee to a summer's day? How do I love thee, let me count the ways. My love is like a red, red rose.* Ida would lie back in her chair gazing at the photo of her young soldier, her eyes brimming with tears and Rita was struck by the sadness of it all. To love meant to suffer, she reasoned. Love was painful, uncomfortable and made you cry. Love was nice at first but then the person always left you or was taken away from you or died or – if you stayed together, all you did was fight and nag at each other.

Like her Mam and Dad. Every night Walter clashed his knife and fork down onto his empty supper plate, stood up, stretched, burped, put on his cap and went off to the club. When she looked at their wedding pictures she hardly recognized the shy young woman smiling up at the soft-faced young man. Where had their love gone? She was certain love meant broken promises, heartache and was definitely something to stay clear away from.

After the poetry came Rita's favourite part. She and George would act out a scene from a book with Ida directing. They'd done Pip and

Estelle, Jo and Laurie, Elizabeth and Mr Darcy, Romeo and Juliet. George was shy at first then soon lost himself in the acting, but Rita threw her whole heart into her character with such enthusiasm that George sometimes stopped her and said, "Don't go overboard." Then he'd look at Ida for support but she just waved her hand impatiently for them to continue. They never touched much or hugged or anything but they used words and gestures that made Rita feel important and beautiful and besides, sometimes George held her hand or kissed it, which was a double thrill for Rita.

She sometimes wondered why George bothered to come to these meetings. She hardly ever saw him on the street. Occasionally she glimpsed him walking alongside his mother carrying the bags of shopping, other times she'd see him shovelling coal into the shed, a scowl creasing his face. Sometimes his Dad would march out the back door and shout at him. Rita had to bite her tongue so as not to march right over and tell him to stop it.

Ella once said George was a loner, "Wi' his nose forever buried in a book" and so Rita decided that George had chosen her as the only person on the street with the class and breeding needed to appreciate his poetry and stories.

On that final horrible day George forgot his poetry book and insisted on reading a black and depressing passage from Milton's *Samson Agonistes*. As soon as Rita and Ida heard "eyeless in Gaza at the mill with slaves" they looked at each other in bewilderment and Ida rushed out to bring in a tray of scones and milk.

"What's eating you up?" she asked. "You're really grumpy today."

George stared into the fire and didn't say a word.

"You're never very happy anyway but today you're worse," she pressed. "At least you usually cheer up when you read but you brought something horrible and boring."

"It's horrible," he said, turning to her, his eyes red and teary, "but it's true."

Rita felt a sudden chill in the air. "I don't know what you're talking about."

"You wouldn't," he answered as Ida walked in, "You're just a spoiled bairn."

Things became worse in their drama session when George refused to say, "I'm not good for much, I know; but I'll stand by you, Jo, all the days of my life..." and just when Rita, as Jo March, had decided to make peace with him. Then for the first time ever in the game they were supposed to hug each other.

"I canna get my mind on this today," said George, standing up and collecting his papers, "I – I canna concentrate."

Rita felt like stamping her foot until Ida made him do it, "Tell him, Ida – tell him he has to do it. I wore my Josephine March pinafore dress today."

Ida only looked disappointed and wiping a smudge of butter from her glasses said, "Next time, flower. Next time."

Once they were out in the yard Rita refused to share her Turkish Delight with George. "You were nothing but a spoilsport today."

"You don't know nothing, you don't," he said.

"What's wrong with you anyway?" she asked, sucking the chocolate off a large piece of sweet, red jelly.

"Something too serious for a bairn to understand – especially a posh one like you."

"I'm not posh, me mam says I'm just refined," Rita replied.

"What's the difference?" George said, kicking the toe of his worn boot against the wall.

"You need new boots," said Rita eyeing her own black patent shoes. "There's a hole coming in your toe."

"I'm getting some tomorrow. Me mam's buying me pit boots."

Rita stopped sucking the Turkish Delight. "Why?" She said.

"I'm starting at the pit on Monday – me Dad made me."

"He's rotten – he's always shouting at you – I've seen him."

George looked angry, "He's a filthy, rotten bugger – that's what he is. A common, rotten old bastard."

Rita was shocked at hearing him talk like that. "But you always said you were going to university to be a doctor or a barrister. Your mam promised you," said Rita.

"Well you'll soon find out that people don't always keep their promises."

"And now you'll be like all the rest of them – like me dad and brothers and your Dad," said Rita, feeling sick in the pit of her stomach.

"I canna believe it's happening but there's nowt I can do about it – and I canna go to Ida's any more – I'll be too busy for playing bairns' games."

Rita looked up at George and realized how tall and grown-up he had become, how he was brushing his hair straight back with something glossy in it – probably Brylcreem, how his jaw had become harder with light shadowy hairs above his lip. She felt like crying but swallowed the tears.

"I don't care," she spat, "Me mam always said your family were poor as church mice – and common too." And with that she turned and walked in the direction of her front gate, trying with all her might not to look back at him. He was the only bright spot in her life and now there'd be no more Saturdays, no more poems by the fire, no more acting. Why did he have to change like that? How could he suddenly grow up and become a miner. He'd soon have rough, dirty hands like her Dad used to have before he got his job in the pit offices.

She'd just opened the gate when she heard the crash of breaking glass. She whirled around. Two men faced each other, the larger man holding a broken beer bottle. On each side of the street people stood behind their gates, craning their necks to see better. Rita froze. George came up beside her.

"It's Jordy Willis and Joe Barker – they must have been playing cards again," he said.

"What?" asked Rita.

"Jordy plays, Jordy wins or else the other man's cheating."

"They'll kill each other," gasped Rita as Jordy lunged forward and knocked the other man down.

"Not likely," said George, "they'll just rough each other up a bit."

"No – no," said Rita, "he has a broken bottle."

"Christ," said George as the two men wrestled, rolling down the street, through black streaked puddles and piles of dogshit. Finally Jordy climbed to his knees and pinned Joe down, then, raising his arm, he held the jagged bottle up in the air and looked around at all the spectators. "Here's what fucking rotten cheaters get," he yelled.

"Do something," screamed Rita, but by then three or four men had rushed out into the street: her dad, George's dad, Jack Danby and some others ran over as he smashed the jagged glass down into Joe's face. The man bellowed like one of the bulls over at Moorsley. She'd seen the farmer shoot it because it had foot and mouth disease. Stiff, cold and lumpy, it slumped over, the whites of its eyes frozen in horror. She pressed her hands to her ears and felt her head reeling.

The men pulled Jordy off Joe and he swung out wildly at them.

"Dinna lay yer fuckin' hands on me."

Joe's wife ran out with an armful of sheets and bent over the writhing figure of her husband, dabbing at the streams of blood that ran into his eyes and down into his mouth and Ella Danby stepped out form behind her gate waving her arms.

"You're a nasty piece of work, Jordy Willis and every bugger on this street's ower spineless to tell yer."

By this time Maggie Willis and her mother-in-law, Hannah were trying to pull Jordy back into the house but when he heard Ella he turned and roared, "What the fuck are you looking at, yer ard whore – I fucked yer sister many a time. That's all yer family's good for."

Rita felt George's hands close tightly over her ears and heard his voice faintly saying, "You don't need to hear this – no need to hear."

Ella led the crowd of neighbours towards Jordy who cursed and jabbed his fist at them. As Hannah, and Maggie tried to drag him inside, he caught Maggie with the corner of his fist and she fell back into the gate. Rita felt George's hands clench into fists as the shouts of the crowd grow louder. In an instant, however, they were drowned out by the loud wail of a siren and all faces turned to the bottom of the street where an ambulance was turning the corner.

The crowd fell silent as the van slowed down and ground to a halt three houses from the bottom. Two men in white coats got out and walked into the Murphy house. Old Mr Murphy had lived on his own since his wife and daughter packed up and left a year ago on account of his drinking, according to Rita's mam.

No one was looking at Jordy now that the mob was moving slowly down towards Murphy's house. Even Joe Barker hobbled along too, holding onto his wife and clutching a bloody towel to his face. Rita looked round and whispered, "Come on," to George and they followed the crowd towards the flashing lights of the ambulance.

Ella stood at the front, straining to see over the wall as the front door of the house slammed open and a uniformed man backed out. The crowd gasped as Miss Jessel, the street midwife and layer-out of bodies, fussed with the white sheet covering the stiff corpse that lay on the stretcher. One of the ambulance men shouted, "Out of the way," to the crush of onlookers.

Ella's voice rose loud above the murmuring. "Found him with his head stuck in the gas oven – slashed his last few sticks of furniture to pieces."

Rita watched in horror. The noise of the crowd throbbed in her ears and the blinking lights of the ambulance sent orange flashes across her eyes. As the stretcher passed by she spied a pair of large bluish feet sticking out from beneath the sheet. The ambulance men were so flustered with the noise of the crowd they fumbled with the stretcher and jammed the feet in the door. The younger ambulance man was breathing heavily and sweating so much, little trickles ran into his eyes. He wiped his hand across his face and pushed the stretcher so hard the dead feet smacked against the metal door hinges, tearing a purple gash into the cold, rubbery skin. Rita's body suddenly felt weightless and the sky crashed down into the street.

When she opened her eyes she was safe in the pink warmth of her bedroom surrounded by the row of dolls who looked down at her with unblinking blue eyes. Her head throbbed and her mouth was dry and tinny tasting.

"Mam – Mam," she called, trying to decide if the horrible things she was remembering were really dreams. She heard the soft pad of her mother's slippers on the stairs. The door opened and her mother appeared, bringing with her the faint whiff of Devon Violets and cigarette smoke.

"Why hinny, yer awake – yer fainted on the street. George Nelson carried yer all the way inside. Nice lad that one – I telt him I didn't know what you were doing watching that dead body being taken out."

"It did happen then," said Rita closing her eyes. "All that trouble with Jordy Willis and Mr Murphy and George. It was all real."

"Aye, it was a bad day on the street today," her mother said, fussing with the pink, ruffled bedspread. "I telt yer Da it's best we get away from this place as soon as we can. It's not a fit place for a young woman. Some of these people are worse than animals – but that Nelson laddie – by he's a canny one – a cut above the others he is. It's just a shame he has to go down the pit. Might have been somebody if his family had some money. Anyway that's enough of my nattering – I'll get yer a nice cup of tea."

Rita looked at the clay pot and the wooden box that George had given her. It was true. She wouldn't see him any more. A small tear trickled down to the edge of her nose but she told herself she wouldn't miss him. She wouldn't ever look for him again. It was over and she wasn't sorry.

9

The sky was still inky black, the street outside silent, and the house lifeless as George slipped from his bed to the pile of waiting clothes. His mother had laid them out carefully. The heavy serge trousers, the white, collarless man's shirt, the old grey jacket that used to be his father's, cut down and mended to fit him and, on the floor, the big, shiny pit boots. Yesterday his mother handed him a new red muffler. It was a gesture of contrition, her eyes imploring him to show some small indication of forgiveness, but he'd barely acknowledged the offering. *Let her suffer with the guilt* he thought, turning away from her.

Later he left the scarf on the kitchen table. Even though she'd spent all her biscuit tin money buying it, she'd betrayed him. Broken the promise she'd made every day of his childhood.

He put on the clothes as if he'd rehearsed this moment many times over and walked towards his bedroom door. Rows of small plastic soldiers were arranged in battle formations on an old wooden board by his wardrobe. *Stupid child's toys.* He kicked at them with the men's hobnail boots and they flew across the floor, scattering into dark corners under the bed. *Let her clean them up now,* he thought just as the door opened, and his mother, wrapped in the dark shawl she wore for cold mornings, rushed in carrying a mug of tea. She stopped and the tea sloshed into the saucer.

"Oh, yer up early, hinny. I was just bringing you a nice cup of tea to have in bed. Summat special being as it's yer first day at the pit."

She said it again. He brushed past her, ignoring the cup she held out to him. A peace offering, he supposed, as he stomped down the stairs. Scuttling behind him, his mother hastened into the scullery; glancing out every now and again to make sure he'd settled himself at the table. He sat motionless, arms at his sides, watching the clock tick away his last moments of freedom. The same clock he'd looked at on school days. Those were happier times – lifetimes away and yet it was only weeks ago he'd stood proudly to receive the school prize for literature, and now boys he'd beaten hands-down were going on to the upper forms and maybe even to university. Only last week he'd walked over to Beattie's shop with Rita and read poems and stories – revelled in the beauty of the language as Rita and Ida gazed adoringly up at him. But that lifestyle wasn't for him, the son of a miner.

His father had decreed, "It's no good trying to rise above your station in life, son. If it were good enough for me to go down the mines then it's good enough for you."

There had been the inevitable arguments about money and how he have to take his proper place in the family as a man. His mother's desperate pleas couldn't shake his father's implacable will and now all the childhood promises she made to him were broken. Scattered like chaff in the wind.

In the tiny kitchen scullery his mother clinked the dishes around then carried in a steaming plate of bacon and eggs.

"A working man needs a good breakfast inside him," she said, her red face beaming as she placed it in front of him. He went through the motions, aware of her standing beside him, her eyes watching his every move. But it was like chewing cardboard. He couldn't swallow anything. The egg yolks congealed into a sticky mess on the plate, surrounded by a pool of bacon fat. Shaking his head, he pushed the plate away and his mother's hands flew up to her mouth. She stepped forward and touched his shoulder.

The Pitman's Daughter

"You'll be a bit worried about your first day but it'll be all right, you'll see. You'll be one of the lads in no time."

Her voice was pleading, and for a moment he wanted to lose himself in her arms and have her stroke his hair, to press his nose into her shawl so that all the bad things would go away, but instead he turned and picked up his bait.

"I'd better be going, Mam," he said, standing and pushing the chair away from the table. His blood simmered. He wanted to scream and curse at her that she'd broken the promise. The promise she'd whispered to him every day of his childhood until he was filled with the certainty of it. *You will never go down there my lovely boy – never.*

He picked up his bag and walked towards the open door. His mother came up behind him. He heard her swift intake of breath as she clasped his shoulders and buried her head in his coat, her whole body shaking.

"Son-------I wish-----."

On the verge of tears, he broke away and stepped out into the silent yard.

"Yer Da would have come with you but they put him on the night shift," she said through her tears, but her voice was lost in the early morning dampness. He didn't even look back at her when he shut the gate, though he knew she was still crying.

The late summer air cooled his cheeks and the sun rose in a cloudless copper sky. Cloth capped men streamed out of the houses carrying their bait bags. They walked obediently, like livestock streaming into a slaughterhouse.

He wondered if the creeping coal dust had suffocated their brains because they marched so meekly towards the giant wheels that turned round and round like a great mangle, squashing and grinding them in its metal jaws.

At the bus stop the men waited in ragged groups. They smoked pipes or chewed tobacco, spitting great black gobs out onto the street. How long before the coal dust coated his insides? How long before he started to cough up black phlegm like the rest of them? How long before he could *never* get his hands clean again?

Suddenly he wanted to turn and run.

In school he remembered Mr Potter, the scripture teacher reading a passage about hell from the Bible. The scrawny old man hissed the words through bluish lips "And in that terrible inferno there will be a weeping and wailing and gnashing of teeth." In a strange gesture of triumph he'd held up a picture showing the raging fires of hell. Charred and tortured human figures shovelled and sweated in endless agony. Now at fifteen George was condemned to hell though his whole future lay ahead of him.

Other young lads not much older than him stood around smoking and chatting, another calmly whittled at a small piece of wood with a penknife. Nobody talked to George and when the bus came swishing around the corner he was pushed forward in a surge of bodies.

The old bus chug-chugged up the bumpy hill towards the pit-head, carrying him along against his will, and every part of him cried out to stop this nightmare. It couldn't be happening. He wasn't meant for this.

His mother had always told him, "Not you, my boy, you're different. With your brains you'll never need to go down there." But the scrimping and doing without had been in vain.

The bus shuddered and stopped, and George stayed frozen in his seat watching the mass of black-clad bodies stream through the gate. If he sat on the bus long enough maybe everything would suddenly disappear like the fireball in one of his nightmares that had rolled towards him, scorching the grass, then disintegrated into the shadows of the night.

"Haway, lad. Thou's gonna be late on thy first day," said the driver.

Now there was no escape. Childhood had vanished. No magical wizards or knights in armour or flying unicorns could save him now and, with his heart clanging against his ribs, he allowed his shaky legs to take him off the bus and up towards the gates.

Sweaty bodies jostled against him as they crowded through the metal gates and swept him towards the pit and a wooden equipment hut where someone thrust a grey metal helmet and a heavy copper lantern into his hand. A voice droned a string of instructions, then someone passed shovels along the line. One for each of them.

The low hum of voices gave way to loud buzzing and whirring and grinding. Suddenly he was standing at the top of a deep shaft at eye level with screeching metal wheels that pulled two rusty chains linked to a cramped cage. George's face dripped with sweat, while his stomach churned the greasy eggs around. Every fibre of his body pulled back in final protest, but the force of the other bodies held him fast. The empty cage swung open and he was pushed into the sulphurous interior. The bitter stink of coal dust burned his mouth and nostrils.

When the cage door swung shut blackness engulfed him and warm wetness spread around his groin. Horrified, he shrunk into the corner as an old man's voice murmured into his ear, "Dinna be afraid, lad, we've all pissed our pants at one time or another!"

For a moment all eyes turned to look at him then they were swallowed into the blackness.

When George came home that evening, his mother was waiting in the kitchen. She sprang at him as he walked through the door, his body aching, its whole surface stinging with cuts and bruises washed raw by the carbolic soap and scalding water of the pit baths.

"I've made you a nice bit of pork – you'll be wanting a good supper now you've had a hard day's work."

"I'm not hungry," he said as he swept by her and ran up the stairs to his room. Flinging himself onto the bed, he covered his face with a pillow and tried to block thoughts of the day from his mind though he remembered the endless, winding tunnels dripping with filthy water. Sharp rocks cut through the knees of his trousers and the burning dust scorched his lungs. He recalled groping through inky darkness as he grasped the shovel and tried to dig among the piles of loose rock and rubble.

"George," his mother called from downstairs, "come down for supper. Yer canna sit up there all night. Yer need to keep yer strength up for tomorrow."

He rolled over and pressed the pillow tighter over his ears. If only they would shut up and leave him alone. They were always nagging at him and ordering him around and they were so pathetic. Both of them with their tired, washed-out faces and humble ways. He hated the way his Da came down to eat wearing his vest and underpants, the way he slurped his tea from the saucer, the way he wore a cap in the house and farted loudly whenever and wherever he pleased. And his mother, forever scurrying around the house like a frightened mouse, wearing the same old faded pinny with the safety pin holding up one side. Trying to please – to avoid conflict at any cost.

Sometimes they looked at him like he was a stranger. Especially when he came in with an armful of books. As if they were afraid to talk to him because he was too clever for their dull minds. They knew that sending him down the pit would clog his brain with dust, would make him accept who and what he was supposed to be. He jumped up from his bed in a rage, "Fuck the whole damn bloody lot of you," he spat and, grabbing a chair, stood it under the little door in the ceiling. He climbed onto it and pushed aside the cover then vaulted up into the attic.

Once his eyes became accustomed to the darkness he could see the sloping ceiling, its square window glowing with the intense blue of the evening sky, dotted with tiny silver stars. Like a torn fragment from heaven, it was a piece of magic here in the top floor of his own house.

Reaching up he pressed his nose and hands against the glass and at that moment a flock of white pigeons scattered like confetti across the sky, soaring and swooping above the houses. Tears began to trickle down his face at the impossible beauty of this sight. He would have pressed the glass out and taken off with the birds. To be away from the earth with its black underground tunnels and into the upper atmosphere was a desire so strong he could taste it and feel it tingling in every part of his body.

He squeezed his fists until the knuckles went white and the sensation ebbed away. Then he sat down and looked around him. Old boxes, toys, papers and photograph albums lay scattered over the dusty floor – the bric-a-brac and memories of other times. In the far corner was an unfamiliar trunk standing against the wall. Crawling over, he pulled it towards him and was ready to open it when he saw a faint light coming from the exposed part of the wall. He peered more closely into the small hole, and then pressing his body to the floor, he crawled through and found himself in another attic room identical to his own.

Piles of old blankets and clothes were tossed into a rusty old bath and beyond was a trapdoor that led down to the house next door. Without daring to breathe, he reached for it, working it back and forth until it slid aside. He peeped through then hastily drew back. Down below, Old man Barker, his next-door neighbour, ran across the hallway in his underwear chasing his wife, Audrey.

"Come here, yer feckless ard woman," he shouted. Dressed in her old white nightgown, her hair in rollers, she panted as she ran into the bedroom then came back out, brandishing a large sweeping brush. She jabbed at his lumpy gut.

"I've telt tha ower many times, yer cloth lugged[5] old bugger, yer gettin' ower ard for that kind of goings on."

George fell back, trying to stifle the laughter that bubbled in his throat.

The old man looked up, "What's that bloody noise? We must be getting rats up there again."

George's face burned. His whole body shook with laughter. It was like being God up here, watching other people's lives as they scurried back and forth in their daily routines.

For a while he remained still, afraid to make any noise, then feeling suddenly chilled, he slid the door back and crept towards the next crawl space. This would take him into the Willis's attic. Their yard was always teeming with ragged bairns. Sometimes Maggie Willis appeared, a slight blonde haired woman with thin arms and a belly always swollen with pregnancy. George's mother said her good-for-nothing husband couldn't keep his filthy hands off her.

Their attic was filled with empty boxes, and the stench of piss was so strong he retched and covered his mouth with his sleeve. He slid aside

---

[5] deaf

the trapdoor and looked down into the dank brownness of the hallway. Children were sleeping on the floor, covered with threadbare blankets – there must have been at least six of them. In the corner, sitting on a creaking rocking chair, a woman nursed a baby. When George leaned forward to hear her soft voice singing a lullaby to the child, he glimpsed the swollen, milky curve of her breast, a perfect pearly globe glowing in the darkness.

He was so engrossed in this vision that he overbalanced and fell against some boxes, disturbing the quiet moment. The woman started and looked up. Alarmed, George scrambled through the opening into Barker's attic and then quickly back into his own. His whole body tingled with an unaccustomed excitement. He stood up, gulping for air and pressed his face to the glowing window, his eyes absorbing the deep indigo sky and its flickering stars.

He felt a step closer to heaven. He could think up here, away from the dark and dirty underground tunnels. Maybe he could start reading again and plan his escape from the life that had been forced onto him. Magic still existed. He just had to find a way to rediscover it.

10

Winter turned the sky grey and Rita was bringing clothes for the Willis children. Rita, the fairy child with the red coat and the hood lined with white fur, who ate cream with her tinned peaches and slept in the clean, white sheets of her very own bed, had no need of these clothes any more. So she brought her castoffs to the children who slept four or five to a bed, fought for every mouthful and never wore socks under their battered old shoes.

She walked solemnly alongside her mother, who grasped the big, brown bag of clothes and nodded smugly at the people watching from behind their gates as she set out on her errand of mercy. Rita was proud of her mother. She looked like a queen, never set foot outside the door without her lipstick on and wouldn't be seen in public wearing curlers or smoking – habits she said were common as muck. In the house she smoked with a cigarette holder. An absolutely glamorous practice Rita had only encountered in Hollywood films.

They passed Ella Danby as she pegged the last pair of Jack's underpants on the clothesline. With clothes pegs stuck in her mouth like wooden teeth and hair prickling with steel curlers, she reminded Rita of a dragon lady. Rita knew that Ella peeped through her lace curtains, stared from her bedroom window and watched the faces of bill collectors as they left peoples' houses. Some folks said Ella didn't sleep at night for fear of missing something.

"Yer gannin' visitin' then, Mrs Hawkins?" Ella asked, eyeing Iris's new mohair coat.

"Just tekkin' some old clothes to the Willis's," said her mother, walking at a brisker pace.

"Lovely coat, hinny!" said Ella's fading voice.

Rita's mam had told her not to talk to Ella ever since the day Rita sat in the yard listening to Ella gossip with Olive Coombes about the Phillips family. Afterwards Rita came in and asked her mother why Harold Phillips had nature's blessing and how come Irma Barker's eyes were all over his trousers.

Next they passed Mrs Mulloway's house. Her husband, Sneck was sitting on the step holding his bandaged head.

"Been in the wars, Sneck?" her mam asked.

"Why no, Iris. I've had a bat off Popeye!"

"What's that Mam?" asked Rita.

Edna Mulloway appeared, pushing an old broom. "Why Archie Nelson did it. His young'un, George, started down the pit last week and Sneck and some of the lads sent him for a cap full o' nail holes. He didn't cotton on and went to Jordy Willis in the equipment shop. Jordy took George's new cap and poked it all ower with a ten-inch nail. Next day Archie comes ower and says which bugger did this to me lad's cap and cracks our Sneck ower the head."

Sneck cradled his head in his hands. "What's the world comin' to if a man canna have a joke?"

Iris smiled and nodded her head as they carried on down the street and Rita felt tears sting the back of her eyelids at the thought of George working with all those rough men.

Soon they reached the Willis's rusty green gate. A row of small hands clung to the top of it while the older children's snot-streaked faces peered over the top. Rita and her mam waited until it swung inwards with the sheer weight of bodies on the other side. There were so many of them all wearing skimpy woollen cardigans gone hard with washing and dog eared shoes with flapping soles. Rita's never played with the Willis children. "Their heads are alive with dickies!" Iris warned. Now, laughing and pushing each other, they swarmed around the shining-faced, round-eyed Rita, who pressed herself into her mother's warm coat.

"Come on, Rita, the children are waiting to see what you brought them," her mother said as they struggled through to the front door.

Once inside, a belt of warm, stale air hit them. The place reeked of piss and cooked cabbage. Clothes, cracked cups and plates, broken toys, and bits of dried bread crusts littered the faded linoleum floor. A dull, yellowy paper, covered with washed-out tea roses was peeling off the wall in damp strips while on the stove a massive cauldron boiled and bubbled, filling the air with a fine mist.

Maggie Willis, a slight pale woman with a nervous squint, wrung her hands together as she welcomed them. Rita had heard her mother gossiping to Ella Danby about how Maggie was always sad and jumpy because she'd been in love with soldier a long time ago but he'd gone away to war and never come back. "And that's why you'll always see her climbing up Whittington Hill – sometimes takes the bairns up there for a picnic. She gazes across the fields hoping he'll come back for her." Ella whispered but Rita heard all of it. "And they say the oldest bairn isn't even Jordy's."

"Well," her mother folded her arms and puffed up her lips, "I shouldn't think any soldier would want her now if that brood of scruffy chickens came along with her." Then they both burst out laughing.

Suddenly Rita felt her mother's fingers poke at her shoulder and she snapped back to reality, realizing that the small brown thing moving behind the curtain was a mouse.

"You'll pardon the uproar, Mrs Hawkins, but my sister came over to help with the washing today," said Maggie, pushing a red-faced little boy out of the way.

Rita tried for a moment to blink synchronously with Maggie's squint but stopped as the effort proved tiresome.

"Oh, don't worry, Maggie, we're just glad to be of some help in these difficult times," Iris said, clutching onto her handbag.

"You'll have a cup of tea then. We'll find a spot for you to sit," Maggie said, sweeping some ragged knickers from the chair.

Rita realized her mother was not about to drop the clothes off and leave. She meant to stay until these slovenly women had a really good look at her new coat with the little bit of fox fur at the collar, and the thistle brooch from Edinburgh with the purple amethyst set into it. Rita knew it wasn't real fur and the jewellery was paste, but she and her mother had so enjoyed shopping for such perfect bargains at Sunderland and no one else knew their little secrets.

Her eyes wandered upwards to a line of clothes that stretched the whole length of the room; though freshly washed, they were ragged and stained. Just below the bubbling clothes tub, a bare-bottomed toddler played in the puddles of soapsuds and on the ragged brown settee an old man sat silently, his toothless gums chewing noiselessly. He wore a flat cap on his head and only a vest underneath his braces.

"Tek no notice of Grandda Willis. He only wears his teeth on Sundays. Don't yer, father?" Maggie raised her voice and the old man looked up, nodded, then spat a shiny, black gob of tobacco into a metal bowl on the floor.

Rita slid off her coat. A fair-haired girl with tawny skin snatched it so quickly that Rita barely had time to protest. She watched as the girl lovingly held it to her grimy face and stroked the soft fur against her cheek. A sharp voice boomed through the bustle of the room.

"Dinna mess up the bairn's coat, our Hazel."

Rita looked up to see a stringy-haired woman standing over by the clothes tub, stirring the steaming mixture, like a witch at her cauldron.

"I swear that bairn's a changeling child," the witch woman said. "Our Maggie must've been playin' around wi' the gypsies." Hazel looked like she was going to cry as she dropped the coat and ran out the back door into the street.

Maggie laughed at Rita's open- mouthed stare.

"Dinna pay any heed to our Eileen. She's got a sharp tongue but she's a big help to me with all these bairns." She leaned towards Rita's mother and whispered, "Twenty-five and still not married. Mother's given up on her, but I reckon it's that tongue of hers. She's too brazen."

Rita tried to listen but her attention was drawn to something much more interesting. She drifted past her mother and Maggie who sat sipping tea from chipped white mugs, past the toddler drinking soapsuds from a spoon.

In the corner by the fire an old, withered woman with skin like dried leather, sat rocking a small baby. A baby so perfect and fragile it glowed. It sat straight and quiet, staring unblinkingly ahead like a tiny statue. Curls of golden hair covered its head, and peachy cheeks curved down to a pouting bud of a mouth. She – *it must be she* – was dressed from head to toe in soft petal pink. Her little head was covered with a satin cap, its delicate lace ruffle framing her rosy face. Tiny hand-knitted booties covered her feet.

The old woman rocked back and forth, crooning softly in her thin, reedy voice. Rita stood transfixed, her hands curling and uncurling, aching to touch this child, this doll of all dolls with the clear luminous eyes that stared unblinkingly ahead.

"She's blind, poor bairn," said Eileen's rasping voice. "Maggie got the German measles in her second month."

German measles. Rita remembered her mother saying, "It's German measles, Rita, but the spots are small. Nobody will see. You must go to school because I have a headache. I have to lie down this afternoon."

And for a few extra pennies Maggie had walked Rita along to the infants' school, holding Rita's hand as she had been asked to and telling her how nice it was to look after a clean and pretty girl with soft hands and silky hair and how she hoped her new little baby was going to be just like her.

Rita walked right up to the baby who held her hands upwards. Had she, Rita, taken away the baby's eyes? The monthly visits with clothing, bits of food and other odds and ends had begun after this baby was born. Rita's mother never missed.

"She hears you, hinny," said the old nut-faced woman.

"Can I hold the bairn please?"

The old lady told her to sit on a wooden chair at the side of the rocker, then carefully offered the precious treasure to Rita. The baby nestled back and turned her rosy face up to Rita's neck, nuzzling and sniffing at her.

The eyes of grown ups turned towards Rita and the baby.

"Grandma Willis never puts that bairn down. She sews for her night and day, brushes her hair and powders her like a little dolly." Maggie took another sip of tea and brushed her hand across her eyes. "I don't know what'll become of her when Grandma's gone and she has to fend for hersel."

Rita held her for the rest of the afternoon, singing songs she knew, and telling stories of magic and princesses with sparkling crowns and forest fairies that sprinkled magic dust on sleeping children's eyes and made the blind children see again so they could run and touch the trees or watch clouds in the sky. In time she watched the infant's lilac eyelids grow weary over sightless eyes. Her own eyes soon felt hot and drowsy as she drifted into the apricot warmth of sleep.

It was dark when she woke to the scratching of chairs on linoleum. The children were gone, the room dark and silent. Her father's overcoat smelled of cigarettes and rain when he leaned over to lift her up.

"Where's the babby?" she asked Maggie, whose white face loomed out of the shadows.

"She's in bed now – she sleeps in Gramma Willis's bed."

She whispered in a little, high voice, "Da, I took away the baby's eyes."

"You're dreaming, flower. You must have had a nightmare."

As Rita was carried out, she imagined the old wizened arms folded around the soft, silky baby.

The drying clothes hung like pale ghosts from the ceiling. All the children were gone – somehow crammed into the few small rooms of the house. Rita wondered how they all fit in, but her eyes felt heavy again and so she drifted back to sleep, thinking of her own silver-haired doll waiting patiently at home on her bed.

1957

11

Every morning Ella stood by the gate, elbows leaning on the half-wall wall that separated her house from the street. She'd finished the cleaning and every surface – every counter – every cup and pan and teapot had been polished to the highest state of cleanliness. And every day she delighted in watching Maggie Willis struggle with her growing brood of bairns in a house that was known to be the foulest pigsty in the street. Worse than that, she had to put up with Jordy Willis, a man who used his fists more easily than his tongue. Why even Maggie's lovely golden hair had gone pale and stringy. Not surprising since all the neighbours said the men in that house got the lion's share of the meat while Maggie and her mother-in-law had to make do with the taties and scratchings. *Where's yer fancy soldier boy now?* Ella wondered as she watched Maggie tiptoe around the yard like a frightened mouse.

Ella still remembered that day fourteen years ago when she'd climbed Whittington Hill and lost the baby she didn't even know she was carrying. All she remembered was her mother, Mabel's voice – so loud the neighbours could hear her screaming the whole length of the street, yelling at the top of her lungs that Ella was a *gormless bloody nowt* and she'd *fettle her* the next time she decided to run away.

Later on she'd heard from Iris Hawkins that Miss Jessel, the street midwife, said it was a crime how the miserable old bugger was railing at poor Ella.

"It was all I could do to clean the poor girl up – what with that old harpy's voice screeching in me ears. And she kept fleeing in and out, slamming the door so hard she upset a bucket of boiling water all over the floor."

Afterwards, Ella played the dutiful daughter role but her blood boiled every time Mabel visited. She kept her mouth shut though. Mabel still had the power to put the fear of God into her.

She couldn't forgive Jack either. When Ella was upstairs writhing in pain, he'd just sat there at the kitchen table asking for his supper. Miss Jessel told him it would be a long time coming since Ella had lost enough blood to fill a bucket and he'd sulked for hours until Miss Quinn brought him some leftover barley hotpot. Ella hadn't forgotten that. She never let him touch her again. She set him straight when he came creeping into the bed two weeks afterwards. Ella was lying there stiff as a board, teeth on edge. nerves twanging like piano wires. The moment his sweaty fingers touched her breast, she grasped his wrist as if she would snap it.

"What the bloody hell?" he gasped, his face like a round white plate in the darkness.

"Dinna put yer filthy hands on me," she growled. "I'll clean for yer, I'll keep yer miserable belly full but yer'll never lay a hand on me or I'll slit yer throat like a chicken's when yer sleeping."

Afterwards she heard Jack's head plop down onto the pillow and then there was silence. Her heart swelled as if it would burst out of her body and tears burned behind her eyes but she clenched her fists and pushed it all inside. The next day Jack crept around the house like a beaten dog and Ella was queen of the household.

She'd watch the comings and goings of all the people on the street or she'd gossip with Olive Coombes, Jesse Nelson, Iris Hawkins and Hannah

Willis. There was nothing her eagle eyes missed. But today's gossip would be cut short because it was Friday and Mabel came round for tea every Friday at four. She was a woman who liked her food so Ella had to start the preparations at one.

She stepped through the stiff, navy curtain that separated the cozy kitchen from the cold outside and went straight to the oak sideboard to get her rolling pin, mixing bowls and her trusty Be-Ro home recipe book. Once they were all spread out onto the kitchen table she licked her fingers and thumbed through the book. Today they'd have Cornish pasties with pickled onions and beetroot, cheese scones, a nice walnut cake and some macaroons. She could picture Mabel filling her fleshy face with the baking and Jack licking his chops at the sight of it all. That would keep them both quiet for a good half an hour she thought as she rolled up her sleeves and started weighing out the ingredients. The fire was good and high now so the oven would be hot enough for baking in about ten minutes. There was no time to waste.

Though the kitchen was stuffy, Ella sang as she folded flour into ivory coloured batters and mashed the corn beef with fluffy boiled potatoes and onions. But no matter how hard she tried to silence it, a little nagging voice kept picking away at her contentment, whispering to her how it was such a shame that there were no bairns in the house to share the bounty and complete her happiness. *Filthy little buggers,* she told herself, *with their snot noses and their mouths forever open like squawking cuckoo birds* – all they'd do was whine and cry and make messes. She was best off without them.

But after losing the baby she'd followed Jesse Nelson down the street every second day when little George was a toddler, just to feast her eyes on his fine golden hair. In her heart she'd ached to touch just the tip of one of those silky curls. She would have made sure his boots were clean, and his nose wiped. She'd have spread disinfectant over every surface so those poor little lads wouldn't have had to live in filth and catch tuberculosis. It was a crime, she thought, that all the dirty people on the streets bred like rabbits and were too feckless to look after their own bairns. Ella remembered the day they carried little Peter Nelson's body away in a small grey coffin. She'd been making stotty cake and had just finished rolling the dough. Something went wild inside her when she saw that small box carrying the child's body. A sparrow would have fit comfortably in it. Afterwards she went inside and slammed the rolling pin across the face of her new mantel clock, then sat in Jack's chair and sobbed for an hour.

Cursing silently, she wiped a stray tear away with a floury hand. *Pull yerself together* she told herself as she slapped the rolling pin down onto the pastry. The cracked clock still remained as a memory of the day she lost control.

Once the macaroons were put into the oven, Ella went to the polished walnut china cabinet and took out her best Sheffield cutlery as well as the willow pattern plates and cups. Jack's mother had left them in her will. They were hers now, she reasoned, so why shouldn't she use them? *Why the bloody hell not?* She took out three cups, three saucers and three dainty dessert plates. They were the picture of elegance with her white damask tablecloth, the gold coronation teapot and the silver spoons. One of Jack's sacred chrysanthemums completed the picture. She'd plucked out the biggest, yellowest flower and placed it in the willow pattern bud vase. Every year Jack entered the flower show and last year he'd won first prize – a red velvet footstool that sat in front of his armchair by the fire. She'd probably picked his prizewinning flower but she'd soon fettle him if he said a word about it.

Then when everything was set out – the pasties in all their golden glory, the buttery cheese scones, and the white iced walnut cake next to the coconut macaroons – it looked like a feast fit for a queen. All she had to do now was to put up her feet for a while by the fire and have a quick snooze. The coalscuttle was empty now since she just put in the last few lumps, but Jack would fill it when he got back from his shift. So once her floury pinny was off and put away to wash, she flopped into his armchair and put her feet up on the red velvet stool, her eyelids heavy with the warmth from the oven and the fire.

In her dream Ella was trying to climb a hill with no summit, but all she could hear was a voice calling her from far away. *I'm up here, Ella, come here* it called from the bottom of a deep, dark well, but her feet were stuck fast as if her shoes were made of iron. She struggled to open her eyes to the cold, dark room. The fire had gone out and when she reached for the coalscuttle it was nowhere to be found. Panicking she stood up and tripped over the stool, landing bottom first on the linoleum floor. *What the bloody...* she thought to herself when she heard Jack shouting out in the yard. "Ella, Ella, come quickly."

Clambering up, she groped her way through the darkness and out into the yard. Jack was standing next to the coal shed where the missing coalscuttle lay on its side. Right by it, Ella saw a large bundle of rags.

Jack was pointing and crying. "Your mam – she tried to fill the coal scuttle."

Ella felt herself floating over to the ragged bundle as if she was still asleep. Once there, she took a close look. Mabel lay twisted on her side by the coal shed door, her face black as the ace of spades and her eyes fixed in an upward stare. At that moment Ella felt something bubbling deep in her stomach as if a huge giggle was about to escape from inside and swallow her. Jack must have thought she was crying because he put his arms around her and whispered, "It's all right pet, it was sudden. The poor ard wife didn't suffer." But the only thing Ella could think of was the mountain of baking waiting inside and how it would come in handy for the funeral guests.

Silly old bugger, she thought as she imagined Mabel complaining about her good-for-nothing lazy daughter who couldn't even fill the coalscuttle. But Jack's shirt smelled clean and nice as she buried her face in it just as the tears started up alongside the laughter.

And Jack squeezed her close to him, not seeing the twisted grin that crossed her face.

12

Sunday morning. The coal oven wheezed and sputtered, warming the kitchen, searing the roast beef and puffing up the Yorkshire puddings. Maggie Willis was busy with the weekly clean up. Using her father-in-law's old underpants, she dusted the scratched sideboard and the iron wall plaques from Blackpool, then tried to sort through the piles of clothes, old newspapers and bits of food that littered the floor.

Sunday dinners were different from the stewing scraps and tripe meals of the week. Sundays meant real meat with all the trimmings – no pigs' trotters or ham bones boiled up for days on end or jam sandwiches with tea. *And wasn't life good with all the men working.* Other folks were worrying about layoffs and pit closures, but not the Willis's. They had enough food and more to spare, but there were always plenty of mouths waiting to be filled, and another was on the way.

Maggie felt the firm swell of her belly and the familiar fluttering deep inside her body; the new life safe from harm for now until it forced its way out, its mewling and crying drowned by the clatter and clamour of the other bairns.

Folks on the street tattled and gossiped about Maggie, looking sideways at her with their sly fox eyes as if she couldn't see them. Talking behind her back and snickering when she walked by with her rag tag line of children. She knew what they were saying: how her man, Jordy, couldn't keep his filthy hands off her, how they were breeding like bloody rabbits without even being able to look after the bairns they had.

Well, those folks were nowt but snoopers and meddlers, the lot of them, always prying and poking into other folks' business and coming up with a pack of lies and gossip. They didn't see the happy faces of her children when she made a big bag of bread and dripping sandwiches, then filled a bottle of water and took them off for a picnic. Or when she kissed the faces of each one before they went off to sleep.

Some said she kept a dirty house. She tried her best, but there was never enough time to look after the holes in the linoleum, or the sticky trail of footprints, fingerprints, crusts and dirt left by the children. And Hannah, Maggie's mother-in-law, helped with the baby but never lifted a finger to do any cleaning. She was happy as long as Jordy had a smile on his face and her arrangement of glass ornaments was clean. Jimmy, her husband won them at Houghton Feast when they were sixteen-year-old newly weds. Three blown-glass swans and a unicorn set out in a tidy row on the mantelpiece above the fire. *Well, let the neighbours talk*, Maggie thought. Her children were happy and their bellies were full. What was wrong with a bit of dirt?

The worst of the gossips was Ella Danby, a right muckraker with her eyes everywhere. She was always bragging about how she kept her husband under her thumb, and how she wouldn't let him get away with any of the filthy kind of behaviour certain other folks were always up to. That's why she'd never had any children – couldn't abide the mess. She kept her front step well polished, and only one or two people ever saw inside her house. Maggie heard the rumours, though, that it was full of china teapots and crocheted chair covers. Maggie's husband, Jordy, said Jack read his paper and smoked his pipe in the outhouse for fear of spoiling Ella's handiwork.

Anyway, Ella didn't know Jordy. When he wanted something, he got it and he wanted Maggie all the time. Aye, one minute he could be a charmer, laughing with the lads at the club or hugging his mam. Next minute the smile would disappear and his entire body was taken over by anger so fierce and rotten that Maggie felt she was being sucked into a black whirlpool.

Some folks called him a 'nasty piece of work' or a 'right arsehole' but she'd learned to tread carefully for the bairns' sake – and her own. When that drowsy look came into his eyes after supper, and he started to rub his groin with a slow, rhythmical motion, she ushered the children into the yard with the older ones in charge, then turned and took off her pinny to walk upstairs with him. He climbed so close behind she could hear his laboured breathing and smell his sharp tinny smell of dried sweat as he guided her up, one hand tight on her shoulder, the other up her skirt. She couldn't deny him or she'd get a good knocking around and another black eye to make excuses about.

But she always wanted the babies, to feel the child sucking at her breast, and the small head with its whorl of dark hair, nestling in the crook of her arm.

Jordy wouldn't touch her when her belly began to swell or when she was nursing. Said it turned him off – like doing it with a cow or something.

But then that time always came when the child finally struggled from her arms, tottering on its own unsteady legs to join the other children and run barefoot into the cobbled street where its soft little feet would soon become hard and calloused, its knees bruised and scraped. Maggie watched, longing for its warm baby smell and the feel of its body against hers, knowing Jordy would be back at her before she could even recover. He'd appear, scrubbed, shaved and breathless, sometimes holding a box of chocolates, but always with that wide-mouthed puppy grin, fresh from the company of some young girl who had shown him her arse in return for a few gins at the club.

"Tek the meat out, Maggie. The men will be getting back soon and nowt's ready."

Her mother-in-law's face glowed beet red, cheeks puffing out with sheer effort as she pounded the suet pudding dough.

Maggie looked out the window at the grey October clouds scudding across the windy sky and remembered the day after her meeting with Chuck. Her mother forced her to go out with Jordy that night. Threatened to throw her out on the street if she didn't buckle under and do as she was told. Finally she agreed to go to the club with Jordy and by eight that night she was sitting at a corner table, her stomach churning and her heart numb. She was wearing a smart navy blue tam o' shanter with matching coat and Jordy bought her tonic water. It had a bitter taste to it but she gulped it down all the same. He bought her another one. Then she'd watched the way his cheeks puffed out as he gulped down his pint of stout and introduced her to the blur of faces passing by the table. She remembered the buzz of voices mingling with the sickly smell of pipe smoke and the terrifying feeling that her body was hurtling forwards on an express train. Suddenly she was gasping for fresh air, but when she stood up to go outside her knees crumpled like cardboard and she flopped to the floor.

Then Jordy's ruddy face loomed above her, breathing stale beer into her face. She turned her head away. "Are yer all right, hinny?" he begged.

A sterner voice said, "Yer should never have put all that gin in the lass's tonic water, Jordy yer rascal."

Maggie panicked. Her mind raced. Images passed by in an orange blur. Some voice inside said he meant to do her harm. But she'd been warned. Her cousin had shaken her finger and said, "If yer marry a man that badly uses you, yer life won't be worth a tinker's cuss."

She tried to get up but her arms and legs wouldn't move and her throat seized when he carried her out and took her home. But he stopped on the way. Took her into a back alley behind the Carlton Picture House, slammed her up against the wall and told her he wanted a bit of what the Yank had. All she could remember was his face pumping in and out of her vision and the rough bricks scraping against the back of her arms.

They were married two weeks later in August. Their first child, Hazel, was born in February of the following year – nine months after her night with Chuck and eight months twenty seven days after the night with Jordy. He barely looked at the baby – not until her hair grew in – and when he saw the fine black curls he swept her up and kissed her rosy face. "Bonny lass," he said. "I always knew you was mine."

Now Maggie shivered, shifting her gaze onto the empty street. All the women were inside making dinner while the men were at the Belton and District Working Men's club. Sunday morning at the club was a ritual for them. Husbands, brothers, fathers, sons, grandfathers, all congregated there and drank pint after pint from 11 o'clock until two. Jordy, face flushed, and stomach bloated with beer, would stagger back home to a full Sunday dinner waiting for him on the table. He spent the afternoon sleeping then they were off back to the club for another session. There was barely time to wash the pint glasses before they were sloshing more stout or bitter until the bell rang for closing time.

Maggie didn't begrudge Jordy this time of rest since most of his waking hours were spent toiling underground.

He needed some time to forget the miserable grind of those long, dark hours. She couldn't imagine how horrible it was down there away from the sky and the sunshine and the children's laughter. Maggie loved the fresh air and always turned her face to the wind when she hung out the bed sheets on a summer day or walked down the High Street in the springtime past the blossom filled apple trees.

Every night Jordy came home, his eyes lined with coal dust and at night he sat in the tin bath in front of the fire as she scrubbed him from head to toe. By the end of the bath he always slipped into a deep, noisy sleep. These were the only tender moments they shared. Once he was tucked into bed, Maggie hung his pit clothes on a line above the fireplace to warm them, ready for the morning shift.

Her cousin, Mary had warned her, "The life of a miner's wife is a bloody life sentence, Maggie, yer'll sup yer share of sorrows. If yer not frettin' trying to scrape a few pennies together to feed yer children, yer'll be worryin' that one day the alarm will be sounding and he'll be buried under a mountain of black dust and rubble. If that doesn't kill him then the black spittle surely will." That's why Mary went off with a man that owned a newsagent's on Kellaway Street.

But she never heeded Mary's advice. Who else could she marry anyway? Her mother said she was soiled goods as far as every sane man was concerned, and at first Jordy filled her head with soft words. Said he'd never have to go to the seaside again because her eyes were blue as moonlight on water. His thick hands stroked her into believing that if marriage was good enough for her mother and her grandmother before her, it must be good enough for Maggie Harris. Mam and Dad had been happy enough for twenty-six years and Dad's gentle nature made her believe all men treated their wives with such tender love. She drifted into marriage without protest.

Hannah knocked Maggie's arm. "Haway hinny. Yer dreamin' again. Closin' time was ten minutes ago and the table's still empty."

When Maggie looked outside again she saw the stream of navy blue suited men shuffling up the street.

"They're coming, Mother. We'd best get the meat on the table for carving."

The roasting pan hissed and spat as Maggie pulled it from the oven, its rich meaty smell filling the kitchen. "By it's a good joint yer got this week. Enough for everyone and meat sandwiches for tonight."

"Aye," her mother-in-law beamed proudly at the dishes of potatoes and Yorkshire puddings, and the bowl of gravy with bubbles of fat gleaming on the surface, "It's a blessing we can feed all these bairns when there's those that have nowt but bread and drippings for their Sunday dinners."

Maggie called to the children who were playing in the front yard, "Yer father's coming, get ready for dinner." Hazel, the oldest, scooped up eighteen-month-old Pearl and the rest followed.

"I'm famished, Mother. Gi's some bread and dip." David was nine and growing out of his clothes faster than Maggie could let them out or down.

"No hinny, let yer father and granddad sit down first. Then it'll be your turn."

The door burst open and Jordy blew in, slack-mouthed and wild, like a blustery wind. His father, Ernie, a short, shrunken figure, padded in behind him.

"I telt that bugger, Archie Nelson, if he so much as breathes on my pint glass again I'll knock his face up his fucking arse."

Maggie's throat felt dry and papery as she ushered the children into the front room.

She could hear her father-in-law's reedy voice, like straw scraping over metal, "Now dinna tek on so, Jordy, he's nowt but a nancy boy."

"Where's Maggie?" Jordy barked.

"She's seeing to the bairns, son."

"Well tell her to get her hind end out here and serve her man some bloody dinner."

Hannah scuttled off to the front room as Jordy yanked off his tie and loosened his braces. Then, sitting at the head of the table, he grasped his fork and knife and stared straight ahead.

"Sit yersel' down, father. After a week's sweatin' at the pit yer deserve a decent bit o' beef for yer Sunday dinner."

The women slid the hot dishes onto the table while the children sucked in their breath and watched through the doorway with hungry eyes.

Maggie stood back, sliding her wedding ring back and forth. She watched as Jordy made a mountain of potato in the centre of his plate, hollowed a small hole on top and poured gravy out until it welled up at the edge of the plate then trickled over the edge staining the white damask tablecloth. Hannah winced and bit her finger while Maggie's hand flew to her mouth. She stepped forward but stopped as Jordy's fist slammed on the table, bouncing his father's plate away out of reach of the old man's fork.

"What the fuck are you looking at with your bloody cow's eyes," he yelled to Maggie.

Hannah pushed the plate of meat in front of him. "It's nothing lad – she's just being careful of the tablecloth."

"I work all soddin' week and if I want to spill a bit of gravy I don't need any miserable slut pullin' a long face over it."

Hannah grasped Maggie's arm, "Say yer sorry, hinny, and we can all eat in peace."

"I'm sorry, Jordy. I didn't mean to bother you," said Maggie, her heart pounding in her ears.

Jordy slammed his plate against the other dishes and pointed his finger at her. "Her frosty bloody face is spoiling me dinner. She canna even crack a smile. Bloody lazy cow stays at home all day while I'm slaving like an animal down the pit. I canna eat it – it'd stick in me throat." He stood up and banged his chair against the table.

"Come on, hinny," begged Hannah, "it's top sirloin."

"I'll choke because she's mekkin' me sick. Sick! So stuff yer bloody dinner."

He grabbed the dripping plate and slammed it onto the fire setting it ablaze with the gravy and potatoes and meat. Hannah flew over to the mantelpiece and swept her glass ornaments up into her pinny then rushed off to the front room.

"What the bloody hell." Ernie's fork was suspended in mid-air – a brussel sprout speared on the end, as Jordy began to empty the dishes from the table, throwing them at the fire one by one.

"Tek that, yer buggers. And that!" he chanted over the splintering sounds of breaking pots.

The little man took his plate and scurried upstairs.

Maggie screamed, "No Jordy! The bairns' dinner!"

Jordy wheeled around. "Shut yer bloody gob or I'll bust it for yer. The bairns – the bairns. Yer think more of them than me."

The floor was covered with potato. Slices of meat slid down the stones of the fireplace and grey puddles of gravy covered the floor. Maggie turned to see the hungry staring eyes of the children, then felt her head yanked back as Jordy grabbed a handful of her hair and pulled her towards the door.

"Time for a bit of fresh air yer naggin' ard wife – thou's nee good to me in here."

Maggie's legs knocked against the table legs and the staircase as he pulled her through the open door, banging her head against the doorpost. Then he pushed her outside and she heard the click of the lock. Frantically, her hands clawing at the window frame, Maggie stood on tiptoes to look inside. Jordy picked up a hunk of bread, stripped off his shirt, scratched his armpits lazily, and then climbed the stairs.

Once the room was empty, Maggie watched the children hurtle out of the front room and scoop up meat, potatoes, puddings from the floor and shove it into their mouths as they glanced with fear-filled eyes towards the dark space at the top of the stairs. Maggie's stomach rumbled as she knocked and scratched against the glass. Sooner or later one of them would let her in, but for now she'd let them eat.

She sat back on the doorstep and rested her head against the door. The pit heap stood at the end of the street – a monument of muck and slag. Her own Da had walked towards it every day. He'd always smile back at her and she'd wave at him until her arms were sore. One day, she remembered, after the big strike of 1926, her brother Ronnie got one of the pit ponies out and lifted her onto its back saying, "Let's go and visit Da now." She'd been overjoyed to hold onto the dusty grey mane and ride up the hill like a princess.

The wall outside the colliery offices was lined with men, standing or squatting against the wall, silent like shadows, their eyes downcast and hands jammed into pockets. Ronnie lifted her down and she ran towards the group, searching for her Da. "Has anyone seen him? His name's Willie," her shrill child's voice cried. She found him, squatting near the gate bowling stones along the ground. He looked so sad and thoughtful she was glad to climb up on his knees and bury her face in the clean, soapy smell of his neck. "Dada, what are you waiting for?"

"Work, hinny. I'm waiting to get my job back."

She stayed with him, wrapped in his jacket, her face pressed against his chest. This time there were no tricks with hankies or sweets or jokes. Just silence and her father's worried glances up and down the street, his strong arms holding her tightly. She was afraid to breathe, fearing he might cry and then she wouldn't know what to do.

"Da," she whispered, "What's a blackleg?"

"Hinny, it's some poor desperate soul that's tired of watching his children starve."

And then there was a sudden rush of noise as if a hundred pairs of boots were crashing over the gritty ground. A fat man in a black top hat waved a metal cane and shouted, "Why are all these men loitering here? Get rid of them." Next minute her father was up and running, yelling for Ronnie to *take her, take her*. Hands grabbed her and she was on the pony again, only this time it was trotting down the hill. She was howling and screaming, "Dada take me back to Dada!" Yelling until her throat cracked and no sound came out. Then a man with ginger whiskers smashed her father over the back of the head with a big stick.

When they brought him home his hair was matted with blood. Maggie could see only the whites of his eyes. "They broke his head, mam," was all she could say, over and over. Her mother cried and tore up all the sewing she was doing for the neighbours. The man with the ginger whiskers was charged and sent away. "Too overzealous in carrying out his duties," was the official word.

They took her father on again at the pit to drive the ponies and he talked to them like they were his own bairns. Some said he'd gone soft in the head, but Maggie knew this was only her Da's real tenderness coming out. It's a queer world, she thought, only the gentle and meek are the victims. They always believe the best of people no matter how rotten or evil they really are.

1959

13

Four o'clock on a damp, grey Saturday in March and the street was quiet. Most of the neighbours were at the football game in Sunderland or out shopping on the High Street. Rita sat on her step, sullen-faced and suffering with a fresh crop of pimples, waiting for gossip and ready to strain her ears for secret information. The stories of things people got up to behind closed doors – sexy stuff that made her heart leap in a sickly way.

In the house her parents were arguing about money again. Something terrible had happened. Something that blasted away the foundations of Rita's comfortable existence with its weekly Girls' Own magazine, the regular shopping expeditions to Sunderland and the endless supply of fresh white socks, underwear and Sunday outfits. The money had run out. The little nest egg her mother cherished had trickled through their fingers like toy pennies, as they revelled in yards of pink gingham to make the flounces on Rita's dressing table. Collections of stuffed teddies and dolls of every shape and size, crammed the shelves in Rita's bedroom and the latest addition to the front parlour was a pale cream cocktail bar made of padded plastic trimmed with gold painted cherubs and studded with pink buttons.

The bathroom cupboards were full to bursting with bottles of coloured bath salts, nail varnish, hair spray and boxes of pastel coloured soaps, but the bank account was empty. "Drained of every penny," the bank manager explained, as they stood empty handed at the counter. His mouth set into a lipless line. "It was a *savings* account, wasn't it," he asked Rita and her red-faced mam. The day's shopping trip was cancelled and the weekly outings ceased.

Inside the house Iris screamed at Walter, "Yer bloody drunkard – yer drank it all away, yer gave it all to the club."

He screamed back, "You – fer ever actin' like Lady Muck. Tekkin' on all the airs and graces. Always in the soddin' shops spendin' money on every bloody thing yer greedy eyes could see."

"But I can't manage on what's comin' in."

"Every bugger else manages on this street – I mek a good wage."

"Yes but I have certain standards to maintain," her mother replied weakly.

"I'll fettle yer standards. You and our Rita had better stop gannin' on all these shopping sprees or I'll have to send you out on the streets to mek yer own money."

There was a scuffling followed by the sound of smashing plates, then Rita's Dad shouted, "I'm gannin' to the dog track – I'll get mesel a better bite to eat down there."

The front door flew open and he brushed past Rita without a word.

Next door Ella Danby stood on her step watching every move. When she saw Iris run out of the house crying she scuttled quickly towards the fence. Rita looked closely at her mam whose face was smudged with shadows and criss-crossed by a web of fine lines and now that the weekly visits to Eileen's Paris Coiffures had stopped, grey hair was growing in from the roots. She'd also developed a slight stoop, aggravated by the hours spent nightly poring over knitting patterns in Women's Weekly while she created a steady stream of dog-eared scarves, socks without heels, and jumpers with one arm longer than the other.

Ella leaned over the fence towards Iris. Ella's eyebrows were plucked to a thin line and pencilled into arches that gave her an expression of permanent surprise.

"Walter gone to the dogs then?"

"Aye – spendin' money he hasn't got."

"All the same, men. Mind our Jack always hands ower half his winnings. I don't even have to put me hand out."

The tinkling of the ice-cream van drowned their voices. Rita's mother turned to her, "Do yer want one flower?"

Rita felt the cold lump of clay in her stomach and shook her head sullenly.

Ella leaned closer, "Just as well, Mrs Hawkins. I telt tha – never buy owt from Valenti – I've heard he picks his nose all the time."

On the other side of Ella's fence Olive Coombes got up from scrubbing the step, wiped her hands on her pinny and leaned over towards the other two women. "Eeh yer never know what yer eatin' these days – and yer know summat else? I wouldn't buy any cakes from Mrs Browning."

Rita's mother pulled her cardigan over her shoulders. It was made of wool scraps from unravelled socks. "But she always ices them so beautiful with marzipan flowers and everything."

Olive scowled and shook her head, "She's got trouble with her tear ducts, that one. I've seen her eyes streaming with tears when she's mixing the cakes – turns my stomach to think of it."

Ella scratched her ear with a raw, stubby hand, "Eeh, there's that many dirty people about." She pushed her face forward, opening her eyes wide so the whites showed in a thin rim all around. Rita strained her ears, knowing something juicy was about to be said.

"Look ower there – Harold Hunt's just gettin' in from the afternoon shift. They say his poor mam's always havin' to gan out since he got married to Irma. She canna even have a cup of tea for the creakin' of the bedsprings and the two of them ruttin' like a pair of dogs in heat."

The other two women turned to look as Harold swung open the door of his house.

"Aye and they say he's got nature's blessing," said Olive.

"He's heavily hung," whispered Ella.

The three women huddled in a little knot as Olive continued. "Just like that Jordy Willis. A prize bull, that bugger with all them bairns. Breeding like rabbits – the pair of them."

"And his wife, the poor soul. Got another black eye and she's just a poor slip of a thing," said Ella, "I heard he forces her to do it even when she's having her monthlies – I'd cut his bloody whiskers off!"

Rita knew what 'it' was. She'd been huddled in the corner of the school playground by the girls' toilets, listening to Jean Basset repeating her 15-year-old brother's explanation. The details of strange noises, naked body parts and nasty smells seemed to have no relation to the perfumed romance and kisses of the Hollywood film annuals Rita pored over every night.

All this talk of dogs in heat and "doing it" made Rita's head feel dizzy and sick. The same way she felt when Mary Wilson died. Mary had lived two doors down and Rita remembered her wedding. She was a picture in ivory lace and apple blossom, throwing pennies to the children who ran up to her waiting horse and cart. Rita, dressed in her best red checked suit, had breathlessly handed her the silver paper horseshoe she and her mother bought in Sunderland. Mary smiled and accepted it, planting a little kiss on Rita's cheek. Six months later she was dead from T.B.

When they went to pay their respects Iris made Rita look at the pale corpse which lay like a manikin in its satin-lined coffin, still dressed in the frothy lace wedding dress, the dead twigs of apple blossom woven through her hair.

"Like an alabaster doll," her mother crooned gently. And for weeks afterwards Rita wrapped her dolls in silk handkerchiefs, and then placed them into shoe- boxes.

Later Jean Bassett said it was getting married that did it. "When he stuck his thing inside her it was so big it burst her guts open."

Horrified, Rita vowed never to get married and, tired of the babbling women she turned to go into the house but not before she spotted George walking up the street carrying a shopping bag in his hand. Dressed in a red muffler and pit clothes, he looked so much older. Suddenly aware of her pimples and lank, greasy hair, she slunk back against the coal shed to watch when he pulled off his cap and nodded to the gossiping women. Rita's face flushed hot at the sight of his wavy, wheat-coloured hair.

"Eeh – he's a lovely lad," said Ella, watching him open his gate.

"And well brought up too," said Olive. "Not dragged up like some buggers I know."

"Bookish too," said Ella, "Goes into Durham every week and spends his money at Andrews' bookshop."

Rita's heart pounded. She'd slipped out of school at least twice this year during P.T class, taken the bus to Durham and gone to Andrews' to buy her Hollywood film magazines. She might have been *that* close to bumping into him, though she would've been stuck for words. Life had become so complicated since she'd entered her teens.

"And I hear he rarely sets foot in the club," said Rita's mam. "Lucky lass that snags him."

He turned round with one last smile before letting himself into the house and Rita was sure she heard a collective sigh from the three women before they started whispering again.

Lucky lass, she thought, the lucky lass will be the one whose hand he kisses because he really loves her and not because some loony sweet shop lady tells him to.

1960

14

It was the day before Christmas Eve and the Number 37 bus swished into Durham Market Place, spattering slush across Lord Londonderry's statue and the crowds of last minute shoppers. George emerged from the smoky bus, glad to be away from the stink of damp coats and mothballs.

The clock on St. Mary's church said four, and though the sky was beginning to darken there was still time to do his Christmas duties and buy a few odds and ends. Bath salts for his mother, some tobacco for his father. Then there'd be time left to walk around the university, to peer in through partly open doors or gaze through the shutters at the students – the fortunate ones. Usually he felt like an outsider in this college town, skulking round the shops knowing that no amount of scrubbing could remove the dirt from under his fingernails. But today he felt different. Today a flame of hope burned inside him from the top of his skull to the tips of his toes. This new inspiration had come from a chance meeting with Walter Hawkins yesterday in the pit offices. Walter was thumbing through the pound notes in his pay packet. "Five for the wife and the rest for me." He stuffed the notes into his pocket. "Bloody wife and daughter gan through it like *watter*."

George had thought of Rita over the past three years although he'd never seen her again. If he wasn't working awkward shifts, he was up in the attic reading and studying. At times though, he remembered the prim little girl with the silver bracelets and starched handkerchiefs and missed her innocent companionship.

"How's your Rita?" he said, approaching Walter.

"Our Rita," he said, shaking his head. "That bairn's got *mair* daft ideas than a cart full o' *cloons*."

Probably still dreams of marrying a millionaire or a visiting prince, George thought, watching Walter take a half smoked Woodbine from behind his ear and knock the burnt end away. And then a faint spark of hope began to tickle inside him. *If she hadn't given up then why should he mope around the place like a "dumb cluck" as his dad said.*

"Yer gannin ter see Jimmy Waites, the union boss? He's doin' a talk down at the club?" said Walter, stepping out into the sunshine.

George just went for the hell of it. But when he walked into the packed room and saw all union men listening in rapt silence, he sat down at the back of the hall. A small, square man, no taller than five foot four, with oily black hair and a rich baritone voice, marched up and down the rows rolling fine words around his mouth like ripe plums. He called them all *brothers*. He used words like *unite* and *rights* and *fight* and *demands*, when he cried out against the greed of the pit managers and the apathy of the government. A master showman, he held the men in a spell that lasted for the full two hours. When he concluded with his fist held upwards in victory the applause exploded from the crowd and every man was on his feet.

George stumbled outside and saw the day in a new light. The hopelessness was gone and in its place were possibilities. Real hope that one day he'd be right up front like Jimmy Waites, but he'd have his own style. In fact he would get to work on it that very night and the next day he'd go to Durham to find books on speech making. He had the ideas, he had the words and Audrey Barker who did the cleaning up at the pit office told him he had the looks, so he was already one step ahead of Jimmy Waites.

Audrey's husband, Neddy was an old miser of a man, rumoured to keep all his money inside at least twenty pairs of socks hidden up in his attic at number sixteen Crag Street – next door to the Willis's. Audrey was forever winking at George and telling him she'd like to mop his floors and clean his whistle. Embarrassed, George usually blushed and turned away but that night he'd taken a good look at himself in the mirror. Looking back at him was a man with clear blue eyes, wavy blond hair and a nose as chiselled as Burt Lancaster's.

Anyway, George wouldn't have touched Audrey with a barge pole. She was forty- eight years old, with red, meaty hands and missing front teeth. He'd also seen her downing Guinness at the club like she was drinking cold tea. No, he preferred to reserve those thoughts for Ruby Allen, the barmaid at the Belton Working Men's club with the jet- black perm and the pouting red lips. Teddy Barrett said she had *titties like Marilyn Monroe and a mouth that belonged around your pecker.*

When George first saw her she licked her top lip deliberately and smiled when he asked for a pint. "At least you haven't gor'a filthy gob like them swine," she said nodding towards Teddy and his mates. "I'll sit in the back at the pictures if you'll tek me," she said, leaning forward so he could get a good eyeful. Only last week he took her to see *Spartacus* and they'd spent the last hour kissing while she massaged the throbbing bump under his trousers.

Now the cold air cut into the exposed flesh of his neck so he pulled his cap down over his ears. Silver rime frosted the town hall roof. Bright red and green Christmas lights framed its windows, revealing glittering trees inside, while over by St. Mary's church a group of carollers sang *O Little Town of Bethlehem* above the sound of peeling bells. It was a slice of paradise far removed from dirt and grime of Crag Street, and the dirt of the pit. Here every sight, every sound, every smell was intensified. He was on the brink of greatness and the nerves in his body tingled with anticipation.

It was half past four when he stepped out from Boots the chemists with a small bottle of lavender water wrapped in tissue paper, and a tin of Woodbine pipe tobacco packed in a brown paper bag.

On an impulse he stopped into Cox's, the baker's, drawn by the smell of fresh pastry and the trays of golden pork pies. He stepped outside, cradling the warm, greasy package. Little droplets of fat trickled down his chin as he bit into the crust, savouring every salty mouthful and wishing the day would never end. If only he could live here his life would be complete. Everyone here had places to go or important things to do. Their lives were significant.

George watched the groups of University students walking together, college scarves coiled round the collars of their duffle coats, books tucked under their arms. *Who are they* he asked himself, that old pang of resentment stabbing at him. *Who are they – these sons and daughters of doctors, these children of businessmen, lawyers, even aristocrats?* They were the moneyed people who glided through their privileged lives, expecting life was always meant to be that way. Their soft palms were greased with easy money, their bodies cushioned with every comfort. *Do they care about us miserable workers struggling to keep bread on the table, a pisspot under our rickety bed and a few pints of bitter in our bellies at the club? Or, worse still, do they know we risk our lives every day to keep their fires burning and their water heated?*

George stuck his hands into his pockets and tightened his muffler. Yes, some people had to fight for a decent life, to better themselves – or claw their way up out of the slagheap and clean off the muck.

He snatched off the cloth cap and the hand-knitted muffler but the thin, navy Co-op suit and the cheap, brown shoes betrayed his class. *All are equal in the eyes of God*, he convinced himself, and turned towards the great cathedral that loomed ahead like a giant galleon. Silent, its immense towers floated in an ocean of stars and its presence moved him. Great and grand sights always stirred him and the bitterness trickled away to a secret corner, set aside for some other occasion of self-pity.

All the narrow streets snaked upwards towards the cathedral, their cobblestone floors overhung by rows of sloping stone university buildings. The doors of the old colleges were closed, revealing only dark shadows beyond. He'd seen behind these heavy old doors one summer day, glimpsing the shady rooms where grand pianos were played and groups of students sat around a dark-gowned teacher. Beyond the rooms were vast and lush gardens, rich with flowers and exotic plants and cooled by the soft hiss of fountains.

On his right was the Three Swans public house, a popular haunt of young mining lads – brawny men and boys who'd come in from the villages on a Saturday night and after a few beers and a round of darts, they'd roll out into the streets and fight. *Too early for that*, he thought, bowing his head in case someone recognized him and tried to call him inside.

Further up was Andrews' bookstore. He usually looked in here, flipped through a few expensive books, read a bit of poetry and checked the University calendar of cultural events. Today, however, he had to find a book on speechmaking.

He stepped into the yellow glow of the shop and breathed in the smell of fresh paper. It was so quiet inside after the bustle of the street. People stood still and took time to think. There was the usual line of people flicking through the magazine rack and over in the poetry section was only one other person – a girl in a navy-blue school coat. There was something familiar about her red-brown curls that drew him over to stand behind her. She was looking through a Hollywood film annual and George saw a rolled-up school beret sticking out of her pocket. Straining his neck to the side, he could see her profile. It was Rita. An older, more sullen Rita who licked her thumb and flipped the glossy pages. She turned around and the strong, dark eyebrows that framed her green eyes startled him for a moment.

"Rita – how are you? I mean – I thought you were at school," he stumbled.

Her face flushed pink for a moment and he noticed the beginnings of pimples around her forehead.

"Oh aye – I left school a bit early – P.E. class – I felt sickly and I didn't feel like vaulting over boxes." She snapped the book shut. "Nice life in California. Better than here anyway."

"Oh – oh yes," he stuttered, trying to find a trace of the old Rita. It was incredible what time could do to a person. Only her eyes were the same, but her hair hung in a lank curtain over one eye. "Won't you get into trouble skyving off like that?"

"Who cares?" she said looking away and pushing the hair behind one ear. Her face was pale and strained and he remembered a day in the pit baths when Teddy Barrett told him, *"Yer can tell when a lass is on the rag, man, all the blood gans downwards and hor fyace is like a ghost's."*

George's face felt hot and he coughed nervously. "Your mam and dad care."

"They don't – they're too busy screaming at each other." She sighed and put the book back. "You won't tell – will you?"

"No – but you don't know how lucky you are. You could be out working instead," George said, feeling suddenly old.

Rita had grown taller, almost to his shoulder. Her coat was open and her school tie loosened. A far cry from the prim and tidy bairn he'd walked over to Beattie's with only three years ago.

༄

"Don't you start going on at me. Me dad does it all the time," she said hitching her satchel onto her shoulder. When he saw the elastic edge of a bra strap George felt his face burn again. He glanced away when he saw the dark brows knit into a scowl. "Wanna picture then?" She said, turning to go.

"Look, I'm sorry – it's none of my business," he said. "There's a tea room upstairs – I'll buy you a pop or something.

"Oh – well," she hesitated, looking first at the door and then at her watch. "I suppose you've got your own money now."

"For old – times' sake," he smiled.

"All right," she agreed, chewing on an ink-stained fingernail.

༄

While George scanned the menu, the waitress, a bleached blonde with buckteeth and pencilled-in eyebrows clicked her chewing gum impatiently and leaned on the back of his seat.

"Pot of tea for one, please," he said.

"Anything to eat?" she asked, inspecting a crimson fingernail. He shook his head. "And what about yer sister?"

"Lemonade, please." Rita asked as she arranged her satchel on the back of the chair.

"Nothing else," said George shuffling the chair forward until the girl stumbled forward.

"Well really," she flounced away muttering to herself, "Some folks…"

George looked at Rita whose expression hovered between pensiveness and boredom. She twisted a piece of hair and sucked the end of it.

"People treat you like dirt when you've got nowt," she said.

"Class discrimination," George replied. "She knows I'm a working man and not one of those professors."

"Doesn't matter who you are. If you have money, people treat you nice," Rita sat back and gazed around.

"Ever see Ida any more?" asked George.

"Never."

"Remember those plays we did," George grinned.

"I was just a bairn – didn't know anything about life then."

"And you do now?" he asked, looking up as the waitress clashed down the tea tray slopping some tea into the saucer. He waved her away impatiently when she tried to mop up the mess.

"What do you know now?" he asked Rita, surprised at his earnestness. There was something pink and transparent about her skin and her pained expression. Something compelling about the heavy, naked eyelids and chewed lips. An innocence that the shiny painted face of the waitress lacked. How old was Rita now? Thirteen or maybe fourteen?

"I know," she said sipping the drink and wiping her hand across her mouth, "I know that life hurts and I hate where I live, I'm fed up to the teeth with my parents and men are pigs."

He cradled his teacup, but suddenly aware of her eyes on his blackened fingernails, put it down and hid his hands under the table.

"Canna get them clean any more," he explained, "but tell me, how did you come to this conclusion?"

"You just have to sit outside your house one day and watch and listen – you'll soon see."

"Look, Rita, the world doesn't begin and end at Crag Street."

"Oh really," she said looking right at him for the first time, "that's why I'm getting out the first chance I can."

"Stay in school, Rita," he leaned closer, "a good education is the best way out. I never had the chance but you do."

"You're dead wrong there," she said, twirling the straw around. "Money gets you everywhere. In fact you're nothing without it and besides, I don't want to end up like the dried-up old biddies that pass for teachers at my school. Studied and never did owt for themselves."

"Whoa – I see you're a bit touchy about that," said George, pleased to get some kind of emotional reaction out of her. Even though he didn't agree with the sentiment.

"What about you then?" she said, as her eyes travelled over his suit, "What about all the fancy ideas you had?"

"I'm gettin' out – I've got a few plans," he said feeling that creeping sense of anticipation again that had been with him since he got off the bus.

"We'll see who does it first," she said, unwrapping a piece of chewing gum.

"I wish you were older," he said, wanting to hug her, talk to her, steer her in the right direction. "I'd take you out for a date."

"Don't flatter yersel' – who says I'd go anyway."

George realized that life had somehow knocked the happiness right out of her.

"Two years – give me two years," he said, "when you're sixteen I'll call on you and take you out to the pictures."

She placed two fingers across her mouth as if trying to stop herself from smiling and looked at him from under her lashes. *She still knows how to be coy*, he thought, remembering the lace hankies, the silver bracelets and the shiny ribbons she'd flaunted as a child.

"If I'm still living on Crag Street I might consider going – as long as you clean the coal dust out of your nails," she said, standing up to go. "Must go now. Me bus is due in five minutes." She flounced out of the room and George choked on his stone cold tea.

The Pitman's Daughter

Once outside again he looked up to the top of the hill where the narrow street turned a sharp right and wound under an ancient stone archway. He made his way towards it, hunching his shoulders and stuffing his hands into his pockets. Seeing Rita had made him feel better. Once she was through the awkward stage he could hardly wait to see how she'd turn out. Two years would soon be over and he could take her out, then he'd make her see the right way. There was so much he could teach her and he'd snatch her away from the horrible prison of the street so that her life would be lovely and bearable again. His head was dizzy with the idea that everything was falling neatly into place

He turned again to the vast Norman cathedral with its massive stone walls and towers – it always took his breath away. A thousand years ago workers like him had died building it and he knew that he too would have been prepared to die to make something this fantastic.

George clasped his hat and scarf and stepped through the oak doors into the great stone halls where the power of the sweeping arches and stone pillars forced him into a pew close to the back of the wall. The deep vibrations of the organ shuddered through him as music rose from the giant pipes. Closing his eyes he felt blood rush into the crevices of his eyes and ears and throat. Words flooded into his head – words he could not sing out to the tune of the organ.

He faltered when the sounds of the choir sliced through the air. The sound was perfect, simple and clear, like water trickling down a mountainside. It seemed that only the present was real, that only this moment mattered. He knew that one day in this city he would move others as he had been moved by the power of this ancient place. With his own words he would inspire some change, some leap of the heart, some rush of feeling. His words would be tossed out like the coins a bride throws to the scrambling street children on her wedding day.

Forty-five minutes later George stepped out through the doors, heavy-eyed and tired but filled with one overpowering resolution: he saw the world as a place waiting to be conquered and now he had the strength

to do it. The night glowed and shimmered around him as he trudged across Palace Green and through the archway.

A small group of students stood under a streetlamp, clustered around a tall young man with a thick crest of curly brown hair who sat on a bicycle. George nodded curtly and walked by but stopped short as a voice called for him.

"Excuse me, my good man, would you be so kind as to join us for a moment of enlightenment?" The tall man beckoned him and George looked around self consciously to see that it was him they were inviting. Seeing no one else he walked tentatively towards them.

"Your name, sir." The tall man demanded.

"George – er, George Nelson."

The other students had turned to look at George and were eyeing him up and down.

"George. A fine, honest name. A name synonymous with all that is great and brave in this glorious country of ours. A miner, I presume. No, don't be ashamed, sir. This is a fine and honourable occupation. You are the salt of the earth, the backbone of our nation. Let me shake your hand."

George felt sick as if a lump of dough was stuck in his throat, yet he stuck out his hand and the tall man pumped it up and down, then with an expression of mock distaste pulled out a handkerchief and made a great display of wiping his hand. The rest of the group snickered. Heat rushed to the top of George's head, making him dizzy and paralyzing his tongue until it seemed to choke him.

"One should never be afraid to touch the hard-earned dirt of the working man and feel the sweat of his honest labours, yet there is an inescapable stink which lingers around the members of the proletariat. Tell me, George, could this have something to do with your unfortunate lack of plumbing. Do you still defecate in primitive earth closets and bathe in rusted tin baths?"

The rest of the group began to snicker. "Come on, Neville, ease off the poor chap," a short ginger-haired man said.

George's felt a rush of anger. "I'm not stupid, you know. I know what you're talking about."

The Pitman's Daughter

Neville threw his head back. He had a large Adam's apple that bobbed with each gust of laughter. "Stupid! Did anyone call you that? Why I'm sure you've had at least five years of schooling before your forays into the mining of fossil fuels. Please share with us, my good man, your reflections of the Trade Union Movement and its effects on the ungrateful working men who aspire to comforts they do not deserve."

Rage gushed into George's throat. He spewed out the only words that came to his head. "Shut your stuck up gob." He almost cried as he wondered why he couldn't have a better comeback or argue with clever words, or even punch him in the face? Anything but this pitiful display.

Neville threw his head back and laughed. "Common little specimen, hanging around our great cathedral, probably trying to pinch something."

George smashed his fist into his palm and cursed aloud. As he turned to go he saw three dark-jacketed figures swaggering out of the nearby pub.

"Hou George me lad, how's the deein'?" said a gravelly voice. It was Jordy Willis and his two mates. Jordy's face was puffed up with drink. George nodded quietly and wiped his hand over his eyes. Sensing some possible danger, Neville started to wheel his bike away. The others followed him.

"What's botherin' yer, lad, somebody been pickin' on yer?"

George looked back at the small group under the street lamp.

"Actually, Jordy, that stuck up bugger on the bike there was callin' us miners dirt."

"Come on lads." Jordy's fists were clenched ready. "Consider it taken care of marrer. Us miners look after our own." They began to walk briskly up the street until they faced the now cowering Neville. Jordy planted himself square in front of him.

"Hou yer milk-faced bugger," he boomed. "That lad ower there has mair brains in his little finger than thou's got in thy whole family. So I'll ask yer to treat him wi' a bit more respect I' the future or yer'll answer to me. Now hadaway home wi' yer so yer can suck yer mammies titty."

By now Neville's eyes were wider than an owl's and he almost jumped out of his skin when Jordy lowered his head, made a rush for him and shouted *Boo*. Within seconds the three students were tailing it down the hill while Jordy and his marrers creased up with laughter. He held a thumb up towards George who carried on towards the market place not daring to look back. A smile spread over his face as he whistled Land of Hope and Glory to himself.

15

"Why did she ask me to be a bridesmaid anyway?" said Rita, sucking in her stomach while her mother pulled up the zip of the eggshell-blue brocade dress.

"Why hinny, it's out of respect. Maggie's grateful for all the things we gave her when her bairns were small," Iris said.

"All the things we gave her including the German measles," spat Rita, choking with spite.

Iris's hand stopped dead then gave Rita a strong shove forward, "You nasty little nowt? Always trying to get under my skin. Anyway that's a lie – there's no proof."

Rita fell against her bed, "Oww – you'll spoil me hairdo," she said, suddenly feeling sorry for her mother in her shapeless navy blue and white polka-dotted suit. Her grey hair looked like straw under her white feather hat. "Sorry mam – I just don't feel like goin'. I look like a great big baby in this dress."

"It's alright, flower, yer just gannin' through an awkward stage. Now they'll be leavin' in ten minutes and I still have to go and fasten yer dad's tie."

Rita stood in front of the mirror and groaned. She'd asked Eileen for a lightly flicked-up hairstyle, but after half an hour of combing, teasing and spraying, her hair looked like a lacquered helmet with a big bouffant on top and two cast-iron handlebars at the side.

"Eeh, you've got natural waves – they're a hairdresser's dream," Eileen said, taking a quick puff of her cigarette as she looked at Rita's reflection. Underneath the elaborate beehive, Rita's face was set in a sulky scowl. "Yer just need to smile and show yer features off – no fella's going to like yer with a face like thunder."

Maggie Willis's second daughter, Marion was marrying a lad from Houghton. Though Rita understood why Marion would want to escape from the madhouse she lived in, it seemed like she was just jumping out of one trap into another – and her fiancé was a miner too. That made it even more hair brained.

"Hurry up Rita – yer Nana's here and she wants to see yer dress," her mother called from downstairs.

"*Bloody hell*," Rita grumbled and flounced out of the room. She felt like a bloated mare and they wouldn't even let her wear a bit of lipstick or foundation to cover up those horrible pimples around her mouth. She was fifteen already. Old enough for makeup. But last time she'd worn some blue eye shadow her dad said she looked like a street corner girl and to wash it right off before he gave her a clout across the face.

Downstairs her grandma was sitting in the chair by the fire while her mother was in the scullery putting on her makeup in front of the tiny mirror. Nana Hawkins, now a widow living over at Belton Downs, usually visited only once a week on Friday evening when Rita's mother opened a tin of salmon, mixed it with vinegar and buttered some dinner rolls, setting them down on the table with a plate of Blue Ribands, Nana's favourite chocolate biscuit. They'd sit for at least three hours listening to her grumbling about the damp weather, her neighbours' smelly dogs that shit all over the chrysanthemums, the skyrocketing price of bacon, the immoral behaviour of young people and her irritable bowel that kept her prisoner inside the house. Today Iris had persuaded her to come to the wedding, to cheer her up a bit. Now she was perched unwillingly on the edge of the seat, her stout body clad in navy crepe, trimmed with dusty net and sequins.

Rita rustled past the kitchen table and her grandma's head swivelled around, sending her heavy pearl-drop earrings swinging back and forth on her fleshy earlobes. Rita's eyes were always drawn to the stretched putty-coloured skin from which hung an assortment of dull pearls or tarnished rhinestones.

"Nice frock – a bit fussy though," she said, squinting through wire-rimmed glasses, "Yer showin' a bit of bustline now – all the lads'll be sniffing after you."

"Mother, she's only fifteen yet," said Rita's mam, struggling with Walter's tie.

"Aye well you were only sixteen when Walter gave you a ring and now the young'uns are having sexual intercourse as soon as they get hair under their arms…"

"Mother do you have to be so vulgar?" said Iris and Rita had to rush into the scullery to get a drink of water before she burst out laughing.

"She's always had a mouth like a navvy," said Walter, mopping his sweaty face with a handkerchief.

"It's true. I read it in the News of the World. Scandalous really," her grandma continued, "they said those holiday camps have orgies goin' on every night – all those young'uns away from home."

"That's enough mam. Rita doesn't need to know about that kind of thing." Rita's mam stood uneasily, rubbing her gloved hands together.

"Aye the world's a wicked place Rita – divn't let any milk-faced bugger come sniffing round without putting a ring on yer finger. Mark my words." Her grandma said, hoisting herself up, "By these eighteen hour girdles bite into the tops of yer legs."

Rita sipped some water, "But Nana, I'm not marryin' anyone from around here. I'm gonna find someone with money."

"Just like I thought, Iris – she's ower big for her own byuts." Nana Hawkins focused her stern eyes onto Rita. Behind the glasses they looked even larger. "Yer mother married a miner. If it was good enough for her it's good enough for you."

"Don't start, mother…" Iris said.

Rita felt that familiar flutter of panic that came every time they discussed her future. It was a suffocating feeling. As if the street was a giant mouth waiting to suck her into its soft, nasty core and if she allowed herself to sink in she'd never climb out again. She always felt headachy and sick when she thought of giving in to their wishes.

Just then there was a loud honking noise from out in the street.

"It's the cars," said Rita's mam, "Maggie borrowed two for the wedding party. Rita you'd better get over there."

"And mind yer don't sit next to that Jordy Willis, the dirty bugger – I'd cut his bloody tail off. Come on let's see yer off," said Nana poking at the space between Rita's shoulder blades.

Rita shrugged her off, irritated at her prickliness. Besides that, her head felt heavy under the weight of the hairdo, the dress was scratchy and uncomfortable, and her shoes tight and awkward as she stepped outside. This was already turning out to be a bad day even though the May sunshine was warm on the back of her neck.

"Lift up the hem of the dress and watch the dogshit," her mam called as they stood on the step waving to her.

All the way up the street, people leaned on their gates watching for the bride, while over at Maggie's the younger children stood in a line by the gate, the boys with shirt collars buttoned tight and damp hair slicked across their head next to the three girls in matching blue brocade dresses. Maggie Willis rushed out the door holding onto her hat and Rita thought she'd never seen her look so pretty. The sun shone on her pale pink duster coat with its matching rose pillbox hat and her smiling lips were slicked with carnation pink lipstick. Her smile made Rita feel better.

"The bride's coming out now. Get ready," Maggie called.

Rita stood next to Hazel who held a small silver horseshoe trimmed with flowers. She looked lovely in the pastel dress; her golden skin glowed in the sun and she didn't have pimples like the nasty ones on Rita's forehead. The boys began to cheer as Marion and her father stepped out into the daylight's glare. Her face was pink and glowing, her brown hair framed with a band of cream roses and her long lace-trimmed satin dress shone like pearls. Laughing and blushing, she waved at the neighbours and then climbed into an old Morris Oxford decorated with white ribbons.

Poor soul, thought Rita. *One day in the spotlight and then she'll be another unpaid skivvy.* Rita had seen it happen time and time again in the street but she pushed the depressing thought to the back of her mind and tried to smile.

"It's oyster satin yer know," said Hazel.

"What do you mean," said Rita, getting into the car.

"Marion's dress is oyster satin – and me mam hand-sewed all the sequins onto it."

"It's lovely," said Rita watching from the back seat as the taxis pulled away and Marion leaned out of the window to throw a handful of coins at the squad of children running after them down the street. When the cars swept around the corner Rita looked back as they wrestled each other for a free sixpence.

༄

After the ceremony, the bridal party made its way to the Club for the reception. Rita found herself squashed into the same taxi with Hazel, Pearl and the newly weds, Marion and Vince. During the entire journey from the church the couple kissed and cuddled and giggled.

"It's a good job our Pearl canna see you two slobbering all ower each other," said Hazel, "Grow up yer sloppy buggers."

"We're married – it's all legal now anyway," said Marion, nibbling at Vince's ear, "Isn't that right flower."

"Aye," Vince grinned and then sucked at Marion's neck.

"Yer just jealous," Marion said to Hazel.

"*Yech*," Hazel grimaced, looking at Rita, "It makes me feel sick."

Rita turned and looked out of the window. There was no two ways about it. Vince was ugly. His mossy yellow teeth could never look clean and he had reddish skin that flared up in patches when he was excited. What would he look like in the morning when he was trying to kiss Marion, his hair all greasy and eyes sticky with sleep?

"Will yer dance with me at the reception, Rita?" said Pearl.

"Why yes, pet," said Rita, glad to look at her honey-coloured curls. "I'll do the foxtrot and the cha-cha-cha and anything you want."

"That's if she can get past all the lads queuing up to dance with her," said Marion as they pulled into the club car park.

At half past eleven the guests streamed into the reception room, the men already loosening their ties in anticipation of a good feast and booze-up. Two women in hairnets and flowered aprons buzzed around setting a big table for the buffet while another filled three huge teapots with boiling water. Children ran around the room sliding on the floor and Marion and Vince stood at the entrance having their first row. Rita had spotted Vince in the bar with his mates, downing a couple of pints and winking at the barmaids, while Marion had been left alone to greet the guests. Vince was trying to grasp Marion's hand but she pushed him aside and mopped at her eyes with a serviette. Maggie came rushing in and tried to console her, but Vince jumped to attention when he saw Jordy lumbering in behind. *What a game it all is*, Rita thought, swinging her own silver horseshoe as she walked towards the table where her mother, father and grandma had already settled themselves. Rita was thirsty but not for tea and not for the watered-down orange squash usually offered for the children.

"Da, can I have some lemonade from the bar?" she asked, nudging him on the shoulder.

"Why, I telt yer Iris, the bairn's spoiled rotten," said Nana, "Yer'll drink what's put in front of yer."

Walter smiled weakly and winked his eye at Rita.

Nana continued. "I see it's another buffet – not like in the old days when it was a nice dinner served at the table. Ham and pease-pudding again and likely the ham's gristly and the pease-pudding's watery and the tea-bags probably used twice-over." Nana's head swivelled as her mouth flapped open and shut without stopping for a moment to take a breath. "And who does Maggie Willis think she is dressing up like a bit lass. Mutton dressed as lamb I call it…"

"Mother, she's only thirty-five and please keep yer voice quiet or we'll have everyone lookin' at us." Rita's mam pulled nervously at her feather hat.

"Why this *tyebl's all claggy*[6] – they haven't even wiped a cloth ower it," Nana blurted.

"By I'm famished," said Walter. "Go and get me dinner flower." Iris got so flustered she dropped one white glove onto the floor. With Nana nagging on one side and Walter whining on the other, Rita sat back and watched as her mother scrabbled about on the floor then emerged again with flushed face and hat over one eye. They were so embarrassing. The whole damn lot of them.

"There he goes again, Iris – ordering yer around like a skivvy. Send the lazy bugger up fer his own pease-pudding. I had them lads trained when they lived at my house," she said, shaking her head and sending her earrings into a frenzy. "What's wrong wi' yer own legs, Walter, yer dumb cluck?"

"I don't know how much to put out," said Walter. "Anyway, I've lost me appetite now. I'm gannin' fer a beer."

"Well we won't miss yer," said Nana looking up as another group of guests arrived. "By there's a canny lad fer you, Rita."

Suddenly the old spotlights on the ceiling spread out like a canopy of stars as Rita watched George walk past the pink frosted wedding cake and help his mother into a chair close to the buffet table.

"Now there's a well turned-out lad – and good to his mam by the looks of it," said Nana nudging Rita. Rita wondered if the old woman could see the way her heart was pounding through the bodice of her dress. She was thankful the lights were turned down or the red flush creeping up her neck would have flashed like a beacon. Over the last two years Rita had seen George only three or four times but she'd thought about him daily. Now that she'd graduated to reading Mills and Boone romance novels, George became the permanent hero – the dashing pilot, the brilliant young doctor, the rugged country squire, the tanned lifeguard or the chiselled Roman soldier.

---

[6] this table is sticky

Once when she was running home during a rainstorm from a late netball game at school, she'd stopped at the ice cream shop with the rest of the team and by the time she left it was seven o' clock and clouding over. The rain pelted down in sheets when she got back to Crag Street and her blazer was sopping wet and so heavy she slipped it off, letting the water soak her thin school shirt. At her gate she looked over at George's house and there, framed in the attic window she could see him standing, his hands flat against the panes, watching her.

At that moment the water trickling down into the hollows of her neck felt like fingers stroking her skin. She dropped her bag and blazer onto the step and walked slowly across the street, coming to a dead stop in the pool of blue light that spilled from the streetlamp. They watched each other for what seemed like minutes and, though his window was beaded with raindrops, she imagined that he blew a kiss to her. The spell was broken when her mam came rushing out with an umbrella, screaming for her to "Haway inside yer daft bairn."

Rita's mam came back with three plates of food. "Here y'are flower," she said, pushing a plate towards her but the voice was only an echo in the back of Rita's mind. *Sixteen. He said he would call on her when she was sixteen – and that was only a few months away – but would he really come?* She remembered sitting with him in the coffee shop in Durham and she'd cursed herself for acting like a sulky child, as if she wasn't interested in him. She'd even insulted his clothes and made fun of the coal dust under his fingernails, and all the time her insides had that same old wobbly feeling she remembered from the Saturdays at Ida's. She needed her head examined for acting so rudely.

She took a good, long look at him. The years of working down the mine had broadened his shoulders and his neck was stronger and more muscular. Like a man, compared to the grinning, skinny boys on the street. He walked with confidence. Shoulders and back straight, chin slightly raised as if ready to tackle anyone who tried to challenge him. His fair hair was smoothly combed to the side and his face looked older with its strong chin and arrow-like nose. He had a *chiselled* face. That was the word they used in Woman's Weekly. In his dark suit and maroon shiny tie he was like one of the faces from her Hollywood film books.

"I see yer gettin' a good look at that lad. Yer want to set yer sights high, Rita. A lad like that's a good prospect. Clean, steady and a good-looker." Nana winked mischievously, showing the large gaps between her teeth. "Good teeth and all."

"Mother, he's not a bloody racehorse you know," said Iris.

"Aye, but he's in the race for union office. He wants to be area representative. The lad's got ambition," said Walter, standing and pushing his chair towards the table. "And he's got brains. When he gets talking about books and all that, half the lads at the pit *divn't na* what he's on about."

Rita grinned, feeling a fluttering inside that was not fear but excitement. She'd stood under his window three or four times since that magic night hoping he'd appear but each time the upstairs window was dark.

By three o'clock in the afternoon the bar was still open, after a brief closure at half past two when the outside doors were shut and the towels put over the beer taps. Five minutes later the towels were whisked off and the bar lights turned on again. Two of the club regulars played the drums and organ and they pounded out a tune while Jordy Willis, tie hanging loose and a pint of beer in his hand, swayed at the microphone trying to sing *"Smoke gets in your eyes."*

Rita danced with Pearl, then a tall boy with pimples, named Robert Gibbons who kept asking her to come outside for a smoke. Next she walked across the smoky hall and past the door to the bar, looking for George. He was inside drinking beer with her brothers. Laughing, he downed the last inch of a pint, wiped his mouth and looked over at her. He smiled and waved then she felt the throbbing in her ears as he came towards her.

"You look smashing in that dress, Rita," he said, putting a hand on her shoulder.

"Liar," she giggled, "I feel like I'm wrapped in a pair of curtains."

"Don't sell yourself short, Rita." When the music started up again he leaned forward and whispered in her ear. "You're going to be a real smasher."

The lights in the room were whirling like rainbows as Rita sucked in her breath, leaned towards his ear, and caught the spicy whiff of his after-shave, "Do you want to dance?"

George grasped her other shoulder and planted a light kiss on her cheek. "You're a bold one, Rita Hawkins," he whispered just as Teddy Barrett thumped him on the back.

"Haway marrer," he shouted, "dinna clart aboot wi' the bairns.[7] Gan back to yer Mam and dad, bonny lass," Teddy said as he dragged George backwards towards the bar.

Rita fell back against the wall and watched him mouth the words *sorry* at her. *What a moment – just like a story.* Her breath was coming out in short gasps. She stayed there watching, peeping around the doorway.

George pushed his empty pint glass towards Ruby Allen, a black-haired, busty barmaid with a real beauty spot and painted Elizabeth Taylor eyebrows. Ruby smiled, George winked and Rita's heart dropped. She felt like a clumsy, awkward bairn. Even Maggie Willis looked more attractive. She'd taken off the duster coat to reveal a matching pink sleeveless dress, then tapped George on the back and pointed to her empty glass. When he handed her another drink, then lit her cigarette, she held his wrist boldly and looked into his eyes. Rita wasn't part of this adult world yet.

Too old to slide around with the youngsters and too young to drink with the adults, she felt a growing urge to rip off the bloody bridesmaid dress and get the hell out of there. She needed to go somewhere to be alone in her misery but when the band started to play "Rock around the clock" there was a rush of bodies from out of the bar. Ruby's brother, Rick and a couple of his mates posed by the door in their Teddy boy jackets chewing gum and combing their greased-back hair with thin,

---

[7] don't bother with children

black combs. Once they were satisfied their hair was shiny and slick enough they grabbed some nearby girls and began jiving.

Rita pressed herself into a corner wishing she could disappear. Tears pushed at the back of her eyes when she watched George pull Ruby onto the dance floor. Ruby giggled and threw her head back while George stared at her throat and pointed breasts. *Just like all the other lads*, thought Rita and yet she felt a sick stab of jealousy. How could she ever believe he'd be interested in her? He hardly knew she existed now he was so important and popular.

A voice at her elbow made her jump.

"Come outside for a tab," said Robert. Even in the darkness she could make out the pimples on his forehead but seeing them made her feel close to him. They were both misfits.

"All right," she said and they slipped outside into the cloudy afternoon. It had begun to drizzle and there were puddles on the ground. Rita sloshed through them, soaking the hem of her dress with dirty water.

"Bloody stupid frock," she said, leaning against the wall of the club. Across the street and up the hill she could see the pit wheels of Belton colliery, cranking and grinding and pulling another cage of men down under the ground.

"I'll be leavin' school in July," said Robert, lighting a cigarette, "Gannin' down the pit wi' me Da."

"Poor sod," said Rita, sucking back the cigarette and coughing. "That's one good thing about being a girl. Yer never have to be a miner."

"Yer've got plenty of other rotten things to put up with, though – havin' babies and all that. Me mam screamed for eighteen hours when she had our John."

"Shut up," Rita said, throwing down her cigarette, "I'm not havin' any bairns anyway. I've got better things to do wi' my life."

"I don't see how yer gonna stop it. When yer get married yer man's entitled to have his needs met – if yer get me drift ."

"Not wi me," said Rita, kicking up a spray of muddy water, "I don't care about rules or contracts. No man's gonna own me."

She bent down, picked up a handful of mud and smeared it down the front of her dress. "That's what I think of marriage." She turned towards the back door of the club, stumbling over some empty beer bottles. "See yer later."

"What are yer gonna tell yer mam and dad?" he called after her.

"That yer threw me down in the mud and tried to fuck me, yer daft bugger," she said, sticking her tongue out so far Robert chased her back to building.

As she opened the side door a waft of smoke, music and heat knocked her backwards. The beer had worked its wonders and everyone was dancing. The men had taken off their ties and loosened their shirts. Wives were clinging with drunken passion to their husbands, children slid around the edge of the dance floor getting under the dancers' feet. The bride and groom had made up and were necking frantically on a chair beside the cake but George was nowhere in sight. Suddenly it all seemed like a big, ugly circus.

She had to find her Mam and Dad because she couldn't stay there one more minute.

16

*E*lla stood, elbows resting on her gate, as Jesse Nelson sent George off on his bicycle to work the afternoon shift. *Poor lad,* thought Ella. It burned her insides as if raw carbolic was coursing though her veins – to see that fine young man wasted down the pit. If only he'd been hers. She'd have scrimped and done without to give him an education. And she'd wear her grey gabardine dress with the starched white collar when she saw him graduate from the university, his hair clean and shiny and his hands soft and white. The ache in her heart was strong enough to suffocate her and she felt that same dizzy feeling again. *Just one of them women's spells* she thought, straightening her apron.

The street was clean today with only a few puddles left from the rainstorm the night before and Jesse was trying to brush away the water from her front step. She was such a tiny woman who looked even smaller wrapped up in that old brown knitted shawl. Ella was sure it was the one her Robert had worn all those years ago. *Poor ard wife,* Ella thought, opening the gate. Since Jack and all the other men had been abuzz with the latest news about union elections she was dying to know if the rumours about George were true.

Jesse was bending over a broken broomstick trying to mend it with twine so Ella tapped on the gate. When she didn't even turn around, Ella realized the poor old bugger was going deaf as well.

"Our Jack says your George is standing up for the union," said Ella, leaning on the gate..

"Aye," said Jesse, breathing hard as she tried to straighten her back to talk. "I always knew he'd mek summat of himsel', he's a good lad, our George."

"Eeh Jesse, yer always looked after that bairn," said Ella, remembering the curly haired toddler climbing up the hill in his dog-eared old boots. By that time, Olive Coombes had joined them at the gate.

"Aye, he's fine young man," said Olive, "better than the last daft bugger, Willie Clegg. He was all brawn and nee brains."

"Eeh," said Ella, "I don't know about that – our Jack says Willie could unload a twelve foot piece of timber down the mine – did the job of two men. He could lift a tub full of coal back up on the tracks with his bare hands."

"Funny thing, though, with all that strength he died of the influenza last month," said Olive. "It's a queer world."

"Aye – a queer world," said Ella, feeling a sudden chill come over her body. The sight of her Mam, facedown in the coal shed had haunted her more than she could ever imagine and she'd woken up more than a few times from dreams in which she'd been filling the scuttle and found an angry black face poking out from under the coal heap.

"Well," said Jesse, "I can tell yer summat else I heard. Last Tuesday his wife, Ethel spoke to him from…" Jesse leaned in towards Ella and Olive and whispered, "the *other side.*" Once it was said, Jesse pulled back quickly and put her finger to her lips in warning.

Ella felt a sharp intake of air rush inside as if her lungs were a pair of bellows and someone had pumped them hard. "How?" she whispered.

"Went to Maria Bell's house," said Jesse.

Ella looked over at Olive thinking surely she would know the significance of this name. Ella prided herself in knowing everyone in these parts.

"Maria Bell?" she asked. "I can't say I know anyone with that name."

Jesse leaned forward again. "Course not – she used to be Maria

Brazinsky – married Jackie Bell after the war – came from Rumania – some say she's got gypsy blood running through every vein in her body."

Ella and Olive nodded. This explained everything. "She's got the gift," said Jesse. "I know because she helped me speak to my dear lost boys." Jesse lifted up her shawl to wipe her eyes.

Ella felt the chill creeping over her again. Perhaps there might really be a way to put things right with her Mam. Her throat felt dry and scratchy as she spoke. "Jesse – can yer take me there – to Maria?"

Olive folded her arms and looked stern. "What the bloody hell d'yer want to be tampering with things that are best left alone. Why Reverend Sykes over at the Heath Street Methodist Church was just saying last Sunday that speaking to the dead was the work of the devil."

"Yer don't understand, Olive," said Ella. "Me Mam canna rest without saying goodbye to me."

"Eeh – you were always complainin' about her frosty face and sharp tongue when she was alive," said Olive.

"I still need to make peace with her," said Ella shaking her head and turning to Jesse again. "Or she'll haunt me to the end of my days. Please Jesse – tek me to Maria's."

"I'd be happy to help yer, Ella," said Jesse, her head shrinking deeper into the shawl. "Nobody understands how hard it can be when the lights go out of a night and the ghosts gather round yer, crying out from the other side. Callin' you from the darkness."

"By yer a right pair of fools," said Olive, starting to take down the washing from the line. "Meddling with the devil hisself."

Jesse ignored her and moved closer to Ella. "As it happens I'm tekkin' Mrs Wilson on Thursday to speak to her poor lass Mary. We'll be settin' out at ten o'clock when Maria's man's gone to work."

"I'll bet he'd fettle her if he found out what she was up to," said Olive, turning to go.

"I'll be ready, Jesse," said Ella, hardly able to wait the two days until then.

Nobody knew Mrs Wilson's first name. Everyone on the street simply called her Missus. Olive said to Ella one day that she was sure her first name was Fanny or Bunty or something embarrassing and that's why she refused to tell anyone. But two days later she met Ella and Jesse with a broad smile on her face, cheeks coloured with pink rouge and lips painted carnation red. Though she was the wrong side of fifty and stumbling on patent leather high heels, she and Jesse Nelson legged it up the street like a pair of rabbits. The two of them rushing ahead as if they were marching to meet the queen while Ella, who'd put a stone on since she'd been married, huffed and puffed behind them. She'd worn her navy suit, matching navy straw hat with the purple rhinestone pin and her best brown Sunday shoes with the heels. No sense in being sloppy when she met her Mam in the other world.

Jesse, her hair wrapped in a ragged blue chiffon scarf, turned to Ella and shouted, "It's just over the road at the school and up three doors – not far now."

By now they were walking down Belton High Street and found themselves in the middle of a busy shopping day. Ella tried to avoid any watchful eyes for fear someone would ask her what she was doing, all dressed up on a Thursday morning. Thankfully they came to the school and crossed the street. Three doors up was a small terraced house with a red painted door and yellow window trim – out of place among the sober greens and browns around it.

"I told yer she's a gypsy," said Jesse, rapping on the brass doorknocker. The lace curtains on the side window parted and a pair of dark eyes peeped out. Ella was suddenly aware of a white smile in the shadows then the door opened to reveal a small woman with wild, curly brown hair and large gold hoops in her ears. She had heavy black eyebrows and eyes that were grey-green and glinting as she smiled with a row of even white teeth.

Ella gasped. "By yer have lovely teeth Mrs Bell."

The lady ushered them in. "Thenk you – ta," she said, correcting her slight accent. "I brush them three times a day with bicarbonate of soda – just a simple trick from the old country."

Ella licked at her own teeth, feeling the gaps where three brownish teeth had recently been pulled out. "Why I'll have to try it meself," she said.

Mrs Wilson fidgeted with her earrings as she directed them to hang their coats on an elaborately carved coat rack, and then showed them into a room, unlike anything Ella had ever seen before. Every wooden surface was polished to a high gloss and decorated with gilded wooden carvings in the shape of garlands and wheat baskets and bunches of grapes. The windows were draped with yellow chiffon curtains and accented with swags of red and yellow satin trimmed with tiny white tassels. Three gilt-framed mirrors decorated the walls and a white lace tablecloth was spread across a table set with polished silver candlesticks and prancing glass horses and unicorns.

The three women stood in silent admiration. "Eeh – it's like a fairytale palace," said Ella, remembering her own plain ornaments and resolving to get the bus into Sunderland next week to do some shopping.

"I bring – I brought many *expenseeve* things from the old country," said Maria, pulling out carved mahogany chairs from under the table. "Please sit down."

The three ladies sat down, in silent awe. For a few moments nobody moved and Maria stood frowning, hand on hip as if waiting for something to happen.

"Is it going to start now?" asked Ella, suddenly feeling stupid as Maria *tut-tutted* with what seemed like impatience. Jesse suddenly snapped to life and whispered, "The silver."

"Oh – yes," said Ella, wondering how she could have been so foolish as to forget the silver shillings she had in her pocket.

"Across her palm," Jesse whispered.

Ella took out the coins and offered them up. The sparkling smile returned as Ella swept the shillings over her palm. When Mrs Wilson followed with a sixpence, Ella was sure she saw a slight narrowing of Maria's eyes. Surely she, rather than that skinflint Mrs Wilson, was about to get her money's worth today. One thing she could definitely say about herself was that Ella Danby was no miser.

"You like cup of tea first?" asked Maria, slipping the money quickly into her pocket.

Ella looked around at the others who were already shaking their heads. Though she was thirsty after the brisk walk, she was ready for some contact with the other world. "After," she whispered. "Are yer alright with that Mrs Wilson?"

Mrs Wilson nodded and, at that signal, Maria solemnly opened the door of her polished wooden sideboard and pulled out the strangest object Ella had ever seen. It was a large shiny ornament in the shape of a hand, and in that hand was held a heavy glass ball. All three of the ladies gasped as Maria turned off the light and sat at the head of the table with her hands stroking the ornament. Suddenly the glass ball glowed pale green. As she closed her eyes and began to murmur in a strange language, Ella began to feel little fingers of fear creeping up the back of her neck. Greenish-grey shadows began to swim around the room and ripple across the faces of the other women. Maria started to breathe very heavily, her mouth slack and open. Then in one instant the most terrible shudder spread through her entire body and her head fell backwards. Ella felt the other hands squeezing hers so tightly they might have drawn blood but nobody spoke. The air crackled. Maria raised her head and, with eyes closed, began to speak in a whiny, breathless whisper that sounded like a girl's.

All the women held their breath as the strange voice spoke. "Is Ermyntrude there?" Nobody spoke. "I need to find Ermyntrude – Ermyntrude Wilson." All eyes turned to Mrs Wilson who sat, her eyes like two white saucers in the dark.

"Ermyntrude? That's yer real name?" blurted Ella, trying so hard to hold in her laughter, she snorted like a pig.

Maria suddenly sat up. "Bloody hell – I lost her."

"Yer evil witch," squealed Mrs Wilson at the red-faced Ella. "That was our Mary and yer scared her away with yer bloody donkey laugh."

"This girl had a white dress – and some kind of veil," said Maria, rubbing her eyes.

"Aye – that's our Mary. Can you get her back?"

"I'm sorry Mrs Wilson. Once the spirit is chased away it won't return – but we can try."

Ella bit her lip to try and stifle the giggle that gurgled deep inside her gut. She sucked in her cheeks and concentrated on the green glow and the rapt faces of the three women. Suddenly Maria started to cry with a whimpering, mewling sound like a sick kitten. Ella's throat felt like a lump of clay was stuck in it. The whimpering continued, filling her ears until she felt as if she had to stuff her fingers inside them to make it stop, but she didn't want to break the circle. And then Maria's face went ashen white and she spoke in a strangled whisper. "Mother – he wants his mother."

Jesse began to cry. "It's my Peter – he's looking for me."

The voice continued. "Not Peter – he has no name – he is unborn."

Ella felt as if she wanted to be sick when Maria's face turned towards her like a blank mask. "She calls you murderer," the voice hissed. "And not worth a pennorth of coal."

"I don't understand," said Ella as the eyes of the other women fixed on her. "Is it Mother? Mother, I fell asleep – I made your favourite cake and I just want to say goodbye properly. Mother."

Maria's mouth hardly moved as the voice trickled out. "Hole in the mat, mend the truss." she said and then fell back into her chair, her eyes rolling upwards to reveal glossy whites.

Ella's cheeks burned like someone had slapped them. Jesse and Mrs Wilson gawped at her with open mouths. "What the bloody hell was that all about?" said the newly christened Ermyntrude.

"I'm sure I haven't any idea," said Ella, pulling her hands away and scraping her chair backwards.

Maria was still lying there in a trance. "Well shouldn't we wake her up?" said Jesse, her head looking from one woman to the other like an agitated chicken.

"They say it can harm them," said Ermyntrude. "I read about it in a magazine."

"Then let's get the hell away from here afore her man comes back," said Ella already putting on her coat and buttoning it up to steady her beating heart.

After making sure Maria was still breathing, the three women slipped out of the house and scurried down the street. Ella said goodbye to them and stopped off at Hutchinson's Flower shop. She bought some lovely cut flowers. Yellow dahlias, orange asters and a spray of baby's breath, then trudged up to the cemetery where she stood in the cold drizzle gazing at her Mam's headstone, which stood next to her father's older, weathered one.

"I'm sorry I loved me father more," she said, placing the flowers against the headstone. "But you never showed me an ounce of kindness – just one little word would have brought me a bit of happiness and light."

She stayed until her coat was drenched, the straw hat limp and misshapen and her eyes swollen with crying, then she turned and trudged through the mud, ignoring the mess on her stockings. The rain had stopped when she got back to Crag Street and the heads turned to watch her walk up the street, a sorry figure, soaked through to the skin and covered in mud.

Later she gathered the dirty clothes up into a bag and went to throw them out into the dustbin, but just as she stepped out the door into the yard, her foot caught on the damp coconut matting at the back step and she almost fell flat on her face but righted herself and went stumbling across the flagstones. After she'd gathered herself together and checked that nobody had witnessed the clumsy moment, she went back to look at the mat. Sure enough there was a ragged hole right in the centre, a rip that would catch the toe of any unsuspecting person – especially someone carrying a heavy coal scuttle. She stood looking at it for a good few minutes, her stomach churning, then swept the entire mat off the ground and threw it into the dustbin with her clothes.

Three men carried Jack home that night. He'd tried to lift an iron girder and ruptured his groin. Ella had already mended the elastic truss that was kept in the top shelf of the wardrobe.

Next day she took a trip into Sunderland and bought herself a pair of high-heeled patent leather shoes and a pair of real crystal candlesticks.

17

George took a deep breath of the fresh November day as he stepped through the gate of Elmway Pit where Sneck Mulloway, Walter Hawkins and Jock the Scot were busy lighting their pipes. He stopped just as Charlie Barrett walked his prizewinning whippet past them.

"Nee work the day, lads?" he asked.

"Union meeting," said George, feeling the excitement rippling through his stomach.

"Bloody National Coal Board tells us we own the mines now – what's the use if we canna get enough shifts to mek a decent wage?" said Walter Hawkins. "We have to make our voices heard."

Old Neddie Barker came up leading his sausage dog, Jennie.

"Bit short i' the leg, thy dog, Neddie?" said Charlie.

"Touches the bottom same as thine, Charlie," said Neddie.

"Cheeky bugger," said Charlie,

"Give ower, yer like a pair of bairns," said Walter. "We need a stronger Union man here. Shake up them lazy buggers ower in Leeds and Newcastle."

"What's the union ever done for thoo, Walter," asked Sneck Mulloway. "The day we were nationalised they said the collieries would be owned *by* the people *for* the people. Thought they were gonna fire all the managers but here we are, still treated worse than shite."

"Dinna mention that day, Sneck," said Walter. "History was made on that day. Justice was done for the workingman. Now we just have ter stop standin' round bubbling like lasses and start usin' some o' that power."

"I agree," said George, raising his voice above the older men. "Now we have rights we don't have to bow and scrape to some fat pit-owner that treats us like dirt under his shoe. We're the owners and we need to start acting like it."

Walter clapped George on the back, scattering loose pipe tobacco in the process. "Well said lad – that's the kind of man we need runnin' things. No more gormless yes-men kowtowing to the management."

George fastened his brown tweed jacket. He'd had it cleaned specially for the meeting.

"Why listen to yer all – yer have it that cushy yer dinna na's yer born," said old Neddy. "I remember the big lockout in 1926 after the General Strike. We thought we'd bring the pit owners to their senses – but they paid us back. Bastards locked us out for seven months. We wouldna stand for it. Grew turnips, taties, cabbages – killed a pig and fed the whole street with it. Schools fed the bairns and we got free bread from Hunter's Bakery. But when we went back it was worse – if yer were a union man they cut yer shifts in half."

"Aye, boys, yer dinna know about real suffering," said Jock the Scot. "My great-grandmother was twenty-two years old and working in the Ayrshire coalfield. They had her carrying thirty pound buckets of coal on her back up a ladder – 180 feet upwards. Half naked she was, beggin' the foreman to give her a rest but he says only them that works, eats and she was afeared of leavin' because her six-year-old bairn was fillin' buckets of coal down below. I'd slit the nasty bugger's throat if I could see him now. Gut him like a slaughtered bull."

"All the suffering," sighed Neddie.

"Aye all the suffering," sighed Walter.

"No need for it now though, brothers," said George, tying up his muffler. "Now's the time to turn the tables."

As he headed down the street towards the meeting hall, he felt their eyes on him and hear the buzz of chatter he'd provoked. He'd soon earn their trust and loyalty. Of that he had no doubt.

Later, he vaulted himself up into the grey shadows of the attic. Moonlight shone through the window. He could straighten out his thoughts here; sort through the ideas that raced through his head and the possibilities that could change the course of his future, which had once stretched out before him like a bleak life sentence. Finally he could see a way out and he meant to grab it with both hands.

On work days he'd always bolt down his supper and, with hardly a word to his mother and father, race to his room and up into the attic where the stillness was interrupted only by the soft coo-cooing of his father's pigeons scratching around the chimney.

Now he needed quiet to reflect on the bold step he'd taken only hours before when, buoyed by the cheers and songs of the other men, he was nominated as a candidate for colliery union rep. Since the day in Durham Cathedral he'd decided to make his mark in the world and earn the greatness he'd always dreamed of and now he was on his way.

Great speeches waited to be written filled with tales of capitalist greed. *Yes, he was equipped and ready to ram the right amount of guilt down the throats of the wealthy, the complacent and the privileged. It was time to reshuffle the cards that fate had dealt him.* But first he had to be elected and that meant long hours working on his strategy. He'd study the speeches of the union giants of the past and there'd be no place for mediocrity in his campaign. Every waking minute would be spent preparing himself for the task ahead and there was no place for courting in his life. Not now, he told himself, remembering a promise he'd made. Besides, he hadn't promised to call Rita on the exact day of her birthday. He'd have to put it off for a while – until the election was over, at least.

Feeling suddenly jittery, he felt the need for distraction and climbed through the opening into the neighbouring attic. He crossed quickly through the Barkers' and on into the Willis's. Here was misery and abuse on his doorstep. Everybody on the street knew Jordy Willis was a bully and George was able to witness it secretly. His stomach lurched with apprehension.

There was a clattering and dragging down below and a sound of loud voices and slamming doors. Easing the trapdoor aside, he glanced into the gloomy, brown hallway. Jordy Willis was down below, hair sticking up like a wire brush, underpants flapping around his legs and right hand tightly clamped around the back of Maggie's neck. He was pushing her towards the stairs, chanting, "Filthy whore, dirty bloody slut."

Like a pinned butterfly, her hands fluttered and grabbed the banister and the wall. He pushed her downwards until they reached the front door and, opening it with his knee, shoved her outside. Then he slammed it shut and climbed the stairs, yawning. On the landing another door opened a crack then quickly shut as Jordy lunged towards it. He turned and went into his bedroom and soon loud, bellowing snores could be heard.

George felt his stomach lurch. *Bloody piece of slime, yellow coward!* When George reached a position of power he'd squash ignorant pigs like Jordy.

He was just about to turn away and go back to his own attic when a narrow finger of light spread across the landing. From the door opposite Jordy's a child stepped out. A slight little figure whose feet skimmed over the linoleum and whose arms were outstretched – feeling through the darkness. It was the blind child, Pearl, who was very small for her age. George froze as she tottered towards the top of the stairs, sleep-walking. She called "Mama, Mama," and in a flash George flipped his legs over the edge of the opening and landed noiselessly in the hallway. In an instant he reached out and plucked the fragile body away from the top stair. She felt as light as a sparrow.

"Who is it?" she said, clawing at the darkness. "Grandad? You're not Grandad."

George swallowed deeply and with the shadows dancing in front of his eyes said softly, "Don't be afraid. I'm a guardian angel."

Pearl gasped and backed away until her fingers touched the edge of the bedroom door. She slipped inside and shut it, leaving George alone in the dark hallway. For one glorious moment he felt as if points of light were sprouting from his fingertips and energy crackling out from the roots of his hair. Then he vaulted back up into the starless attic and scuttled into the safety of his own house with its familiar old boxes and photographs and the sleeping remnants of his lost brothers' lives.

His head throbbed with the sensation of power. Out of four boys he'd been chosen to survive. He was the lucky one, the chosen one and that gave a special purpose to his life. There were so many people to help, to save, and he thought of Maggie shivering outside, her white body huddled in a thin blanket. Perhaps he could go and take her some warmer clothing. He grabbed an old knitted bedspread and, looking at the patchwork of bright colours, realized that in another life he could have draped her body in the brightest silks.

18

Maggie stood at the gate watching Jordy cycle to work. His wheels swished through puddles, spraying sludgy water into the air and soaking his work trousers. As he rounded the corner at the bottom of the street and disappeared from sight she let out a deep sigh. The sunlight suddenly burst through black clouds and the day was hers now. She marvelled at the freshly rain-washed street, the shiny grey rooftops and the white clouds in the pinkish sky. Even the usual clip-clop of the milkman's horse and the clinking of milk bottles had a comforting ring. Yes, today would be a canny day. Happiness swelled deep inside, like a tiny fist of dough waiting to rise and fill her with joy. For last night something wonderful had happened to her.

It started when Jordy put her out again after she said she was too tired to do anything more than have a hot cup of tea and lie down. And just when she'd got all the bairns to bed. She'd sheltered in the outhouse, listening to rain drumming on the corrugated roof. The sharp, acid smell of piss and disinfectant was worse on a wet day and the night air chilled her to the bone. She closed her eyes, trying to get her mind away from the icy draught blowing under the door. But all she could think of was Jordy's face, thrust close to hers, and his mouth spitting out filthy words. Then he'd grasped the back of her neck, forcing her down the stairs as she grabbed at the wall, the banister, anything to steady herself. Once he'd pushed her outside, sheets of freezing drizzle slashed across her face, soaking her thin nightdress as she ran across the yard.

She'd spent many other nights outside. Just looking at him the wrong way when he was in one of his savage moods would start his yelling and cursing. Then she stayed silent, afraid to scream for fear of waking the bairns, afraid to cross him for fear of feeling his fist on the side of her head. Usually he just shoved her outside like a dog and there she'd sit, waiting until he was safely asleep and Hannah or one of the children let her back in.

Last night something very strange had happened while she shuddered in the dark, worrying at the howling of the wind that sounded like the crying of her babies. She was afraid they were out there in the driving rain, lost and scared. That's when she heard a faint voice calling, "Maggie, Maggie." But the wind took the sound and bounced it back and forth like an echo. It was a young man's voice and if she closed her eyes it reminded her of a summer day years before when another young man had called her name in the half-light of a hotel room. She kept her eyes tight shut for fear that the dream would go away again, but the voice was closer now – coming from her own yard. It was a gentle voice with a cultured edge to the usual street accent.

Instinct caused her to push the door open and she cried, "Here, here," into a flutter of cold wind and raindrops.

Now that the rain had slowed down to a fine drizzle, the water ran in rivers to the drain then gurgled and sloshed down into the sewers below. Maggie heard the scrunch of boots on the flagstones and looked up to see George Nelson. He carried a rolled up blanket that he offered to her, his hesitant eyes gleaming pale grey. His collarless shirt shone bright white in the bluish glow of moonlight. She stood tongue-tied, wondering how he'd known she was there. Again he held out the blanket. It was hand crocheted. Probably something Jesse had made when he was a bairn.

"I heard him put you out," he said and she watched his eyes flicker as if caught in a lie, then fix momentarily on her body. She blushed and covered herself with her arms, feeling suddenly vulnerable and bedraggled under the damp, clinging nightdress.

"The blanket," he said again, "I brought it for you."

And still she hadn't spoken. Just stood there like a tongue-tied fool, wondering why any man would be interested in seeking her out. She, who'd been called filthy whore so many times she believed herself ugly and worthless. Standing there with rain-sodden hair, haggard face and a body like a wrung-out piece of washing.

But there was something magical about this night. Something about the foggy darkness that muffled all sounds except the steady drip-drip of water from the outhouse roof. Something about facing a young man alone after so many years, and having him look at her with those hungry eyes. He held out the blanket and then finally, astonishingly, wrapped it round her shoulders so gently and so carefully he could have been draping her in silken webs. Strange, she thought, that he should wrap her so deliberately and so delicately that she felt like a queen. His face was close enough that she could see the shine of his cheek and the full curve of his mouth – so close she could see a small mole just above the top lip.

She closed her eyes and gave herself to the wrapping, caught in a moment that seized every inch of her tired body. For the few seconds his hands brushed her shoulders and breasts, she could have buried her face in his chest and smelled the clean, young smell of his skin. Swathed in that soft blanket, she floated away from the clutter-filled yard and Jordy's devilish moods..

"Will you be all right now?" he asked, tipping her face up towards him. She knew it. He meant to go. Sliding away as noiselessly as he had come – afraid of being discovered there with her. How was he to know that she could have wrapped her arms around his leg and begged him to take her anywhere, away from there. She could have grabbed onto the hem of his jacket and pleaded with him, clawing the ground like a mad woman. That's how desperate women would behave – women in storybooks and films – but not Maggie Willis. All she could do was to stand there like the doormat she was, not crying or begging or covering his face and hands with kisses. No, she'd push it all inside like she always did, until the bitterness choked up inside her.

And so she pulled herself away just in time to hear David calling her from the front door.

"Mam, he's asleep. Come in Mam, yer'll catch yer death out there."

Finally she whispered, "Thank you," in a small, cracked voice, afraid that her heart would leap out of her throat.

George slipped away and she stayed still for a moment, her fingers running over the soft, worn blanket.

At breakfast that morning Jordy came up behind her and put his hands on her shoulders, his mouth hot and close to her ear.

"I'm sorry, flower. I'm sorry. I dunno what gets into me. I'm a weak man. I'll not put you out there again."

Maggie felt the urge to turn and spit square between his eyes but she gritted her teeth and said without looking at him, "It's all right. Get away to work now."

"You're too good for me, Maggie, but I'm gonna make it up to you. You've got my word on it. Things'll be different around here."

He went off to work with the swagger that comes from a conscience cleared of guilt. He kissed all the children, hugged his mother then set off with a head full of promises and plans to go to the seaside next Saturday and take the bairns to the shows.

But today Maggie had something new to think about as she watched him cycle away – hatred for him burning deep in her gut. Hatred that spoke to her in an evil little voice that told her one day the alarm bell would ring and he'd be buried under a mountain of coal or he'd get so drunk after a night at the club he'd walk in front of a bus. She even pictured her reaction. She'd cry and wear black so folks wouldn't talk, but inside she'd be screaming with joy and so giddy she could sweep all those bloody glass ornaments off the mantelpiece and watch them shatter into a thousand pieces.

But today was different. Today she had George to think about. She had only to say his name to herself and the breathless feelings came flooding back until she took herself to the fence to watch for a glimpse of him on his way to work. Nobody else could know about this, for she could imagine the scandal travelling up and down the street. Maggie Willis, the scrawny slut thinking such a fine lad would fancy her. And her a married woman – doesn't she get enough already?

Then she remembered something from about a month ago. She'd been listening to some music on a B.B.C. radio classics show. It was Spanish. Low and throbbing like hot blood pumping into your heart and it made her imagine two people facing each other, moving slowly together, holding scarves of scarlet silk, until they met and swayed body to body, mouth to mouth. *Bolero*, they called it. Now she had a partner to dance with in her dreams and she smiled just to think of the secret that no one else would ever know about.

19

When George left his house two days after the rainy night in the outhouse Maggie Willis was watching him from behind her gate. He didn't know whether to smile or wave – and so he just swished by her and nodded his head. As he turned the corner at the bottom of the street, she was still gazing after him.

That night in the rain something magical had happened. He'd wrapped the old blanket around her shoulders and she closed her eyes, leaning her head back with a look of pure bliss lighting up her face. He never dreamed he could have the power to make a woman sigh that way. If only she'd known, just minutes before, he'd saved Pearl from a bad fall down the stairs.

And afterwards, images of Maggie's body filled his mind as he lay in bed; the thin vulnerable arms, the pale face with dark shadows under the eyes, contradicted the swollen breasts and the rounded belly pushing against the sodden nightdress. She aroused him more than the other, younger women he'd taken out. There was something pathetic but compelling about her – something wonderfully grateful about those frightened eyes. He was reminded of feelings he'd had years back in his scripture classes when the teacher had introduced the boys to all the words in the bible that smelled of sex. Words like *begat, fecund* and *harlot*. Smutty words the boys looked up in the dictionary and sniggered at.

His scripture teacher was a florid faced man named Mr Graves with silver hair bordering a bald, pink head. Mr Graves' lips smacked together when uttering words like *harlot* and *fornication*. He rolled them from his tongue, lingering over them as if he were licking each word. George remembered the verses from the Song of Solomon he and his friends had read over and over until the page was torn:

> *Thy two breasts are like two*
> *young roes that are twins...*
> *... he shall lie all night*
> *betwixt my breasts.*

Last night George slept restlessly as the words drifted through his dreams leaving vague images of creamy naked bodies and the silky feel of skin on skin.

Cycling to work, he thought about Jordy and imagined him forcing Maggie to have sex. He pictured the thickset man crushing her thin body and could hear the grunting and puffing as his lips sucked at her skin. Jordy's lips were unusually full and red for a man so hairy and muscular. Firm and swollen like two pieces of rubber tubing. George remembered his Dad saying that men with thick lips weren't right. "Nivver trust a man wi' thick lips. There's summat funny about men like that."

When George asked his Dad why, Archie tapped his pipe on the table impatiently and said, "I just dinna like them, that's all – they're not right."

But Jordy was popular with the other men at work. He was the kind of man who had a wisecrack for every situation and jokes at the tip of his tongue. George supposed it was easier to be Jordy's friend than his enemy because his mood could change in a matter of seconds.

Jordy treated George in a fatherly way, looking out for him in tricky situations. George wasn't sure what he'd done to deserve this treatment but thought it might have something to do with a Valentine poem he'd written for Jordy a couple of years back. The big man looked awkward when he came to George with the request.

"Summat romantic, tha na's, to do with blue eyes and flowers and all that," he said, scratching at his ear. "Just dinna go too far with the lovey dovey stuff."

George thought it might be for Maggie but wasn't sure because everybody said that Jordy boasted about the number of women he'd been with.

Jordy read the finished poem over four or five times, his brow wrinkled in thought, his big lips pouting. "By that's beautiful," he declared and looked at George with damp eyes. From that time they maintained a respectful distance from each other.

It was half past six when George sat down in the changing room and waited for the morning shift to begin. The room was plain with grey stone floors and a row of double hooks along a stark, whitewashed wall. A string of bottle-blondes posing in swimsuits was plastered one side. He'd never understood the fuss about dyed blonde hair. He preferred brunettes and those glossy, red lips were far too brassy for his taste.

He drank the last gulp of bitter tea from his thermos flask, then dug into his paper "bait" bag, and took out a jam sandwich. His mother was always up at least two hours before he opened his eyes, lighting the fire, brewing tea, carving big hunks of bread with her sharp knife, and making porridge for breakfast. He would have given anything to curl up in front of the fire after breakfast with a big mug of tea and the day's papers. Instead he'd taken to lying in bed until the last possible moment, then cycling to work with his empty stomach growling.

Now he sat in the quiet changing room thinking of his future. Some of his best speeches were composed in the pale morning light.

A loud voice boomed into the silence, "Keep your strength up lad, we need someone with brains and energy to give us a good showing in the union." George looked up to see Jordy Willis standing above him, plucking at his thick, black moustache. "Hey marrers, what say we tek this young'un out on the town if he gets in. He might be well educated with the books but he needs catching up with the lasses if yer na's what I mean."

"Aye and you're the prize bull best suited for that job, Jordy," Joe Barker said, nudging Jordy and winking at George. As usual the men gathered around Jordy, laughing as they took off their coats and slung helmets over their shoulders. George packed away the remains of his sandwich, unable to stomach another mouthful when he thought of Jordy grasping Maggie's neck and pushing her down the stairs.

But outside, the cold air shocked his body awake and he jammed his helmet onto his head, then joined the queue of men waiting for the lift to come up. Their breath rose like steam into the morning chill and George stood dreaming about the way the moon had cast a silver blue shadow over Maggie's face so her cheeks looked like wax.

At the sound of the clanking lift, a few men threw away cigarette butts, crushing them into the mud. George took several deep breaths of clear morning air before entering the suffocating atmosphere of the pit shaft.

The cage jerked down into the gloom and the shades of light faded from dimness to gloominess to darkness with only a few naked bulbs giving off a weak yellow light. The other men chatted about the club, the dogs, the brass band, dart games and card games while George studied the shaft walls trying to see some beauty in the hard black glitter of the coal face.

When the lift touched down, George's eyes slowly accustomed themselves to the wet glare of electric lights reflecting on the damp walls and floor of the narrow tunnels. After five years the bitter smell of coal dust still caught in his throat.

Grasping his shovel, he made his way towards the clanking and skimming of the coal cutter. He nodded at the machine operators, then the tub loaders who shovelled the piles of coal into the waiting containers. George was still a "back-end man", cleaning up the mess after the cutting machine had worked its way across the coalface.

At first he'd been fascinated by the dark ribbons of coal spanning the rock surface. He marvelled at the miracle of its origins; the crushed bodies of giant prehistoric trees and creatures lying layer upon layer, compressed into dense black rock. Sometimes he would find a pale fossil curled into the rock and his mind would fill with images of a Jurassic ocean teeming with ancient crustaceans and waving fronds of exotic sea plants. Often the foreman would dig at his shoulder and call him *glaky* or a dreamer, then hurry him on with the shovelling.

The men worked as a team down here, like a brotherhood, looking out for the oldest and youngest workers. This had made life bearable for him in his first years as a miner and though his fear gradually seeped away, the bitterness remained.

Though they were deep under the ground and in constant danger of explosions and rock falls, the men joked and chatted, oblivious to the tons of rock above them. At the farthest end of the tunnel, Jordy Willis's bulky form leaned back against a tub as he adjusted the tool belt around his waist, then bent over to pick up his container of explosives.

Jordy was a shot firer. He handled the explosives tenderly, his thick fingers respectful of the treacle-like substance. It was the only time he was quiet. It was like watching another person, someone separate from the bully who terrorised his wife and children.

George was so lost in thought he didn't realize how fixedly he had been staring at Jordy and, with a jolt, dropped his shovel when he found the eyes of the big man upon him.

"Hou lad, does tha' fancy thysel' as a shot firer. There's a few year afore yer'll be ready fer that. Eh, Harry." Jordy nudged Harry Dodd, the driller, a thin man with massive shoulders and a shock of reddish hair falling over his forehead.

"Aye, dinna get ahead of yersel, son," echoed Harry.

George's face burned. "Oh – no I didn't mean anything."

Jordy stepped closer. "Yer see, son, this dynamite's like a woman. Yer handle her softly, a little tickle here and there and she starts ter heat up – but yer mek the right connections – press the right buttons and it explodes with power like yer've never seen. Teks a man with experience to handle that, lad. Catch me drift?"

"By, Jordy, there's only a couple of things on your mind – drink and lasses," said Harry. "Nee wonder yer've got a house full o' bairns."

"And a few more round the town," Jordy boasted as he pulled wire from his toolbox and clipped it to the right length. "It teks more than one lass to satisfy Jordy Willis."

Jordy was just a swaggering bully. George felt the anger rise in his throat, so he picked up his shovel and attacked the piles of rubble with a new burst of energy.

Working in silence, he was usually able to separate mind from body till he became a machine: shovelling, scraping and loading while his mind composed speeches to packed Union gatherings. Today he couldn't centre his thoughts on his latest speech and instead created passionate scenarios with Maggie. He imagined her kneeling gratefully at his feet, her hair brushing his shoes, and then he picked her up like a baby, swept her up into his attic and made love to her.

There was a sudden rush of movement as men scattered to the far end of the tunnel. It was time to blast a new part of the seam. George picked up his shovel and shuffled towards the others, his mind still in an attic filled with silver moonlight.

The loud voice of the foreman bounced off the stone walls, "Clear the way, lads. We'll be firing the shot in two minutes."

The men filed around to the other side of the safety gate while the detonator adjusted the generator ends, connecting them to the terminal. The foreman shouted into the black hole of the tunnel where the new coal-face was to be blown out.

"Haway Jordy lad. We're all waiting – ger'a move on."

Jordy's faint voice echoed from the shadows of the tunnel. "All right, divn't get thee knickers in a twist, I'm comin'."

The detonator looked at his watch and moistened his lips with his tongue. "Haway, man, what's he deein'?"

Heavy footsteps echoed along the corridor and Jordy appeared, hitching his tool belt over his belly.

"Tha's ower slow the day, Jordy. Hadaway out o' the tunnel and get behind the gate," the foreman shouted, "It's gonna blow any minute."

"Dinna worry yersel', I na's this stuff like the back of me hand." He slowed down to a lazy swagger.

"Get out of the bloody way..." the detonator yelled. George sensed danger when he saw the man stumble backwards and he threw himself behind the gate, joining the other men who were halfway down the tunnel just as a deep rumble then a deafening explosion boomed behind them. A thick column of reeking smoke swelled into the tunnel and a shower of jagged coal fragments pelted like tiny arrows into Jordy's face. When the smoke cleared, Jordy's body was doubled over, hands first covering his eyes then clawing at his cheeks. He bellowed like a wounded bull until the foreman ran up with a bucket of water and pushed the screaming man's face into it. When Jordy came up, choking and retching, his swollen face was gouged with deep black lines. He swayed for a minute like a tree in the wind then slumped heavily onto the ground, his tools clattering around him.

The foreman's voice snapped into the chaos, "I need four men to get this poor bugger up to the top. The rest of yer get back to work clearing this rubble or we'll be stuck here. Harry you're in charge."

Harry opened the safety gate and ushered the stunned men back to the work area. George watched from the corner of his eye as four men half carried and half pushed Jordy to the lift while he moaned and cried, "Me face, me face."

The shift was strangely silent all that morning as the men silently shovelled the rubble away until all traces of the accident were gone. The morning had been another reminder of the dangers of their job, though the whispers had already started that Jordy had brought the trouble on himself.

George stayed quiet. He'd never join in with the gossip.

God has his own way of dealing with bullies and abusers, he thought to himself, and he attacked the coal seam with more vigour than he'd ever exerted before.

20

The howling finally stopped. The doctor had been over and it took two sleeping pills to knock Jordy out. Now he lay in bed snoring, his face cleaned and covered with bandages.

Maggie, Hannah and David held him down while the doctor tried to pick out the bigger pieces of grit with a tiny pair of tweezers but the bellowing had been awful.

"Me eyes are on fire," he screamed as black tears streamed down his livid cheeks, but the swelling was so bad the doctor couldn't get a close look at the injuries. He explained that they'd only be able to see the extent of the damage to his eyes and face when the swelling had gone down. Until then he was to rest and keep his face clean and covered.

Hannah sat by the bed holding Jordy's hand, sniffling quietly and blowing her nose. "Eeh – what's happened to me bonny lad's face. It's all black and ruined."

Maggie stood watching, her heart like a hard stone. To see him lying there like a blubbering baby didn't give her the satisfaction she'd imagined and the thought that only this morning she'd wished for such an accident, was a heavy burden. She felt no pleasure in his agony.

"Mother, get away to bed now. We'll need all our strength in the morning. Come on, pet," she said, taking the old lady's arm.

Hannah allowed herself to be guided away to her room. The four youngest were sleeping soundly on the bed settee, two one end and two the other and the air was warm with their breath.

Maggie shut the bedroom door. Jordy lay powerless here in his own house. She didn't have to tiptoe around, feeling his prickly presence, afraid of setting off the swearing and shouting and hitting.

Out in the empty hallway, light from the streetlamp stained the shadows blue and the distant wailing of a siren signalled the start of the night shift. Maggie felt at peace, like a ghost drifting through the familiar spaces. The house was so quiet she wrapped her arms around her body and remembered the other night when George had draped the shawl around her shoulders. She'd felt like a blushing young girl for she hadn't felt such gentleness in years and tonight she was free again just like she had been that day on Whittington Hill. Before Jordy came into her life.

On a whim she walked over to the girls' bedroom and pushed the door open. The air was warm with the hum of regular breathing. At the far corner of the room, behind a rough woven curtain, was a small cupboard filled with old boxes of papers and dusters, broken toys and ragged clothing. At the very back of this cupboard was a small biscuit tin with a wartime picture of George VI and Elizabeth on the front. She felt the prickle of tears when she touched the smooth surface.

She carried it back into the hall, sat down on the old rocking chair and started to rock gently, back and forth, back and forth stroking the lid. As she rocked and watched the bands of white light whipping around the wall when the bus or a car went by, she hummed a song she'd sung to all her babies.

Dance to yer Daddy, sing to yer Mammy, dance to yer Daddy, when the boat comes in. You shalt have a fishy on a little dishy, you shalt have a haddock, when the boat comes in.

She pried the lid off the tin. Inside were two small rhinestone hairclips, a scrap of creamy fabric dotted with lilac flowers, some letters and a picture. It had been at least eighteen years since she'd looked at Chuck with his bright smile, his eyes squinting against the sun and the huge fish that dangled from a metal hook. Perhaps he was skimming across some lake at that very moment unaware that he'd ever met her.

She closed her eyes and held the picture against her heart. It wasn't long before she drifted off for five minutes or was it an hour? She didn't know.

"Maggie," a voice whispered, and looking up she saw the ceiling open as if by magic. George's face looked down. "Maggie are you alright?"

She couldn't speak. If this were really a dream she would do exactly as she wished. She pushed an old chair under the opening and the air was velvet around her as she stepped up and lifted her arms high.

It was so easy to spring up there once she felt the ledge around the attic opening. George's strong arms pulled her upwards and she was led, her fingers just touching his, through dark spaces and into a tiny moonlit room.

Holding hands they sunk onto warm blankets and Maggie closed her eyes to imagine that they lay outside in a beautiful clearing somewhere. He slid her faded, blue nightie up to her waist and somewhere in the distance she heard his voice gasping, "Touch me here, here Maggie." Then she felt the whole weight of his body roll over onto hers. His knee pushed firmly between her legs then he moved slowly inside her, whispering words into her ear, his hands brushing against her breasts. She smelled clean soap on his neck, felt the satin skin on his back and damp curls of hair round his ears. Her body was alive, every nerve tingling as she clasped his face and kissed his mouth hungrily.

Behind his head light from the window lit up George's fair hair. And her own hands looked pale and silvery when she touched him. As though, somehow, they'd been cut from moonlight.

1962

21

On Rita's sixteenth birthday she stayed in the house the whole day. Even when her mother asked her to come to the shops in Belton and promised to buy her a sundae at Valenti's, she refused, choosing to sit in her bedroom, reading film annuals and comics and waiting for a knock on the door. But by eight o'clock that night there was no such call and so she cried and clawed at her pillow, then stuffed it into her mouth until she fell asleep, fully dressed and clutching Wendy who, by now, had lost one eye and had a loose left leg.

The next day she woke up with a hard lump of anger where her heart was and decided it was time to say goodbye to the old Rita.

Three hours later she emerged from Eileen's Paris Coiffures and looked sideways at her reflection in Wilson's window. She barely recognized herself with the platinum curtain of hair hanging over her cheek. The frosty hair and tight baby blue, angora jumper made her feel like an ice queen and she walked coolly down the High Street, past a knot of pit lads still in their work shirts, waiting for the bus home. Clucks and whistles erupted.

"Yer can scrub my back anytime, flower."

"She can scrub summat else for me."

Rita swept by, hair fanning out like a silken veil, her cheeks warm and her stomach scrunching tight. It was not an unpleasant feeling, but new and unfamiliar. She floated past them, like a being from another world. It was all right to be looked at like this – but not to be touched. There was real power in looking sexy and glossy like a photo. As long as you could keep your distance and stop before the groping and heavy breathing started.

Some of Rita's friends from school were standing by the leek hut. Lads were smoking, wrestling and combing their hair, while the girls chewed gum and held up pocket mirrors to put on lipstick. Rick Allen slouched over the handlebars of his new racing bike. He'd dropped his teddy-boy image and gone crazy over Elvis since Blue Hawaii was showing at Sunderland. He'd even got the Elvis sneer and with his big sweep of greased, black hair, blue eyes and cigarette dangling from his lip he'd become quite a celebrity in Belton. He'd never so much as looked at Rita before, but now he straddled the bike open-mouthed watching her walk towards him. Robert Gibbons sat on the kerb next to him, head down. Robert was laying low since the rumour had spread that his parents had used their new council-issued toilet seat as a frame for his Nana's portrait.

Rick's lips gathered into a puckered 'O' as he whistled loudly. Robert chewed his gum and grinned as Rita swung her hips.

"It's Marilyn Monroe," said Rick. "By Rita, yer look smashing. Just like a film star."

Rita felt a small rush of excitement. Now she was finally getting the attention she deserved.

"Sexy, sexy Rita – yer good enough to eat," Rick said, snapping his gum.

"Shurrup, the pair of you."

"No, I really mean it," said Rick, with the slightest hint of an American accent. "With that hairdo yer a knockout. Want a tab?" She took out a cigarette, leaning forward for him to light it, and caught hold of his hand lightly. Then she threw back her head and blew the smoke upwards as she'd seen Lana Turner do. She knew their eyes were on her.

"What's going on inside there today?" she asked, nodding towards the hall.

"Some union meeting."

"How come yer not in there – yer both in the union."

"It's ower borin' – just talkin' talkin'," said Rick. "Since the pits were nationalized every wet-eared bugger thinks he can run the place, but soon there's not gonna be a pit left to run."

"Aye me da says the pit's likely to close within a year," said Robert, lighting another cigarette.

"What does that daft bugger know?" said Rick. Robert retreated into silence again. "I'm not bothered about that. I'll just gan ower to Hartlepool. As long as I get my pay packet I'm happy. Half for me Mam and the rest for beer and tabs and a few nights out. That's my life. Shouting and speechmaking is for the old'uns and the married ones with nowt better to do."

Rita stuck her hands in the pockets of her navy school raincoat. "Aye, there's nowt doing in this dump. Yer get stuck here for the rest of yer life and yer old before you know what's hit yer. Just like me mam – she's finished."

"There's a real up and comer talking in there. George Nelson from your street," said Rick, "That upstart's come from nowt and now he's climbing up in the union, hobnobbing with the big boys in Newcastle."

Rita face felt hot and the angry feeling swelled up inside. "That's all he's good for," she said, taking another drag, "talkin' all day and preachin' at them poor sods. That's not gonna make him rich." She flicked her cigarette at the wall.

"Aye, he might think he's summat special but his shit stinks the same as thine, eh Robert." Rick spat out his cigarette and ground it into the gravel with the heel of his pit boots. "Or mebbe I should ask yer Nana's opinion. She's closer to it than any other bugger here."

"Get lost, marrer," said Robert shrugging his shoulders as he got up and left, dragging his feet as he walked.

"Do you always talk to yer mates like that?" Rita asked, fascinated as he took a thin, black comb and began to slick his hair back.

"Three's a crowd, hinny. Anyway our Rob's got a hide as thick as a horse." He swung a lanky leg over the crossbar and leaned the bike against the wall. Rita's throat felt tight and dry as his body swung closer to her, so she had to tilt her head back to see his face.

"Yer look smashing, Rita. Different-like." He reached out and flicked the silvery hair. "I swear I never looked at yer before, but now... yer look mair like a woman." He pursed his lips up again and whistled.

Rita felt a downward pressure in every part of her body and a sensation that the daylight had changed colour – shifted gears with a crisp *click-click* as Rick moved closer, all long, jean-clad legs and sweet Brylcreem smell. She bit her lip and squeezed her knees together to stop the tingling below. He smelled of cigarettes and chewing gum and the warm tickling of his voice vibrated in her ear.

"Haway, hinny, leg's go behind the hut – we can look through the window at all the fools inside."

Rita allowed him to guide her around the corner and with one sudden, swift movement, he pushed her against the wall. His tongue was all over her, licking her lips, cheek, neck like a big lazy cat and her insides were full of warm, gushing liquid. She tried to tell him to stop but her throat felt as if it was stuffed with cotton wool. Struggling, she tugged at his arms but he held on tighter, sticking his hands under her sweater. He pulled up her bra from the bottom and flipped out her breasts so that she gasped at the sudden cold and the freedom of it. His head burrowed between her breasts and she felt suddenly detached from her body.

"You must educate yourselves – understand your rights," George's voice boomed out through the open window, "for that is the only way to escape this life of misery and oppression forced on us by profiteers and scoundrels." The voice sliced through Rita's fuzzy consciousness. Suddenly Rick's face felt clammy, his smell suffocating.

"Get off," she tugged at his hair but he nuzzled more deeply into her neck, cupping her breasts with her hands. "I said get off."

Rita pushed Rick with all her force and he stumbled back gasping, "What the hell..."

"If you ever touch me like that again, I'll kick you in the balls." She pulled her bra and blouse down, aware that her heart was pounding hard in her ears.

"You're a real cock teaser." He said, rustling through his pockets and taking out a shilling. Flipping it towards her he turned his bike to go. "Ta for the feel – you know you really liked it."

She backed away, edging towards the front of the hut. Suddenly the thought of him touching her body made her feel sick. *Why did everything feel wrong? Why couldn't she fit in like the other girls who would've done anything to get Rick's attention? Why did she always feel mean and prickly?* The questions crowded into her head until she couldn't think straight. All that mattered was to tidy her new shiny hair and sneak a look into the meeting room. Men were pressed against the walls and doorways watching George who stood at the front silhouetted against the window, his head framed with light. He looked like a gorgeous film star but she hated him for it. He'd built up her hopes then let her down. But it would never happen again. She wouldn't let a man use her or lead her on. Never.

The tears welled up in her eyes but she pushed them back with a clenched fist and looked down at the coin Rick had thrown at her. A shiny shilling. *I don't need you, George*, she thought. *I'll make my own way without the help of any man.* She flipped back her blonde hair and without looking back, ran out to catch the bus for the next feature presentation at the Palladium.

22

Boxing Day, 1963. Rita sat on the red velvet sofa rummaging through a half-empty box of Black Magic. All the nutty, caramel ones were long gone and only a few sickly orange creams were left. The Christmas tree leaned over at an angle, its decorations thrown back on. Lennie had drunk twelve bottles of Newcastle Brown on Christmas Eve and fell against it before crashing to the floor dead drunk. Strings of cards hung crookedly across the wall and limp crepe-paper streamers dangled over the doorway. The spirit of Christmas had sputtered out like a fart from a deflated balloon.

Her Dad and brothers were at the club again, boozing it up. Still coasting along drunkenly on the last gasps of Christmas cheer, and in the kitchen her mother was carving up the remains of the chicken and ham from yesterday's dinner. The men would be in soon shouting for a plate of fried potatoes, meat sandwiches, and plenty of pickled onions.

Walter would be the loudest and first to sit down at the table, even though he weighed twenty stone and the doctor had told him to cut down a bit and lose some of his beer belly. But telling him that was like pissing in the wind. The club was his second home and beer was his lifeblood. Lifting the pint of stout to his mouth had become a religious ritual. He'd set his knife and fork down on his supper plate and fill his pipe, then he was off out of the house without so much as a word to anyone. *Poor Mam, slaving in the house day after day, hands all dried up and back bent with scrubbing. For what? A lazy drunkard with nowt to say to her.*

Her brothers were both cut from the same cloth, all right sober but get a few pints inside them and they were all talk and hot air. Shouting the odds about what the union was going to do for them, then rushing out to plan strikes at noisy meetings and rallies.

She rustled absently through the chocolates in search of coffee creams then licked the bitter filling while she scanned the fireplace. Everything looked cheap or drab. The shiny pink metal plaque from Scarborough or the set of flying ducks with jewelled eyes that flew up towards a dark print of fat cows drinking from a muddy river. *Like something from the rag and bone man's cart*, she thought – not like the lovely, modern, sleek furnishings she gazed at in magazines and Hollywood annuals. *Jesus*, she sighed, *this rubbish life isn't for me. I'm not gonna be a martyr like Mam.*

She'd already started to make the right connections and that was the first step. Closing her eyes, she thought back to Christmas Eve and the smart Newcastle nightclubs she'd gone to with Dickie Francisco, a dance-hall singer from down south.

They'd met at the Sunderland Palais de Danse. Her friend, Marion had left an hour before with a pipe-fitter from Shafton Colliery who bought her three Babychams and had his hand on her bum within an hour. So Rita was left alone to reflect on the disappointments of the night and come to the conclusion that there was no romance left in her life – no mystery, no passion. Was it only Marilyn Monroe or Audrey Hepburn who bewitched men by the twitch of an eyebrow? Hadn't she studied the Women's Weekly then bought the best push-up brassiere and the newest shade of stockings in American Tan. All that effort just to spend two hours of agony sipping on the same gin and bitter lemon while her net petticoat scratched the hell out of her legs and her roll-on girdle bit into the tops of her thighs.

The band started up again for the last set, and the glass ball suspended from the ceiling, began to turn, scattering snowflakes of light across the dance floor. Dickie appeared in a smooth, black suit and bow tie, crooning into the microphone, to the tired couples locked in sweaty embraces, who stumbled around the dance floor. His dark hair was slicked back into a smooth wave and with eyes half closed he swayed his hips to the music.

A line of girls pressed against the stage, looking upwards, following his every move, sighing when he ran his hands through his hair or moved his free hand over the curves of an imaginary girlfriend. When he fell down on one knee pleading, the audience screamed with delight and one girl started a brawl when she ripped her petticoat on the edge of the stage trying to climb up. The bouncer tried to pull her down so her boyfriend jumped on his back and pulled off the big man's toupee. The stage lights went on and Dickie carried on singing as the fight picked up steam.

Rita couldn't believe her luck later when he stopped his car at the deserted bus stop as she was struggling with a broken stiletto heel.

"Pretty bird like you can't get home in that state," he said ushering her into the soft leather interior of his car.

After she introduced herself his eyes travelled down her body and he said, "Rita – hmm – Must have named you after Rita Hayworth with equipment like yours."

Instead of driving her straight home, he took her on a tour of Newcastle.

She clung to Dickie's arm when he breezed into the smart Newcastle nightclubs. Inside she remembered red plush seating, pink neon lights, rows of bevelled cocktail glasses, and ice. Buckets full of it. Mountains of cold, frosty crystals, smoking faintly. There was something clean and luxurious about having all that ice at your fingertips. She marvelled that someone had actually taken the time to make this pile of tiny, sparkling ice cubes. Sucking one after the other, she relished their clean, cold taste. They didn't have a fridge at home. Nobody on the street had one and at The Colliers' Arms gin or whisky was warm as stewed tea.

Dickie threw his head back and laughed at her. "She's like a kid playing with a new toy," he said to the club owner, "I bring her to the fanciest place in Newcastle and all she wants to do is suck the bloody ice cubes." He reached over and tweaked her cheek.

At one place she drank something sweet and fizzy called a pink lady. After two of those she felt a bit giddy, so giddy she couldn't stop herself talking and hugging him. And laughing – she'd laughed all night and danced barefoot across the dance floor till her feet were wet with beer. Everything sounded funny and wonderful, and she knew Dickie liked that because he had kissed her lightly on the nose and said, "There's nothing I like better than a bird with a good sense of humour. Not like those stuck-up tarts down in London."

She'd walked out of that place like a film star and ridden home on a cloud. As the car swept over Gateshead Bridge she gazed at the dim shapes of the ships moving like ghosts along the Tyne, and the stars shining through the high metal girders.

The endless streets of houses were dark, all the families now sleeping, all the empty milk bottles placed safely out on the step waiting for another morning to begin in its safe monotony. Rita felt at that moment that she could never put out another milk bottle in the same way – that her life was now measured by some new standard and her glimpse into another kind of life had changed her forever.

She must have drifted off to sleep because the next thing she knew Dickie was nudging her, telling her they were driving through Belton. Opening her eyes, she saw the harsh orange light of the streetlamps and the grey terraces of Belton Downs. Her head ached, but the warmth of the car felt safe and comforting as they turned the corner, passing the old blacksmith's and the lonely, flapping sign of the Colliers Arms. She shuddered and snuggled further into the seat.

"I live in a rough place, Dickie – it's not what you're used to."

He put his hand over her lips, "Don't say nothing', luv. I'm no snob. When I was a kid we was brought up right near the Poplar tube station. Our flat looked out onto the back of Jerry's jellied eel restaurant."

Her house was dark when they stopped outside and, without warning, he reached over to her with one arm, the other remaining draped over the steering wheel, and kissed her full on the mouth, sticking his tongue in so deep that she gasped. He tasted of mint and ashes and she ran her fingers through his hair like Lana Turner did to John Garfield in the Postman Always Rings Twice.

"You kill me, Rita," he said afterwards. "You're just like an innocent kid and that's what I like about you. Now run along or yer Ma'll be worrying about ya."

Rita slipped into the quiet house. Her heart raced as she tried not to step on the creaky floorboards and in the tiny room at the top of the stairs she fell onto the bed, stuffing the pillow against her mouth to stifle the scream of joy that threatened to burst from her.

"Rita – Rita," her mother's voice cut into her daydream and the glamorous images were wiped away when Rita saw Iris holding a knife in one hand and an onion in the other, eyes red-rimmed and streaming from the fumes. Rita squeezed her eyes shut but the pictures wouldn't come again and now Iris was calling.

"Rita – Rita – put some coal on the fire – it's nearly out – then come and put some pickles in the dish – yer've been sittin' dreamin' all mornin'. Lazin' around the place like Lady Muck."

Rita slouched into the kitchen and reached for a large pickled onion. "I'm tired, Mam."

"Aye, yer've a good right to be. Ella Danby says she saw yer gettin' out of a fancy car the other mornin'. Late," she said. "Three o'clock in the mornin'."

The sharp vinegary taste of the onion caught in Rita's throat. "I'll swear that nosey old bugger never sleeps for fear she'll miss summat." Rita licked her fingernail and held it up in front of her.

"Eeh, yer getting' far ower big for yer boots, our Rita."

Rita knew a lecture was about to begin, and put on the blank face that stopped her Mam in her tracks. Just in the nick of time there was an urgent knocking at the door. Olive Coombes rushed in, one of her pink plastic curlers unravelling across her forehead.

"Iris – Iris , it's yer man. He's comin' down the street and weavin' something awful on his bike. Yer'd better come along before he kills hissel'."

Rita sighed, "Not again, Mam." But Iris was already out the door, and through the cracked brown gate. Rita followed her to the step, and they were just in time to see her father swish by, pedals whizzing around like windmills, wind blowing in his scarlet face and feet flailing out to the sides as he headed directly towards the wooden fence bordering the allotments at the top of the street.

"Walter, Walter---- stop Wal---."

There was a splintering crash as his front wheel drove straight into the wooden posts and became tangled up in barbed wire. He was catapulted over the fence into Ned Barker's fresh pile of steaming manure, then lay motionless.

"Eeh – Rita, he's dead," her mother wailed.

"More like dead drunk," said Rita as neighbours moved onto their steps or leaned over gates to find out what all the commotion was about. Passing Ella Danby's house, she heard her whisper to Maureen Clegg, "Walter Hawkins got his arse caught in the fence again. Up to his eyes in beer I'll warrant."

Furious, Rita ran to the top of the street where old Neddy Barker was trying to pull her Dad out from the mud but as soon as Walter got to his feet his fists went up and he started growling.

"What's everybody gawkin' at? I'll fettle any bugger that teks me on. I'll give him a good bat on the head."

He shuffled around, poking and jabbing with his fists then one of his boots fell off and he was ankle deep in mud and manure.

"Ger out of the clarts man," Neddy shouted and a few of the spectators began to snicker.

"Aas the gaffer here," Walter yelled, "and I'll clip yer lugs if yer come near me."

Rita's face was flaming hot as her Mam clambered over the smashed planks of wood, wading through the mud in her slippers and holding her hands out as if to a wilful bairn.

She turned and stomped back to the house. Time to go. Time to get out of this circus today before her Mam asked her to fill up the tin bath and help to pull the drunken old sod up the stairs.

Pink, she thought. Pink ladies, iced glasses, and hot neon lights. Suddenly the street faded away into a rosy fantasy of cocktail lounges and plush hotels.

1964

23

When George finished his speech to the packed house at the club, the place erupted in a roar of cheers, whistles and coughing. Hats flew up into the air and George had to fight his way through them to the doors at the back of the hall.

On the way out, men ruffled his hair and pumped his hands up and down until his head was so light and dizzy his eyes ached and his jaw was sore from smiling.

Outside, the sun burst through ragged clouds and shone through the exit doors, bathing him in its brilliance. His heart swelled and he threw his arms upwards in triumph. The rush of victory coursed through his blood faster than the strongest whisky.

Leaning against the wall, he closed his eyes for a moment, trying to realize what had happened. He'd finally done it. Now he'd never have to go down the cursed pit again, for today he'd been elected Union Secretary for the whole of Durham County. That meant a salary, clean work in an office and a room in one of the agents' houses at the Miners' Hall, the grand building in Durham City.

To live in Durham was a dream. He'd wake up every morning with a view of the cathedral from his bedroom window. He'd buy his groceries down at the marketplace and walk among the students, businessmen and clerics.

Crag Street would slide away into the past, fading away until it was nothing more than a vague memory; a grimy row of soot-smudged houses filled with nosey, ignorant gossips. Of course he'd still send money to his parents but the ties would be severed and he was glad of it.

He looked down at his navy suit – the shiny, frayed cuffs and the mended knees. He'd throw it out the first chance he had and buy one of those quality made-to-measure ones from Blackwell's in Durham.

"I canna believe that was my son in there," a reedy voice said in his ear. George looked up to see his Dad, Archie, staring at him with an expression of pride and bewilderment. He crushed his folded cap in his wrinkled hands. George was speechless for the first time that day. It had been so long since they'd spoken more than two words to each other.

Archie clasped George's hand and George took a good, long look at him, wondering when his neck had become so wrinkled and his sharp, blue eyes so pale and watery. There was a sudden surge of movement behind them and Archie let go, muttering, "All the best, son." Then he was swallowed up in a sea of bodies.

Walter Hawkins manoeuvred all twenty stone of himself in front of George. "On behalf of me family and mesel' I'd like to congratulate you and if yer can manage it – come ower for a bit o' supper tonight."

George tried to push his back closer to the wall to avoid the blast of stale, beery breath. Lenny and Bill grinned from behind Walter like two bookends. "Me wife, Iris and me lovely daughter, Rita are mekkin' a beautiful roast beef."

George stammered an acceptance then was immediately surrounded by men requesting, suggesting, arguing and shoving. A new banner was needed before the next Big Meeting as well as uniforms for the band. Someone had to put pressure on the Coal Board to stop the closure of Belton Colliery, wages should be higher, hours shorter, conditions better and they needed a bigger voice on the National Executive. George began to feel so faint at the pounding throb of voices, he slipped out unnoticed in the middle of an argument about changing the band's colours from silver to maroon.

It was three o'clock when he told his parents he was leaving. Facing the fireplace, he studied the pipe rack on the mantelpiece and the barometer from South Shields. They were old familiar things, souvenirs of childhood when he was happy to be the centre of their lives. For a moment he remembered begging to clean his father's pipes – setting them all in a row and gently working the pipe cleaner around the bowls. Or walking along the front at South Shields holding both their hands as they swung him into the air and squealed, "Oops a daisy."

He pictured the two of them sitting behind him now, his father grasping the arms of the old rocking chair, his mother perched on the edge of the oak footstool still holding an unpeeled potato and knife. Silence weighed heavily in the air and pressed on his heart like an accusation.

"Of course I'll make sure you're well looked after," said his formal, new voice. *When did I suddenly take charge*, he wondered. "I'll send you something every week to help out and I'm only a bus ride away." He knew then that he might as well have been going to Land's End or New Zealand and he turned to see his mother rise and come to him holding out her arms.

"I knew you'd mek something of yourself. You were the blessed one. I always knew it. My golden boy was never meant for a life down the pit." And she held him close, her head heavy on his shoulder, her tears making a damp patch on his shirt. It was a relief. She'd finally let him go.

Around five o'clock that evening George lay on his bed and looked at the two cracked, brown suitcases piled high with clothes and books. *It was going to be a messy leave-taking.* He'd been careless with women. First there was Maggie to think about. It had been over a year now they'd been going up to George's attic to make frantic love while Jordy was working the night shift, "Like a pair of young ferrets," Maggie said one night, crouching down on the old blanket. George's stomach lurched at the analogy but he still smiled and unzipped his trousers, excited by the tragedy of her.

In the darkness he imagined her to be one of the poor wretches climbing the metal ladder with a bucket of coal on her back and every time he plucked her from out of that godforsaken house of hers he'd shower her with tenderness. She was so grateful and his head was always felt clear afterwards. Clear enough to get on with his union business and not worry about sex like some of the other lads at the pit. And now he was used to looking Jordy Willis square in his ruined face and saying good morning without flinching a bit.

The relationship with Maggie had been so easy – so uncomplicated. She made few demands on him outside their meetings and he rarely spoke to her on the street. Just the odd hello. A smile or a wave when he'd catch her watching him cycle to work. Staring at him with those faded blue eyes that squinted nervously when she became excited.

It has to stop, he realized. *There's no place for it in my new life.* She was thirty-eight and had seven children. The whole idea was ridiculous, even distasteful to him now. It was a mistake – something he wanted to wipe away like an accidental smudge, and so he decided to slip out early in the morning to catch the first bus. There'd be no fuss, no crying, no empty promises made to appease. He'd just shrug off the old life like a butterfly shedding its cocoon or – a small voice nagged at him – like a snake shedding its first skin.

There was one more messy detail to take care of. Supper at the Hawkins. He had to go since Walter was one of his biggest supporters and influential with the other men. But he knew he'd slighted Rita. He'd hardly spoken to her since the day of the wedding and he'd never carried out the promise he'd made. Too many important opportunities stood in the way and besides, she'd have probably expected marriage after a couple of months of serious courting. There were too many complications. Walter would've run Rita down the aisle to get her married off and once the babies started to arrive that'd be the end of his union career.

Stop worrying, he told himself. He'd heard rumours that she'd turned out to be a common sort anyway with her bottle blonde hair and tight jumpers.

The Pitman's Daughter

She probably had a swarm of flashy lads hanging around her. Comforted by that thought he jumped up and began to fasten his new red tie.

At half past six that evening George arrived at the Hawkins' house and realized the family were in the middle of a fight. He could hear the shouting from out in the street.

"You'll bloody well stay in tonight." Walter was shouting. "Yer not gallivantin' off like some street girl with any Tom, Dick or Harry that buys yer a few Babychams."

George waited for a few minutes before he knocked. There was a scuffling sound then Walter came to the door wheezing and wiping the sweat from his forehead with a red handkerchief.

He coughed and sneaked a quick look behind him then opened the door wide. A rich smell of beef and drippings wafted outwards.

"Pushin' a few chairs around yer na's. I'm not up to it the same as I used to be. Fancy a bottle of stout?"

He showed George through the kitchen and into the front room where rows of beer bottles stood on top of a pink and cream padded bar studded with gold buttons. Faded motifs of cherubs were painted across its front and chipped gold scrollwork curled around its edges.

"The wife," Walter nodded his head towards it. "Likes to collect things."

The whole room was crammed with ornaments. Wall plaques, beer glasses, candlesticks and tea sets. Unfinished frames of embroidery and tapestry nudged up against an ornate toasting fork with a metal carving of Blackpool Tower on the handle. There was barely room for Walter to move. He flipped the top off a bottle of Newcastle Brown and held it towards George.

"Oh – if yer'd rather have a glass we've plenty of them here."

George shook his head, conscious of the furry layer of dust on the surface of every shelf and ornament. He took a long swig from the bottle then sneaked a look inside the kitchen where Iris Hawkins was trying to persuade a thunder-faced Rita to help set the table. He noticed her heavily made-up face and carefully arranged platinum hair and realized she probably had other plans for the night.

"She's a canny lass but she's headstrong that one – I don't know who she got that from," said Walter. "All the women on my side were saints."

Five minutes later George sat in the cluttered kitchen in front of a mountain of roast beef, Yorkshire puddings, mashed potatoes, parsnips and boiled barley. Rita looked sullen and tottered towards the table dressed in high black heels and a skin-tight black sheath dress.

"Why the hell they wear them bloody stupid dresses I'll never know," Walter said as he shovelled a whole Yorkshire pudding into his mouth.

Rita poured the gravy from the porcelain boat that said *souvenir of Harrogate*. George watched her closely. Under the heavy layer of foundation and the crimson slash of lipstick was an attractive, determined face. The dark, arched eyebrows contrasted with her pale hair, the hazel green eyes were widely set and the well-shaped mouth curved downwards in a pout. But there was something about the way she moved – something pushy and aggressive. He decided that she'd become the kind of girl he'd always tried to avoid. The cheeky kind who thought nothing of swearing and smoking in public. The kind who, on Big Meeting days would wear a cowboy hat saying "Kiss me quick" and drink beer from a bottle as she danced through the streets. He'd seen lads at the pit go out with girls like this. Watched them kiss and grope in front of everyone's nose. Teddy Barrett's girlfriend was one of those brazen types. She'd knocked out one of his front teeth play wrestling with him.

He must have been staring at Rita because she glared at him and he dropped a gravy-covered parsnip down the front of his good white shirt. "Damn it," he muttered without thinking.

Walter jumped up. "Rita, take George into the scullery and wash the lad's shirt front. We canna have him looking hacky when he's due at the Miners' Hall tomorrow."

Rita clashed her fork down, splashing gravy over the tablecloth.

"Rita," squeaked Iris, "that's me best cloth."

"Don't worry about it – I can wash the shirt when I get back home," protested George.

"She'll do it," said Walter through gritted teeth, "she's not gonna sulk around here like Lady Muck."

"Aye, she's always flouncin' around here like she's better than us," chimed Lenny as he stuffed a whole pudding in his mouth and a thin line of gravy trickled to the end of his chin.

"It was my fault," said George as he followed Rita into the scullery.

She ran the tap, wrung a dishcloth under the water then turned and began rubbing his shirt, her eyes downcast. He could smell strong perfume. The kind he'd bought at Woolworths for his mother.

"I'm sorry – I – I can be clumsy sometimes," he stuttered.

Her green eyes flashed directly at him and he stumbled backwards.

"The way they talk about you round here, people would think you're perfect," Rita snapped.

"Yes, your Dad's been a loyal supporter – I have to say that for him," said George wishing she'd finish wiping soon.

She glared at him again, "Loyalty – hmmm – that's something you wouldn't know much about – eh?"

He gulped, determined to set things right between them. "Look, Rita, I can explain what happened."

She wiped harder, almost knocking him off balance and dousing the front of his shirt with soap suds, "That's the trouble with this cheap material – trying to pass itself off as the real thing – attracts the dirt like flies to muck. Well that's the best I can do." She flapped the cloth and laid it out flat on the sink. "Better get back to your supporters and by the way – yer'd better make sure you keep the promises you make to *them* or they'll drop you like a piece of cow clarts."

George cleared his throat and followed her back into the kitchen where Walter, Lenny and Bill were arguing about union business. Mrs Hawkins was clearing the supper plates away while Rita stood sulking in the scullery pulling the threads out of an old tea towel.

"Why don't they ever have to help?" she asked her mother. "They all ate too."

Iris shrugged and the conversation continued.

"Why if the pit closes George'll look after us," said Lenny, "We can get a transfer to Hartlepool. I'm partial to sea air – it's close to Crimdon as well – by I saw a good looker at the Lido there last summer."

"Yer not pickin' a holiday camp yer na's," Walter said, jabbing at his potatoes as Rita whisked the plate away, "You're talkin' about the livelihood of a hundred men – wi' families too – we canna allow our pit to close down – what do you say George?"

"I'll see what I can do," George said weakly.

"And the banner for the next Big Meeting day," said Bill, "We should get that one with the lion lyin' on its side and the bees buzzin' around it – yer na's – the one that says "out of the strong comes...."

"That's the bloody picture on the treacle tin," said Lenny, "yer don't want lions on the banner – yer want a miner standing proud at the top of the mountain with his lamp shinin' in the darkness." His hand reached towards the ceiling in a grand gesture.

Rita was cleaning her nails with the end of her knife, "More like standing at the top of a slag heap with a full pint glass yer mean." She giggled and chewed on the end of a nail.

"Cheeky madam," said Walter, "If yer haven't got anything better to say then keep yer gob buttoned up."

"I'm just tellin' the truth – yer just have to read the paper to know it's a dyin' industry," Rita continued. "We're into the sixties now – things are changin'."

"Aye well some thing don't change – yer still have to eat and this is my house – so keep your ideas to yersel."

George was having trouble with the jam roly-poly. It stuck in a doughy lump at the back of his tongue, "Er – I was wondering if you'd like to hear some of my ideas on the Coal Board's employment policies." He noticed Lenny and Bill's eyes darting to the clock and realized it was only fifty minutes to closing time, "But I'm sure we can go over that the next time I see you."

There was suddenly a loud honking from outside and Rita rushed to the window, "It's Dickie – I have to go Ma – Da, come on – he's driven over from Sunderland to see me."

Iris pulled aside the lace curtains, "By that's a smashing car, pet. Go on have some fun."

"Aye just because the bugger's got a few pound yer think he's alright," said Walter straining to see outside.

"Money talks Da, and one day I'm gonna have plenty of it – you'll see," said Rita. She fastened a pink chiffon scarf around her curls and dabbed at her lipstick.

"Aye – yer'll have to learn the meanin' of hard work then," said Walter, "summat yer don't know owt about."

Rita turned to go out of the door, shaking her hips, "Have a smashing night all of yer – don't stay up for me – *Tarraa*."

The door slammed and George stood up, "I must be off – see my mam and dad before they go to bed."

"Bloody cheeky little madam," said Walter, "Her mam bought her everything she wanted when she was a bairn and now she's spoiled and brazen."

"There yer are again – blamin' me – I did my best for her and you were down the club all the time wi' yer drunken marrers," Iris snapped.

George got up and went to get his coat. They were still arguing when he came back, fastening his scarf, "Thank you very much, Walter – Iris."

But they kept on shouting so he slipped out and was halfway to the gate when the back door opened and Walter yelled, "We'll be comin' to see you in Durham in the next few months."

But George hurried along the street hoping they'd forget the address.

24

Ella Danby ran so fast out of her gate that she knocked over Jack's new leek seedlings arranged in a neat row of pots along the wall. Well she'd just clean that up when she'd taken care of some very important business that couldn't wait.

All morning she'd been watching out the window for George. Ever since she heard he was moving to Durham her mind had been working overtime and she'd sat in the front porch counting and recounting the money in her tea caddy. All told there was £260, saved from twenty years of pinching pennies from the grocery money. When she first started saving it she'd planned to run away to America, but as she got settled into the routine of the street, the idea had fizzled out, especially after her Mam's death. The thought of Jack, helpless and alone at an empty kitchen table had been too much for her to bear and so she kept putting the money aside knowing some purpose would finally reveal itself to her. Now it had.

She watched the Nelsons' rickety gate squeak open on its broken hinges and cursed the pair of them for their slovenliness. That was one thing about her Jack. He was a spotless man. Never sweaty or smelly like some folks and he kept the house in tip-top shape so that every hinge was oiled, every nailed tapped tightly into its hole and every surface freshly painted.

The Pitman's Daughter

It was a wonder the Nelsons' laddie turned out as well as he did. So her heart leapt a little when she saw George slip out through the gate, his fair hair brushed shiny and smooth and a small cloth bag in his hands. He was not equipped for the position he was to fill and she knew it. But her gift would change all that.

By now the wind had whisked up a cloud of grit and papers that scraped across the broken pavement. There was a blue-grey light in the sky. It would be a dull day today, she thought watching him fiddle with the gate latch. She had to catch him now. Before it was too late. She ran up the street. He stopped, frowned and tipped his hat awkwardly. "Morning Mrs Danby," he said in a polite tone.

She beckoned him towards her and her heart was in her throat as he crossed the street. "Did you have some questions about the union?"

She shook her head and felt the fat envelope in her pocket. The words were not coming to her. "I want to – I want to – ," and then she remembered. "I've watched you since you were a little bairn runnin' up the hill with yer mam. I couldn't have a child of me own – so I want you to have this." She thrust the envelope towards him though his eyes seemed not to comprehend what was happening.

"I don't understand," he said, looking at her.

"Open it," she urged. "When you get to Durham you'll need a good suit, some new shirts and ties and real leather shoes. The wrong shoes can let a man down especially when you're meeting with the bigwigs."

He pushed aside the envelope flap with the tip of his finger and gasped when he saw the thick wad of notes. "It's too much – I can't accept it," he said, pushing it towards her.

She sucked in her breath and took his hands. Looking at his fine, smooth cheeks, the slim curve of his nose and the slight blue shadow above his lips she allowed herself to imagine he was her son. This was how she would feel saying goodbye to him; heart in her throat, tears pushing against the backs of her eyes.

"Go on – take it. All I ask for is that you invite me to one special do – mebbe a luncheon or an afternoon tea. So I can see you in your new things. And I won't shame you. I have good clothes and I know how to behave mesel. Just so I can imagine I'm yer mam. Your own mam, bless her soul, can never do that and you know it."

He looked down, his cheeks flushed. "I do," he said quietly.

Just then a big black car swished up the street – a shiny, black Austin that pulled up outside the Hawkins' house. They both turned to watch its progress. A man sat alone in the driver's seat, smoking. His head tipped back as he blew out curls of smoke. Just then the Hawkins' door opened and Rita tiptoed out wearing a white raincoat, her hair covered with a tangerine chiffon scarf. She ran towards the car with her suitcase but stopped dead when she saw George. They stared at each other for a few long moments and George thought she would speak to him but she pursed her lips, threw the case into the back of the car and ducked down towards the open door. The car moved off and George's eyes followed it down the street. Ella watched, realization dawning on her. "It's for the best she's gone," she said. "She would've spoiled everything."

He nodded as he watched the car sweep round the corner.

"You'll meet a lass of better standing," she said.

Ella thought she noticed tears in his eyes and for a moment felt she could break down too. "Now get on with you," she said, brushing a piece of fluff from his jacket.

"I can't thank you enough for this," he said, leaning forward and kissing her cheek. Her heart felt as if it would burst. "And I'll invite you to something. Don't worry."

And then he was gone, swinging his bag and walking at a jauntier pace. She watched until he turned the corner and stood there staring at the place he had last been visible. Then she heard a reedy voice calling her. "Ella – I canna find me work socks."

She sighed with her whole body and turned back to her house. Now she'd have to start saving again, for the special invitation could come at any time and she had to be ready for it.

25

Dickie took Rita's shoes away.

"You ain't goin' nowhere," he said, twanging the elastic of his black bowtie. "No parties for birds who don't put out. It's as simple as that."

Though her feet felt cold and clammy on the linoleum, she watched his car pull away, the rear lights two unblinking red eyes in the dusk. It was six o'clock in the evening in Tooting Bec and crowds of workers poured out of the tube station, putting up umbrellas to shield themselves from the grey rain. Everything here was a drab, weathered grey. The streets, the sickly trees, the streaked windows of flats and houses. It was worse here than in Crag Street where at least there was a field close by.

The other day he'd taken her coat.

"I don't want yer goin' anywhere – especially down to the Palais," he said, combing his hair and smoothing after shave over his chin.

It was getting to be a game, this taking things away. He'd already spent her money. They'd drunk it all in three nights of binges at the Hammersmith Palais. She watched him sing, then he came right down off the stage and kissed her in front of all the other girls. She felt like a princess. But that was over a week ago.

When they first got to London the flat had been a shock. It was one small room with a sloping roof, leaky sink and a small gas ring on the third floor of a row of terraced houses in Tooting. The place was equipped with a foldout bed and an electric meter that ran out regularly. Usually in the middle of cooking, plunging the room into complete darkness. At least there was a bath but you had to put sixpence in the meter to have a hot one. She thought he'd live in one of those fancy penthouses with teak shelving units, white couches and plenty of potted plants and fancy lamps.

The first few days they'd come home at four in the morning then passed out on the bed, drunk and giggling. On the fourth day she found herself kneeling on the bathroom floor in a pool of vomit and she knew she had to stop. Afterwards she stumbled to the bed where Dickie lay snoring so loudly the bedposts vibrated. She couldn't sleep and, rubbing her eyes, she noticed something odd about his hair. The glossy, black wave was really a toupee that had somehow come unstuck and was pushed over his eyebrow. Her head ached so much she imagined it was a wet rat flopped, dead as a doornail over his forehead.

After that she wouldn't drink with him at night so he sulked and began to hug other girls instead of her. Then she had to drag him back home and up the stairs to the faded room with its posters of Frank Sinatra and Dean Martin and its smell of after shave and Vic's chest rub. The only good thing about the booze was that he was too drunk to come on to her and too hung over in the morning to give her a second look. But at the end of their weeklong binge he tried to grab her breasts one morning and she pushed him away.

"Get yer hands off," she yelled and he smacked her hard on the face.

"Don't lip off to me yer little cow," he snarled and pushed her onto the bed, pinning her arms down on the bedspread.

All she could think of was her Mam, her Dad, Lenny, Bill, Maggie and George and Pearl. She ran their names and faces through her mind over and over while he rammed and grunted, crushing her body until she was breathless. Somehow she made herself float away from her body – away from the pain between her legs.

Afterwards he said, "I didn't know it was yer first time – yer never struck me as a virgin. I'll buy yer some flowers... come on luv."

The Pitman's Daughter

But she'd just wanted to sit quietly and stare out of the window, her eyes swollen and dry, her insides turning over. She'd made a stupid mistake. After all her high and mighty vows she'd landed in a grubby old room with a toupee-wearing drunk who'd raped her.

That was the first night he took something of hers. "I don't want yer runnin' off now." And he'd wrapped her coat in a bag, locked the door then carried the package out to the car, leaving her like a prisoner with no means of escape.

At first she slammed her body onto the floor and sobbed until her whole body was limp. Then she lay staring up at the ceiling with aching eyes. He would never touch her again, she vowed. *No one would touch her like that – ever*, said a hard little voice inside her.

She'd felt soiled and dirty. So dirty she'd sat in the bath crying and scrubbing at her skin until it was covered with red welts. Then after she'd patted herself dry and put on her clothes, she rooted through the cupboards. Dickie usually stopped at the chippie for cod and chips or a steak and kidney pie with peas so the only thing she found was a lone tin of beans, a jar of pickled herrings and half a loaf of Hovis. She made some toast and sat slowly chewing the bean-soaked bread while thinking of a way to get out of the mess she was in. She had to get money. That was the first priority. When she went through all his jacket pockets and the chest of drawers opposite the bed she scraped up a few coins. About ninepence all told. It wasn't enough to get her anywhere and so she sank down onto the couch wishing she could be back home listening to her mam and dad arguing. She wondered if they'd forgive her for running off without a word. All she'd left was a note saying Dickie had found her a good job and she'd write soon.

Dickie didn't come home. Not until three o'clock in the afternoon when he stumbled through the door, cigarette hanging out of the corner of his mouth, clutching a bunch of pink flowers. She was sitting on the couch hugging her knees as she listened to Children's' Story Time on the wireless.

Dickie took one look at her swollen eyes and lurched towards her, a wounded dog look on his face. "Oh Christ – look at my sweet baby girl." He went to kiss her but she turned her face away. "What, still mad at old Dickie? Here, luv, get a sniff of these beauties," he said, thrusting the carnations at her, his bloodshot eyes squinting in the daylight. He stunk of stale tobacco and booze. Rita slammed the flowers down and turned up the radio.

"Hey – don't turn yer nose up at me yer little tart. I'm tryin' to be nice."

She simmered in silence hoping he'd just take the hint and leave her alone but when he grabbed her arm and yanked her onto her feet something snapped inside. Her whole body went rigid. "Don't you fucking dare touch me," she hissed through gritted teeth and he stepped backwards, stunned, his eyes blinking in disbelief. After a moment of tense silence he threw his head back and laughed. That's when he took her shoes away.

"You'll come around," he said, "Once you've 'ad a few days of being cooped up in here. Roughin' yer up ain't my style luv – but yer lucky – some other bloke would've given you a good crack over the jaw for that little performance."

Half an hour after he left she went through his wardrobe and found a pair of black, shiny men's shoes. She stuffed the toes with toilet paper and walked around the flat trying them out. They'd be all right with her stretch navy trousers. He was so stupid, she thought. As if taking her shoes would stop her. He must think she was a right dumb cluck as her Nana would say. Grumpy old Nana. Rita almost longed for the old lady to be here. She'd fettle him good and quick – *cut his tail off* if he dared to come near Rita again.

She fastened her raincoat, picked up her case and went to leave but the door was locked and Dickie had the key. Not so stupid after all, she realized. Now she was good and trapped. Running from room to room she panicked, as she looked four floors down into the street from every window. The only place with access to the back fire escape was the tiny bathroom window. She opened it as wide as she could then climbed up onto the toilet seat. Once her head was through she wiggled from side to side until she squeezed her body out to freedom.

It was a gusty night. The wind pulled at her scarf and sent blasts of chips and vinegar and petrol smells into her face from the street below.

Halfway down she slipped on the oily steps and sent her case hurtling three storeys onto the pavement below. "Christ and bloody dammit," she hissed as a wiry mustard coloured terrier shuffled up and sniffed at it, then cocked its ragged leg and pissed over all four metal corners. Rita picked up the nearest stone, threw it and the mangy little mutt scampered away.

Half an hour later her feet began to ache from the shoes and the walking. She'd reached Clapham already but had no idea where she was heading. With only one and sixpence in her pocket she had no idea where she'd sleep. Phoning her parents was impossible. Nobody on Crag Street had a phone and none of them ever came down to London except for band trips or union business. If she could find somewhere to stay for just a few nights she might be able to find out if there was a brass band contest or a union convention coming up soon. She'd swallow her pride to hitch a ride back up north with them.

Then just as she passed the grey dome of Clapham Common Tube Station a red shield caught her eye. It glowed from a billboard and advertised a Salvation Army Hostel nearby. She remembered seeing the Sally Ann people back home. They'd come into the pubs on Saturday nights, dressed in their prim, blue bonnets, to sell copies of their magazine. Rita never laughed at them like her friends did but instead bought the paper and found she actually enjoyed it. The assortment of crosswords, games and bible stories had kept her entertained on many nights. She was glad she'd supported them because right now she needed their help more than anything. They claimed to help the homeless. Well she didn't have anywhere to go tonight. She decided she'd take them up on their offer and she hoped they were ready for her. She was counting on them tonight.

26

When Maggie came back from buying the Woman's Weekly at Minnie Wilson's shop she found the front door shut and the yard empty. Doors were only closed here in times of war or plague. From the crack of dawn till the last rays of light faded from the sky, peoples' doors were left wide open, so in a day a person could travel the whole length of the street picking up news, passing gossip and drinking tea.

Maggie hesitated before trying the door. If it was locked then something serious was up so she twisted the handle. It wouldn't budge. She'd left Hannah busy, darning work socks so what could possibly be wrong now? Since Jordy's accident the whole household had turned topsy-turvy. First old Grandpa Willis had dropped down dead in the front garden while he was weeding the leeks, then Hannah started wandering about the house moaning. She slipped out the front door one day and they found her halfway to Belton High Street with her slippers on. Then Jordy kept getting awful headaches and took to sitting up in the attic for long hours, hardly speaking to anyone. The only time he'd come down was when Pearl sang to him while he rocked in the old chair in the upstairs hallway.

It was a relief to Maggie that he didn't touch her any more but with one bairn after another leaving the house to get married, and George going off, she felt all dried-up and empty inside.

She waited for one more minute then crossed to the window and stood on tiptoes. It was black as an undertaker's inside but she could see something moving under the table. It was Hannah, squatting underneath, shifting her weight from one leg to another, like an old broody hen. She was holding onto Hazel and their eyes burned brightly from the shadows.

Maggie went back to the door and opened up the letterbox.

"Mother what are yer doin'? Open the door – it's Maggie." There was a scraping and shuffling and the door opened slowly. Hannah's face peered around the side of the door, a face so thin and hollow she was all eyes. "Eeh – Maggie, I thought it were robbers comin' through the gate but it were the happy clappies and I was all by mesel'."

Maggie pushed her way in and tossed the magazine onto the table. Every few months people from the evangelical mission visited all the houses on the street. "But they're harmless mother." She went to fill the kettle.

"Aye but yer canna get shot o' them once they're in preachin about the gospel and I were all confused what wi' Jordy gannin' off in such a rush."

"Where to?" Maggie asked spooning the tea from the brown tin canister.

"Why off to the dog track. He says George Nelson's gannin' there wi' some of the union men."

Maggie's hand shook, scattering tealeaves across the table. Jordy couldn't know anything. Nobody knew.

"Aye, said he wanted to shake his hand personally. Even dressed himself up a bit. Took out his good navy blue tie." Hannah held her mug out as Maggie stirred the tealeaves around. "Pour us another one, Maggie. I'm parched."

Suddenly all Maggie's wanted was to get down to the track and see George. She could taste him – smell the clean scent of his skin. She fumbled with the teapot, scalding Hannah's hand in the process. *She had something to tell him – a small suspicion that maybe....* She'd checked the Co-op calendar and calculated that her period was really fifteen days late and it had been six weeks since she'd seen him for the last time. *She*

183

couldn't look after this by herself – not with Jordy and the neighbours and her own bairns.

"Oww – yer all of a tither, Maggie," said Hannah rubbing the small red spot. "Must be one o' them women's spells."

Maggie realized she was holding the teapot in mid- air and dripping it all over the floor. "Eeh, sorry mother – now look – I have to get down to the track to tell Jordy summat. Give Hazel some of that soup and have yersel' a bit o' this fruit and nut bar and I'll be back in an hour."

She left the old lady quietly chewing on a piece of chocolate and ran into the scullery to check her face. Her eyes were wild, her cheeks flushed, her lips pink and open. But she looked her age. In two years time she'd be forty and it showed. Shameless hussy, she thought as she combed back her hair. But she was beyond caring now. What did it matter if she made a fool of herself? She had only a few good years left and then nobody would give her a second look. She tied a pink chiffon scarf over her hair, buttoned up her coat and hurried out of the gate.

It was ten past six when she reached the dog track and one of those clear nights when she could hear the buzz of the streetlamps. Everything glowed gold and orange. She could taste the vinegar in the air from the chip stand and her throat was dry with excitement.

Inside, the place was packed. Bright floodlights cast a brilliant white light over the crowds as if they'd been frozen in the flash of a camera. She felt like an actress in a black and white film and quite separate from the everyday Maggie. People jostled her but she didn't care as she floated weightlessly between bodies. Somewhere deep in her pocket she found a few coppers so she headed towards the booths to have a bit of a flutter on the next race. As she was taking her ticket she felt a sharp poke between her shoulder blades.

"Hou – what's thee deein' here?" a voice rasped and she turned to see Jordy. She wasn't afraid of him here and looked him right in the eye.

"I like to have a bit of a fun too yer know." She stared at him till he lowered his eyelids.

"Bloody fool," he hissed, scratching his head under his cap, "Dinna bother me and me marrers," he said under his breath as he turned and walked away.

Somehow it was easy to be brazen here. She'd never acted that way before, but since George had left without a word, she felt more reckless and now she was going to watch the race to see if today was her lucky day. If George just happened to walk by she'd do or say the first thing that came into her head. *Take a risk, being a doormat got you nowhere.*

On the second race she won a pound and had to hold herself back from squealing with joy when the bookie handed the money over. This was the best time she'd had on her own since she was a girl and so she bought sixpennorth of chips and slathered them with vinegar. She was just finishing up the crispy bits on the bottom of the paper when the clubhouse door opened and two men came out; one had red hair and a beard, the other was George. They talked for a minute and the red-haired man looked at his watch, George patted his shoulder, they said goodbye then Maggie saw George pushing towards her. He hadn't seen her but she screwed the chip paper into a ball, threw it down and manoeuvred herself into his path. His mouth dropped open when he saw her.

"Maggie," he muttered, looking around to see if anyone was watching. She took in the expensive navy suit and starched, white shirt. He didn't even try to smile and she felt suddenly sick.

"Don't worry – I'm not gonna make a scene," she said, "I just want to talk to you – somewhere private."

George glanced quickly from side to side.

"You worried about someone seeing us?" she said.

"Oh – no – it's just – I'm here on business you know," he said, not meeting her eyes.

"You've got business with me," said Maggie, "I'm gonna wait for you behind the sheds at the far end of the track."

She walked away without looking at George but bells were jangling in her head. How had she dared to speak to him like that? *It was easy, he bloody well owed her something.* Leaving without a word after she'd given everything to him and she'd never ever asked for anything in return – until now.

It was quiet by the dog sheds and away from the crowds. She slipped a piece of chewing gum into her mouth and pushed the wire gates open. Between the sheds was a narrow, shadowy gap, and once she was hidden there she turned to the wall to press her whole body against it. Her skin was buzzing, the nerve ends tickling so that she had to open her mouth to breathe. Despite the minty taste of the gum her mouth was dry. She felt like a drunk thirsting for a cold glass of gin.

At the crunch of shoes on the gravel she panted more quickly. A tall shadow spilled across the opening and George looked around the corner. "Maggie?" he asked.

She flew at him and threw her arms around his shoulders. His arms moved slowly around her waist.

"I need – I," she stuttered, "I missed you."

He put his hand softly over her mouth and made a shushing sound, but when she pressed her body hard against him, as if she could climb inside him, he flinched and pushed back against the wall. She fumbled with his trouser fastening, feeling the fine silky wool then slid her hand inside – into the warmth. Holding close to him, she pressed her face into the curve of his neck, burrowing like a hungry animal but he turned his face away and grasped her wrist.

"Don't do this, Maggie – we can't do this anymore." He whispered, his voice husky against her ear. But she felt his hardness and, pulling down her knickers, guided him inside her. His body thrust with such force she knew he'd denied himself for some time and she felt complete again for this one moment.

His whole body shuddered and when she cried out into the damp air a strange thought came to her; the suit – his new suit – it must be marked, stained, rumpled even torn, since he'd braced his back against the rough, brick wall. With tears pouring down her face, she began to smooth his tie, his jacket – to brush his sleeves and hair.

"No – no – don't – it's alright," he stammered, zipping up his trousers, "I'm sorry – so sorry."

"But your suit – your new suit – it's a good suit." Maggie was frantic.

"I said leave it – I'll see to it." He ran his fingers through his hair, then spit on his hand and wiped away some dust.

"You'll have to get it cleaned," she said feeling small and scared.

"Maggie," he said in a hard, strange voice. "I've got responsibility now – the men are depending on me to put more bread on the table, improve the working conditions – I've got no room for personal ties."

"Aye." She felt hot and cold all at once. "Of course I know."

His face was blank. "I'm sorry – *but this is what I've always wanted.*"

He backed away from her, touching his tie and collar. *Checking for hairs or lipstick smudges,* she thought.

"You're a good mother, Maggie and I've no right to use you any more and I'm sorry about *this.*" He motioned towards the wall they'd been leaning against. "Don't get in touch with me again – do you understand." This time he looked right at her with narrowed eyes.

"Yes," was all she could manage. All the bluster and bravado was knocked out of her and the chips sat like a greasy lump in the pit of her stomach.

He turned and walked away from her. He never looked back, but took the time to flick a piece of grit from his shoulder. Bending almost double she was sick all over the grass. When she stood up again he was nowhere in sight. She wiped her mouth with the chiffon headscarf then threw it away. She needed a drink and she needed it soon.

Beside, the buzzer had just sounded. Another race was about to begin.

27

From the third floor office of the hostel Rita watched the place empty out around eight o'clock in the morning. Doors opened and spewed out a rag-tag line of bedraggled men and one or two women onto the streets of Hammersmith. Some had given up. Wearing long tattered hair and filthy clothes they set out in quest of a drink – cooking wine, rubbing alcohol, even nail varnish remover might do. Others tried to keep up their appearance, tying stained ties over frayed collars and inking over scuffed shoes. They sat in greasy hole-in-the-wall teashops drinking stewed tea and poring over the situations vacant section of the paper. Rita watched them when she went to fetch the tea for the office.

Captain Webb – the administrator – had taken one look at Rita the night she walked in and promptly offered her a job keeping the books in exchange for free board and lodging and two pounds a week. Her room was in the staff quarters so she had no contact with the rabble downstairs.

A single bed, a washstand, a soft-sided plastic wardrobe and a two-door metal chest of drawers were crammed into a lemon coloured cubicle no bigger than seven feet by seven, There was a permanent smell of stale tea and sweaty sheets but the food was free and the place was quiet. The

The Pitman's Daughter

only drawback was the one-hour sessions she had to sit through when Captain Webb pulled out his morocco bound bible and began preaching to her. He walked around the room, circling her chair, leaning closer to emphasize a point. Generally the stories were about Mary Magdalene and other *fallen women.*

At the end of the sessions he'd slam the book down to mop his sweaty face with a large paisley handkerchief. Rita was sure he never cleaned his uniform because as his face grew redder the tinny stink of sweat flooded the small office. As her Nana would have said, "yer could cut the air with a knife and spread it on yer bread."

One night she'd been lying in her miserable cubicle trying to pluck her bushy eyebrows, when the curtain dividing her area from the rest of the quarters, swished open and he stood there holding two large china mugs. "Horlicks?" he inquired, inclining his head like a large hairy dog. He was thinning on top and wore a large hank of hair plastered over the bald spot. She could imagine him swimming or running in the wind with the thick lump of hair swinging loose. He was also forgetful in matters of personal grooming and often had bits of toilet paper stuck to shaving nicks or dried gravy dribbles down his tie or his top trouser button undone showing a patch of wobbly white belly.

On the Horlicks night he was wearing his patched and mended white shirt with the three silver pens in the top pocket. He held out a lime green striped mug to her. "Mother bought these in Skegness," he said like a sad-eyed dog. Rita didn't have the heart to say no to him. Though he was an odd soul he meant well.

After forty-five minutes of listening to endless chronicles of his childhood camping experiences in the Lake District, Rita's eyelids began to droop. "Enough, Miss Hawkins," he blurted, jumping up and knocking over her tray of tweezers and face cream. "I leave you with a demonstration of strength." Rita's eyelids snapped open again.

"You may not know that I am a pocket Hercules and despite my short stature I have the strength of a six foot man." Directly after this announcement he proceeded to lunge towards the floor with his hands and flip his legs up in the air. The next thing she knew he was standing on his hands, legs pointing directly skyward and veins on his neck bulging like swollen ropes. As she'd expected, the large hank of hair had come unstuck and was hanging down – a lank horse's tail flopping onto his left nostril. "Get down," she cried. "Think of your blood pressure."

"All in a day's work," he gasped, flipping himself upright to reveal a face that would put a pickled beetroot to shame.

Today she watched the men file out, then made her way down to the tiny office. With a bit of luck she could squeeze in a cup of tea and a quiet cigarette before he interrupted her for a preaching session. She liked sitting alone behind the desk. Though the walls were painted a sickly lemon colour and the filing cabinet was a bit rusty, there was something satisfying about putting papers in order, slipping them into neat, brown folders and filing them. There was an order to it, and after the chaos in her life, she needed a bit of that. Within a week she'd whipped that messy office into shape. She leaned her head back and inhaled the cigarette, watching the smoke spiral upwards to the ceiling. Then she took a sip of tea and was ready for a day spent entering the daily expenses in the ledger.

Half an hour later the heavy clump of boots thundered along the hallway and Captain Webb burst into the office, his face sweating. He was always overheated from hurrying around so Rita made a mental note to open the window next time she heard him coming .

"Miss Hawkins you are a veritable hurricane. You have cleared out the unwanted debris from this office and left in its wake a tidy, modern place of business." When he flopped down on the wooden chair opposite her there was a loud creak. The legs wouldn't last much longer with all his weight crashing down on it.

"Mother insists on serving bread and butter pudding for dessert," he said, adjusting his waistband." Rita was sure he lifted one side of his bum to let out a fart, which he covered up by coughing. Within seconds, however, the office was filled with a putrid stink and Rita was forced to light a match, which she held out for a long time before lighting her cigarette; a trick she'd learned in childhood when there was always a box of matches handy in the outhouse for when her Da or brothers had been in there.

Captain Webb was oblivious to the stink and continued on with his rambling. "Mother also insists on listening to the Victor Sylvester request show every evening," he continued. "Do you dance, Miss Hawkins?"

"I've never learned proper ballroom steps," she said, licking her finger and turning the page; an action Captain Webb watched closely.

He leaned forward and cleared his throat. "I hope you won't think me too forward, but would you call me Bert?"

"Is that proper?" she asked. "After all you are my boss."

"You have a point," he said, sinking back into his chair. "Perhaps you might restrict it to when we are alone."

She looked up, unable to concentrate on the tiny black figures that seemed to swim around the page. "Will there be anything else – Bert?"

He quivered at the sound of his name on her lips, and then jumped up sending the chair skittering across the floor. "Of course – you must get on with your work and I have a meeting with the Women's Volunteer Corps." He rescued the fallen chair and then backed out of the office, nodding furiously. Once the coast was clear, Rita lit two matches and waved them around all over the office. Then satisfied the stink was gone, she returned to work.

At half past twelve she walked across the street to the little café she'd discovered. They had cheap but decent ham sandwiches and the old woman always put in an extra slice of meat for Salvation Army people. She sat in the window chewing the bread, drinking her tea and watching the world go by. She was desperate. It would be two or three months, she calculated, before she could save enough money to pay for her bus ticket to Durham. And she didn't have the guts to hitchhike. She had to get out before Bert asked her home to meet his mother and then before she knew it he'd offer his hand in marriage. Though he was more of a gentleman than any other man she'd met recently, the idea of pledging her life to the plight of the homeless didn't really appeal to her at this time. And she was certain that Mother Webb was probably a meddling old cow when it came to her beloved son, Bert.

No, she had to get back home. Now she knew what she wanted; a business of her own with an office, a typewriter and a smart new filing cabinet. And a ledger in which she'd enter the money she made with her own sweat. She'd watch the totals increase until she was rich. For now she knew money was the key to success and the only way to be independent. She'd learned a lot from her own *stupid gormlessness* (as her grandma would say) and had come out of this experience a changed woman – more ruthless and not likely to believe the empty promises of any fly-by-night Romeo who might think he could charm her with a bit of cash, a flashy suit and a lot of false promises. She never wanted to depend on any man again. There was always a price and with Dickie it had been too steep.

Someone had left a newspaper on the table in front of her so she reached across and took it. On the front page was a picture of a Russian rocket ship. They were at it again – sending men up into space. It was incredible that people had actually been shot up so far into the air they'd reached the blackness of space. They'd sent animals up there. But people. That was different. Her grandma hadn't believed it. Said it was government people making it up. Rita flipped through the pages but her eyes rested on a smaller story. The headline read *Pit Closures Accelerate: NUM Meets to Consider Action*. Her eyes scanned the story for the conference location and she found it in the last sentence. It was in Luton.

"Where's Luton?" she asked the grey-haired woman behind the counter.

"About thirty miles away," she said looking up from the sink.

"Any buses going there from here?"

"Just coaches, luv and trains."

Rita thanked her and walked back to the office where Captain Webb was sitting again, in the wooden chair opposite her desk.

"Miss Hawkins – I'm – I'm..." Captain Webb jumped up and reached for his bible. "Let me read you a passage out of Hosea, chapter eight, verses..."

"Not just now," Rita replied, plunking herself down into his chair and turning to him. "Do you know how to get to Luton?" she asked.

The Pitman's Daughter

~

Two hours later Rita sat in the passenger seat of Captain Webb's three-wheeler Riley Elf, clasping her suitcase and watching the giant wheels of transport lorries come within a foot of her shoulder. Only a pane of glass and a cheap metal side panel came between her and the thundering traffic of the M1. *I hope to hell he's got a steady hand*, she thought. *One wrong move and we'll be mangled.* Her neck ached with the worry of it.

"Do you think your father will be surprised, Miss Hawkins?" Captain Webb shouted above the roar of engines and the draught blowing in through the window.

"Father? Oh yes – father," Rita stumbled over the words, almost forgetting the little white lie she'd been forced to tell. "Oh yes – me dad loves surprises and he only gets down here once every few years for the band contest."

Captain Webb grasped the wheel more confidently. "I'm looking forward to meeting your father. I shall have a lot to tell him about you – good things of course – it will be a pleasure to get to know him and I've been thinking about ..."

Christ, thought Rita, *not here in the car*, and suddenly she saw her life spread out ahead of her. A string of groping sessions in Bert's shabby bedroom with Mother Webb holding a glass to her ear on the other side of the wall. Worse still was the thought of him naked. Standing there with his wobbly tummy, hairy chest, his hands clasped over his willy. She almost choked at the thought.

"Can you stop at the next services," she said, "I have to pay a visit."

Captain Webb's hands clenched the steering wheel again and he cleared his throat, "Don't want you to be uncomfortable, Miss Hawkins – or might I call you Rita?"

"I don't mind," she answered, "but just put your foot down before I pee meself'."

They almost missed the turn-off so Captain Webb had to swerve at the last minute, bumping over the kerb and nearly tipping them over. Rita held onto her suitcase and prayed for the moment she could get out of this three-wheeled death trap. It sputtered to a halt in the car park and Rita almost fell out of the door in her haste to open it.

"Must go," she said in a breathy whisper, holding tight to the handle of her case.

"Your case," he said, bowing down to look at her, "just leave it here."

"Personal needs," she whispered, "feminine supplies."

She saw his face flush red and for a moment she felt a pang of pity for him. "Oh – er – I understand," he stammered.

As she hurried away she heard him shout after her, "I'll get you a tea."

"No, don't worry, just wait there," she called. *Be a good boy* she said silently to herself.

Poor soul, she thought as she entered the lobby, a busy, glassed-in area reeking with the smell of burnt sausages and baked beans, but she wasn't a bit hungry so she ducked into the pink tiled women's toilets. *Poor sod*, she thought, *he can't be more than forty and never married.* He was probably desperate for someone to darn his socks, wash his underwear and oblige him at least once a week while he sweated dutifully on top and called out to the Lord.

Shuddering at the thought of this she decided to hide out in the Ladies toilets for a while, to plan out the next step. *Maybe he'd get tired of waiting and just pack up*, she hoped.

In the toilets she sat on a bench, leaned against the wall and rested her arms on her cases. Her life had become one scrape after the next and now she had to think of a way to get out of this one.

"Got the monthlies?" said a tall, gangly girl about her own age with puffed-out blonde hair, pink twin-set and mauve toreador pants.

"I wish," said Rita.

"Fag?" the girl asked, holding out a pack of Capstan.

Rita reached her hand out. "Don't mind if I do."

"Not pregnant are yer luv?" she said, lighting up and taking a long, deep drag. "Me sister Stevie got knocked up at fifteen – couldn't stand the smell of tea or brass polish."

When she spoke the smoke came out of her nostrils in small dragon puffs. Rita was fascinated at her jewellery – a charm bracelet of gold poodles, large bevelled gold hoops in her ears and a gold pendant with the letters BF in gold. "Billy Fury's my fave rave. My boyfriend looks just like him – we're going to see him in Manchester. Wanna come? Merv won't mind."

Rita had a brainwave. "Look – er.."

"Janice – Janice Watson."

"Janice – me dad's outside in the car – the three wheeler. He wants to take me back to Newcastle…"

"I knew you was a Jordy girl – I'm London born – Stepney – east of the river."

"I don't want to go with him. Since me mam and him split up he's been acting really horrible – touching me and all that. To tell the truth I'm scared to go with him – but if I could get to my sister's house in Luton…"

"Don't say another word – that old bastard's bloody disgusting – someone ought to cut his bollocks off. D'you want Merv to rough him up a bit?" Janice was now stamping hard on the smouldering cigarette end and Rita felt a giggle rising in her throat.

"No, I'll deal with him. You and Merv get the car ready and I'll meet you at the other side of the restaurant."

"No time to waste," said Janice, teasing up her stiff lacquered beehive. "We'll be waiting – and watch out for a grey Morris Minor," Edna said. "Merv's really smashing – looks like Billy Fury's brother."

Rita slipped out of the toilet and bumped smack into Captain Webb who was standing there, ruddy faced and holding two plastic cups of tea.

"Piping hot – just brewed, though it's not Tetley's." He sniffed at one of the cups and Rita let out a loud sigh. He started forward, offering her the tea. "Are you all right – is it *ladies' problems* you're having."

Rita was looking straight through to the other side of the restaurant and could just make out the nose of a grey Morris. *I have to do something quick.* "The gift shop," she mumbled. "I need aspirin."

"I'll wait right here… Rita."

She could see the frayed sleeve of his uniform as he held up the steaming cups of tea. *Lecherous old sod*, she thought, *but this is a matter of survival.* She stumbled into the gift shop, which was filled by a party of elderly women. Rummaging through the confectionary shelves, she kept an eye on the outside and saw him standing stiff as a sentry guard.

"We're the Clacton and District Women's Spiritualist Society," said a white haired ex-gym teacher type to the cashier. "Each one of us has become widowed in the last two or three years."

"Well what d'ya want to bring the old boys back for?" said the cashier, a lumpy woman in her fifties. "Have yerselves a good old fling now there's no-one lookin' over yer shoulder."

When the gym teacher backed away saying, "Well really." Rita stepped towards her. *This was her last chance to escape.*

"Excuse me," she croaked.

"You're addressing me?" she said with the kind of snooty tone Rita remembered from some of her old teachers.

"You see that man out there – the *distinguished* man in the Sally Army uniform?" said Rita.

"Why yes," said the tall woman, straining her neck to look. "The gentleman with the thick, wavy hair."

She must be blind, Rita thought but continued in her most charming voice. "Well he's my uncle and he's one of the most well known mediums in the Spiritualist Church. As soon as we drove up to this service station he said he'd been drawn to it by a messenger from the other side."

"Oooh...." The woman began to beckon her friends over.

Rita continued, surprised at her storytelling ability. "He came into the lobby and said *The power is over in the gift shop* and when he saw you he said *that woman is a force field – she is a transmitter of messages from the other side and I have someone who wants to talk to her, someone whose name is...*and then he stopped and told me to fetch you."

"Maxim – Maxim – it must be." By now all the friends had gathered around them and suddenly the whole group migrated from the store like a screeching flock of gulls to swamp a flabbergasted Colonel Webb. Rita took the chance to race across the restaurant, knocking over chairs in her wake until she threw the glass doors open and fell into the upholstered comfort of Merv's Morris Minor. Merv, a large-jawed lad with shiny black hair and a permanent sneer cranked the gear stick and Rita huddled down into the back seat, not daring to look back. She felt a bit guilty but realized Bert probably hadn't had that much excitement in years and besides, they were all widows. Who knew what might come of it?

In Luton, Merv and Janice took her for a sandwich and an ice cream sundae and they sang to Billy Fury songs on the jukebox. When they dropped her off at the hotel Janice said, "Mind you tell that sister of yours to look after you instead of letting you wander around like a gypsy. Yer never know what could happen." Then they pulled away, snapping their gum and waving at her.

Rita felt scared and alone, but relieved. It was almost noon and the steady procession of cars rumbling down the High Street was giving her a dull headache. There was a smell in the air that wasn't like home. A greasy smell like old cooking and petrol. It was always warmer here, but it was a stuffy warmth and she missed the fresh, cold air of home – even missed the sharp tang of coal smoke. George was her best hope of getting home *but why*, she moaned inwardly, *why did everything have to be so difficult?* She was sick of scrounging favours. But she vowed this would be the last time.

The sky was already blotched with jagged, angry clouds, knitting themselves together to start another rain shower. Shivering, she stepped into the stuffy warmth of the hotel lobby and headed towards the safety of the teashop with its familiar clink of stainless steel pots. Tea was tea wherever you went and she needed a strong cup before throwing herself on George's mercy.

28

For the first time since George had gone, Maggie was having a good time. In the floodlit world of the dog track anyone could be a star and under the silvery glare everyone's face was flushed with excitement and the thrill of winning money. Maggie was on a winning streak, living recklessly and dreaming of making enough to take the bairns away and leave Jordy.

Even he was happy at the track. She stayed out of his way of course, but she could see him laughing, drinking a few pints, joking with his mates and cheering at the dogs as they streaked around the track after the electric hare. It was like watching another person, because once he was at home he'd grind his teeth with the awful headaches.

The doctor said that some of the coal fragments had blown into his eye and lodged behind the eyeball. His face took on a more serious expression when he said the pieces might work their way into Jordy's brain tissue. There was no way of getting them out now. "Let nature take its course," the doctor said, "The body cleanses itself." Jordy just growled at him and the old man scurried off to his next patient.

But the crashing headaches became worse. Some days he'd lie flat out on the couch with a wet cloth over his eyes and everyone stayed out of his way because he'd come to sometimes like a mad old bear. Other times he'd sit up and look at them all with a blank stare as if he didn't know them. Then he'd go up to their bedroom and Maggie would hear him rooting around in the wardrobe or opening drawers. She didn't know what he was up to and she didn't care.

The night she'd seen George at the track, Maggie stumbled, afterwards, into an old junior school friend, Vera Brown. Vera said Maggie was looking a bit peaky and bought her a glass of Guinness. "Plenty of good, rich iron in this, pet, yer blood needs building up a bit." Maggie gulped it down and was amazed at how it filled her with new energy.

"Another one," she said, holding her glass out, then Vera showed her how to earn extra gambling money by hanging around the betting area and going up to the men there, offering to stand in the queue for the tickets in return for a tip.

Once Maggie got over her first awkwardness she soon learned to spot the easy touches. The lazy ones who were happy to let someone else run after them while they read the racing form over and over, or the ones who were flush with new winnings and didn't mind giving out a shilling or two. And tonight she'd even made herself a bit extra, but Pearl needed new shoes and she was trying to put away every penny. *In case she had to get away from Crag Street in a hurry.* She told Vera about missing her period – two months in a row. But Vera just held up her little hand mirror and applied a thick coat of scarlet lipstick, then smacked her lips together to spread it out. Vera told her it was nothing to worry about, "Probably yer change of life come early – that's why yer anaemic, hinny," she said, handing Maggie another creamy Guinness.

"But I'm not even forty yet," said Maggie, watching the white bubbles pop on the surface.

"It's different for everyone," said Vera, touching the back and sides of her stiff, black backcombed hair. "Like it?"

"It looks lovely," said Maggie

Maggie's worries floated away when she won five pounds on the last race. Vera hugged her and Maggie bought her two gin and tonics and all the men stared as they staggered, tipsy and giggling through the gates.

It was after eleven when Maggie turned the corner and hurried up the street towards home. There were no neighbours out spying at this time of night and she felt a secret thrill sneaking past the darkened windows and closed doors, avoiding the yellow pools of light thrown out by the streetlamps. She pulled her scarf tightly around her ears to keep out the wind then slipped in a Polo mint so nobody could smell the gin on her breath. She'd sobered up a bit with the long walk but she still felt her stomach turning somersaults when she touched the five pound note. It didn't really matter though, because she was late enough to miss the gawping faces of the miserable old blatherers, who often pushed back their net curtains so they could sneak a glance at anyone who was daring to have a bit of fun on the side.

The house was dark. Jordy was probably in bed, snoring already. He always slept with his mouth open, legs splayed all over the bed. No matter – she'd get in with one of the bairns. She'd not slept with Jordy for a few months now. It turned her stomach to look at his puffy, flushed face with the damp patch of spittle leaking out onto the pillow. And it certainly didn't feel right sleeping next to someone who felt like a stranger to you. *Sleeping with someone was an act of love and there'd been none between him and her for years.* She doubted that she'd ever loved him and now all she felt was bitterness and hate. A hate so strong that some nights she felt she could creep into that room and slit his snoring, quivering throat. Then and only then the snoring would stop and she'd finally have some peace.

Careful to stop the gate from clashing, she tiptoed across the yard and slipped her key into the lock but the door creaked open. Funny, she thought, maybe Jordy wasn't in yet. She'd leave it unlocked for him. Inside, the kitchen was warm and the last embers of fire glowed pale orange. She went to put her gloves on the sideboard but her heart almost flew to the roof of her skull when she saw Jordy sitting motionless in the armchair staring unblinking into the fire. He didn't even move, his eyes never flickered, as if he was in a waking sleep. But there was something different about his face – something strange and doll-like. Maggie leaned in closer and saw the black lines had almost disappeared –

covered in a thick film of pale beige foundation. She shivered half in fear, half in disgust at the sight of him sitting there like a painted clown. She felt a sudden need to get out of the hot, stifling room and went to pick up her gloves again, but his hand clawed at the hem of her coat. He pulled her back and she turned to face him.

He spoke slowly and quietly, "You've got the stink of another man on you – I know about you and your whoring ways."

"I just went to the track tonight – with Vera," she spat back at him, hating the way the breath whistled through his swollen lips.

"People see things," he hissed.

"What things – there's nothing to see," she whispered, gulping back the fear.

"I've been reading – reading things – I know that one day I'm gonna tear the filth right out of you." He chanted the words like a robot.

"What the hell are you talking about," she said, pulling her coat away from his hands. "You're going mad."

"I've been reading up there, up in the attic – and I know you and all the painted bitches are gonna burn like they *fucking deserve to.*"

"And what's that stuff on your face?" she said, realizing he wasn't even talking to her. His eyes were fixed on the dying fire. The reddish light fell across his cheeks making the sweaty layer of make-up look like thick butter spread over his face. "You've been using my foundation."

He pulled himself up from the creaking chair. "Dirty whores – all you women. Ya paint your face and spread your legs and you think you're in charge. You've got it comin' though. Any day now."

He padded up the stairs, his head bent. The bedroom door shut followed by the thud of his body as it flopped onto the bed. *Oh, Christ,* she thought, *did someone see her at the back of the dog sheds?*

If only God could make a miracle for her, she could be rid of Jordy for good, because now the burrowing coal grit was turning him mad, sneaking and tunnelling into the folds and creases of his brain. With luck though, one day it might hit the right spot and put a blessed end to him. Then and only then could she be free.

29

Rita was on her fourth cup of tea and feeling queasy. Two weeks of hostel food had left her starving for something wholesome and home cooked. Something like melted butter on hot stotty cakes or a big plate of roast beef swimming in gravy. The deep brown type, rich with onion and meat juices. Not like the thin grey stuff they served in the hostel, made of half an Oxo cube or a teaspoon of Bovril in a pan of boiling water.

She slopped her tea all over the tablecloth when she spotted George coming out of a meeting room opposite the cafe. He strode to the counter to order and the lady behind the counter winked at him then gathered up two or three silver teapots onto a big tray.

He wore a smart navy suit with a deep red carnation in his lapel and was well tailored from his freshly cut hair down to his polished shoes. She glanced down at her own feet, sweating in the shiny men's shoes with the crumpled toes. Why did she always feel grubby and common beside him? It hadn't always been that way. Not at Beattie's sweet shop, when she was the pretty child with the ringlets and he was the one with darned socks and patched elbows. She checked the mirror of her powder compact. Dark hair roots were starting to show – a thin stripe of brown against the platinum dye job – and her raincoat was so crumpled it looked like she'd slept in it. Which she had a few times when she'd found cockroaches at the hostel, scurrying around behind the old wooden bedposts.

She took a last glance at herself, smacked her lips together to smooth out her lipstick, and strode up to him. He was stealing a quick glance at his reflection in the silver hot water urn and smoothing down a stray lock of hair. She tapped him on the back and said, "Don't worry – you look smashing," He wheeled around suddenly with a jug of milk, spilling some of it down the front of her raincoat.

"What the heck – I'm sorry," he said. Rita's heart fell at the vexed look on his face. He put down the tray and began to feel around behind the counter. "I'll get something to wipe it."

"Doesn't matter," she said trying to mop it off with a serviette, "I think I did the same to you last time I saw you."

"I remember," he said taking the damp serviette from her.

"Seems like a long time ago, doesn't it," she said nervously.

"What on earth are you doing here?" He didn't wait for an answer but continued, never meeting her eyes. "Your Da isn't here, Rita. He stayed up in Belton this time." He was glancing around at the other people in the restaurant. "Look, I've got a very important meeting going on so I'll tell Walter you called in to visit – he was saying you'd found a job down in London. Lovely to see you, Rita." He went to take the tea tray and Rita felt a stab of anger.

"Don't give me the bloody brush-off like that. I came to see you," she called.

He turned quickly, his brows knit together. "You don't seem to understand – I'm involved with something *extremely* important and there's no time for personal issues here."

"I need your help," Rita continued, lowering her voice. Now the grovelling had to start, but this, she swore, would be the last time.

"What do you want from me?" he asked, turning his back to the door as if to hide his face.

"I have to get home – I've no money – nothing."

"And you pick now – here – to come and announce this." He was becoming more agitated.

"I had nowhere else to go." Something inside of her wanted to scream at his smugness.

Some other men in dark suits and red carnation buttonholes came in through the door. George fumbled in his trouser pocket, "Here's my room key," he thrust it at her. "Wait there and I'll be up in a couple of hours. Don't say anything to anybody." He went off to join the group of men at a large round table by the window.

Rita stood open-mouthed at his nerve. He'd changed – and for the worst. There was no trace of the gentle, humble lad she'd known back on Crag Street. Ambition had turned his head. She'd had it up to here with men and their selfish concern for their own bloody skin. She walked towards the door, arms tired with the weight of the suitcase and her mind exhausted from thinking. *How could he think he was a cut above her, sitting with his fancy new friends and treating her like dirt?* Well some day she'd show him.

The upstairs hallways were carpeted in plush pale blue and the soft swish of the lift doors told her that this was an expensive hotel. That's where all those union dues were going – to keep the top brass in fancy living quarters while the poor working stiffs like her dad would never even get to sniff the inside of a place like this.

The numbers were stamped in gilt on the door and she slipped the key into the lock as quietly as she could. It was like paradise inside. Soft carpets, gilt-framed mirrors and *wonder of wonders* – a private bathroom. She'd practically had to bathe clothed at the hostel since she'd caught wind of a rumour that Captain Webb had peepholes all over the place, including the staff bathrooms.

The hotel bathroom had lights above the mirror and tiny wrapped bars of soap lay next to the sink. Even a towelling dressing gown with the hotel monogram on it, hung on a brass hook by the door. This was the life she wanted for herself. To be able to buy luxuries, to pamper herself, to sail straight into a place like this and demand the best suite and all paid for with her own money earned by her own sweat.

She'd always known money was the key — ever since those childhood shopping trips with her Mam. And George knew it too. She remembered when they were at Ida's — the way he looked at her clean, pretty dresses and her bracelets with the silver charms. He liked new expensive things too. But she'd made the mistake of thinking she had to rely on a man to provide them for her. *Well she didn't like the price* — and there was always a cost. *Open your legs luvvy and show your gratitude, then you can have whatever you want.* Well as far as she was concerned she wasn't for sale. At least once she got back home. Today she'd still have to grovel a bit.

She ran a scalding bath then sprinkled in some lavender salts from a pink packet on the sink. Stripping off her clothes she briefly caught sight of herself in the mirror. The weeks of bread and margarine and thin chicken soup had slimmed her out. *Not bad*, she thought and slid into the perfumed water, letting the steam clear away the panic and worry of the past few weeks. She'd survived it all so she could survive anything. No one could shake her confidence or beat her down. Not even George and his hoity-toity ways. He was so busy trying to make believe he was something special — trying to wipe the dirt of Crag Street from his shoes. She could see right through him.

After the bath she wrapped herself in the soft dressing gown and walked over to the window. Outside it was raining — cold grey rain — the kind that soaked right through thin raincoats like hers and chilled her body to the bone with a bitter, sodden cold. She shuddered and turned to the bed. She'd get in just for a minute — only a minute. It would warm her up. Settling down under the blue silk cover she wondered what it would be like if she was really here as his girlfriend. Waiting for him to come back from his meeting. Maybe they'd get dressed up and go out for dinner. Somewhere fancy. And after a few drinks and a lovely, juicy steak they'd come back here and he'd take her in his arms and .... . Her heart ached. It would never happen. So she closed her eyes and fell asleep to the hum of the vacuum cleaner somewhere in a distant hallway.

Rita was running down a street somewhere in London. The road was uneven and full of deep potholes and behind her ran Captain Webb pounding on a huge drum strapped to his shoulders. Closer and closer he came until the sound was so deafening she crumpled to her knees holding her hands to her ears. Bang, bang, bang went the beat, never stopping until his pudgy, distorted face pushed itself into hers, the swollen lips rooting around her cheeks and neck. She opened her mouth to scream but only a gasp came out. The weight of his body crushed her, then the face turned into Dickie's and he was thrusting at her until she couldn't breathe, squeezing the air from her lungs until she choked and clawed at the air and then she heard a small voice coming from somewhere near her face. She struggled to open her eyes

"For Christ's sake it's me, George. Wake up Rita."

Somewhere between the state of sleep and waking Rita reached up and grasped the shoulders that loomed over the bed. She woke, clinging onto George's jacket and sobbing.

"Sorry, sorry," she said over and over again and he held onto her like a baby.

Once she was able to stop crying George placed her back down on the bed and went into the bathroom. She lay looking at the moon that hung full and heavy in the window. *What time is it?* She wondered. *How long had he been watching her?* He came back out with a damp cloth and sat down on the side of the bed, mopping her face.

"You've had a bad time of it then?" He asked, wiping her forehead.

"I just want to go home now."

"I thought you were trying to get away from Crag Street."

"I've been stupid, *stupid, stupid...*" she felt the tears pressing at her eyes again.

"Give yourself some time," he said, ruffling her hair. "You're not ready to go it alone yet – you're only eighteen and there's too many rotten bastards out there for you to deal with."

She sat up, her head woozy with sleep, eyes fat with crying, "Like you?"

George stood up and walked towards the window. "Things crop up – things you never know are going to happen and then everything changes."

"I'm never gonna believe any man again." She said, reaching for her clothes.

"It's a good lesson, Rita. Welcome to real life, flower." He handed her a clean towel. "Now go and clean your face up then we'll sort out how to get you home."

When Rita came out of the bathroom George was on the phone. He looked up at her, mouthed *wait*, and then went on talking. *It's no good*, she thought, her insides always went fluttery when she was close to him and she had to struggle for the words. She stood holding the towel like a child after its bath.

He put down the phone and came over to her. "You look like the old Rita again – the little girl with the lace hankies and the prim manners."

"That's all gone," she said, thinking of Dickie and suddenly the guilt and shame welled up inside. "I feel *fucking lost* now." She buried her face in the towel and began to cry. George put his arms around her and they stood there, not moving until her crying had turned to a shudder.

"Rita – you and I both come from the same place," he whispered. "But when we find a way out we have to take it and nothing can get in the way – *nothing.*"

"But I have to go back to that filthy hole again."

"*Whoa – I bet* next time I see you, you'll be out of there. You're a feisty lass. Knowing you, you'll claw your way out. Whatever it takes. Now come on – I'll give you your train fare home and order a taxi to take you to the station. Ten pounds," he said leafing through his wallet. "That should be enough to get you back."

"Thanks for the pep talk," she said, reaching her face up and pecking him on the cheek. "I knew you'd help me."

She had a warm feeling inside when she went back into the bathroom to repair the damage from the crying. "I could do with some wet teabags for these eyes," she shouted, feeling a small hope inside that maybe she *would* really see him again and when it happened she wouldn't feel like a wrung-out dishrag.

George was changing his tie when she came out. "Going somewhere?" she asked.

"Dinner," he replied, brushing his hair.

"Nice."

"Yes."

"I'll be going then," she said, feeling a hard lump in her throat as she picked up the ten-pound note. "Thanks."

"All right luv," He squeezed her hand and she saw herself reflected in miniature in those sea blue eyes. She winced at the sight of herself with the crumpled raincoat and the brassy hair.

There was a sudden tapping then the door opened quickly. George jerked his hand away and Rita gasped as a tall, dark haired woman walked in, carrying a leather overnight bag, a suede coat slung over her arm. Her diamond earrings sparkled against perfectly teased hair and her slim black dress was accented with gold buttons.

"George," she said in an accent that Rita associated with the boarding school girls from her childhood books, "Train got in early...". She stopped and looked Rita up and down. "And who in the hell is *this*, darling?"

"I was just leaving," Rita said catching hold of the door.

By now the woman was grabbing George by the sleeve, "I don't think you quite heard me – *who is this person?*"

Rita chuckled to herself as George stuttered for words, "One of the chambermaids – she left an earring in here."

"You're not very convincing – are you," she said, her voice escalating.

"Fiona," said George. "This is not what you think…"

"We've got a regular farce going on here," spat Fiona. "Floosy exits stage left and fiancée enters stage right."

Rita picked up her cases, conscious of Fiona's open-mouthed stare. George stood behind her, holding her shoulders, "Fiona, I'll tell you all about it when Rita's gone."

Spineless coward, Rita said to herself and, pulling herself up tall but then he'd helped her and she couldn't overlook that, "He's telling the truth luv, I noticed his north-eastern accent and we just got talking."

Fiona shrugged and Rita turned and left them to it.

30

Jimmy Bishop was enjoying a booming business since television had hit the Northeast in a big way. He was into equal rights for the working class and if the rest of the country was tuning in to Coronation Street then why shouldn't the workers. By that time Jimmy was waiting to cash in with a ready supply of twelve-inch black-and-white models.

Everyone was on the hire-purchase plan, known as the 'never-never'. Never put out the money up front and never finish paying for the damned thing until Jimmy had collected the principal amount together with a whole lot of interest. All he needed was someone to collect the payments every Friday, in person, door to door. When Rita answered the ad, he took one look at her teased platinum hair, baby pink twin set, tight black skirt, high-heeled gold sandals and knew he'd found the right person. A person with guts, glamour and plenty of showbiz allure.

Rita loved the job. She could do herself up and waltz, without invitation, into everyone's house, pick up gossip as well as their money and then sweep out of the place leaving the smell of her perfume and a lot of clacking tongues behind her. Her London escapade was popular fodder for gossip and people looked forward to her visit to spice the day up a bit.

Marjorie DeLuca

One lukewarm Friday in July, Rita was doing her collection wearing a new pink Crimplene two-piece she'd found at Joplins. The salesgirl told her Crimplene was the latest fabric, produced synthetically – never wrinkled or went baggy. Today she'd colour coordinated her entire outfit and proudly flounced up to Mrs Willis's gate in a froth of pink. Hannah Willis was standing there with Ella Danby and Olive Coombes and Rita knew for a fact they'd been gossiping about her because they stopped talking and watched her sway towards them.

She nodded at Ella who squinted at her with narrow eyes then, suddenly conscious of the old bucket in her hand, shuffled back to her step. Hannah opened the gate and Rita stepped through.

"Afternoon, Mrs Willis."

"Aye – yer'll find the money inside on the kitchen table."

"Is Maggie in?" asked Rita.

"Why no, I wouldn't leave money out on the table with her around. I'd never see it again – bloody feckless wife she is – teks every spare copper and bets it on the dogs."

Rita turned to go into the house, thankful she'd remembered to wear plenty of Lily of the Valley cologne for the inside smelled like piss, old laundry and rotten vegetables. The breakfast table was still covered in dirty dishes so she sat herself at the table and cleared a space with her hanky so she could sort through the payment books. First she took out her mirror to check her make-up – pink spots of blush on her cheeks, the silvery-blue eyelids with the thin black liner extending out like cat's eyes, lips a bright rose-pink curved in a deep Cupid's bow. Her pink painted toenails peeped out from her thin gold sandals. Just then the door opened and Maggie fluttered in nervously, holding her headscarf tightly around her chin. Mary, the youngest at ten, followed her in and, seeing Rita, rushed over and hugged her.

"Mam, I think Rita's really beautiful."

Rita was shocked to see how thin Maggie had become, her hands fluttered like a pair of transparent butterflies and her blue eyes were sunk into deep shadowy sockets.

"Why yes, hinny – Rita's gorgeous."

"Oh, go on," Rita said, embarrassed and took out a pink, shiny powder compact, holding it out to Mary, "Do you like this, flower, I won it at the Pleasure Beach in Blackpool. It has a picture of Elvis inside. Do you know I used to go with a famous singer?" Rita looked over at Maggie then continued. "I could've been living in a big place in London instead of staying in this dump. Aye, that's where the high life is – big cars and posh nightclubs – places stay open all night – and the lights – bright colours flashing and people dressed in fab clothes dance the night away."

Maggie took her scarf off and pulled at her wispy, faded hair. "Eeh, Rita, I don't know why you'd come back here to this muck hole after being down there. A long time ago I once had the chance to get out of here and go to a place where the air's so fresh you can hang out your clothes without fear of dirtying them more."

Rita smiled and then licked her thumb delicately to flip over the pages of her coupon book. "You'll have to tell me that story sometime."

Maggie nodded and went into the scullery to get the kettle.

Rita took out a brightly coloured pencil.

"See this, Mary, that's Blackpool Tower." She held the pencil out to the child, "By, that's a smashing place – always summat going on. Last time I was there I saw the ballroom dancing competition. Eeh, all the dresses were lovely. Our Sandra – that's my cousin – was in the Paso Doble wearing salmon-pink net and all the sequins were hand-sewn. Our Sandra says ballroom dancing's the way to get somewhere. Before you know it, you can be in London dancing at the Locarno."

Both Maggie and Mary were sitting, staring at Rita, who kept on talking. "Of course, Dickie, that's the singer bloke I was goin' with, said I was wasted up here. London's the place for a girl like you, he says. But – things didn't really work out the way I'd planned and that's another story so I must be going," She jumped up quickly, taking the envelope of money.

Maggie blinked her eyes nervously and returned to the present, "All the best to yer mam. Tell her to pop over for a cup of tea next week."

"Mebbe I'll take the bairns to the next ballroom competition, if that's all right, Maggie. Your Pearl would love the music."

"Oh aye, Rita. I'd love that. I don't get out much these days – there's not much money now Jordy cut his shifts and I want the girls to have every chance possible to... " She stopped abruptly and looked towards the window. "It's Jordy, you'd best be on your way." Maggie's mouth set in a tight line as if she was grinding her teeth.

Needing no more warning Rita got up and walked through the open door, her shoes click-clacking over the grey flagstones. Outside, Jordy Willis was talking to Hannah. Rita looked out from the corner of her eye to see the ruddy face criss-crossed by spidery-black lines and the full lips curled into a sneer. He didn't turn his head to look at her as she walked by but simply said to his mother, "What's that bloody stink?"

Lilies of the valley, you big clod, Rita thought as she stepped out onto the street and made her way to the Phillips' house, thankful to be away from the dank atmosphere of the Willis's.

The Phillips had become very popular on the street since they'd installed a bookie's machine in the pantry and old Mrs Phillips would take the bets over to the bookie's in a tattered shopping bag. Any winnings were paid out the next day so people were always coming and going to and from the house, much to the embarrassment of old Mrs Phillips who had to cope with the noises that came from her son Harold and his wife Irma's room when Harold was home from work. Harold's reputation as having God's gift and using it as often as he could was well known.

Rita stood by the crammed sideboard watching the Flowerpot Men on the grainy television screen along with old Mrs Phillips when Harold came in from the morning shift, his face pink and shining. Patting Rita fondly on the backside he nuzzled at her neck and whispered, "By yer look smashin' hinny. Some feller's blind not appreciating what he had here."

"Ta Harold, I'm feeling lucky today. I think I'll splurge a shilling or two on the horses."

"I would, hinny." Harold said, "Mam, where's our Irma?"

"In the scullery mekkin' bread," she said turning back to Rita. "Bloody stupid program, this one. They say it's for the bairns but yer canna understand a word of it. I prefer The Woodentops."

"Well tell her I'm away upstairs," he winked broadly at Rita.

"Aye."

Mrs Phillips pushed the racing forms across to Rita who scanned the pages looking for a name that would smack her in the eye. London Laddy, that looked good, that struck a chord. She could see herself with an armful of pound notes standing in the winners' circle, her arm around the horse's rosette covered neck.

The old lady took Rita's money into the scullery where Irma, obscured by a cloud of flour dust, was pounding bread dough and singing, "Keep yer feet still Jordy Hinny." She moved out of the way so her mother-in-law could open the pantry and take out the clocking machine. It was supposed to be a well-kept secret but everyone on the street knew that it brought in a bit of extra income and paid for her annual holiday in Harrogate.

"By that's a really lovely place – posh tea rooms and places to sit and think. I was born in the wrong time, Rita – manners was manners in those days," said Mrs Phillips.

Irma wiped her forehead with a floury forearm, "Eeh, this bread's takin' a lot of poundin' mother."

"Why hinny yer should be watchin' them American shows. They've got electrical doo-dahs for everything. Yer just sit back and the gadgets do everything in the kitchen, they even have them big refrigerators. Can yer imagine that – gettin' ice out any time yer like and everything's kept cold – eh."

Rita was just writing out the payment receipt when there was a faint voice from upstairs.

"Irma, can yer fetch us a cup of tea? I'm parched."

Irma slapped down the dough, "Bloody hell, the dirty bugger's after it again. I'll never get back down here again."

"Irma, Irma, come up here? I'm dry as a wooden god."

Irma took off her apron and washed her hands. "Watch the dough, mother."

Mrs Phillips waited till Irma was out of earshot then leaned over to Rita, saying, "It's been ten years now since they were married and they're still ruttin' like a pair of rabbits."

Rita began to feel nauseous from the strong smell of yeast and the steady creak – creaking from above. She excused herself hurriedly.

"Pay out tomorrow if yer win, flower," Mrs Phillips called as Rita gathered up her book and the payment envelope. "And dinna' tell a soul. I try to keep this hush-hush."

Once outside, Rita looked up to the sky and thanked God she was free and single. She was meant for better things and that was sure.

She set off again down the street, clutching her bag of money and papers. She'd finish her collecting and go to Nuttall's, the chemists to buy some new talc and bath salts. Tonight she'd soak herself in Devon Violets and read the latest copy of Valentine.

Two weeks later, Rita finished her collecting late Friday morning and took her usual trip to the High Street. Lloyd's Bank was always busy on Friday lunchtimes. The spenders were there taking money out for a couple nights of drinking at the club, a trip to the pictures, an hour or two at the dog track and maybe shopping in Sunderland and a football game.

You could easily fritter away a whole week's pay in a matter of two days, especially if you were young, single or courting and most folks never used the bank, living from one pay-packet to another and scraping by as best they could. Rita was different. She saved religiously, putting aside every penny for a the future of her dreams.

She loved the clean, papery smell of the bank – the smell of money, of business and prosperity. Each week she deposited her pay, checked her bankbook and gloated over the little black numbers that multiplied and grew like busy, black ants. Brilliant, she thought, for this week the total had reached £565 saved over the last few months from her weekly pay, and her winnings on the horses. She'd had the best winning streak ever, so good that Mrs Phillips told her not to come any more.

"Gan ower to the bettin' shop – bonny lass." So Rita had sent Jimmy over to Ladbrokes every other day at one o' clock with her bets.

At first she'd kept the money at home under her bed but her brothers soon ferreted it out and got into the habit of borrowing half a crown here and there when they were short of beer money. Most lads their age were either married or at least courting, but not Lenny and Bill. They were too attached to their Da. The three of them were like a team with two interests in common – beer and Union politics.

Rita put the bankbook back in her handbag and snapped it shut. She'd taken out enough to treat herself to a shampoo and set at Eileen's and her appointment was in half an hour.

It was a mild spring day. A pretty day with pale blue sky framing the few blossoming trees clustered around the old church in the High Street. Their branches burst with clumps of flowers the colour and texture of thick ice cream. Rita had watched on many a Saturday as young brides burst out from the church flushed pink with hope, their veils a froth of white gauze, their hand clasped tightly onto the arm of a freshly shaved young man in a shiny new suit. They'd duck to avoid the clouds of confetti raining down on them and race off to their reception, followed by a few days in Blackpool if they were lucky. Then the dream was over. How many times did she see the same girl six months or a year later – confined to three rooms of a dingy house, servant to a mother-in-law or husband, pregnant, exhausted and fed up? To Rita marriage was nothing but a trap – a life sentence of hard labour.

Checking her watch, she realized she had only twenty minutes before her appointment. Enough time to pop over to the bus terminus and buy some chewing gum and a Woman's Weekly. She crossed the street in time to avoid the groups of pitmen who stood around or crouched down on their haunches by the War Memorial. Today she was wearing a new tangerine crochet sweater that clung so tightly to all her curves she could hear the catcalls and whistles from across the street. Ignoring them, she swept by and headed for the bus station, two shops away from Eileen's.

Dammit, she thought as she focused on a tall, stout figure entering Eileen's pink and gold door. There was no mistaking Ella Danby who nowadays wore a black knitted tam o' shanter and had taken to sitting for long hours in the newsagent's shop or Eileen's, listening to everyone's gossip. Rita's mam said Ella's husband Jack had hardening of the arteries and Ella was worn out with the queer way he behaved. Poor thing, thought Rita, that's why she stayed away from home more often.

At the bus terminus Rita had to visit the ladies toilet, a stinking place at the best of times, but she held her Nights in Paris-soaked hanky up to her nose and rushed inside. One of the cubicles was closed and she could hear someone moaning. Spots of blood dotted the concrete floor leading to the cubicle. Someone was in pain and Rita stood confused, not sure what to do. Should she go and keep her appointment or help the person who was in trouble? Another moan clinched the decision and she called, "Are you all right in there?"

A weak voice asked, "Is that --- is that Rita?"

"Yes --- Maggie – what the hell are you doing in there? What's the matter?"

"Rita, I'm sick – I canna get up. I just canna."

"What's happened? Did you have an accident or summat?"

Maggie begin to cry harder.

"No, it's something terrible and no-one can know about it. That's why I canna call the doctor."

"Come on out and I'll get a taxi to take you home," Rita begged.

"I canna go home. They'll know and Jordy'll kill me."

"I'll take you somewhere else, then," said Rita thinking of the flat above Jimmy's shop. "Come on, it's filthy in here."

The crying stopped for a moment and Rita waited, listening to the rustling of Maggie's coat. Her eyes were drawn to the scuffed, brown shoes peeping underneath the door – a pair – but only one had its own brass buckle, the other had only two staple holes in the place where the buckle should have been.

The bolt on the door shifted and Maggie lurched forward, falling against Rita's chest. Rita gasped at the sight of her chalk-white face, the limp hair plastered against her forehead like stringy weeds and the sweat dribbling down the sides of her face. Her red-rimmed eyes were so swollen they were almost closed. Rita could smell her fear.

"What have you done?" she gasped at the sight of Maggie's blood stained legs.

"Just take me somewhere – don't let anyone see me," Maggie begged.

The Pitman's Daughter

Rita half walked, half dragged Maggie's limp, dead weight out of the bus station and two doors down to Jimmy's place. With the morning rush over, it was quiet on the street and she was able to get there without being seen. She pushed with her shoulder at the front door of the shop and burst into the display area where Jimmy, a portly man in his forties with a thick head of iron grey hair, was sitting hunched over a box of electrical plugs and chewing on a hot Cornish pasty from Dickins the baker's. He stopped suddenly, his full mouth gaping, "What the hell...?"

Rita stood panting as Maggie swayed and almost fell.

"Well stop stuffing your face and help me get her upstairs, will you."

"I don't like this Rita. What happened to her?"

"She had an accident. She just needs somewhere to rest for a while. Come on, flower; I'll owe you one. I'll go to the dog track with you."

Still frowning, Jimmy came over and slipped his arm around Maggie's shoulders. "I telt yer – I don't want any trouble with her husband – that bugger's a nasty piece of work." Then he helped Rita drag the moaning Maggie up the stairs to a tiny room crammed with boxes and packing cases. In the corner a foldout cot was piled high with papers. Rita swept them off onto the floor, then covered the bed with a white sheet and lowered the unconscious woman down onto the mattress.

"Don't worry love," she said to Jimmy, "I'll clean up afterwards. You go back downstairs and don't breathe a word of this to anyone. There's far ower many nosey ears and eyes around here already."

When Jimmy left, Rita pulled up a packing box and sat watching Maggie, whose face was crushed into the pillow, her bony, bruised legs splayed out on the mattress. How could such a frail, tiny woman have borne so many children and put up with Jordy for so many years. He was a pig and a brute. No wonder her poor body was all used up and tired from all the babies sucking the life out of it. Rita wrapped her arms around her own firm body. Since Dicky it was untouched, like a fortress.

She awoke with a start at the sound of muffled crying and saw Maggie, face buried in the pillow, her body shaking.

"So bonny – he would have been so bonny," she sobbed.

"Who, Maggie? Who?"

The sobbing grew louder and more desperate.

"I could have had his baby. I wanted him so bad and he would have been a beauty... but I couldn't."

Rita stroked Maggie's back. "Calm down, Maggie. Tell me about it."

"The baby – I killed the baby, Rita. I went somewhere and I let them stick something inside me and they killed him before he even had a chance to grow. I let them kill him because I was too scared of Jordy. He would have known it wasn't his."

Maggie's sobs grew louder as she clawed at the pillow, crying in rage.

"Maggie, whose baby was it?"

"I canna say," she whispered. "But it doesn't matter any more. They flushed him away and I canna forgive mesel now. I want him back – back inside and I'll keep him – if only I could get him back again – my baby boy – my bairn..." By this time Maggie was screaming and pounding her hands against the wall. Rita lunged forwards and grabbed her, turning her so that the sobbing woman's face was pressed against her shoulder.

"There, there, you had no choice. You had to do it. Ssh – ssh." Rita rocked her back and forth, humming and stroking her hair because she couldn't think of any words to comfort her.

Later, at dusk, when Maggie had cried her eyes dry, Rita helped her clean herself up, borrowed Jimmy's Rover and drove her home. It was raining a steady drizzle and that meant they'd be safe from prying eyes.

Maggie huddled in the corner of the seat like a bundle of rags as Rita turned the corner into Crag Street. "Maggie, tell me which bastard ran out on you like this?"

Maggie's face was a pale triangle in the dark. "No, Rita. He was kind and gentle and he loved me. He went away and he didn't know about the baby."

"All the same," said Rita, "if he loved you he shouldn't have left you. But that's men for you – get what they want and then bugger off."

"One day you'll understand, Rita. When you meet someone you really love."

"Never, "Rita replied," No man's worth it." She reassured herself with those familiar words but a stab of loneliness touched her in some deep, secret place.

When they arrived at Maggie's house the front door was open and Rita held tightly to Maggie's arm as she hobbled across the yard. A belt of cigarette smoke hung in a hazy band above the kitchen table where Jordy and four friends were playing cards. A pile of empty beer bottles was stacked in the centre of the table and an ashtray overflowed with cigarette ends. Hannah was sitting in front of the television watching Coronation Street, a bag of crisps in one hand and a bottle of beer in the other. Nobody looked up.

"She's had a bit of an accident, she'll have to rest," Rita shouted over the T.V.

Jordy belched loudly. "Bugger off then *Ritaaa*." The other men sniggered. "Maggie mek yersel useful and get some more beer from the kitchen."

Maggie nodded at Rita, "I'll be all right," she whispered. "And thank you. Go on now."

"You heard her – now piss off – I dinna want her gettin any of your fancy ideas."

Rita left, exhausted, head throbbing. She was still thinking of the unformed baby, still alive when it was torn out from its own mother's body. The place that was supposed to be safe. Her heart clenched inside her. How could Maggie have killed the innocent bairn? But then what kind of life would the poor mite have had with Jordy? It was better not to think too much about things like that because they only brought pain and grief. She'd learned that lesson as a child in the sweetshop, when Ida cried about her long lost love and her poor, dead bairn. *How could she forget it?*

1965

31

Rita put the finishing touches to her make-up. A final layer of crimson lipstick, a few extra strokes of eyebrow pencil and a poke and prod of her comb so the blonde beehive hairdo stood stiff and poufy.

She pulled aside the lace curtains. It was a warm Friday evening, the end of a hot and dusty day spent traipsing up and down the street collecting the week's payments. The late summer sky glowed crimson streaked with gold. Like those exotic pictures of Hollywood skies she always looked at. Places where Annette Funicello and Sandra Dee romped on ocean-soaked beaches with Fabian and Troy Donahue.

It was going to be a good night. Jimmy Bishop, her boss was taking her to the dog track. On Fridays he always felt flush and they'd sit in the comfortable clubhouse, away from the rabble, drink gin and orange and watch the dogs. They had a good arrangement. Jimmy didn't bother Rita since she'd put him straight the first week when he'd tried to slide his hand under her skirt. Once he'd known there was to be no funny business he'd been satisfied to take her out, show her off and spend some of his extra money on her. He'd had a few lonely years since his wife passed away suddenly of lung cancer and Rita was happy to indulge the middle-aged man's fantasies. She'd dress up in her most clingy outfits, do herself up like Marilyn Monroe and let him take her out somewhere.

Happy with her makeup she turned to her bed, still stacked with the teddies and dolls of her childhood. Damn it, she cursed, she'd forgotten to pack them up in a bag and take them over to Willis's house to give to Hazel and Pearl. Poor bairns needed a bit of spoiling.

Downstairs her father and brothers were in a tight discussion. Rumours of pit closures had them panicking and arranging emergency union meetings. Rita walked downstairs, hoping they'd be too engrossed to see her but her Nights in Paris perfume wafted into the air and three heads craned round to watch her as she teetered over the braided rug on steel-tipped stiletto heels.

"Gannin' out wi' the ard man tonight?" said Bill, taking a swig of Newcastle Brown. "Yer'll knock the poor ard sod out wi' that stink!"

"Wily ard bugger, that Jimmy Bishop. Couldna wait till his wife's body was cold i' the ground afore he's got his hands all ower some lass's arse," said Lenny.

Rita snorted through her handbag. "Shurrup the pair of you. Just because yer never looked further than yer own backyard – yer think yer na everything. Where's me Mam?"

Her father slammed his fist on the table making the beer bottles jump. "She's outside gossipin' with all the other ard wives on the street – probably about you shamin' our family, knockin' around the place with that smarmy old bugger. You'd be best off concernin' yourself with important matters like whether we'll have food on our table after they close all the pits down and we're out on the streets wi' only the clothes on our backs."

"But Da," said Bill, "George Nelson was speakin' at the union meeting today and he told us that Belton isn't on the list of closures. He says he's done everything he can."

"By there's a powerful man," Walter said, his eyes uplifted as if addressing God himself. "And if you'd played yer cards right, yer could have been Mrs Nelson – but no, instead yer gan buggering off like a painted twopenny whore wi' some fly by night puff of a singer, the night George comes ower here for supper."

Rita felt the blood rush to her face. "Yer think he's so great. What kind of a man goes away and leaves his family and acts like he's too good for them? His mother stands out on the step day in and day out, poor old soul. She's waitin' for a word from him. He was in Belton today but he never came to see her. That's yer big man for you."

Walter stood up, sloshing his beer over his trousers. "He's got more important things on his mind. He's a leader – with the jobs of thousands of men in his hands. He's a great man and great men have to make sacrifices. But that's summat you'd never understand, yer Mam taught yer to be selfish."

Rita was getting ready for another screaming match when there was a honk of a car horn and she looked out to see Jimmy Bishop's sleek maroon Rover outside. The street was alive. People were leaning over their gates watching as Rita walked out waving at the open mouthed audience. Jimmy, polished and Brylcreemed in a navy pinstripe suit, rushed around and held the door open for her. His face was red and glowing, the stiff, white collar cutting into his fleshy neck. He slammed the door shut and dipped his head in a shallow bow towards all the gossips. Rita laughed and lit a cigarette, tossing her head back and blowing the smoke out in rings.

At the track it was a relief to get through the throngs of pitmen, and the haggard women nervously searching for a few coppers to make a bet. They dodged the hawking and spitting to reach the carpeted comfort of the clubhouse. Jimmy pulled out a chair for Rita. "What'll you have, flower?"

"Gin and orange and a bag of cheese and onion crisps," said Rita, arranging her skirt so her stocking tops weren't showing.

Jimmy glanced longingly at her slim legs, clad in American tan nylons.

"Hadaway, yer dirty ard man," joked Rita, looking through the window at the dogs that ran like brown streaks after the electric hare. "We've got some serious betting to do."

After an hour of betting Rita was up thirty-five pounds and on her third gin and orange. Jimmy was losing but having the time of his life. That's what Rita liked about him; he had a sense of humour and was always laughing and joking and generous to a fault. Then to top it all he kept his hands to himself. Christ, she thought, if Jimmy would really keep off her she'd have married him – but as soon as you got that ring on your finger most men thought they owned you.

"Another one, flower?" asked Jimmy.

"Get one in, chuck, – I'll have to pay a visit first."

Rita walked out to the ladies toilet, just beside the main betting hall. She was about to open the door when she heard loud voices and scuffling.

"Hadaway – gan back home and look after your family," said a rough man's voice.

Around the corner Maggie Willis was kneeling on the floor in the middle of a mess. Loose peanuts, old betting slips, cracked lipstick cases and a broken comb were scattered across the floor and Maggie, face flushed, eyes squinting furiously, was scrabbling around trying to sweep it all into her shabby white handbag.

Two men – strangers that Rita had never seen around the track – walked away from the scene shouting back at her, "Bloody pain in the neck – asking for money. Just another scrubber." Then they were lost in the crowd.

Rita rushed over and, crouching down, began to help Maggie.

"Come on, Maggie. Let's get yer away from here before yer make more of a spectacle of yersel'. Come on and I'll buy yer a cup of tea or summat stronger if you want it."

Rita sat Maggie down with a stiff gin and tonic.

"Drink that and yer'll feel better."

"I was only doin' what the others do, Rita. Yer just ask a man if he wants yer to put his bet on for him – you know – stand in the queue for him – and then he gives you sixpence tip or summat. All the women do it. It's the only way to mek some money for betting."

"Aye, but you have to mek sure it's a feller from round here, Maggie or they might think yer after summat else," said Rita, looking at Maggie's stringy hair, now streaked with grey. Her clothes looked washed out and rumpled as if they'd been left to dry after going through the mangle.

Rita lowered her voice. "You need to clean yersel up, Maggie, you're all to pieces. How come yer down here all the time? Your mam says you're here every night. What about the bairns?"

Maggie took a gulp of the gin. "It used to be alright – I could put up with him before, because of the bairns. Even when Jordy was in his blackest mood I could look at their faces and be happy. Now it's no good any more. None of it. And the bairns are leaving – one by one. What'll I do when they're gone?"

"Is Jordy knocking you around again?"

"Oh no, hinny. He never bothers with me now – he spends all the time up in his room or even the attic. I don't know what he's doin' up there. He's gone that queer, and he only brightens up when our Pearl sings to him."

"Then yer should be happy, flower, yer free of him."

"I'm lost Rita. I've lost my heart. I can't feel anything any more."

"Pull yersel together Maggie – your children love you."

"I've been a stupid, stupid woman, Rita. I've made a complete fool of mesel and – you know after that terrible thing I did," Maggie looked around quickly and leaned closer, "You didn't tell anyone did yer, Rita?"

"No, Maggie, I didn't breathe a word."

"I think I've done some damage to mesel – I canna even think about it. I've got pains there all the time as if something's tearing at me insides." Maggie drank down the rest of her gin and stared at Rita with clouded eyes.

"Why don't you go to the doctor's?"

"I canna, Rita – I canna tell him what I've done – I'll get into trouble for it."

"God – Maggie – just make up a story."

"I'm too ashamed – and to tell you the truth – I canna be bothered any more. It doesn't matter what happens to me now – there's nowt worth carin' about."

Rita lit a cigarette and took a long draw at it, "Maggie whose baby was it? Why didn't you tell the heartless bastard?"

"I've got my reasons for keeping it to mesel and now I'm not worth a tuppenny damn and I don't care about mesel or anybody."

"That bugger – whoever he is – deserves to have his balls cut off for puttin' yer through all this."

"Rita, not everyone's as strong as you. You don't tek any nonsense. But I loved him. He was so good to me and so gentle. I couldn't believe he'd even look at me."

"He must have been a sly one – I bet he wormed his way into yer affections."

"No, Rita. I've never known a man like him." Maggie began to sniffle softly.

"Don't start all that again," said Rita, handing her a tissue. "Now promise me if the pains are still there next week yer'll let me tek you to see a doctor I know – no questions asked – all right?"

"All right, love – you're a good person, Rita – a real friend."

"And I'm gonna borrow Jimmy's car – he's off to Torquay for a holiday. I'll come round soon and take you and the bairns to the ballroom dancing contest at Brentmoor."

"That's lovely Rita."

Rita fumbled in her handbag and pulled out some coins.

"Here's a few shillings for yer betting – no need to do any begging."

Just then there was a huge commotion as a crowd of punters rushed towards the door. Rita tapped the shoulder of a young man who was standing on tiptoes to see over the crowd. "What's all the fuss about?"

"It's George Nelson, the big union man – he's here on Union business. He stopped them closing the pit."

"Bloody hell, all that fuss for one man. I canna believe it."

But when she glanced down again, Maggie's eyes were wide open and her face white. "I have to go Rita. Ta for the drink... thanks."

Rita stood up, knocking her leg on the table. "Ow... Maggie... wait."

But she disappeared into the crowd, head bent and face down. Rita craned her neck and spotted George Nelson surrounded by an escort of pitmen, her dad right at his shoulder. *Taking in every word from the great one*, she supposed.

As she looked at the carefully groomed hair, the smooth-shaven face, the passionate way his hands moved as he charmed his followers with every word, a flicker of suspicion crossed her mind. Maggie had fled like a frightened rabbit as soon as he showed up. Could he be the mystery lover – the heartless coward that used Maggie and threw her aside? She looked again at his immaculate navy suit – the kind that could only be bought in the best shops in Newcastle. No, it wasn't possible. Someone like George wouldn't take a second look at Maggie. A dark-haired girl in a tailored blue dress stood beside him, her arm linked closely in his. It was Fiona – the girl from the hotel in Luton. Everything about her screamed class – the small string of pearls, the pale coral lipstick and the silky wings of chestnut hair. *They'd been seeing each other for more than a year, then.*

Touching her own blonde beehive of hair, Rita felt suddenly brash and common. The thick layer of make-up felt dry and caked like a clown's mask, the three gin and tonics turned sickly in her stomach. Why, she asked herself – why did she feel vulgar and cheap whenever George was around and she'd been having such a wild time with Jimmy. *Why did he keep showing up in her life and turning things upside down?* "Jimmy," she bawled at the top of her voice, "Jimmy, where the hell are you?"

George and his entire entourage turned to look at her, then her dad whispered something to George and dismissed her with a wave of his hand.

"Jimmy," she said as he scuttled across to her, the suds slopping out of his pint glass. "I'm parched. Get me another gin."

Jimmy came back, a gin in one hand and a grin splitting his face from one cheek to the other. "Rita – Rita yer won – a hundred and twenty pound on that last outsider."

"Smashing, Jimmy," she said, downing the drink in one gulp. "Let's celebrate – somewhere else. This place is getting to be that full of riff-raff I feel like going somewhere fancy. Haway, chuck." And with that she took Jimmy's arm and swept past George with her head held high and not a second look behind her.

32

Ella stood in her front room holding the invitation. Her heart was beating so fast she thought it would burst. He'd remembered. He'd kept his part of the bargain and here it was – an invitation to a garden party in Darlington. Far enough away so no prying eyes from around here would bother her. The invitation was on stiff white card with a silver edging. Very smart, and expensive. It showed the kind of circles George was mixing in. There was a small handwritten note along with it. She read carefully.

> *Dear Ella,*
> *This is a small luncheon and afternoon party with some business people and influential women's charities. Dress smart but not too fancy. They asked about my mother. You know what to do. Pick you up at Darlington station at eleven.*
> *Keep this to yourself.*
> *George*

She checked the calendar and realized she had only two days to prepare for the most exciting occasion in her life since her wedding. In her haste she almost turned her ankle rushing upstairs. She flung open the wardrobe to see if she had anything to wear but there was nothing suitable. It was all cheap, shabby Crimplene. She'd have to pay a visit to Durham today and go to those fancy clothes stores down by the Royal Hotel. There wasn't a second to waste, she thought, pulling off her hairnet and teasing out her perm. She'd have to get her hair done tomorrow — at a place where nobody would ask questions. Then she needed shoes. Good leather ones.

Back downstairs she turned out the contents of the biscuit tin. In two years she'd saved up another hundred and twenty pounds. That would be more than enough. Jack was making more money now and eating less so she'd stepped up the saving to be ready for her special moment. Within five minutes she had her best raincoat on and her patent leather handbag slung across her arm as she rushed down the street to catch the ten past ten bus to Durham. Olive Coombes and Hannah Willis called out to her when she bustled by but her eyes were trained straight ahead for there was no time for gossip today. It was her turn to do something exciting that other folks might gossip about.

When the bus pulled into Durham Station she got out and looked around realizing it had been years since she'd visited. North Road was bustling with shoppers. She even went into one of those new ice cream shops that smelled of coffee. A crowd of young people hung around the jukebox listening to that American singer with the sneery lip and wavy hips. She ordered an ice cream from the handsome Italian owner then walked along the street happily licking it, past the Essoldo cinema where *Carry on Cowboy* was playing and along to Framwellgate Bridge where she stopped and looked down at the River Wear, then up at the Cathedral. It was so beautiful she wondered why she hadn't come here lately with Jack. But it wasn't too late. Any Saturday or Sunday they could just get on the bus and in half an hour they'd be here, walking arm in arm.

And then she realized how troublesome that might be. He was going a bit soft in the head since the doctor said his arteries were hardening.

Some days he was all right. In fact at work he was fine. It was second nature to him, getting in the cage and going down into the darkness underground. He said it calmed his demons. Demons. She didn't even know he had any. Come to think of it she didn't really know much about him at all. He was a quiet man, happy to sit in front of the fire and smoke his pipe while she bustled around in the background cleaning up. She felt a little twinge inside when she thought one day he might be gone. But she'd made him contented. Hadn't she?

She scolded herself for being soft and turned away from the river and the beautiful view to make her way up the narrow cobbles of Silver Street, climbing up towards the marketplace, which was thronging with people even though the market wasn't on until Friday. She stood and looked at the statue of Lord Londonderry on his horse and then turned onto the street that led to Elvert Bridge. At the other side was a row of gleaming little shops. The kind you didn't walk into unless you were serious about buying.

Ella pushed open the door of the first one and found herself in a fancy room with an ivory carpet. A thin older lady dressed in a tailored black dress came out from behind the gilded counter. Ella was suddenly conscious of her stout figure and her thick legs. The shop assistant looked Ella up and down quickly appraising her cheap clothes, while Ella saw the wrinkles underneath the heavy layer of foundation and realized the woman was just *mutton dressed as lamb*. There was a momentary standoff between them and then the lady broke the silence.

"Can I help you – modom?" she said, affecting a posh accent.

"I'm going to a special garden party," said Ella. "I need something suitable to wear."

"Of course. And your price range?" she asked.

"Up to £110," Ella answered, taking the shoes and hairdo into account and feeling very smug when the woman raised her eyebrows in surprise.

"Well in that case, would Modom like to take a seat," she said, ushering her towards a white chair padded with plum coloured velvet. "My name is Edna and I'll see what we have for the fuller-figured woman."

Ella sat back and crossed her legs then a thought suddenly hit her, causing her to have a sharp intake of breath. She'd been in that much of a hurry she'd forgot to put on her girdle. Now there'd be rolls and lumps of flesh to deal with. And she'd be so embarrassed if that woman looked in while she was changing and saw her standing in her old navy blue knickers. Well, she'd just bloody well keep her out of there!

She heard the rustle of cellophane and the clink of coat hangers and then Edna returned with an armful of garments, which she hung up in the changing room. "If modom would like to try these," she said, holding open the curtain to reveal the striped wallpaper and glittering mirror beyond. Ella stepped through the crimson silk curtains into the magical room and looked around, catching sight of the infinite reflections of her stout body in the mirrored walls – her thick legs in the lisle stockings, the cheap navy raincoat and her grizzled grey hair under the navy felt hat. For a moment she felt a fluttering of panic in her stomach. What if she couldn't go through with it? Or what if she went to the garden party and showed George up?

The bright new clothes hung on a gilded hook. She slipped off her grey skirt and navy jumper and stood there in her old petticoat cursing the rolls of flesh that ringed her middle. The first outfit was a bright peach suit in a shiny silk fabric. The skirt was far too tight. She couldn't even get it past her hips. The second was a spotted dress that reminded her of a clown costume with its starched white collar and ruffle around the cuffs. The third was a lovely deep purple dress in fine wool with a velvet collar. Ella gasped as she pulled it over her head and smelled the fresh newness of the fabric. It fell smoothly over her hips, the cleverly tailored seams hiding her lumpy body. It was perfect from all angles.

"How is modom doing?" Edna enquired from outside.

"I've found the perfect dress," said Ella opening the curtains.

Edna clapped her hands. "Fits like a glove – and very flattering I must say."

Edna flitted around the store gathering gloves, a printed silk scarf and the sweetest little grey hat with a small brim and purple ribbon trim. Ella stood in front of the mirror marvelling at Edna's handiwork. It was the most beautiful outfit she'd ever seen. The tears pricked at the back of her eyes and she thought again of the child she might have had. Edna coughed a little then reached for a tissue that she handed to Ella.

"It's for my – my son," said Ella. "He has to make a speech and I'm very proud of him."

Edna tilted her head and smiled. "You're a lucky woman – Mrs – Mrs?"

"Danby," said Ella.

"There's many a woman would give anything for a fine, handsome son," said Edna straightening the collar gently.

Ella stopped in at a teashop for a ham sandwich and pot of tea. The dress was wrapped in tissue paper then folded into a white box with the hat, scarf and gloves. She'd also picked up a pair of soft grey leather shoes. While she was chewing on the sandwich a troubling thought came to her. How could she get the packages home? It would be next to impossible smuggling them past all the prying eyes of the neighbours and then there was Jack. He knew nothing about the biscuit tin money and she'd have to face his blank-eyed bewilderment when she couldn't come up with a reasonable explanation. And then what about the next day when she was all dressed up in her finery? The tongues would never stop wagging when she walked down the street. She checked her purse. There was forty-five pounds left and she still had to get her hair done. And then it came to her. She'd find a room – either a bed and breakfast or a small hotel, book it for two nights – tonight and Thursday – and leave the clothes there. Then she'd return on Friday morning, get changed and be on her way to Darlington. She felt a rush of excitement. This was better than gossip, for now she was the person doing something that other folks would actually talk about. On the way out of the teashop she asked the lady at the counter about suitable bed and breakfasts. The lady wrote down two addresses that were nearby and Ella set out to investigate.

Her feet were beginning to throb as she made her way down past the County Hotel and its posh sandstone exterior. Far too dear, she thought, glimpsing into the plush lobby. This was where all the bigwigs stayed during Durham Big Meeting day and where George as union representative would make a speech one day from the wide balcony at the front. She continued and further up the street found the Three Tuns Hotel. On a whim she stepped into the warm interior where cream walls and polished oak wainscoting flanked a cosy fireplace. Comfortable chairs upholstered in red were arranged around the fire and she had a sudden desire to stay there just one night. Tomorrow night. To put her feet up by that very fire and enjoy the luxury of it without Jack yammering in her ear or sucking on his teeth after supper.

Gathering up her courage she went to the desk and enquired about rooms and within ten minutes was the proud owner of a key to a room on the main floor. This was far better than a bed and breakfast where some busybody landlady would ask too many questions.

On the way to the room she checked her watch. It was already two o'clock and the bus went at twenty past three. She slipped the key into the lock on the cream panelled door that swung open to reveal a clean square room with oak wardrobe, oak dressing table and mirror and a nice bed with a pink brocade bedspread. By the bed was a chair upholstered in red striped material and a little desk with its own chair by the window and even some writing paper. She sat on the plush chair and looked around. Never in her life had she stayed anywhere like this. She hastened to hang the lovely dress in the wardrobe, stroking the soft wool and arranging the scarf around the neck. The shoes sat on the floor of the wardrobe and the hat and gloves on the dressing table.

On the way to the bus station she'd find a hairdresser's, then be back on the bus and home in time to make Jack's supper. Her heart raced with the thrill of the adventure and she couldn't wait until she was back here tomorrow in this beautiful room of her own.

When the bus stopped at the bottom of the street Ella's head was spinning with all the excitement of the day. From Edna at the dress shop to the blazing fireplace at The Three Tuns – the images were clear and bright in her mind, propelling her past the houses where her gossip friends stood scratching their heads at her absence. But she was so busy thinking she barely noticed their puzzled faces.

There was hardly any time to make Jack's supper so she opened up a tin of beans and fried a couple of pork sausages. He'd probably complain but she'd make it up for him tomorrow when she'd leave him a slap-up roast beef supper while she was away – for a whole night on her own. She still had to make up a good excuse, so when Jack came stumbling in complaining of a headache her heart fell. Surely he wasn't going to fall ill on her so she couldn't go. She sat him down by the fire with a pot of tea and two aspirin tablets. He was asleep in an instant; snoring like one of those motorbikes the young'uns rode fast round the Lanes.

While there was time, she went upstairs and packed a small overnight bag with some makeup, her nightdress and knickers, nylons and her newest girdle. Then she reached up into the back corner of the wardrobe shelf and took down her father's box. The wallet with the Empire State Building lay on top of his scarf and gloves. With her heart beating she took the wallet and slipped it under her girdle in the overnight bag, then a lovely pearl necklace he'd brought back from France. He was the only one that would've appreciated the adventure she was about to embark on and she decided she'd have a drink in his name while she was sitting in front of that fireplace in the hotel lobby.

Jack winged and whined so much during supper she thought she'd scream, but she held it in and announced at the end. "Our Irma from Bishop Auckland's poorly,"[8] she said casually.

Jack just kept chewing his sausage.

"Did yer hear me?" she repeated.

"What's that?"

"Our Irma. She's poorly."

"Who's Irma?"

"Me second cousin – she lives in Bishop Auckland. She wants me to stay there tomorrow night," said Ella slipping in the important part of the message.

Jack's large, hollow eyes looked up at Ella. "Why how'll you do that?"

"I'll get the bus there. It's just for one night."

"I'll be on me own," he said. "And I'm not feeling too clever."

"I'll tell Olive to come in to get yer tea for yer," Ella said, impatiently.

"Yer'd better wait till next week," he said. "I'll feel better then."

---

[8] sick

Ella's nerves were screeching. "I'm gannin' tomorrow and that's that. She's expecting me."

Jack went up to bed with a long face, like an injured bloodhound. But she wouldn't be taken in with his act. It was done. Now all she had to do was get his food ready for tomorrow and then she'd be off on the great adventure. After she'd peeled potatoes, got the beef ready, made Jack's sandwiches and laid out his clothes for two days she stopped for a moment and wondered if George would ever realize just how much effort it had taken for her to accept his invitation. Still, it would be worth it.

The next day she got Jack off to work though he was still protesting about his headache, then went round to Olive's and gave her instructions about Jack's tea and breakfast the next day.

"I've left Friday's bait[9] in the pantry," she said, avoiding Olive's questioning eyes.

At last Ella walked down the street holding her overnight bag. The gossips were out again and she heard whispers of, "She's staying with her cousin in Bishop Auckland." She stopped at Jesse Nelson's house where the shrunken little woman stood with Iris Hawkins.

"Gannin to yer cousin's then," said Jesse, her toothless mouth stretching into a crumpled smile.

"Aye, she's suffering with angina," said Ella pitying the shabby woman but feeling a slight sense of annoyance that she'd squandered an opportunity Ella would have killed for. Jesse could have been the one going to see George but she didn't even have the sense to look after herself and he wouldn't want a shabby old scarecrow coming to his fancy garden party. "Anyway, I'd best be off," she said, impatiently. The bus was due in ten minutes and she wanted to be in good time.

---

[9] packed lunch

Ella had a lovely day in Durham. After she dropped off her bag at the hotel she got her hair done at a small shop near the marketplace. Looking in the mirror she felt transformed. Her brown hair, though streaked with grey, looked shiny and full with its smooth curls. Eileen's in Hetton always dried the life out of her hair but this place had worked wonders.

Elated, she made her way through the streets and up towards the cathedral. She marvelled as she looked up at the magnificent towers framed against the pale blue spring sky. There were even tourists there – families taking pictures of each other with the great building in the background. One man asked Ella to snap a picture of him and his wife and two bairns and she was excited to oblige. Ella had never felt so alive and vowed to herself that she'd do this again. She'd save her money and come through to Durham, stay in her own hotel room and buy some nice things for herself. Maybe she'd even convince Jack to come.

Inside the shadowy interior of the cathedral she got talking to a very distinguished old man. She reckoned he was about sixty, eleven years older than her, but he was tall and had the nicest head of white hair with a dashing silver moustache. He told her he was a retired pilot and now he worked as a guide at the cathedral showing visitors around. "Of course I had to learn a lot of history to do the job but it was worth it," he said, looking so pointedly at her hair she felt the colour come to her cheeks.

"Still – it must've been interesting," she said, admiring his dark blue robe.

"We all have to wear these," he said laughing. "It makes me feel like the vicar."

She laughed, surprised at finding herself talking to a strange man. He stretched his hand out to shake her hand. "Colonel Ralph Carson," he said. "Are you staying here in Durham?"

"At the Three Tuns," she blurted, suddenly embarrassed she'd told him everything. "I'm meeting my son tomorrow in Darlington."

"Lovely," he said. "You must be looking forward to that."

"I am," she said. "I'm very proud of him."

"I sometimes go to the Three Tuns for a drink," he said. "Mebbe I'll see you there tonight."

Ella felt a small pounding in her head. Nothing like this had ever happened to her before. "Yes – maybe," she said. "But I'd better go now." He smiled and nodded when she looked back at him and then she found herself back outside in the bright sunlight, cheeks flushed and heart racing.

On the way back to the hotel she stopped in at the bustling marketplace, thronging with Friday crowds. A young man was up on a wagon trying to sell knives. She knew these fly-by-night types. They'd show you a good set, then sell you rubbish and you couldn't get your money back once you'd handed it over. But her eye was attracted to a clothing stall nearby. Hanging on a long rack were some beautiful printed blouses in bright shades of pink and purple. She could wear one tonight with her grey skirt and the pearl necklace her father had brought her from New York. She bought the last one in her size and then picked up some lavender bath salts and a couple of extra pairs of nylons just in case of accidents. When the marketplace clock struck five she was off back to the hotel realizing she hadn't worried about Jack for the entire day.

After a long, luxurious bath in the lavender scented water; she put on some makeup and dressed herself in the grey skirt and the new blouse. She looked like a different person when she stared into the wardrobe mirror and wondered why she'd waited all this time to step away from the street and really enjoy herself. She thought of all those wasted years of gossiping and almost cried at how stupid she'd been, but rather than let the tears ruin her foundation, she pulled herself together and made her way downstairs in time to enjoy a nice supper of shepherd's pie and braised parsnips.

There was a bar inside the residents' lounge and, though Ella had never gone for a drink alone, she had no trouble walking up and asking for a gin and tonic. That's what all the glamorous women on the telly asked for. There was a nice song playing on the radio – something called *Up on the Roof* – and Ella went to sit on the upholstered armchair by the fireplace and raise her drink in a silent toast to her father. The drink was bubbly and delicious. After a couple of sips her head felt light and happy but she had to struggle to keep her eyes open. She'd best be careful, for tomorrow she'd have to be on the ten o'clock train to Darlington to get there by eleven. This would be her one and only drink and then she'd make her way upstairs and have an early night. By eight o'clock she was ready to turn in, though she did feel a bit disappointed that Ralph hadn't shown up. Oh well, she thought, tomorrow was going to be exciting and she wanted to look fresh and rested.

As she elbowed her way through the crowd of drinkers at the bar she felt a light tap on her shoulder and turned to see Ralph looking even more suave than she remembered, in a light checked jacket and dark green cravat. His hair and moustache were brushed to shiny perfection and he shrugged his shoulders in bewilderment. "Surely you can't be leaving so soon, Ella."

She forgot that she'd introduced herself to him. "Well I do have to get the train quite early," she said, feeling her neck go very hot.

"Just have one before you go up," he said, indicating the empty chair beside him.

"All right – I'll have a bitter lemon," she said.

In an instant he was up at the bar, ordering the drink. Ella looked around, hoping that no one from Belton was here among the Friday crowds, then seeing nobody familiar, she sat back as Ralph descended carrying his beer and two other glasses. "Gin and bitter lemon," he said, holding the glass out to her. She was about to protest that she'd actually asked for just the bitter lemon but decided not to make a thing out of it.

"I like a chaser with my beer," he said, sipping at the small glass of whisky and then gulping the beer. "All the boys in B-Brigade enjoyed a good shot of Johnny Walker."

Ella had never laughed so much. He told so many stories about the other pilots and all the scrapes they'd got themselves into in France and Belgium during the war. Of course he was one of the more experienced pilots and he'd had to teach the young lads a lot about flying *and* life. Soon one drink led to another and before she knew it, Ella's head was spinning as if she was rushing along on an express train. Then it all happened at once. First she heard him say in a slurry kind of way. "I must tell you that blouse looks very fetching."

Next she felt his hand on her thigh, working its way upward, but her arms were so heavy she felt powerless to stop it. His face was close to hers and she stared at the hand as if it was a creature separate from him. The next terrible event was that when his hand was all the way up her skirt and she was just sitting there like a block of wood, she looked up and saw that brazen hussy Rita Hawkins standing only a few yards away at the bar with Jimmy Bishop. Luckily Rita hadn't seen her yet so Ella stood up suddenly and knocked Ralph's beer over onto the table and right down his trousers, then onto his good leather shoes.

"I'm sorry," she said, handing him a clean handkerchief from her bag then backing away from him. "I don't feel very well." Wasting no time she rushed out in the other direction away from Rita, into the lobby and along the hallway to her room. Once inside she ran straight to the toilet and vomited up everything – meat, parsnips and all.

What a stupid fool she'd been, she thought, catching sight of her bright red sweaty face. She'd risked being seen by that blabbermouth Rita who visited every house on the street to collect the telly payments. It wouldn't take five minutes before Ella's story spread down the street like the jungle telegraph and then she'd be the talk of the neighbourhood.

Relieved at her narrow escape, Ella washed her face and changed into her nighty. She climbed into the cool sheets and was asleep within minutes.

Next morning Ella awoke and sat up in bed with a jolt. It was already half past eight and she wasn't even ready. She'd never slept in this late. Not since she was a girl and that was rare – what with her mother always poking her in the back at six o'clock in the morning. She bolted out of bed and took a good look at herself. The lovely hairstyle had lost a bit of its lustre and her eyes were a bit red, but she set about washing herself vigorously and applying a coat of foundation. With a bit of lipstick and a few flicks of her comb she was back to normal. The slippery lining of the dress slid down over her body and the scarf was a silken feather around her neck. Next she placed the hat over her hair and slipped on the soft shoes. This person looking back at her didn't belong on Crag Street. For once Ella felt proud of herself after all the years of hearing her mother call her plain and stout. She took one last look at the room and committed it to memory before she left. Her own room that was waiting for her any time she chose to come and use it. Shutting the door, she decided that she'd need a taxi to get to the station in time for the train.

Ella wasn't thinking about George on the way to Darlington. She sat back in the carriage and thought about Jack. After last night's escapade with Ralph she'd realized how much she appreciated her husband. He was a clean man. That was important to her. And though he had very little hair, he had fine dry skin – not clammy or sweaty like some men. He liked to wear after-shave lotion and Ella appreciated the little scented whiffs he gave off when he passed by her. He never burped or farted in public like Olive's husband. Olive said her man farted so much after a heavy supper their bedroom would explode if you lit a match at night. Also, though Jack sometimes whined a bit, he didn't interfere with her or put his hands on her like the other brutes. He was a gentle old soul and Ella's heart caught in her throat as she thought of him. When she got back she'd cook all the things he liked and spoil him a bit.

The train began to slow down. Darlington was the next stop and Ella looked out the window to see if George was waiting on the platform. When she climbed down from the train there was no sign of him so she made her way towards the exit, through the gate and onto the street outside. She checked her watch. It was five to eleven so she sat down on a wooden bench to wait.

The station was a busy place. Cars swished by as well as scooters ridden by young people in those army-style parkas. Some people came running to catch a train, checking their watch, their coats flying out behind them while others walked at a leisurely pace reading the newspaper. Ella was just beginning to wonder if George was coming when a black car slowed down at the kerb. Ella's heart skipped as the door opened and George stepped out in a smart navy suit, his fair hair swept back and gleaming. He smiled a nervous, wobbly kind of smile, then held out his arm. At once Ella got up and took it and he escorted her to the passenger side, opened the door and she got in just the way she'd seen Joan Crawford do it on those Sunday afternoon films.

"You look really nice, Ella," he said, closing the door and she sank back into the leather seats, her heart racing with joy.

Ella sailed through the garden party, a lovely affair in one of those country inns. She'd even learned how to handle a teacup and a plate of sandwiches without spilling anything. And what sandwiches. There was egg and cress, cucumber and salmon – but not the salmon from a tin – and some meat paste the waiter called pate – made from duck parts. She loved every one of them and even held out her little finger as she nibbled at them. George urged her to slot her arm in at his elbow as he toured around the crowd introducing her as his favourite aunty since his mother was indisposed. When he got up to make his speech he left her at a table with the rich widow of an iron foundry owner and the wife of a local politician. They admired her dress and even asked her where she shopped.

"It's a lovely little boutique," she said using a word she'd seen in the Woman's Weekly fashion pages. "Down by the County Hotel."

"I just love those darling little shops," said the politician's wife. "Such personal service."

"Yes," agreed Ella. "You must ask for Edna if you go there."

The two ladies nodded their heads and just then a hush came over the crowd as George took his place. Ella observed his new confidence. The way he held his shoulders back, his chest swelling and his chin held high. He was a handsome lad – there was no mistaking that and she'd seen to it that he'd been able to buy the best clothes to make the right impression otherwise he'd have been skulking around in his cheap suit. If there was one thing she'd learned this past few days it was that good clothes make a world of difference – especially among these circles where appearance counted for everything. She'd also learned how much she missed Jack and was surprised to realize how much she wanted to get back to him.

Ella had been so lost in thoughts about Jack she'd missed most of George's speech and only caught the ending. He raised his arms up in triumph as he delivered his last few lines.

"And so between the years 1957 and 1963, no less than 264 collieries were closed, while the number of miners fell by nearly 30 per cent. During this six-year period, Scotland lost 39 per cent of its pits, while 30 per cent of those in South Wales, Northumberland and Durham were wiped out. We have lived with these hardships ladies and gentlemen and our workers have suffered. That is why we ask for your help. A strong union will fight to secure jobs and ensure a strong future for our industry. This great country was built by the sweat of its workers. We cannot abandon them now in their hour of need. Please donate generously and do your part to keep Durham and the north-east strong."

Applause thundered through the room and suddenly George was the center of a crowd. People patted him on the back and shook his hand.

"You must be very proud of him," said the factory owner's widow.

"Oh I am," said Ella. "He's a canny lad and he's destined for greatness."

The two ladies nodded their heads and Ella felt more gratified than she ever had. It was possible, she realized, to be completely happy and content with your lot in life. *My cup runneth over* was the thought that kept flashing across her mind. So that suddenly the idea of gossiping felt mean and spiteful.

She felt a tap on her shoulder and looked up to see George flushed with the thrill of victory. "How was it?" he asked, beaming from ear to ear.

"Lovely," she said, feeling her eyes tear up. "Right from your heart."

"I can't thank you enough, Ella." He slid his hand into hers and squeezed her palm. "I may need you again some time. Would that be all right?"

"Aye," she said, "I can truly say I've thoroughly enjoyed myself."

"I hope so," he said, offering his arm again.

She got up and made her way out with him, noting the admiring glances of the other ladies. She'd always known that one day her luck would change and she hadn't been wrong. Now all she had to worry about was what to make for Jack's supper.

1966

33

Rita locked the shop door and put the keys in her handbag. She stood in front of the plate glass window, looking at her reflection. The woman that looked back at her was trim and tailored in a neat red suit, her hair brushed in shiny wings that framed her face. The stiff blonde beehive was gone and with it the old, common Rita. What a difference it made! She felt like one of those air-hostesses in a romance novel – the type with cascading chestnut hair who fell for the pilot. *Classy and professional* were the two words she'd use to describe herself now. New look, new life and new hope. She'd found a good hairdresser in Houghton who'd quickly advised her to go back to her natural red-brown colour.

Her eyes took in the whole span of the window display with its shining row of black and grey televisions. The blank screens waited for a quick turn of the dials to jolt into life, bringing glamor and magic into dull lives. Poor sods! This was all some folks had. It was their only view of life outside the North East. In the centre of the display sat the latest deluxe model with teak casing and roll-around doors. She'd had her eye on this one for the last two months. When she made enough money to buy her own house she'd get it. She'd only allow the best of everything in her home. There'd be no cheap, inferior merchandise.

The shop was hers – well almost. Jimmy's letter had come just last week from Torquay. He'd only been there three weeks and had already fallen head over heels for the landlady of his bed and breakfast. She was a widow who had, from the start, given Jimmy extra rashers of bacon at breakfast time and had gone out of her way to serve hot Cornish pasties and real Cumberland sausage for supper to make Jimmy feel at home. His letter had been all bubbly and happy as if he was a young lad again:

> ... Rita you wouldn't believe it down here. It's summer all year round and it's that clean you could eat yer supper off the pavement. There are even real palm trees along the streets and the sea's so blue you can actually swim in it. Now Doris – she's been very good to me and she's a smasher and all – used to be a cabaret singer before she was married. We've got so much to talk about and then she plays the piano of an evening and we all have a good singsong in the guests' sitting room. I haven't had such a good time in years and so Rita you won't mind looking after the shop until I decide if I'm staying here. I always knew you were interested in it...

She was so interested she moved three suitcases and four wooden crates of her bits and pieces from her parents' house and into the small flat above Jimmy's shop. Her Dad donated the padded cocktail bar.

"Get that bloody piece of rubbish out of this house for good," he said, ignoring Iris's protests. "I'll be glad to see the back of that sodding thing. Yer canna even balance a dozen beer bottles on it. It's made for wine-drinking fairies."

Now he could have his Union meetings at the house without fear of ridicule and he'd lose the nickname, Cock-Tailed Walter.

Rita also had the use of Jimmy's old Austin Traveller. Of course he'd taken the Rover down to Torquay – and today she was taking Maggie and the girls to the ballroom dancing finals at Brentmoor. It was the least she could do. Since the incident at the bus station she'd become closer to Maggie. She loved treating the two girls and it helped ease the guilt she felt when she looked at little blind Pearl.

She'd also considered taking on Hazel, Maggie's oldest girl, to do some collecting on Fridays. Hazel was different – a solitary girl given to taking off on long walks up the hill or along the railway tracks. She was a good looker too; tall and slender with long black wavy hair, honey coloured skin and the iciest blue eyes Rita had ever seen. What's more, she was wasted in her job at the newsagent's on the High Street. With the loan of a few smart clothes she could be a real asset to the business. Rita had no more time to do the collecting. Her plans to expand the company would take every spare minute – reading trade magazines, poring over business manuals at the library, talking to contacts on the phone. She wanted to be ready to take over when Jimmy decided to hand over the keys.

She turned the key of the old car and pulled out the choke. The engine revved into action and, with a thrust of the gear stick, she was sputtering down the High Street, past the church and the chemist and all the other dark shop windows. At six o' clock everything was closed for the day except the pubs. The Hare and Hounds was already filling up with early drinkers. If it wasn't the telly it was the booze or the dog track. What else was there to do here?

It had been a relief for Rita to leave home. They'd lived on top of each other for over twenty years and everyone in the family got on her nerves. Now she didn't have to listen to her Dad's insults when she dressed herself up or have the union business rammed down her throat every waking minute. Her brothers lost no time taking over her bedroom. Only her mother looked hurt and abandoned.

"Don't get yourself into a state, Mam," Rita told her. "I'm only a mile away and you can call in any time for a cup of tea and a bit of quiet." That seemed to calm Iris down a bit and she even slipped her a bag full of new sheets, towels and tee towels she'd been storing for Rita's wedding day.

Today Rita had instructed Maggie to meet her at the bottom of the street to avoid the gossips. In the early hours after supper they were usually out in full force. In fact, last Monday evening, when she moved out of the house, Ella Danby, Olive Coombes and a few others had taken note of every stick of furniture being taken into the moving van.

"Yer'll know the inside of me flat better than I will," she commented as she walked by the little knot of women, "There'll be no need to invite you over for a cup of tea then."

Approaching the end of the street she could see Maggie and the two girls, Hazel, dark haired and dusky and Pearl, who was thirteen years old now, with the palest blonde curls and the sweetest voice this side of the Tyne.

Rita swept up to the kerb and they rushed forward to meet her. Pearl and Hazel got into the back seat and Maggie joined Rita in the front.

"You girls look lovely," said Rita, noting their freshly styled hair and shining faces, "I see your Mam's been curling your hair."

Maggie smiled, "It's all thanks to you, Rita, I don't know what I'd do without the clothes you've given us. We'd be dressed like beggars."

"Your girls would look bonny whatever they were wearing, they've got natural beauty, not like me, I've got to wear a ton of make-up to look half decent," she said setting off down the street.

"Eeh, Rita, you've always been a good looker – I mean all the men fancy you, but you're too good for anyone round here," said Maggie staring straight at her. "And you've got that much class since you did your hair. You look like yer just stepped off the London train,".

"Thanks, hinny, you've just made my day." Rita glanced sideways at Maggie. The dark circles under her eyes were deeper and the lines around her mouth more tight and drawn. Today she'd persuade Maggie to go to the doctor's whether she liked it or not.

The Pitman's Daughter

Once they reached Brentmoor the streetlights changed from blue to orange, filling the car with a warm electric glare. Rita wondered why some villages had blue lights and other orange, but she had always felt a sense of excitement at night when the lights were on.

The dance hall was at the top of the High Street and people were already crowded around the entrance.

"What's it like Hazel?" begged Pearl, when the car slowed down outside the building.

"It's a big, brick building but it's lit with golden lights and people are piling in the front door," said Rita. "It looks like we're in good time."

Rita knew the lady at the front door and so they swept past the rest of the queue and were shown to the second row of seats.

"Our Sandra – that's my second cousin – was champion here for three years in a row. They think the world of her – always give the family good seats and they ask after her all the time."

"Where is she now?" asked Maggie, fumbling with her handbag.

"Down in London for the summer then she's working for a big shipping line in the autumn – entertaining on them Mediterranean cruises."

"Eeh, that sounds so glamorous," said Hazel, "She's lucky."

"Hazel, it just takes determination and you can go anywhere you want," said Rita.

"You girls listen to Rita," said Maggie, "and you won't end up like your mam."

"Shurrup, mam, you're not as bad as you think," said Hazel, squeezing her mother's arm.

"What's happening now?" asked Pearl, craning her neck and searching the room with blind eyes.

"Sorry, flower," said Rita, "we won't forget about you any more. The band's just tuning up and the announcer's clearing his throat, adjusting his bow tie and walking up to the microphone." She turned to Maggie and whispered, "Recognize him – that's Charlie Carter all done up in a dickie bow tie – fancied himself as a singer – Jimmy told me he went down to London and ended up at the Elephant and Castle singing backup to a striptease act – lasted two weeks and he was back. Did ten years at Butlins in Filey as Uncle Charlie, judging knobbly knee contests and then they let him go the day after his sixtieth birthday."

The band swept into a smooth version of *Come dance with me* and Pearl began to sway with the rhythm, clasping her hands tightly in front of her, as if she could feel every note.

Rita dug into her handbag and brought out a box of violet cachous. She offered them around.

"All the elegant touches," said Maggie, slipping one into her mouth. "You're a real lady."

The dancers swirled onto the floor for the foxtrot in a flurry of organza and tulle. The women's hair swept up slickly into elaborate buns or teased into gigantic pouffes fixed with glittering combs and pins. Their faces were painted like china dolls with glossy red lips. The men looked suave in black tails and white bow ties.

"The dressed, the dresses – what are they like?" asked Pearl.

"Like a rainbow, flower. All pink and green and orange – like sucking a bag of sweets all at once."

"That's beautiful," said Maggie, "you have a lovely way with words, Rita. Just like someone else I used to know."

"Who's that?" asked Rita, watching Maggie's faraway look as the band played *Smoke Gets in Your Eyes*.

"I'll tell you another time, pet."

The dancers finally reached the waltz section of the program and the music slowed down. Then the lights dimmed and the mirror ball began to rotate on the ceiling sending little dots of white scattering into the darkness and dappling the glittering sequined gowns with tiny rainbows of light.

"That's gorgeous," cried Hazel, clapping her hands.

"What is, what is?" cried Pearl.

"It looks like a whole roomful of white snowflakes and feathers," said Rita who leaned across to Maggie and whispered, "I could kill for a drink."

The band had just begun to play *Autumn Leaves* when Maggie got up quickly and asked where the ladies toilet was. She looked purposeful standing there holding her handbag in the crook of her arm, tightly against her hip and she motioned to Rita to follow her. "Come on then. The girls will be all right here."

Rita followed her into the small bar outside the main ballroom.

"Let me buy you summat for a change, Rita – I had a good night at the dogs on Tuesday."

They stood with their drinks, watching the dancers swirl across the floodlit floor, their brightly coloured dresses leaving traces of colour in the darkness.

"Autumn leaves," hummed Maggie, "I always feel sad when I think of autumn – it's a time when things go away isn't it? I used to watch the birds when they flew away down south for the winter and I wished I was going too – to get away from the cold and the damp."

"That's where Jimmy is. Walking by the palm trees, soaking up the sun and taking his new lady friend to the Black and White Minstrel show every Sunday. He's even taken up Old Time dancing. Says he's never been so happy in his life."

"I'm glad for him. He's had his share of troubles. His wife suffered that much before she passed away," said Maggie.

"I doubt we'll ever see him back here. He's landed himself in paradise and there's nowt left for him up here," said Rita feeling a little pang of sadness knowing he was gone for good.

"Just like every decent person from these parts. Sooner or later they all go away. You'll go too Rita. And it'll be soon. You're already moving up in the world."

"Sometimes I feel like a wild animal in a cage ready to burst out and fight the world," said Rita, "But I'll always help you with the girls – with money and all that – don't ever worry."

"As long as Jordy doesn't find out."

"I know he can't stand me," said Rita, chewing at the plastic cocktail spear. "He's always giving me the evil eye."

"He hates everybody except his bloody mother – and Pearl, of course. He comes in, eats his supper, then climbs up into the attic and just reads the bible or rummages around all the old boxes."

"What's he looking for?" said Rita laughing. "Your secret lovers?"

Maggie drained the rest of her drink and began to fumble in her handbag again, "Give us a tab, Rita. I need a smoke."

Rita took out a slim, green pack, "Sorry Maggie – did I say something wrong?"

Maggie leaned forward as Rita held out her lighter, and then she took a deep drag of the cigarette, blowing out the smoke with a big sigh. She leaned across to Rita, "When Jordy was on the nightshift – I'd wait until he was down the street and then I'd go up into the attic and meet the man I told you about."

"Get away with you," said Rita suddenly feeling a bit chilled.

"It was like heaven up there."

"Sounds like a line from a Hollywood film," said Rita, trying to work out who lived near to Maggie.

"And it was all worth it – every minute of it."

Rita could only stare at Maggie in disbelief.

"You think I'm a slut or summat – I can tell by your face," said Maggie.

"No – no Maggie – the man's just as much to blame…"

"He didn't make me do it. I went because I wanted to – I loved being with him. You only go around once yer know."

"But Maggie, all men are just after one thing, then when they get it…"

"No, Rita – not all men – there's some good ones – believe me. Me da's a lovely old man, gentle and kind. And I met a soldier over twenty years ago. He was a real charmer. Trouble is they all went away and left me with Jordy, the nastiest piece of work in the world."

Rita was only half listening. She was still trying to work out who would have crossed through the attics to meet up with Maggie.

"One day you'll fall in love, flower. Don't close yersel away from men. Yer'll miss out on the best things in life and yer canna protect yersel from pain all yer life," said Maggie, squeezing Rita's hand. "Now I'll tell you a secret if you promise never to tell anyone."

"Swear on me great-grandma's grave," said Rita, holding her hand up to the barman for another drink.

"Jordy isn't Hazel's father."

"I knew it," said Rita, taking another drink. "She's so different from the others."

"Her dad was a Yankee soldier named Chuck from Wisconsin. He was half Swedish and half Ojibway Indian."

"Of course with that hair and those eyes. My God – does she know?"

Maggie's eyes were filling with tears. Rita squeezed her shoulder. "What is it, pet? You can tell me everything."

"I've tried to tell her – but I've put it off so long she'll be angry at me for hiding it from her. She'll have to know sooner or later though, she's a restless lass – always searching for something far away." She stopped and took a long pull of the cigarette, then wiped her palm across her nose, "If anything ever happens to me Rita, swear you'll tell her about it if I haven't."

"Don't talk so morbid, Maggie. You've a long way to go yet."

"I have this feeling I'm not going to live long, Rita. I always felt small and weak – like I could be wiped out easy, just like a smudge of dirt on a window."

"Maggie, don't say that. Come on, let's hadaway back to the girls – yer'll have the both of us bubbling[10] before long."

Rita walked behind Maggie, studying her thin shoulders and pale, wispy hair. The dancers whirled around the floor, flinging their arms in the dramatic poses of the paso doble, but to Rita they looked fierce and grotesque. Maggie's words had brought back that old childhood terror of the strange, sickly secret things that had made her dizzy with fear; sex and marriage, childbirth and passion – they were complicated, messy and painful.

She longed for the safety of the shop and the comforting smell of money.

---

[10] crying

1970

34

When the renovations on the house at Roker Avenue were finished, Rita sat back on the tapestry sofa and realized she was meant to live alone.

She gazed in awe at the butter yellow walls, the sage velvet curtains, the walnut sideboard with its solid brass carriage clock and the arrangement of Waterford crystal reflected in the mirror. And as she drained a solitary glass of champagne she admired the burst of tangerine tulips in the centre of the polished occasional table and made a silent toast to her new life. Hell, now she could afford to down the whole bottle if she wanted.

She felt so peaceful here. In a way she'd never felt in the cramped flat above the shop or the messy chaos of Crag Street. Each carefully chosen picture frame or china cup was a reminder of success. To touch the cool, delicate surfaces. To enjoy the luxury of fresh flowers, polished wood and starched damask sheets. Every piece of finery gave her so much pleasure yet asked for nothing in return. It was safe and painless to love material things.

Business had been good. Jimmy taught her everything he knew about T.V. rentals and since she'd opened up her fourth shop in Sunderland, she'd moved her offices into the city centre on Fawcett Street.

Every day she drove down Roker Avenue, loving the grand old houses with their solid mahogany and stained glass doors. So when the house came up for sale six months ago she called Johnny Hill, the estate agent, to show her around. Johnny was in his early thirties – slick, successful and persuasive with a liking for flashy ties. He drove with one manicured hand on the wheel and the other draped across the back of her seat.

"You and me we'd be magic together, Rita," he said, but even though she'd managed to hold him off, the tension between them smouldered in the air.

Of course when she first looked at the house it was a mess. Hadn't her mam always said, "When yer move into a house it's ten to one the people before yer were pigs." The floors were covered in cracked linoleum, the old wood was painted shit brown and a thick furring of dust covered everything. Apparently the previous owners were an old couple that just smoked and read newspapers all day until their unemployed son had eventually carted the poor souls off to a nursing home and sold the house.

Rita bought the place for a song and promptly hired a crew to restore its original beauty. The carpenters and painters were unused to taking orders from a woman and, at first kept asking to speak with Mr Hawkins over the specifications, but after a few weeks of receiving prompt cash payments from Rita they were like putty in her hands. Rita always paid in cash. Peeling off the notes one by one as if to keep track of every pound. For each one had been earned by dedication and hard work. She'd slaved night and day for the past six years and discovered a thirst for money that shocked her. Now it was time to enjoy some of it.

Six months of elocution lessons at Miss Pauline Draper's voice studio had prepared her to move into the business world. All the rough edges smoothed, vowels rounded, accent cultivated until she stripped away the commonness and only said *bugger* in extreme emergencies.

She'd been living in the house for three months now and leaving at eight o'clock to get to the office but today she had to get out half an hour earlier to look at a small bungalow on the sea front at Seaburn. Her parents had always wanted to retire to the seaside and spend their days strolling by along the front. Retirement for her dad was still a few years away but Rita thought it might be a good investment to buy now so they could start spending weekends there.

Her gloves lay on the antique walnut table in the front hall below an arrangement of purple irises. She'd first fallen in love with the entrance hall with its grand oak banister, the black and white mosaic tile floor and the stained glass panel on the door. Today the morning sun shone through it, spilling a rainbow of colour onto the polished wood floor.

Grasping the gloves in one hand she checked her reflection in the mirror and pulled one heavy wing of hair behind her ear. Satisfied, she walked to the back of the house, past the formal dining room and through the small, neat kitchen with her teapot collection lined up on the Welsh dresser. The new Rover was parked in the back. It was a gleaming bottle green with camel leather upholstery. God, she loved the smell of it and the sound of the engine purring to life when she turned the key.

It was early March and the sky was gorgeous – clear blue and no trace of the coastal frets that usually blew in from the sea. At the end of the avenue was the North Sea, a rippled sheet of grey-green, stretching out to France and Holland and the sign she'd always looked at as a child. The post pointed out to sea saying Paris 300 miles, Amsterdam 450 miles. Along the front the brightly coloured chalets were all closed up for the winter. In the summer they sold winkles, cockles and prawns. You doused them with vinegar and ate them with salty fingers. Her dad always loved the whelks – great rubbery things you'd pick out of the shell with a pin.

"They make me sick," her mam always said, "just like eating a live worm or slug."

Good times, Rita remembered, looking at the white framework of the Big Dipper at the end of the promenade. Good times when the taste of a toffee apple, a stick of candy floss or a good scream on the ghost train was all it took to make the day seem perfect. She remembered when her dad took her on the Horror House ride for the first time – just climbed into the too-small car and put his arm tight around her shoulders. She felt safe then. That was a happy time when Da was the biggest hero in her world and not someone that picked on her every move like when she came back from London. He didn't speak to her for a week and when Jimmy left her with the shop her Da flew into a rage. "What did yer do to get that then? – Jimmy Bishop doesn't pay a high price for nowt."

Rita remembered her mam standing in between them, her hands held up in a panic. Her dad went on, "Don't ever give us any of it – I'll nivver tek a penny from a painted whore."

That was when her mam slapped him square across the face and he stood there holding his swelling cheek. Rita was speechless.

"Don't you ever talk to your own daughter like that," Iris screamed, "You're nothing but a miserable old bugger that canna stand to see a woman do summat for hersel'. Well it's the seventies now and women don't have to wait for a man to mek all the money. It's called women's liberation."

At that point all Rita's old admiration for her mother came flooding back. Good old Mam. Those Women's Weekly magazines had taught her something after all.

The incident was quickly swept under the carpet but Rita soon noticed a change between her mam and dad. He looked at her in a different way. As if he were measuring her up, checking the way he spoke to her. He even started to help with the dishes. Things were changing and none too soon.

When Rita swept into the office at two minutes to nine, Hazel was already making a cup of tea. Hazel had been working for Rita for three years now and was a real peach. She'd even moved into the flat over the shop after Rita moved out. Rita would love to have moved Hazel's whole family out of Crag Street but they were bound to Jordy with a strange combination of fear and loyalty that Rita could never understand.

"Get Johnny Hill on the phone, Hazel," said Rita hanging her coat on the brass coat stand.

"You're finally gonna give in then," laughed Hazel.

"When hell freezes over," said Rita touching up her lipstick, "Tell him to arrange an appointment to view the bungalow at Seaburn."

"Right," Hazel answered, pouring the tea. "Want a cup?"

"I could kill for one, flower," said Rita, "or as Miss Draper would say 'Why thank you darling, I'm terribly thirsty.' Orange pekoe, is it?"

"Tetley's best," said Hazel holding up her little finger as she passed Rita the striped mug. "Me mam sent some Eccles cakes. Says you're not looking after yerself."

"She's a gem. I'll have to pop by and say hello," said Rita, cradling the cup with her chilled hands.

"Aye but not when me da's there – strangers aren't welcome in our house any more," said Hazel. "He just sits there glowering at them like a big black crow, until they go away."

"Your poor mam," said Rita. "Let's take her out for the day on Saturday. Do a bit of shopping, have a bite somewhere. Go and see that new Peter Sellers' film."

"Smashing," said Hazel, "I'll tell her."

When Hazel brought the paper and the morning post in to Rita she hovered around the desk more than usual.

"Are you waiting for something, chuck?" said Rita, fanning the letters out across her desk.

"In the paper today – an old neighbour of ours."

"Someone from Crag Street in the Sunderland Echo?"

"Page three – far left column."

Rita quickly turned the page, straining her eyes to find a familiar name. "Where – where?" she asked.

Hazel pointed to a small article with the headline "Prominent Union Leader involved in breach of promise suit..."

"George," gasped Rita, "George Nelson."

"Dead on, love," said Hazel, "It seems he was engaged to marry a Miss Annabelle Stott, beloved daughter of Sam Stott, shipbuilder of

Newcastle and he called it off – three months before the wedding."

"The ruthless bastard," said Rita. "He goes from one girl to another."

"Did you ever go with him?" said Hazel, her brows knit in a puzzled expression.

"My dad had hopes for us," said Rita remembering the old times. George reading love poems at Ida's, sitting across the table from her in the bookstore in Durham, whispering into her ear at Marion's wedding, making a passionate speech in front of the crowd of union men, holding her while she cried at the hotel in Luton. He kept cropping up like a disease. She'd think she was clear of him then suddenly he'd come into her life again, spreading discontent in his wake.

The phone rang in the outer office and Hazel went to get it. "Supper at Davis's wine bar tonight?" Rita shouted after her, forcing herself into some kind of routine.

"I'll be there," said Hazel.

Rita glanced back at the article and read, "Mr Nelson stated, 'I have dedicated my life to the union cause and I regret there is no place in my life for personal relationships if we are to succeed in our battle with the Tories."

"Typical," sighed Rita, sitting back in her chair and wishing she hadn't read it. The mere mention of his name had disrupted the quiet order of her life.

By six thirty that evening Rita and Hazel had each finished a plate of scampi and chips and moved on to glasses of white wine. Wine bars were still a novelty, attracting young suit-clad office workers and mini-skirted secretaries. The Monday evening supper together had become almost a ritual with Hazel and Rita, a chance to loosen up over a few glasses of wine and chat up some of the local men. Usually everything went fine until they found

Rita owned her own business. That's when they sloped off with one lame excuse or another.

"I'm not that frightening," said Rita after two trainee accountants had rushed off in a great hurry to catch a train.

Hazel was on her fourth glass of wine. She always talked more when she was tipsy – giving advice on the state of Rita's personal life. "It's not that, Rita – it's just – just that you're too much for them. Too independent."

"So you think I should play stupid – bat my eyelids and say "Ooh you're so interesting" when really they're boring the tits off me."

"Miss Draper, Miss Draper," said Hazel wagging her finger.

"I know – let's forget about Miss Draper – I'm talking about no dates for the past three years and no male contact other than Johnny Hill's hand on my knee when he's changing gear."

"You need someone with more power. Someone more mature – you know – equal status," said Hazel. "Someone who's not so predictable – like an artist or a politician maybe." She downed the rest of the wine.

"Someone like George Nelson, I suppose," said Rita, getting up to order another glass for Hazel. She lost herself in the crowd of people standing at the bar. Smoke hung thickly in the air mixed with the heavy smell of patchouli oil from a group of hippy girls dressed in beaded, flowery dresses. It was a heady, dizzy smell and Rita made a mental note to buy some of the incense sticks she'd seen in the market.

Hazel looked deadly serious when Rita came back with the wine.

"What the hell happened?" said Rita plunking down the glasses.

"He's a bastard."

"Who?" asked Rita pulling her chair in.

"George Nelson," said Hazel taking a drink. "I need a cigarette."

"You don't smoke."

"I do sometimes."

Rita went up to the bar again and bought a pack of cigarettes. Johnny Hill was standing there with three or four friends. He looked over at Rita and winked. Rita nodded her head and turned back to her table. He'd be over soon – no doubt about that.

Hazel took a deep drag of the cigarette. "You'll burn your lungs out at that rate," said Rita.

"George is a real bastard."

"Why do you keep saying that?"

Hazel leaned in close to Rita, "It's not the drink talking now. This is the truth. He messed around with me mam and then just up and left her."

The noise of the bar crowd suddenly became a loud buzzing in Rita's ears as she struggled to hear Hazel. "How – how do you know?"

"I saw them. I heard a noise on the upstairs landing one night when me dad was on the night shift. So I opened the bedroom door a crack and you'll never believe…"

"What," said Rita, aware of a tickling, nervous feeling in the pit of her stomach.

"Me mam was out there. She climbed up onto a chair then he pulled her up into the attic. They were kissing and touching each other. Me grandma thought we had rats up there but I knew it was them. I was only a bairn – too scared to say anything."

"How long did it go on for?" asked Rita, needing to put it all into a context of time – to relate it to events in her own life.

"I don't really know – over a year I think – maybe more. But when he went away to Durham she never saw him again. He just left her without saying goodbye. She moped around the house for weeks after that. Hardly stirred herself out of the chair. Just sat there staring into the coals and I'd say, 'Mam come and play a game wi' me' but she never seemed to hear."

Rita needed to get out of the heat and smoke right away. All she could see were mouths opening and closing. The noise buzzed in her ears. "Haway – let's go," she said quickly, leading Hazel through the tightly packed bodies to the front door.

Out in the street she felt the cold slap of the night air on her face. George and Maggie had been at it in the attics above the heads of their families, friends and neighbours. George was the father of Maggie's aborted baby. George had made love to Maggie and Rita was sick with envy. And while the two of them were busy having a secret, sexy fling Rita was floating around moping over broken promises. She was furious with Maggie and but wanted to scream and curse at herself for feeling jealous. That's all it was – plain, wicked old jealousy – and it had never burned this fiercely in her before. All this had happened right on her doorstep and now the secret was out. She felt like a useless fool. Passed over and rejected.

"What's up Rita? Yer look like a ghost," said Hazel, wobbling a bit on her platform shoes.

"I'll have to get you home," said Rita. "I don't feel too clever."

The Pitman's Daughter

Rita was silent all the way back to Belton. Hazel passed out beside her, mouth wide open, breathing loudly. She drove right past the flat on the High Street and kept going until she reached Crag Street where she stopped outside of Maggie's house. It was already dark outside when she tapped on Maggie's door hoping to hell Jordy wouldn't answer. The lights were on in the kitchen so she knew someone was up. She heard shuffling noises then the door creaked open. Rita was shocked at how thin and tired Maggie looked, but the angry feeling wouldn't let go. She refused to feel any pity.

"Rita – Jordy's here – I canna talk," she said glancing behind her. "He could come down any time."

"I don't care about that bastard," said Rita. Her voice sounded sharp like she was speaking into a tin can.

"What's wrong?" Maggie looked scared.

"You like to keep secrets from friends," said Rita. "You like to carry on with men when you're already married. When you've already had your chance. And then you steal someone else's."

"Rita – what's this all about?" Maggie opened the door wider.

"You and George – up in the attic. Up there. Like two scheming rats. I know about the two of you."

"Who told you that?" Maggie's voice was hoarse and she was squinting frantically.

"And you kept it all a secret while I was waiting like a stupid schoolgirl, hoping he'd call on me."

Maggie's eyes gleamed in the darkness, "I swear I didn't know you were interested in him."

"I'm not – I don't care a damn about the bastard."

Suddenly someone thumped the ceiling above them and there was a loud shout. "Who the bloody hell's callin' at this hour Maggie. I'm coming down."

"It's Jordy – you'd best be away from here."

"Don't worry – I'm going," said Rita feeling the tears start up. "You're nowt but a scheming slut."

"I never thought I'd see jealousy get the better of you, Rita Hawkins," shouted Maggie, "but then you were always spoiled."

"At least I'm not a used up old floosy," screamed Rita slamming the gate. Lights were going on in some upstairs rooms as she slammed the car into gear and screeched down the street.

～

Rita drove back to the High Street with tears streaming down her cheeks. She woke Hazel, who'd slept through the whole thing and saw her to her door. Back in her car she considered the idea of driving back to an empty house. She couldn't do it.. Tonight she needed company. So she drove towards Sunderland trying to blank out the image of George and Maggie together in the attic.

She stopped at Houghton where Johnny Hill lived on the top floor of a large house just off the Front Street. Banging hard on the door she ignored the faces of neighbours pulling aside lace curtains. Johnny came down the stairs, running his hands through his black hair. His tie was undone and a gold cross glinted against his chest.

"Rita – what's up?"

"Let me in for a drink, Johnny," she said, hanging her head and pressing up against the doorway. "I feel like some company tonight."

Johnny opened the door wide and beckoned her in with a nod of his head. She stepped in and he pinned her against the wall. "About time, flower," he said kissing the tip of her nose. His cologne was sweet and musky and his lips so soft, she snaked her arms around his waist and pulled him close to her.

35

Ella stood behind her gate keeping an eye Rita Hawkins' flashy new car. Cheeky bairns crept up to stroke its dark green, shiny surface. One brave little beggar said, "Posh snob," and spat on the gleaming metal then rubbed it dry with the dirty cuff of his shirt. Next minute Rita came tearing out of her front gate but the bairns were off running like tomcats. That's what happened when you tried to show off on this street, thought Ella smugly to herself. You were soon brought down a peg or two. And even if Rita didn't have that brassy hair any more, she still belonged to Crag Street and she'd never wipe off the stink no matter how much money she had.

It was late July and though the schools had broken up for the summer there was more activity than usual for a Tuesday afternoon. George's mother, Jesse, the poor old wretch, had died suddenly last night and now the two old ladies, Miss Jessel and Miss Quinn, scuttled like a pair of black crows towards Jesse's house. Their thin, beaky faces focused on the ground as they crossed the street on creaking knees. It was a wonder Miss Quinn was even on her feet still.

She'd told Ella all about her swollen kneecaps. "Eeh by supper time they're like a pair of balloons," she said, lifting up her flowered pinny to show Ella a pair of bony yellow legs.

For fifty years they'd lived together at number 3 Crag Street. Some folks said they were half sisters but Ella knew there was more to it than that. One Monday afternoon about ten years ago she'd called round with some spice cake from her niece's wedding. She'd knocked on the door for a good five minutes but nobody answered. Ella knew they were definitely in because she'd watched all the comings and goings that day and she hadn't sighted them at all. Feeling a bit concerned that they'd maybe had a bad turn or something she walked all the way down the street and went up to the other side of the houses. The garden at the front was bursting with leeks and cabbages and all manner of vegetables. That's how the two old biddies lived without spending a penny. They probably had a goat or something tethered up by the coal shed because she'd never seen the milkman stop there.

Ella crossed quietly through the garden but this time she pressed her nose up against the window of the front room. At first her eyes couldn't make out the white shapes in the gloom but when she finally focused she almost fell back into the tatie patch. Miss Jessel and Miss Quinn lay entwined in a sleeping embrace but they were naked as the day they were born. Ella could hear the snores through the window and see their wrinkled old breasts resting on each other's skin like dried up flour sacks. She had to run fast to get away from there before she started hooting with laughter. *The sly old buggers* she thought. *All prim and proper but they're really a pair of lesbians.*

That day she'd been bursting to tell someone about what she'd seen but even she realized that some things are best left unsaid. *Let the poor old biddies live the rest of their lives in peace* and really, she supposed, it didn't matter what folks were up to behind closed doors. There were probably worse secrets than that on Crag Street.

Besides, over the years, the two of them looked after the street in a way nobody else could, delivering babies and laying out the dead. But now they were on their way out too. Nobody knew how old they were. Some said they must be over eighty-five because Miss Jessel always claimed she still had a frock that her grandmother had worn on Queen Victoria's coronation day.

Nobody really used them any more; only those that couldn't afford the high price of the funeral home and with all the money Jesse's son

The Pitman's Daughter

George had, there should have been a smart, black undertaker's car there. But George hadn't been seen around the street in two or three years. Ella hadn't seen him since the garden party. So today the old ladies would make poor Mrs Nelson look respectable for her last appearance on earth, then give out tea and stale cake to the mourners after the funeral.

Ella had been at the gate for a good two hours already. Funerals usually meant there'd be family drama like long-lost relatives showing up to claim their piece of the leavings. At funerals emotions ran at fever pitch. Now she wondered why Rita Hawkins had showed up. Surely she hadn't seen anything of George lately. Ella caught Rita's eye as she came back from chasing the bairns. She motioned her over and pointed at the Nelson house.

"They say she died poor as a church mouse. Not a stick of decent furniture in the house," she said. "Tragic. Sold it all off piece by piece after her man, Archie died."

"So where was George when she needed him?" asked Rita. "Now he's a big union man he doesn't have time for his own mam."

Ella looked at Rita's expensive navy outfit. It was a nice, fitted wool dress with a matching jacket. Probably from somewhere in Newcastle. "Why there's a lot of folk rely on him for their jobs yer na's. He canna always pick up and come over here."

"You sound like me dad and all the other folks brainwashed by the great George Nelson," said Rita as her mam came out to join them.

"Why yer na's, she was thin as a stick," said Iris. "Selling her bits and pieces to buy a scrap of food for herself. Only had the milkman come once a week and pigs' trotters or a few oxtails was all she bought from Lakey."

Lakey was the butcher and Ella thought she was the only one that kept tabs on what people bought from his van.

By now Miss Jessel had stepped out of the house carrying a rusty old biscuit tin. She saw Ella and the others and made a beeline for them.

"Eeh – I canna believe me eyes. Poor old soul. We found a tinful of money – nearly two thousand pounds in a biscuit tin. Seems George was sending her something every month and she never used it – poor old soul." She held the tin out. It was stuffed with five and ten pound notes. They all stood silent.

"Mebbe she'd gone soft in the head," said Iris.

"That's all very well sending money," said Rita, "but why couldn't he spare a minute for her when she was alive?"

"Mind Mrs Barker found her," said Ella, " says the place is filthy – she could barely lift a finger, poor old soul, she just fell over in the yard."

"Eeh she was like a bird – all bones and no meat," said Miss Jessel. "Edie laid her out on the table by hersel' she were so light."

"Well I hear George is coming up from London tomorrow," said Iris. "Poor lad probably thought he was providing for her all this time."

Ella imagined his face when he saw the pigsty his poor old mam was living in. She didn't have the heart to make him suffer like that. They had to do something. "We'll clean the house," she said, feeling the old excitement bubbling up in her stomach. "We canna let Jesse down. We'll paint it and spruce it up a bit so it's respectable for after the funeral."

༺

Within an hour a steady stream of people marched over to Mrs Nelson's house carrying buckets, rolls of paper and paintbrushes. Maggie Willis stood on the kerb with two heavy buckets, one in each hand.

"Maggie," Ella said, shocked at how skinny and pale she'd become. "Yer poorly. We can do it."

Maggie shook her head. "I'm gettin' me hands dirty for the sake of Jesse's memory – poor soul. She's got family coming and we have to make it look decent."

Maggie joined the procession and Ella followed, bucket in hand. It was common knowledge that she'd been soft on George and her with six bairns too. Ella thought Maggie should be ashamed to set foot inside that house and yet she meant well and she hadn't had much of a life, poor lass. Not worth a tinker's cuss living with Jordy.

Then Ella looked at Jack shuffling along in front of her. His boots were polished, his hair tidy and his shirt clean. He turned to her and smiled. "Haway lass, it's thy good deed so you lead the way."

And Ella's heart swelled to bursting as she took her place beside him. Swelled with pride and a feeling that she knew must be love. After all these years *Count your blessings* she thought to herself. *Count your blessings.*

36

On a chilly Thursday afternoon Rita sat at the back of the crematorium chapel. Sunlight shone through the stained glass flowers spattering blobs of coloured light onto the black clothes of the mourners.

Her mother sat beside her dressed in a musty, black woollen suit. It was a relic from the fifties. Bought on one of their many shopping trips to Sunderland. It gave Rita a bit of a twinge to see her mam sniffling and wiping a hanky over her eyes. At the end of the pew her dad and brothers sat, solemn-faced and stiff in their Sunday suits.

On top of the simple wooden altar stood a magnificent arrangement of white lilies and chrysanthemums dotted with crimson roses and carnations. Just below was the pale wooden coffin, closed and festooned with creamy wreaths of lilies and gardenias.

George sat right at the front, his shoulders hunched and his face resting on one hand. She knew so much about him. About the attic and the secret affair up there with Maggie. About the baby he'd never known, and the filthy conditions that his mam spent her last days in. Yet he was still a mystery to her. He'd given his life to the miners' struggle but he'd sacrificed everyone he'd ever loved for the good of the cause. Was it the power and prestige he loved or was it his survival instinct?

His way to escape Crag Street? She couldn't criticise him for the last reason – she'd done the same herself.

Flecks of dust danced in a golden halo above his head and Rita felt dizzy. The outlines of his back and the side of his face were edged in sunlight and the familiar churning in her stomach started up again. She tried her hardest to direct her attention to the vicar who was speaking about Mrs Nelson.

"Jesse was a devoted wife and mother who fought against all odds...Sacrificed her own comforts... produced a son who has served this community loyally and aspired to greatness..."

She wondered suddenly if all these people had come to show respect to the mother or the son? She knew why her Dad was there. He'd come cap in hand, greasing up to George, the saviour of the collieries, and enemy of the Tories. Paying lip service to the old lady who had walked her little bairn to the top of Whittington Hill every day to save his lungs from T.B.

The whole street had paid their respects to the old lady earlier in the morning when the undertaker's car came to take Jesse's body away. People lined the streets watching George, immaculate in his dark suit, stride out of the gate. The car pulled away with everyone waving as if he was royalty. The undertaker, top hat in hand, marched solemnly beside the hearse until it reached the bottom of the street when he flipped up his tailcoat to climb back in beside the driver.

Rita snapped out of her daydream, her mind in turmoil. One moment she detested everything he stood for but the next minute she felt like a nervous fool at the thought of talking to him and so it came as a shock to her when the coffin suddenly lurched and shifted out of sight through a trapdoor in the floor. George's head bowed down into both hands. Rita gasped loudly and everyone turned to look at her. Cremation was so final. She would never want to be burned away to a pile of ashes when you didn't know what you needed in the after-life.

"Everything's burned except the bones and the rings," Ella had said years ago. But who scrapes around in the ashes for those, thought Rita?

The congregation stood as George made his way out, accompanied by a withered man in a shiny navy suit and a stout woman in a feathered hat. His aunty and uncle on his father's side.

"Come down from Tynemouth to see what they could lay their hands on," said Ella Danby.

As George passed by he glanced at Rita. She turned away but not before noticing the bluish shadow above his lips as if he had not shaved that morning. Her face flushed with heat or was it embarrassment?

Behind the crematorium were manicured lawns – cropped, green velvet criss-crossed by winding stone pathways and dotted with headstones. The mourners stood in small groups chatting and trying not to look as a puff of black smoke blasted from the chimney. Jesse's spirit flew above their heads and up into the clouds

Her dad and brothers joined George, shaking his hands and hugging his shoulders. When a man brought the ashes out in a small, metal urn, George's face turned sheet-white but he held out his hands to take the container and, clasping it to his chest, marched back to the car as if he was heading a union delegation. *He's good*, thought Rita, *a real pro. Only a few cracks in the armour today.*

Rita had always detested funeral teas – walking into the houses of the bereaved where people sat balancing teacups, eating stale cake and not knowing what to say for fear of causing offence. They pulled up outside the Nelson's house and she breathed out a sigh, throwing her head back, relaxing her neck.

"I'll just stay in the car," she said, "I've no stomach for these things."

Walter leaned forward from the back seat and snapped, "No daughter of mine – no matter how fancy she is – shows disrespect for the dead. Get yersel' inside."

Following them into the house, she noticed the smell of fresh paint, applied only two days before. The neighbours had done a good job, painting the walls a pale yellow and pasting on a border of yellow chrysanthemums. An old, grey settee, borrowed from the Barkers next door,

The Pitman's Daughter

stood against the wall and her mam had loaned the large trestle table, now covered with plates of triangular sandwiches and sliced Madeira cake. Miss Jessel was pouring tea from Ella Danby's large, silver teapot into an odd assortment of china teacups borrowed from different houses on the street. Walter took a cup, balancing the china saucer in his thick fingers like an eggshell that could be cracked if he squeezed too tightly.

"Where is he?" he asked Miss Jessel, leaning forward and slopping his tea on his saucer.

"Upstairs, Mr Hawkins – he wants to be alone. Taken it very badly you know."

Rita took a cup of tea and went to look out of the window. It was easier to look thoughtful that way and avoid any conversation. Funny, she thought, in all the time she lived on the street she'd never set foot inside this house. George's family had kept to themselves and Jesse was always out on the step waiting to catch some gossip.

The company sat grim-faced and silent, chewing sandwiches and cake. The stout lady, George's Aunt Minny, was still wearing her hat and watching when people took extra sandwiches, "I telt our George it's a blessing," she said, "she never had much, … just a few bits of things, so then there'll be nowt to fight over. Isn't that right, Charlie." She dug her husband's ribs and he, chewing on a large piece of Madeira cake, choked and spilt his tea.

"Daft bugger," she spat and stalked into the kitchen scullery, returning with a cloth, which Miss Quinn tried to wrestle from her.

"Of course," said the aunt, mopping at the carpet and her husband's shoes, "I'll be choosing summat of Jesse's for a keepsake. To remember her by, yer na's – and I always did admire that silver teapot, didn't I Charlie?"

Ella Danby's eyebrows shot up as she swiped the silver teapot from the table before Minnie could lay her hands on it.

"Aye, yer did go on about it – aye," the little man wheezed, nodding his head furiously. "And I was partial to the plaques from Blackpool, wasn't I Minnie?"

"And yer shall have them, my pet," she said, patting him with a blunt red hand as if her were a pet dog.

Rita turned back to the window. *What a bloody comedy show.*

There was a sudden change of atmosphere in the room as George came down the stairs. He was freshly shaved; hair brushed neatly back and wearing a clean, white shirt. A sweet smell of cologne wafted through the room. Expensive tastes, she thought. Men's colognes were her specialty.

"Please everyone – please carry on eating," he said, motioning for those who had risen to sit down. Walter had been one of the first, almost upsetting his teacup and plate in the process.

Miss Jessel rushed to offer him a cup of tea but he waved her away.

Rita watched, fascinated as he worked the room like an expert, handing a small box of antique port glasses to meddling Aunt Minnie as a memento. She giggled like a girl when he planted a kiss on her forehead and knocked her velvet hat askew. He sat with Walter and passed on the latest union news, then circulated around the guests shaking hands and thanking them for their concern. *What would she say when he got to her?* When he did turn and walk in her direction she was forced to take a gulp of tea to steady herself.

He held out a hand to her. "I'm glad to see you here," he said, smiling, "I've heard all about your business exploits." He looked her up and down and she fumbled with the button of her jacket.

"I'm the talk of the neighbourhood," said Rita, flipping back her hair and regretting her words.

"You changed your hair," he said.

"Blondes aren't taken as seriously in business."

"It's very dramatic with your hat." Rita felt the weight of the black wide-brimmed hat. Maggie had said black was Rita's colour, and it looked rich with her chestnut hair.

"And your clothes – fine quality. I see I'm not the only one who enjoys fancy tailoring."

"Makes life worth living," she replied curtly.

"Of course," he added, "but there *are* more important things in life than material possessions. One must also have ideals to strive for – a cause, if you like."

"I have one," she replied, "Plain and simple – make pots of money and have a bloody good time doing it!"

A slow smile spread across his lips, "Still blunt as ever, Rita – no pretences."

"That's me. What you see is what you get," she snapped.

"An apt cliché," he said, smiling.

"I have another rule," she said, longing to knock that smile off his face.

"And what's that," he said, leaning closer.

Rita noticed her father staring over at them, mouth open, and ears cocked. She bent forward and whispered in a silken voice, "Rule number one – family comes first, and causes come second." Then patting him on the cheek, she handed him her empty teacup and turned to see the whole room watching her. Sensing a blush coming on, she walked towards the door feeling a foot taller – or was it just the hat?

"I'll see you out in the car," she muttered to her father and stumbled out, oblivious to the stares of the assembled guests.

Outside the air was charged with excitement and those who weren't at the funeral tea were leaning on their gateposts or fences watching the comings and goings from the Nelson house. So many eyes charted her progress through the newly painted gate that Rita fought the urge to wave one hand from the wrist like the queen did on state visits. She was just fumbling with her car keys and cursing the depth of her handbag when she noticed Maggie Willis rushing across the street towards her. Shrunken and swaddled in a hand crocheted blanket, she scurried like a rabbit, stealing furtive glances back at her house.

Rita stopped rummaging through her handbag. She hadn't spoken to Maggie for so long. Not since they'd fallen out over George. "Maggie, you look like someone's after you."

Maggie's chest was heaving like a pair of bellows. "I've been meanin' to give up smoking but I canna sleep without one before bed."

"You didn't come and pay your respects to George's mother, Maggie," said Rita, searching her face for a reaction.

"You know I canna see him – ever," she told Rita. "But I wanted to make things up with you, Rita. While there's time."

All Rita's old bitterness seemed to melt away when she took hold of Maggie's hand. The bones felt dry and fragile, almost lifeless. "I'm over it," she said quietly. "Don't fret about it."

Maggie tried to smile but it took an effort. "I'm glad," she said, wincing and holding her stomach.

"Maggie yer should be resting," said Rita. "Have you got some medicine?"

"I canna rest, Rita. Jordy knows something. He just watches me all day when he's in – sits in his chair by the fire and follows me with his eyes."

"Promise me you'll leave him," Rita begged. "I'll set you and Pearl up somewhere – somewhere lovely."

"He'd come after us, pet. It's safer if we stay," said Maggie stroking Rita's black suit. "By, I'm certain when George got a look at you, his eyes were out on stalks, flower. You're a real treat for the eyes now – he'd be blind not to fancy you."

"Get away with you," Rita said, feeling a pounding in her chest.

"Anyway, Rita – there's something important I need to ask you." She reached into a pocket in her pinny and pulled out a small envelope. "It's the picture of *that man I told you about before*."

Rita knitted her eyebrows together. "Who?"

"*Him* – Chuck – I can hardly say the word – you know I told you when we were in Brentmoor – Hazel's real dad."

"Oh yes," Rita said, "But what do you want me to do with it?"

Maggie thrust the envelope into Rita's hand just as Jordy's voice bellowed Maggie's name across the street. "Take it, Rita – I have to go now."

"Something's wrong Maggie," said Rita, her heart jumping as Jordy loomed out of the shadows and stood between the gateposts. "Has he hurt you again?"

"No – no – but he knows now."

"Knows – knows what?"

"About George and me."

Jordy yelled again and they both heard the sound of the gate creaking open. "Get into yer car Rita and get away from here – oh and promise me – if anything happens you'll make sure to tell Hazel about her dad – it's all explained in this note and – give her the picture too."

Rita hardly had time to answer before Maggie scurried back across to the waiting figure that was now beating one clenched fist on the gatepost. Then Pearl came out from the back door and took Jordy's arm. Maggie took the other and walked him back into the house.

∽

"What did he say to you?" was her dad's first question when the supper dishes were being cleared away. He'd been too busy feeding his face to make conversation before and now he lit a cigarette, sucking back so hard on it his cheeks sank with the effort.

"Who?" said Rita, adjusting the waistband of her skirt.

It was half past nine in the evening and they'd just finished a late supper of baked ham, boiled leeks and fried potatoes followed by creamed rice pudding and two cups of tea laced generously with brandy. She felt as if the zip of her skirt was ready to burst.

"Marley Cock Jackson – who do yer think? George Nelson."

"I told him I always put family first," said Rita. "And business second."

"Why that's a bloody lie," said Lennie. "We hardly see yer nowadays."

"And a stupid bloody comment as well," said Walter, stubbing out his cigarette onto his dinner plate. Rita grimaced. She knew how her mam hated cleaning up leftover potatoes mixed with cigarette ashes. "Christ, – spendin' all that money on elo- elocution and yer come out with a daft remark like that."

She grabbed the plate away. "You can never find a good word to say about me – can yer?"

Lenny and Bill got up from the table. "Ower much bickerin' here," said Lenny.

Walter pushed his ashtray away, "You two buggers need a haircut – yer look like two fairies – the pair of yers."

"Long hair's in Da," said Bill. "The lasses like it."

"I don't care," said Walter, "it's not natural – yer need a clean cut look – like – like-"

"Like George Nelson," said Rita rustling through her handbag. "You'd think the sun shines out of his arse the way you talk about him."

"See – what did I say," said Walter, ambling over to the couch. "Yer'll never get the street out of yer blood. It's bred into yer."

He lowered his rear end slowly, undid his braces before he stretched out in front of the blazing fire, closed his eyes and began to snore. Rita snapped her handbag shut, picked up her hat and thanked God for her quiet, orderly house on Roker Avenue. Lenny and Bill stood in front of the mirror; smoothing back billowing locks of hair. "It's the Robert Plant look, Rita," said Bill.

"Like a pair of male tarts," said Rita, envying them a bit.

"Dead right, sis," said Lenny, "Haway Bill, else he'll wake up and see we've gone without him."

"Canna chat up any lasses wi' the ard man taggin' along," Bill said, glancing at the bulky shape on the couch that jiggled and shook as the snores roared from it.

"I thought he'd be a real draw," laughed Rita. "Maturity, experience and all that."

"Like hell," said Lenny. "Spot us a few quid, sis. We're poor working lads."

Rita dug into her purse, fished out a twenty-pound note and flicked it at Lenny. "Go and find yourself two nice girls and settle down."

The door shut behind them leaving the room filled with the heady smell of Brut after-shave.

Rita let herself out after saying goodnight to her mother who was upstairs quietly knitting a pink bed jacket. "Just in case I get sick and have nothing good to wear," she explained.

The street was quiet, almost peaceful after the excitement of the day and for the first time in her life Rita realized there were no trees to shade the houses or soften the view. She'd grown used to the giant elm trees around the back of her house on Roker Avenue and often fell asleep at night to their soft rustling.

Here on Crag Street everything was bare and exposed. Life here was raw and tough and, God knows, she'd tried hard to smooth out the rough edges she'd been left with. Money could do a lot for you. You could dress yourself up or pay a few pounds to change your accent but the prickliness remained like nettle leaves on skin.

It was time to pay Jimmy a visit. Getting away to the seaside would be good for her. She could see it now. A deckchair on the beach, a drink in her hand and the sun on her face. That would warm her right through. Besides he always knew what to do to calm her worst worries. He always saw the best in people which was rare in these parts.

She was just about to get into her car when she noticed a light flickering in the attic window of the Nelson's house. She remembered George saying he'd be clearing out the whole place from top to bottom, ready for new owners. She could picture him sorting through his mam's bits and pieces. Would he remember her sacrifices? Would he cry for leaving her to die alone?

Inside the car she kept a small transistor radio and she fumbled with the dials, listening for the whistling sound as the radio tuned itself to the scratchy sounds of Luxembourg. Everybody listened to Luxembourg. Pirate radio was big. *Pirate radio – did that mean the deejays were out at sea somewhere near Luxembourg or were they sitting in some tiny office overlooking a cobbled medieval square?* She wondered. *Where was Luxembourg anyway?* She caught the end of a Kinks song. Her grandma hated The Kinks – said they looked like they needed "a good wash." Next song was the Rolling Stones singing, "*Let's spend the night together.*" She hummed along with the melody until a sudden, steady buzz of interference cut off the song and she imagined the sound waves bouncing through the night, crossing over Europe and the North Sea to her. Lost in thought, she was jolted by the sound of shouting and went to switch off the radio but she turned the dial the wrong way, sending out a blast of distorted noise.

"Damn it!" she cursed, swivelling the knobs. "Damn it..."

She could make out the Stones singing

Let's spend the night together
Now I need you more than ever
Let's spend the night together now...

Then the sound of screaming became louder – an old woman's thin scream and a young girl that sounded like Pearl, crying and crying. Rita scraped her ankle as she clambered out of the car and ran across to Maggie's house. She heard voices shouting, "Rita, Rita – it's me mam – come in." Pearl was fumbling with the gate – feeling her way around the brick wall – groping at thin air. Hannah moaned and hid her face in her apron.

Rita held Pearl's flailing arms. "What is it – what's happened?"

"Inside," screamed Pearl, "Quick – he'll murder her."

Rita put Pearl in the corner of the yard and told Hannah to stay put, then, with a sickly feeling in her stomach she went into the house. It stunk of mouldy food. She stopped at the kitchen table and almost puked at the sight of an open jar of jam with a fat blue fly buzzing over it, hovering and diving into the sticky jelly. Floating up the narrow stairs she felt as if she was drifting into a nightmare. There was a moaning, whimpering sound coming from the end of the dark, windowless landing. A dim light shone from the loft door above and down below Maggie was splayed out on the floor her face pale and waxy, her mouth pulled into an oh-oh shape, head bent to the side and chest heaving hard and fast. Rita rushed to touch her but Maggie's face went grey with pain. "Wait, Maggie, I'll fetch a blanket," she said rushing into the musty bedroom where she forced open the window and shouted out to Hannah, "Quick – quick, take Pearl and phone an ambulance from my mam's house."

Back out on the landing she covered Maggie with the patched brown eiderdown. "There, there," she whispered, "just breathe easy and someone will be here." But Maggie's eyes suddenly opened wide and fixed onto the ceiling at something up above. Her mouth was moving furiously but only a wheezing sound came out – like air whistling through broken lungs.

"What is it – what?" Rita said, then looked up to see the attic opening filled with a big, black shape. *Christ almighty,* she gasped. It was Jordy looking out at her, his dark-ringed eyes looked out of a face that was plastered with makeup. He was yelling and sobbing at the same time. "I telt her she had it coming – punishment for the harlot – and for him too – the adulterer." Rita stepped forward but drew back when she saw him brandishing a heavy stick. He thumped it against the ceiling and swung his legs back and forth.

Once he had one foot over the edge of the opening Rita blinked her eyes. She couldn't believe what she was seeing. A hysterical giggle bubbled up inside her. *Jesus Christ,* she gasped, *he's wearing nylons under his nightshirt and suspenders and everything.* She was riveted to the spot.

"You're a lunatic – you're off your rocker – get away," she screamed, trying to shelter Maggie from him but he was a big, fat insect, waving his legs, slamming the stick and rocking like one of those laughing clowns in a glass box outside the funhouse. Back and forth, back and forth he went until he tipped over too far, his hands tried to claw onto the ledge and he clattered down onto the old rocking chair, buckling its legs and smashing its back with his head. He landed in a heap across Maggie's legs.

When the ambulance men came they took them both away.

Next evening Rita had drunk her way halfway through a bottle of gin when there was a knock on her front door.

She didn't want to talk to anyone. Not today. Not after watching Maggie slip away this morning. Drowning in the water that filled up her lungs. All the bairns surrounded her, laying their heads on her small tired body to hear her breathe her last breath. The sight of them all gathered there made Rita realize why Maggie stayed with Jordy. It was always for the bairns.

She put down her glass and the chiming started. *The stupid fancy door chimes* she'd put on the front door that played *London Bridge is Falling Down* every time you pressed the button. When she got up, the furniture seemed to tilt to one side. She was far-gone. Riding the drunken express train that raced you along, stomach churning and head reeling, towards the nearest toilet.

Managing to open the door, she held on tightly and opened it to find George standing there in jeans and a black raincoat. The rain fell in sheets behind him. Before she could say anything he pushed past her and into the house. His hair was dripping wet.

"Hey," she called after him. "I was gonna ask you in."

He sat on the couch and started to play with the Newton's cradle, setting the balls clack-clacking against each other.

"I need a drink," he said. "A big drink."

"I was just about to pour myself another one," she said, slopping the gin across the glass table.

"Steady, steady," he said, grabbing her hand.

When he'd gulped down half the gin and tonic he said, "She died this morning, didn't she."

Rita cleared her throat, "Yes."

George buried his face in his hands and began to cry. "They took Jordy away too?"

"To Sedgefield – he finally cracked." She drained her glass and fought the tears. "Bit late though."

"I never believed he'd actually kill her." said George blowing his nose.

"You cared for her?" asked Rita.

"I did once. But really I felt sorry for her," he said, stumbling over the words.

"I know," said Rita.

"Nobody knew – who told you?"

"Hazel – Hazel saw you."

"Christ – who else knows?"

"Why? What are you worried about? Your precious union job?" Rita gulped back the drink, knowing she was getting more and more drunk.

"Yes – my precious union. Thousands of men depend on me," he said, sloshing his drink around in the glass, "You don't realize the importance of what I'm doing."

"You are so fucking arrogant," blurted Rita, bolstered by the gin.

George drained his glass, "I'm committed and I'm fighting for people like your dad – all the working men – they're being exploited by...."

Rita stood up and felt sick, "That's not all there is to life," she said feeling as sick as she had once on the ferry over to Ireland. "What about the people that loved you?"

"I know you think I have no feelings but I do care. That's why I gave up all my time so they could have a better way of life," he said, almost pleading with her.

"You and your causes," she continued, pointing a shaky finger at him. "Well I take care of those men after a hard day down the pit. They get home, put up their feet and watch one of my tellies." She noticed a nick on his cheek – a little scar of dried blood where he'd cut himself shaving. "And so do their wives – the ones that slave with the house and the bairns all day."

"I suppose you do," he said, looking around the room, "and you're making a pretty good living at it."

She stood up so suddenly the room seemed to spin around. "Don't dare judge me. We're both cut from the same cloth, you and me. We've both done well out of the working folk. Only I don't pretend to be a bloody saint." Rita sat back down and felt the whoosh of alcohol in her head. She began to giggle. "We should go into partnership."

Don't close your eyes, she told herself, *don't or that'll be the end of it*, but it was too late. Her body felt like it was hurtling down a long tunnel and at the end of it she could hear George saying, "We're on the brink of something very big – over the next few years we could change the course of history in this country and I can't give that up for anything – anybody."

The train stopped for a moment when she opened her eyes and he was standing at the fireplace, hands dug into his back pockets, then she heard her voice saying, "Not even for your own baby." It was out and she couldn't take it back because he was holding her shoulders and shaking them. His face looked white and scared, the eyes big and dark blue.

"Which baby?" he whispered.

Rita couldn't really remember anything at that moment – only the bus station, "In the bus station she was bleeding." She wanted to put her head down and sleep. "I can't remember – I need to sleep." She closed her eyes again and was sucked into blackness.

At one point she remembered him carrying her upstairs and she'd pressed her nose against his neck. She remembered his clean, soapy smell. He placed her on the bed and covered her with a blanket and the last thing she heard him saying was to sleep it off because she'd have a hell of a headache the next day.

Marjorie DeLuca

❀

Her alarm clock clanged like a great church bell and she woke with a start, only to thud back down onto the pillow as a sharp pain circled her head. When her mind cleared, she pieced together the events of last night. The gin, George. He'd carried her up here. *She must have passed out cold – but where was he?* She cried out softly, "George – George," but the house was empty. He'd gone. Just put her up here and gone after she'd told him about the baby. She lay back as tears squeezed out of her eyes. Today she'd stay in bed. There was nothing worth getting up for.

37

She spent the next six weeks in Manchester, Liverpool and Leeds on business, dragging herself from one meeting to another, dealing with suppliers, viewing new product lines and dodging the advances of married salesmen on the lookout for a warm body and a night of fun.

Finally, exhausted, she took time off to visit Jimmy. She lay in the sun on the Torquay beaches and let his new wife, Doris, fatten her up her with breakfasts of bacon, sausage, fried egg, fried bread, baked beans and anything else that could be crammed onto a nine-inch plate. Rita strolled down palm tree-lined streets and watched happy couples wrapped up in their whirlwind holiday romances. For a few sun-drenched days the daily grind of dull jobs did not exist, all clothes were new and dreams became reality until the coaches and trains took them back to the realities of home.

On crowded beaches the heat of the sun slowly warmed her, and the sand coated her tanned legs like frosted sugar. Though she felt the sting of sunburn it made her more aware of her own body. She lay back in the striped deckchair, lifted her face to the sun and dreamed and with the dreams came sadness. She grieved for Maggie and for herself. She'd stayed clear away from any real chance at love. Her heart was curled tightly inside her, feeding on vanity, bitterness and pride. George had been her one hope and when he let her down she'd spent the next eleven years hating herself.

She turned these thoughts over in her mind, and they became a torment to her on those hot nights when the sheets were sticky with heat and she could hear every sound through paper-thin walls. Jimmy and Doris's bed creaked for a good hour every night and Doris always whistled when she made breakfast while Jimmy patted her behind as he set the table.

"You must be in love, ducky," Doris said to Rita at the breakfast table, "you've buttered the same piece of toast twice."

At Durham station Rita struggled to the car park with her cases. Thank god her Dad and Lenny had dropped off her car. She was free to go anywhere and the night was in full swing but she was lonely.

Pulling out onto North Road she went in the opposite direction to home and found herself on the road to Redhills. At the traffic lights she checked her reflection in the mirror. She was dressed carelessly in a white T-shirt and black slacks, her hair pulled back with two tortoise-shell combs. Her face looked unfamiliar. A deep tan and dusting of freckles across her nose made her feel like a new person. Could she find the courage to walk right up to George's grand house and pay a casual visit without blushing, stammering or searching for words?

She drove towards the redbrick hall wondering what on earth to do when she got there. It was difficult to imagine herself walking straight inside and finding him, bent over papers at a desk or studying the text of a speech. What would she do?

The house was dark except for one brightly lit wing at the west side of the house. Rita parked the car at the side of the driveway and crossed over the paving stones to the wide open windows. There was a low murmur of voices. Inside was a large meeting room where George, at the head of the table, presided over at least eight other men, including her Dad. Piles of papers littered the table and the air was blue with cigarette smoke. George's hands were raised as if was sketching out an argument. She could hear brief snatches of conversation, "-got the power now – the membership has taken enough – ready for a vote – time for a walkout."

He slammed his fist down and Rita ducked away from the window, pressing her back flat against the cool, stone wall, "That's the spirit lads" she heard him say, "we'll bring them to their knees. They can't buy us off with their promises – one minute they agree to better wages then in the next breath they're closing down the pits because they say they're losing money."

"Aye," said her Dad, "you can trust the bloody Tories to take it out on the workers."

Rita recognized the rough scraping of Ned Barker's voice.

"Wait a minute, lads." Rita heard chairs shuffling. "We're gettin' ower greedy now. We've got everything we need – tellies, flush toilets and all that. There's enough food on the table. Why I remember the days after the big strike in 1927 when men roamed the fields snaring rabbits or poaching sheep because they couldn't earn just a few pennies to feed their families and -"

"All right Granddad – that was another world then," said a young voice, "Technology's takin' over now – we're fighting for survival."

All this talk, though Rita, and for what? To save a dying industry. Every week she read, in one business magazine or another, about the development of oil as an alternative to coal. But these men hung on to the mines like bairns clinging to an old blanket. If there was one thing she'd learned in business it was to be flexible and move with the times. That was the way to make money.

And George was wasting himself. She'd run into plenty of company presidents who would have hired him in minute for an executive position. She shifted her feet and stumbled on the gravel, banging her shoulder against the open window just as the men were raising their hands to vote.

"There's spies out there," her Dad said and she managed to slip into an open doorway before they got to the window and spotted her.

She found herself inside an oak-panelled office lit by a brass table lamp. A large mahogany desk in the centre was covered with papers, files, newspapers and framed photographs. George's jacket hung over the back of the padded leather swivel chair and Rita touched the fine wool that carried the familiar scent of soap and after-shave. She ran her fingers over the brass and wooden photo frames. There were pictures of his mother perched on a fake metal horse with her husband standing by holding the reins. Pictures of George making speeches, receiving awards and holding banners. She buried her face in George's jacket again and reached her hands deep inside the pockets. The cool silk lining made her shiver as if she was reaching inside his clothes and touching smooth skin.

At the sound of approaching voices she jumped up and slipped outside in the direction of her car. The last thing she wanted was to be found here, by her father and the other people from the street that knew her. *Coward, coward*, she screamed feeling like she would suffocate if she didn't drive away that very minute.

38

Durham Big Meeting 1971 fell on a Saturday when midsummer trees leaned over the river banks, trailing their leaves into the River Wear. On this day all the miners from Durham County decked themselves out in their Sunday best to converge on the stately old University city. The sudden rush of visitors always forced the shopkeepers to board up their windows and doors while the pubs ordered in extra kegs of beer then threw their doors open wide to welcome the coachloads of miners, their families and the thirsty members of at least fifty-two brass bands.

Rita stood on Elvert Bridge watching the punts and rowing boats float lazily across the water, their oars slicing the surface. She'd make the most of the quiet because in less than an hour the streets would fill with crowds and there'd be dancing and singing and the music of brass bands.

Rita loved the excitement of Big Meeting day. She'd been every year of her life, right from when she was a baby in her mother's arms, dressed in her Sunday best or waving a flag and toddling beside her Dad. Then for a few rebellious years she'd flaunted a cowboy hat and danced with a line of rowdy teens in front of the band. But this year she was carrying an invitation to a reception at the County Hotel, an honour reserved for people with money and an opportunity to hobnob with Labour Party bigwigs and Miners' Union executives.

The invitation had been a complete surprise. When it plopped through the mailbox, with the Redhills letterhead on it, she hadn't rushed to open it. Instead she carried it into the kitchen and propped it up against the Wedgewood flower vase in the centre of the table. Then she made tea and toast and settled down to slice open the cream-coloured envelope. The invitation was simple and formal, an embossed card with a thin gold border. Tasteful but not too extravagant. It was a union function and excess had no place in these times of wage demands and unrest.

Attached to the back of the card was a small handwritten note from George. She read eagerly.

Thank you for telling me about Maggie and the baby. The timing was lousy but I'm glad I heard it from someone I trust. I know you're honest – painfully so sometimes, but I deserved to be told off. I'm ashamed of the way I've treated people who cared about me and I need to talk about it at a quieter time if you'll let me. Come to the reception. It'll give me a boost. There's always plenty of wine, food and political hot air. You're my link with everything that's real. Everyone else has gone. There's only you left.

George.

Rita read the letter over and over again then went out to buy a new dress.

Since the crowds had started to line the streets she set off towards the hotel, a pale gold building with ivy covered walls. Most of the smart shops along the bridge were boarded up like fortresses, their owners afraid of brawls and flying beer bottles. It was probably justified. Her Dad told her that in the past there'd been occasional clashes. Some years ago visiting miners had thrown the Bishop of Durham into the river.

Apparently it was a way of paying the old bugger back since he'd made some rude public comments about miners' wages being too high.

She checked her watch. It was too early for the reception, scheduled for half past ten. She had half an hour left to stop and watch the first bands march through. Try to capture the rush of excitement that always hit her on this day. Placing her cream leather handbag beside her, she smoothed down the skirt of her navy and cream dress. She'd dressed carefully that day, pulling out the silk crepe dress from its plastic cover. Its simple empire line bodice was edged with a cream satin ribbon and a large, soft bow lay just below the swell of her breasts.

That morning she'd floated down to her car then sunk back into the leather upholstery and set off along the sea front, then inland towards Belton where she drove down the High Street, past the Hare and Hounds, past the bottom of Crag Street and up towards Whittington Hill.

She didn't have to call for her Mam and Dad who were enjoying the second-hand Morris Minor she'd bought them. In fact they were hardly ever at home nowadays. If they weren't going out for drives in the country they were off to the seaside with a flask of tea and a few sandwiches packed up in a picnic basket. Walter had sworn off the drink since he passed his driving test. It was one thing to smash his bike into the fence at the top of the street but his car was another matter.

They'd set out to Durham over an hour before so that Walter could get himself hitched up to the new colliery banner that he'd be carrying for its first appearance. An honour he'd lobbied for with great enthusiasm. *Typical Da*, she thought, smiling.

The sound of a drum rumbled like an earthquake and lifted her heart into her throat. The first band was on the way and she stood up to get a better view of the bright silk banner flapping down the street. The smooth harmonies of cornets, trumpets, and trombones glided through the air filling Rita's head with images of heather covered hills and bustling country marketplaces under cloudy skies.

The banner of the next band was edged in black. There'd been an accident at that colliery. Nine were dead and the band played with mournful tones. The sound of a brass band could fill her eyes with tears and make her heart ache with pride at the sheer beauty of the music.

The Edinburgh pipe band followed, fronted by two Highland dancers, then the Yankee jazz band that'd returned for the second year in a row after causing a sensation last year with their fast-paced jazz. A group of bobby-soxers danced around a baton twirler in tan-coloured tights. The crowd clapped and yelled at the sight of their plumed hats and choreographed marching even though some of the old folks muttered that the whole thing was just modern Yankee showmanship and not really in keeping with the proud tradition of the miners.

Rita glanced at her watch for the tenth or was it the twelfth time? Today was a good day – when all the good things in life ranged through her mind like the items in a Christmas catalogue. Today she could allow herself to be happy for the first time in months. She felt attractive, had a purse full of money and would soon see George. She glanced at her watch again and noticed it was already half past ten, but not wanting to appear too eager she waited for the Belton band, which had just rounded the corner of Old Elvert.

At the head, carrying the banner was her dad, puffed up with pride and bursting out of his suit, his hair slicked down with so much Brylcreem that little rivers of grease were beginning to run down his cheeks in the heat. Her mother, who insisted on marching along behind, was sweating in a newly crocheted multi-coloured waistcoat as she plodded along to the strains of "The Blaydon Races." Both of them stared so doggedly ahead they didn't notice Rita waving as they swept by. *Charming*, she thought to herself and, tired of the endless stream of marchers, turned away from the cheering crowds.

As Rita approached the hotel she noticed the crowds were gathered around below the third floor balcony. A group of dark-suited men stood up there looking down onto the street. One was Anthony Wedgewood-Benn, an up and coming star in the Labour party standing next to George who was in the middle of a passionate speech. His face glowed above a vibrant red carnation in his buttonhole. She stopped to catch his final words.

"We find embodied in the machine the skill, craft and hard physical work of the previous generation, and what it took ten men to do a decade ago can now be done by half that number. But I ask you brothers and sisters, does this mean that the labour force in our mines should be drastically reduced, putting more men out of jobs and bringing increased hardship to families who have sacrificed their lives for generations to work the mines? No. On the contrary we must deploy our labour force more efficiently and keep our productivity competitive with the miners of Poland and Kentucky. This great union of ours has done away with the unfair and divisive system of piecework and brought in a standard shift rate for face workers, but we still have work to do to ensure parity for all. Many challenges face us. We have warned the present government repeatedly about the economic madness of depending on imported energy from the Middle East, but up to now this has had little effect on a government that seems determined to introduce their so-called coal rationalization program..."

His hands cut through the air as he emphasized each point – just like years before when she had watched him speak at the club. He'd taken her breath away then and now the crowds faded to a blur and she focused only on him.

Finally, dazed from the glare of sunlight, she stumbled into the reception. A waitress passed by with a loaded silver tray and Rita snatched a large glass of white wine. The drink, a cheap Sauterne with a vinegary after-taste, didn't seem to calm her jittery nerves so she took another one and gulped it down. The day took on a rosier haze and she was starting to feel a little tipsy.

Holding the empty wine glass she scoured the crowded room. The mayor, a local butcher and well-known womaniser stood resplendent, the square gold chunks of his chain of office spanning his broad shoulders, his thick brown brush of a moustache speckled with flecks of beer foam. His wife, a small woman dwarfed by an enormous hat made entirely of magenta silk gardenias, stood by anxiously clasping her handbag. He talked loudly to two blondes in chequered blue shift dresses and only addressed his wife when he asked her to light his cigarette.

Rita, suddenly aware of her empty stomach, made her way to the food table that was spread with plates of cocktail sausages, pickles, pink curls of ham, large cheeses and baskets full of Scotch baps. The wine had made her hungry so she tore open a large bun and filled it with meat, cheese and pickles, then, oblivious to the other guests, she took a huge mouthful, chewing and savouring the tangy taste. Pickled cauliflower had always been her favourite.

"Have we laid enough food on for you?" a voice asked and George stood watching her, his face tanned and shining from the sunshine outside.

Rita's mouth was so full she could barely speak and the ball of food in her mouth so dry she couldn't swallow it. She began to laugh and choke while trying to point at the water jug with both hands. Smiling, George fumbled with a glass of water, sloshing it over a plate of salmon sandwiches. "I've lost my coordination," he spluttered, pushing the water towards her and she gulped it down together with the lump of food while he tried to mop up the soggy bread with a serviette.

"What a pair of ninnies," she laughed, "I don't usually make such a pig of myself. I was famished – I don't know what came over me." By now they were both shaking with laughter and Rita realized this was the first time she'd seen him really relax.

"You looked charming," he said, "And incredibly comfortable in a room full of stuff-shirts. Every woman here thinks she has to cock her little finger when she drinks a cup of tea. I mean it's a long time since I saw someone really enjoying food – I mean – actually relishing it."

Rita grabbed another glass of wine from a passing waitress. "Don't get carried away – I was only eating a sandwich." She gulped the wine, spilling a dribble of it down the front of her dress.

"You'd better watch it – too much of that and we'll be carrying you out soon," he said moving closer. The wine and the faint smell of his after-shave were making her giddy and she wondered if she'd ever noticed how well shaped his lips were.

"If you promise to be the one to carry me out I don't mind."

"Then let's get out of here," he said, clasping her wrist. A small man with wiry red hair and a badly fitting grey suit came up behind them. "George, Arthur wants to talk to you – says it's important.

"Tell him I'm busy – it can wait." He watched Rita intently, his eyes never leaving hers to look at the little man. "Come on – it's too crowded in here."

He guided her through knots and clusters of people who stopped their conversations and waved their hands or strained their necks to attract George's attention. Brightly coloured hats passed by her in a rainbow blur as George pulled her by the wrist, ignoring the voices around him.

Outside, she was hardly aware of her feet touching the cobblestones as they ducked under the overhanging lilac trees in the courtyard and through a small gate into a cobbled backstreet. Sunlight dabbed pale gold shadows on the old sandstone buildings and up in the eaves troughs she could hear the throaty coo of pigeons.

She followed him, as he pulled her along and studied his glossy hair and the hollow of his cheekbone. Suddenly he stopped, loosened his tie and took her by the shoulders. "I want to look at you, closely – the way you've been looking at me."

For a few moments they studied each other closely *for the first time ever*, thought Rita. *And after all these years.*

"I was just thinking how different we are," she said.

"And how alike," he replied.

She smoothed his hair away from his forehead and he pulled her towards him.

Together they stumbled and fell against the wall their bodies pressed so close they fit like two lost pieces of a puzzle. He kissed her eyes, her nose, her ears, her neck and she tasted sun and salt and fresh air. The smell she remembered from the years at Ida's.

"Where's your car?" he whispered as somewhere above them a window opened and the faint sound of laughter rippled the silence.

"Parked near the Three Tuns," she said.

"Let's drive somewhere," he kissed her fingertips, "Tell me where you'd most love to go – somewhere quiet and beautiful."

"Bamburgh," she replied, touching the outline of his chin. "A castle on a beach. The sea and the white sand. I remember my Dad took us there."

"I didn't realize you were such a romantic," he said, "Let's go now. I want to get you out of here – kidnap you before someone else takes you."

"My feet are killing me," she complained, kicking off her high heels and running barefoot alongside him. "Don't you have to make another speech? Won't they miss you?"

"No – I've said my piece already and I don't care if they're looking for me. I can't let you go now."

They ran down the smooth cobblestone street. Barefoot, Rita dangled her shoes in her left hand – George carried his jacket notched on one finger and slung over his right shoulder.

All around was the smell of summer flowers and walls of pale honey stone leaned inwards over the narrow lane, their surfaces covered with fronds of ivy and vine creepers. Somewhere in the distance a brass band was playing and a faint wave of cheering and applause floated across the city.

They stopped to look at a cracked stone gargoyle with tiny blue and white lobelia poking out from its mouth and nose. George took long garlands of the tiny flowers and draped them in Rita's hair and around her neck.

Her whole body tingled when the flowers touched her skin as if she was sparkling from head to toe. Her skin shimmering – on a summer day in a quiet old city.

They didn't make it to Bamburgh. A farmer with a large herd of sheep was blocking the main road just outside of Alnwick, so they turned back to the village and parked outside a little bed and breakfast place. They'd barely spoken on the way there, just touched every now and again, George's hand trailing over Rita's hair and shoulders and lips, her fingers brushing across his ear and smiling. She couldn't stop grinning from ear to ear when she looked at his face, grinning so widely that she felt he might think her a fool. But his face was so dear and so familiar to her she could visualize it even when she looked at the road ahead.

The Pitman's Daughter

It was a relief to get out of the car, run in through the front door and scrawl their signatures – Mr and Mrs Bishop – in the guest book. They scrambled, breathless and giggling up narrow back stairs to a room at the top of the house where cream muslin curtains flapped in and out of the small casement window. They stumbled and hopped as they pulled off socks and stockings, fumbling with the tricky elastic of braces and suspenders until, naked, they faced each other and Rita remembered Maggie once saying, "A body that's done hard, physical work takes your breath away."

The shock of skin touching skin was like sliding over a shiny satin sheet or slipping into warm water and she felt waves of pleasure gushing through her body before he was even inside her – over and over again, until she could have turned herself inside out for him. They made love, greedy for the taste of each other until finally they lay back, gulping for air, bodies streaked with sweat, hair plastered to their foreheads.

"Now I know," he said, "what it's like to make love to someone you've always adored."

Rita couldn't speak.

"Food tastes better after making love," said George coming back from the shops with fresh stotty cake, butter and jam. They ate huge wedges of it washed down with cold bottles of lager.

"Reminds me of the bait I used to take down to the pit," he said, wiping a smudge of butter from her chin. "The first jam sandwich of the day always tasted the best – '*smashinbaitthat*' my dad would say when he picked up his bait bag from the kitchen table."

They fed each other spoonfuls of jam for a lark, licking the stray droplets from their faces and bodies.

Afterwards, stretched out on the bed they talked and talked – sharing stories about their memories and their separate lives. George described the horror of going down the pit for the first time and how the fear and terror soon changed into the monotony of scraping and digging for eight hours straight. Rita told him how she despised the street and the gossiping interfering women. "I didn't want to end up like them – spending the afternoon leaning on the gate watching time pass by – I fought like hell to prevent that."

"Rita," he said, "We both wanted the same things."

"Then why did it take us so long to get to *this*?" she asked, trailing a finger down the small hollow at the base of his back.

"I suppose I was afraid of you, in a way," he said. "I always thought of us as being like two lions stalking each other, circling around, afraid to touch for fear we'd tear each other to pieces."

"Very poetic," Rita said. "Rrrrrrrrooar."

George laughed and moved his arm across her shoulders "But the funny thing was Rita, I always knew where you were and it comforted me to think of you walking through all the familiar places. I suppose I knew sometime we'd both conquer our pride and make a truce."

"You are *very* dramatic," said Rita. "Ida said you were a budding poet."

"You're right – I was poet laureate at the pit for all those lovelorn miners. *Shall I compare thee to a summer's day at the top of Whittington Hill* and all that…"

Rita rolled over and pulled him down onto her. Then they made love again and slept until late afternoon.

Later on the way to Bamburgh they stopped at a pub on the edge of a steep hill. Inside the lounge with its red, flocked velvet wallpaper they listened to Beatles' songs and ate shepherd's pie covered with H.P. sauce. In the middle of *Yesterday* they began to neck and kiss with such gusto the landlord came over and told them to, "Tek yer necking and slobbering elsewhere – this is a respectable establishment." They ran out red faced and howling with laughter.

At Bamburgh they stood looking down over the walls of the castle, onto the white strip of beach where foam-flecked seawater washed the sand into deep ridges.

"The air is so clean here," he said. "Reminds me of Whittington Hill. My mother tried so hard to keep me healthy."

The Pitman's Daughter

Inside the castle with its suits of armour, ornate silver candlesticks and dark brown and maroon walled rooms, George drifted aimlessly from one display case to another. "Don't you like schmoozing around stately homes?" asked Rita

"Reminds me of why I got into the fight in the first place – it looks like a mine-owner's place here, furnished with the sweat and blood of men, women and children. Let's get the hell out."

Once outside he chased Rita down the hill. The sunset was brilliant, dappling the water with golden discs of light. "Look, George," she cried. "Real gold from the sky. We don't need money any more – we can live off the land – live on love."

"Fantastic," he shouted, tearing off his socks and wading in the water. Soon they were splashing around like two giddy children.

"Remember Burt Lancaster and Deborah Kerr on the beach in that film *From Here to Eternity?*" she said, catching him around the waist.

"I'll freeze my arse off in here," he said, splashing her. They dried off in the grass and drove back to the town square where Morris Men were dancing, and they stood watching, feeling the ground shake as the dancers banged their wooden sticks on the cobblestones.

"Isn't this some kind of fertility ritual?" asked Rita, marvelling that such husky rugby types would actually wear ribbons and twirl hankies in the air.

"I believe they're trying to wake up Mother Earth by banging their staffs on the ground."

"Fascinating," said Rita.

"Yes, fertility rituals are fascinating," said George moving closer to Rita so that his hand rested in the small of her back. "I think I'm ready for one of my own. How about you?

On Sunday morning Rita stood at the hotel window brushing her hair and looking down at the mess of rotten fruit and vegetables scattered across the market place.

"Place needs a good clean up," she said. "Everyone's gone to church and left the sparrows and dogs to do the job." She looked round at George who was stretched out on the bed, face buried in the pillow. His hair was sticking up on one side, his cheek pink and creased from the pillow.

"I can't get used to seeing you all mussed up like this," she said. "You were always *so* perfect. Even when we used to go to Ida's your hair was always combed and plastered down."

"Now you're really embarrassing me." He rolled onto his back and threw the pillow at her. "What about you, Miss Prissy with the silver bracelet and lace hankies."

"My mam's fault. I was her dolly."

"I used to dream about you and your chestnut ringlets."

"No – really?" said Rita, flopping down on the bed beside him.

"I loved to walk along the street with you – loved your clean dresses and your rosy cheeks and your imperious little voice. You were like a tiny empress."

"And I thought you were a young Prince Charming with your clean shirts and your neatly-combed hair," said Rita stroking the soft hair that curled over his ear.

"We were both just bairns. Each with a mission to escape from Crag Street before it knocked the fight out of us."

"Hey – it's Sunday," she said, kissing his chest, "What do you usually do on Sunday?".

Turning to prop his head on one hand, he smoothed back his hair with the other.

"Sunday – Sunday – sleep in, read letters, write speeches, read more letters then write a few."

"Don't you ever go anywhere? A drive – a pub – for dinner?" said Rita resting her face on the pillow next to him.

"I'm a recluse. I gave up all that social stuff for work," he said, smiling so broadly her heart turned a somersault.

"This is so strange," she said, "being here like this together and not sniping at each other."

"I like it," he said, lazily tracing the line of her collarbone. "And what do you usually do on Sundays?"

"Sunday's not Sunday without Mam's roast beef, a game of Newmarket with the family and a good row with the old man. At least when

The Pitman's Daughter

I'm not away on business."

"I envy you and your family life."

"Seriously?" asked Rita, sitting up and crossing her legs.

"Seriously – I feel like a drifter – no anchor -nothing," said George. "All the union boys call me brother but when the meeting's over and the talking's stopped they all go home to their wives and children."

"I thought you said once there's no room for commitment in your life," said Rita, shuffling closer to him.

"I'm beginning to reconsider," he said, catching hold of her shoulders and pulling her onto him.

"I could kill for a cuppa," she spluttered.

"Later," he whispered.

∽

They were sitting by the window of the Northern Hotel restaurant looking out onto a courtyard. Tall fuchsia bushes bordered the window and the front garden was dotted with pansies of every colour. A gardener's wheelbarrow piled high with tools and gloves and broken old plant pots stood by an ivy-covered wall.

"That's what I would've been if I hadn't gone into the union," said George.

"A gardener?" asked Rita, spooning out the last of her sundae, and then tipping up the glass to enjoy the last few drops of strawberry juice.

"I love the way you eat" said George, catching hold of her hand, "You're so voracious."

"It's all part of my wild beast image – remember – the circling lions and all that," teased Rita.

"You'll never let me forget that – will you?"

"No – but anyway – why would you be a gardener?"

The early afternoon sun was streaming into the courtyard, throwing yellow shadows across the hotel walls. It looked like a scene from a Van Gogh painting. Rita thought of sunflowers.

"I'd love the quiet. I love the way plants open up to the sun – and of course I'm an expert digger. All those years down the mine haven't been entirely wasted. Besides, I feel good when I put something back into the soil."

"That's lovely," said Rita. "You'll have me in tears soon."

"You're a complete cynic," said George, folding his serviette. "Not a scrap of sentiment in your body!"

They spent the afternoon browsing at a small antique fair at the village hall. Rita admired a pair of rhinestone earrings in the shape of ladybirds and George insisted on buying them. "Right from New York – made in the early twenties," said the vendor, a pudgy man with thick, grey eyebrows and a dyed black wig. "Real Art Déco."

George kissed her earlobes as he fastened on the sparkling insects.

"My first present to you," he smiled.

"First?" asked Rita.

"First of many," he announced.

Rita felt a tiny core of fear inside. Tomorrow was another workday when everything would have to go back to normal, the regular routine. *But how could it*, she asked herself? George was making plans that included her and she had no idea how to deal with commitment. What would happen when they had to consider the practicalities of their lives?

"I'll take you back to Durham," she said. "I'm tired of this place."

"Right," said George, "and maybe we can catch evensong at the cathedral. I love the choir on Sunday night."

Driving home, Rita's stomach wrapped itself in knots. She'd look at George and a flood of emotion squeezed at her heart. He chatted about his work and Durham and the Tories while she listened, worrying about how today would end. Would she really see him again or would she be just like the other women – sacrificed for the grand cause? She remembered those poems of her childhood and those messages that told her love hurts, love is painful, and love is desperate. For twenty-seven years she'd avoided it but now she was beginning to panic.

They parked the car on the castle green and walked towards the cathedral.

"I love this place," said George, sliding his arm round Rita's shoulders and kissing her cheek, "it fills me with the spirit of those early Christians – Cuthbert and The Venerable Bede. Whenever I feel lost I come here in the evening and sit inside for a while. It calms me down."

Fading daylight filtered through the high, narrow windows and the white surplices of the choir glowed bluish in the semi-dusk.

"Let's sit at the back," Rita whispered, pulling at George's sleeve.

"No, over here," he said, motioning towards a little stone chapel off to the side. "The Durham Light Infantry chapel – we'll still hear the choir."

"Why do you want to sit on your own," asked Rita, looking up at the tattered banners – relics from the Battle of Waterloo or something.

"I need to talk and this seems to be the right place," he said, bowing his head down as they passed the high altar and sat on the shaky metal chairs. "Tell me about the baby."

She knew he'd ask her sooner or later and so, starting from the time she found Maggie at the bus station, she told him everything. He never looked at her the whole time, but stood up when she was finished.

"I have to go outside," he said in a breathless voice. "Stay here – I'll be back in a minute." He disappeared behind a stone pillar.

Telling him should have cleared the air but it didn't. It was as if Maggie stood there between them, reminding them of her pain and ruining their pleasure, saddling it with old memories.

Everything had been so simple in the bed and breakfast place when it was just the two of them. Now there were three.

The shadows grew darker in the chapel and the choir more distant. Rita felt completely alone in the great thousand-year-old building. She could have closed her eyes and drifted off into a peaceful sleep, just like the reclining bishops lying on their stone tombs with hands held together in petrified prayer. In the ancient chapel time seemed irrelevant and she drifted into a state of half-sleep. She woke to the sound of George shuffling into the chair beside her. His face was white with fear or maybe panic. She knew something was wrong.

"I feel like a penitent coming to confession," he said. "I have to tell you something more about Maggie."

Rita felt groggy – disoriented, "George, I know everything – I don't want to keep going over it."

"I've told nobody else, Rita – only you. But I'm plagued by this. I have been since Maggie died. I keep imagining her – dreaming about her – the way she was on that last night. Listen to me Rita. She saved me up in the attic."

"Just calm down," said Rita, "and tell me slowly."

"After the funeral," he said, falling back into the chair. "It happened then. I went up into the attic to clean up some things – a few old suitcases and such. I heard a noise in the next-door attic – the Barker's place. I thought it was Ned clearing up but then I heard someone calling my name. More like howling it. My first thought was that Ned had hurt himself getting up there so I pushed aside the old door between the attics."

"You mean you can cross through from one to the other?" asked Rita, feeling shivery and nervous.

"You could run the whole length of the street if you want to," continued George. "Anyway, I crossed through Ned's attic. I couldn't see anyone, but the door to Maggie's attic was open. I couldn't make much out in the darkness but it looked like someone was moving about in there. I crept closer and saw a big, dark shape – and it was *him.*"

"Who," Rita asked, suddenly afraid now the shadows were deeper.

"Him – Jordy. He was like a great horrible clown sitting there, waiting for me. His face was white and pasty."

"With make up – I saw him too," said Rita, wincing at the memory of the face she'd tried to forget.

"He was holding a big bag and laughing 'I'm packing up Neddy Barker's socks' he said holding up an old grey sock that was stuffed full of something. 'He's got over three thousand pound up here and I'm gonna clear it out for him,' he said then started shouting that if I ever breathed a word of it he'd tell everyone what I'd been doing up in the attic – above his own head, with his own wife. Then he started crawling towards me so I grabbed a broom handle. I didn't know whether to poke him in the chest or hit him over the head with it. I held it up in the air and he just started laughing. His whole body was shaking as if he was having a seizure, and then he lifted up the long shirt he was wearing, called me a great nancy boy and showed me the women's stockings and lace suspenders he was wearing. He said he was going to – sorry Rita – *give it to me up the arse* and called me a *fucking fairy*. So I yelled at him – told him he was mad, sick, needed a doctor and that's when Maggie came up behind him. She screamed at him then leaped onto his back. Just launched herself onto him, tore at his hair, grabbed and clawed at his face and eyes. I couldn't move – I couldn't leave in case he killed her and I was *afraid*. I felt so useless. The big hero – the saviour of the miners couldn't even defend a frail woman. Anyway, she must have drawn blood. He roared like stuck pig and threw her off onto a pile of old bricks. She was hurt. She whimpered and then started to crawl towards the opening. I remember picking up the stick and holding it up to hit him. I reached back *so far* to hit him – hit him hard enough to knock him out *but I couldn't bring myself to do it*. That's when he laughed at me again and pushed his face right into mine. By then the blood was dribbling down his cheek, and he grabbed the stick from my hands. We struggled for probably a few seconds but I couldn't hold it. When he got the stick he cracked me across the back of the head and I blacked out."

"That's when he chased her and threw her out of the attic. He pushed her so hard she cracked her ribs," said Rita feeling tears prick at her eyes.

For a while they both sat, speechless. The spirit of Maggie filled the empty space around them. Then George got up and pressed his body against the old stone wall, his cheek squashed against the deep ridges and his arms spread out like the branches of a crucifix. The scene impressed itself on Rita's memory like an old black and white snapshot that would one day fall out crinkled and dusty from the pockets of some family album and awaken painful memories.

Later, when Rita dropped George off at Redhills he held her for a long time.

"Stay with me tonight."

"It's too soon," she said, "I need time to think. We can talk tomorrow."

"I'll phone you at your office," he said. "I'll want to know everything you've been doing since we left each other tonight."

She watched him turn and wave goodbye and when he disappeared through the door she got back into her car and drove sobbing back to Roker. They would *not* talk tomorrow because she'd already decided to catch the seven-thirty train to London. Perhaps it was self-destructiveness that made her listen to the nagging voice telling her it wouldn't work – *could never work* between them. Or *was it the picture of him standing like a coward up in the attic – doing nothing to help Maggie?* All she knew was she had to put some distance between herself and George. So she ran. Hopped on the London train and ended up at a party in South London – Blackheath Village to be exact – at the flat of one of the television sales reps from the London office.

39

After drinking a bottle and a half of German wine Rita lay back in one of those huge wicker chairs, her mind drifting as she watched the action. The air was thick with marijuana smoke. People smoked it through water pipes, rolled fat joints or even sprinkled it over food and ate it. It was then she met Mark. He squatted beside her and held up a thick, messy looking cigarette. He had a long, thin face, a mass of brown curly hair and wore black. "Wanna drag," he said in a strong Southern accent.

Rita took a few puffs as the music changed and the room filled with throbbing sounds.

When she woke up the next morning he was sleeping on the floor beside her. He took her back to the hotel in a grey Alfa Romeo, fed her a drink that took away her sick hangover and she was eternally grateful to him.

Mark was a graphic designer and terribly trendy, with friends that included a girl who claimed to be David Bowie's ex-hairdresser and two heavy beer drinkers who were distant cousins of one of the Queen's polo pony trainers. He hung around with debutantes and music promoters and Rita soon found that sex with him was like having a haircut. Mildly stimulating, fairly relaxing and fully deodorized. No body odours of any type were allowed. Mark insisted on perfumed cleanliness, often bathing her before making love and looking after meticulous details like bath oils and body creams and fruit flavoured soaps.

They shopped and lunched – Carnaby Street, Chelsea, Biba's and Kensington Market. In a marijuana-fuelled, patchouli-perfumed haze they floated from one party to the next and Rita's pain at leaving George gradually subsided into a dull ache.

One Saturday night Rita had a little get-together with Mark and a few friends in the flat she'd leased near Fulham Rd. They'd had dinner, drank a lot of wine and were getting totally wasted on pot. Good stuff now she had enough money to keep her dealer coming back with the best Lebanese Black around. Since she'd started to commute between London and Sunderland her business had boomed. She'd stay up north for the first two or three days of the week – do the paperwork, make the phone calls and show up for dinner at her Mam and Dad's new bungalow in Seaburn. Iris Hawkins had rediscovered shopping and was doing up the new house in mint green and old rose so she always greeted Rita with a tableful of wallpaper books and paint samples.

On Thursdays Rita would come back to London where she found a kind of refuge from the old painful memories. This was the place for new business connections and Rita threw herself into moneymaking with such enthusiasm she barely had time to sleep. Mark was always hanging around smoking marijuana or drinking Belgian lager with a few friends when she came back from the office. Tonight it was the ex-hairdresser, a couple of T.V. sales reps, their girlfriends and some earl's son who worked at Harrods' and did Morris dancing for a hobby. They'd all sunk a few gin and tonics because of the heat, and the earl's son started dancing, twirling a couple of Rita's scarves in the air. Connie, the hairdresser, joined in with him. *She's a real vamp*, thought Rita.

Blonde hair piled high, tight black dress, eyes ringed in kohl pencil and strings of turquoise beads. She lived on cocaine and tried to get Rita to sample it but the whole thing had been a disappointment when Connie rubbed it on Rita's gums. All it did was make Rita's mouth numb as if she'd just come from the dentist's office.

The men watched Connie as her braless breasts bounced like two small beach balls, the joints were passed around and eventually she flopped onto a P.V.C. beanbag chair in a sweaty embrace with the Morris dancer. Rita could feel Mark's cool, dry hand on the back of her neck as the music closed in around them like fog. She was immobile – limbs like lead then there was a brisk knock on the door.

"Get it," said Mark to one of the sales reps.

"Turn up the music," said the Morris dancer.

"Get me another drink," said Connie.

"I feel sick," said the sales rep's girlfriend and threw up on the floor. Rita still couldn't move.

"Rita," she heard the sales rep say. "Rita there's a man here to see you."

"Christ," she sputtered when George walked into the room.

"You must be Rita's bank manager," said Mark staring at George's suit. "I didn't know you'd asked him."

The hairdresser stopped necking with the Morris dancer and looked up. "Mmmm – I love financial experts in *shhuits*," she slurred. "Are you married?"

"Bitch," said the Morris dancer and slipped his hand down the front of her dress. She started to wrestle with him again.

George just stood there blank faced.

"Lighten up, man," said Mark. "Want a drink?"

"No," said George. "I came to see Rita."

"Oh – it's one of your school chums from back up North," said Mark faking an accent.

"Shut up," Rita said, cringing.

"Can I talk to you – outside?" George said, sidestepping the pool of vomit.

"Roll another one, Teddy," said Mark. "I'm losing my buzz."

Rita tried to pull herself up. *I feel like shit,* she thought, trying to command her legs to move. Once outside George held her by the shoulders.

"What the hell are you doing here?"

"You're such a fucking prude George – these are my friends. We're just chilling. What else is there to do?"

"Looks like I came here just in time to rescue you from a bunch of junkies."

"Just like always – Mr Perfect. Always think you know what's best for everyone." Her head was pounding.

"I want to know why you walked out on me without a word – nothing. Just buggered off after everything that happened between us."

"Don't like that treatment, do you?" she teased.

"Grow up, Rita. I thought it all meant something when we were together."

"Ask yourself," she spat the words out. "You've run out on plenty of people before. What's it feel like to be the poor sod scrabbling around in the dust?"

"So that's what was worrying you," he took her by the shoulders and went to kiss her but the door opened behind them and Mark came out.

"Hey, poor class, man – get your fucking hands off my girlfriend," he shouted.

George whispered to Rita, "Come back to Durham with me tonight. Come now."

She began to cry – sobbing and shaking – *like a stupid fool.* Something told her *not to give in.* Something like revenge, Old Testament style.

"Buzz off, mate," said Mark. "See how you've upset her."

"Rita come with me now," said George, but Rita's feet were rooted to the spot.

"She's not your wife, arsehole, now get lost." Mark pulled her back towards the door and for a moment she wanted to turn – grab George's hand and run away but she couldn't take that one step. As the door shut she caught a last look at his face. He stood there looking broken, as if she'd dug a knife in deep and then gouged his heart with the blade.

The Pitman's Daughter

She sucked back the dry marijuana smoke and told herself it was best that they forgot about love. They could never be together. All they were ever did was hurt each other.

A year later, Mark straightened out. He gave up drugs, threw out his junkie friends and discovered he actually had a talent for business. With his tall, slim figure clad in a well-cut suit and newly cut hair he was the picture of elegance. Rita barely recognized the man who had once been a pot-smoking hippie. Mark was also creative and had some great ideas for marketing campaigns, so it seemed natural that he should join Rita in her company. Next they decided to get married. Mark called it a personal and commercial merger.

A week before the wedding, when the dress (a floaty chiffon mini-dress edged with daisies) was bought and the cake ordered, Rita was threading some pearls onto a headband and watching the evening news. The conservative government was under siege and the miners were celebrating. She watched as Arthur Scargill delivered a speech telling how the Tory government had rejected the miners' demands for a 43% pay hike and now – for the first time since 1926 – miners from all over Britain were coming out on strike. There at his right shoulder was George, his face set in the smile that made her heart jump. She dropped the box of tiny pearls and watched them scatter across the floor, rolling into the corners where they lodged under the legs of the chintz sofa.

The miners were meeting at the Strand Palace Hotel and Rita knew she had to see him one last time before she was married – *to make sure*. She ran out in the rain wearing only a thin smock top over her jeans and flagged down a taxi.

The lobby of the hotel was packed with screaming revellers, sloshing beer and champagne over the floor, blowing party horns and throwing streamers up into the air. She pressed herself up against the wall and stood on tiptoes. A young man with a droopy moustache thrust a drink into her hand, dropped a party hat on her head and tried to dance her inside the great ballroom.

"The iron workers are coming out on strike in solidarity with us miners," he babbled. "Us young'uns have really shook up the N.U.M and we've George Nelson to thank for that."

That's when she saw him, being carried around on the shoulders of three or four swaying union men. He was holding a bottle of champagne up high then swigging it down – didn't look so immaculate either. For once his tie was undone, his shirt collar open but that broad smile made her twist the engagement ring hard around her finger. *You've finally done it*, she thought. *You got where you wanted to be after twelve years total sacrifice. Was it worth it?* She wondered, watching him hold up his arms in victory and then she suddenly felt something wet on her hand. Looking down she saw her ring finger was dripping blood.

Before anyone saw her she slipped out and went home to pick up the pearls. The hairband had to be ready in less than a week.

1973

40

Rita was running late and cursing the Prime Minister for calling a state of emergency. Her Dad had kept her on the phone for half an hour, breathless with excitement.

"We're finally gonna bring those Tory bastards crashing down," he said, blasting her eardrums as he shouted down the phone. "We came out last week because they wouldn't give us a 7% raise and now Heath's bringing in the three-day working week."

"I already know," said Rita, trying to put on lipstick and listen to her Dad and David Bowie at the same time. "The buses and tubes are in a real mess and people are cursing the greedy miners."

Walter wasn't even listening to Rita. "George says Heath's gonna call a General Election."

Rita's heart thudded a bit as it always did when she heard George's name. "Well – and what do you predict the outcome will be?" she asked, satisfied with the reflection of the sleek woman dressed in a long, slim halter-necked evening dress made entirely of midnight blue sequins.

"Of course we'll bring them down," said Walter. "They're finished. Harold Wilson will be prime minister. He'll appoint Michael Foot as Secretary of State for Employment and good old Mike will give us everything we want."

"And what do you want, Dad?" asked Rita, checking her watch and calculating that Mark would be at the hotel in about ten minutes.

"Respect – first and foremost," he said, his breaths coming in rasping gulps. Too much time down the mines had coated his lungs with dust.

"I'm sure you're looking for something more than that," said Rita. "Or we wouldn't all be suffering like this."

"Well – of course we want the pay raise – but we're asking for compensation for all those poor buggers suffering with black lung – and we want a superannuation scheme so your broken-down old Da can finally retire for good."

"Well George has been working hard for you," said Rita, impatient to get away. She asked after her mam and finally got Walter off the phone. She'd be lucky to get a taxi in this chaos, but the doorbell chime told her it was finally here and she threw on her fur wrap and made her way out of the elegant mews flat with its cream furniture, buttery walls and glittering mirrors. The February air was brisk as she held up her skirt to cross the wet cobblestones. The taxi driver held open the door for her. "The Dorchester," she said, arranging her skirts carefully on the seat. She exhaled and rested her head back, finally able to relax for the first time that day.

She'd been married to Mark for two years now. They'd had a small registry office wedding – just a few friends and immediate family. She'd dreaded seeing her Mam and Dad sitting next to Mark's middle-class parents who lived deep in the suburbs of Purley, but Walter and Iris showed up larger than life and Rita had to laugh when she saw Iris's navy blue dress with the giant white polka-dots, next to her Dad whose swollen pot belly strained the buttons on his suit. Mark's mother, Mamie and his father Jim could barely get a word in edgeways once the Hawkins started chatting and when Walter got a few beers inside him she was worried he might start patting Mamie's bum.

They'd bought the mews flat in St. John's Wood a year later and Mark had spent months supervising its renovation. The results were breathtaking. So much so that he began to get requests to design other interiors. Rita helped him set up his own office and in the next year he worked hard and set up a successful interior design company. Hard work was the core of their lives and as the taxi pulled into Park Lane, she realized that Sunday was the only day they ever actually spent time together. During the week they were so exhausted from travelling and working late they collapsed into bed and were asleep within minutes. On Sundays they read the papers, took a walk in Hyde Park to listen to the speakers, then had lunch together.

Life had settled into a routine of sorts but Rita still felt emptiness gnawing inside her. Her friends told her she was lucky. Women flocked to Mark, attracted by his laid-back elegance, but he stayed true to her. Now tonight he'd be waiting at The Dorchester where she was to receive an award for Excellence and Vision in the Field of Electronics Marketing. As one of the leading retailers to support the introduction of home videocassette recorders, she predicted they'd revolutionize home viewing. She'd been right of course and the whole industry was poised to usher in the new era. She and Mark made a perfect team. They rarely raised their voices to each other and he was very accommodating. At times, however, she found his politeness cold – like living with a friendly stranger. Sometimes she longed for a blazing row of the type she'd seen daily as a child on Crag Street. A bit of cursing, a few plates thrown did wonders to clear the air.

The taxi pulled up outside the pale grey façade that glittered with rows of white lights. The uniformed doorman swept up and opened the door, assisting her as she climbed out and, within seconds of her arrival Mark burst from the front doors holding an umbrella out to shelter her from the drizzle. His long face looked gaunt. She made a mental note to make some hearty home-cooked suppers to put a bit of meat on his bones. "Cutting it a bit fine, darling," he said, taking her arm and guiding her into the brightly lit lobby.

"Dad was on the phone – he's ready to bring the government to its knees," she said, smoothing her hair down. "How do I look?"

"Gorgeous as ever," he said, kissing her temple lightly and holding the banquet room door open for her. "They're going to bring the country to its knees with their ridiculous demands."

"Well they've sacrificed their health so we coddled southerners can be warm," said Rita, feeling the hairs on the back of her neck bristle.

"I suppose that's the usual argument," he said, looking suddenly tired. "But what makes them different from a farmer or a factory worker?"

"You wouldn't know," said Rita, regretting she'd ever mentioned her dad.

"Darling – let's not fight. No more talk of miners. This is your special night. Look." He turned her around to see the banquet room in all its splendour. Crystal chandeliers sparkled above tables covered with white damask cloths. At the centre of each table was a slim vase containing a single white lily surrounded by ferns. Candles flickered and guests in evening dress mingled around the tables.

Rita grabbed a glass of champagne from a passing waitress and quickly drained the glass. She reached quickly for another one.

"Hey – take it easy," said Mark. "You'll need a clear head to make a speech later."

"Don't worry," said Rita, wondering where that nagging sense of alienation had suddenly come from. "It'll give me inspiration."

They sat close to the front next to a couple from Swansea. The husband, a florid though handsome man in his fifties had a successful string of TV repair shops in South Wales. His wife was much younger – probably in her late twenties. She was a small, curvy blonde woman with sugar pink lipstick, matching nails and a cleavage that was bursting out of her bodice.

Mark was an expert at small talk and was chatting like an old friend to the man who introduced himself as Owen while Rita sat silently wondering what on earth she could say to Roni (with an *i* she emphasized). It was Roni who finally broke the silence. "So Rita," she said in her Welsh twang, "What do you do while Mark is working his long hours?"

Rita measured up Roni's stiff platinum curls and her cheap silver dress with the large diamante clips at the shoulders. Suddenly she felt sorry for this girl who was simply an accessory for her husband's arm

"Oh – I tinker around with my own business," said Rita being deliberately vague. Telling the truth would kill any hope of conversation.

"Owen says he might help me start my own manicure business. I think that would be so exciting – I mean every woman loves to be pampered, don't you think?" she said, suddenly animated.

"I suppose so," said Rita feeling her mind drift to her speech and the world of videotape formats. "Excuse me a moment." She stood up quickly, almost upsetting her glass of wine in the process. She bent down and whispered in Mark's ear. "I need to go and rehearse my speech." He nodded and she slipped away, thankful that another couple had taken a seat at the table and occupied Roni's attention.

Outside in the lobby she took a deep breath, looked around and headed towards the bar where she ordered a large gin and tonic. It was her dad and his talk of the union that set off these dark feelings and the old emptiness had come back at just the wrong time. She turned away from the bar and looked around the oak-panelled room with its little red-shaded lights. Businessmen in dark suits were huddled at tables probably talking shop. She'd been in many places like this over the years, enjoying the transience and anonymity of it, but now she was tired of it. One hotel bar was like another – places you passed through and left no mark. And then, just as she placed her empty glass on the bar, she had the distinct feeling someone was watching her. Glancing to her left she saw George standing at the door staring at her. She felt a downward pull throughout her whole body – a dizziness that didn't allow her to trust her own legs. He walked towards her, his eyes never leaving her face and then, miraculously, he was there – right beside her. His face was unchanged, and though the beginnings of small lines had formed around his eyes they were still the same calm grey-blue they'd always been.

"Rita," he said, touching her arm and sending a thrill through her body. "You look amazing."

"What are you doing here?" were the only words she could muster.

"I could ask you the same question," he said, smiling at her.

"I have to go," she said, feeling panicky.

"I just came from a meeting,"

"I'm due to make a speech in about five minutes."

He dropped his hand from her arm. "I'm staying at the Strand Palace," he said. "Come and see me tonight."

Rita looked hard at the face she'd known for so much of her life and felt as if a strong hand was squeezing her heart. "Maybe," she said. "I'll see."

And then she was rushing through the lobby, nearly tripping on the hem of her dress, pushing at the wrong door and almost sobbing. Pull yourself together, she told herself, but it felt as if every nerve ending in her body was on edge. She got back to the table just as the soup course was being served. Mark looked at her expectantly. "Something come up?" he asked.

"Just ran into one of the buyers from Durham," she said, grabbing the water glass and almost knocking it over. Roni was already deep in conversation with a petite redheaded woman so nobody else had noticed Rita's absence. She tapped her foot up and down and began to chew at her fingernails.

"Last minute nerves darling?" said Mark, spreading his arm across the back of her chair.

She nodded and began to spoon the soup into her mouth, not tasting a drop of it.

After her speech Rita was conscious of the applause that accompanied her back to her seat, but it seemed to come from another place far away. She must have been persuasive enough because Mark was up on his feet clapping. "Terrific," he said, embracing her. "You're an inspiration."

Roni's expression had changed into one of total awe now she'd realized the extent of Rita's "tinkering" in the business world and was looking at Rita with wide-eyed admiration. Suddenly it became an absolute necessity for Rita to get out of there and go to the Strand Palace Hotel, though Mark's gentle encouragement filled her with such guilt she could barely look at him. She took his arm. "I need to go somewhere quiet – be alone for a while," she said, kissing his forehead. "I'll stop by the office on the way home – just to get my head together."

"Sure," he said, disappointment colouring his face. "I'll stick around for a bit and talk to Owen."

She said her polite goodbyes and then, wrapping her fur around her shoulders, made her way through the lobby. The doorman hailed a taxi and she was off down Park Lane, willing the taxi to move faster.

The Strand Palace seemed darker than the Dorchester and she attracted some stares as she swished through the lobby in the sparkly dress. George had whispered the number to her as she left the bar and she was hoping she'd remembered it correctly. The thought of finding some unfamiliar face at the door was a terrible one since an embarrassing scene at the front desk would inevitably follow. The receptionist would take her for a highly paid call-girl.

Going up in the elevator she had no clue what she would say to George. But some force was driving her upwards – as if she was returning home.

The elevator doors whooshed open on the fourth floor and she felt a quick rush of heat to her face when she stepped out, her heart pulsing and her eyes stinging with unexpected tears. Room 405 was halfway along the hall and she stood outside studying the many scratches on the oak-panelled door before raising her fisted hand and knocking gently. There was a rustling sound inside and for a moment she wondered if he had another woman in there, but suddenly the door opened and he stood there in his shirtsleeves, his top button undone. By now the tears streamed down her cheeks as she stepped in and fell into his arms and then she was kissing him as if she wanted to taste every part of him again, her hands fumbling with his shirt buttons, pulling off the shirt, stroking the sinew of his arms and pressing herself to him as he undid the zip at the back of the dress letting it flop to the floor in a sequinned puddle. With one swift action he scooped her up into his arms and carried her to the bed where they ripped off the remaining clothing until their naked bodies slid together in the natural way she'd always remembered.

Afterwards they lay close together as if any distance between them might drive them apart. Rita kissed the hollows near his collarbone then propped herself up on her elbow to look at him. Now halfway through his thirtieth decade, his face had become more angular, the jaw stronger, his cheekbones more defined. His hair had darkened to a sandy blond and curled at his temples, but his eyes were still the same clear blue with grey flecks and the tiny network of lines at their corners drew more attention to the smile he now directed onto her.

"I must apologize," he said, grinning, "I forgot to say hello."

"Your body said it for you," she said, tracing the circle of his nipple.

He cupped her breast in one hand. "Watch out or we'll be replaying the whole greeting again."

"Well it's so nice to see you, Mr Nelson," she said, sliding her hand downwards and in an instant he had flipped over onto her and they made love again until she cried out with pleasure.

She must have drifted off to sleep because when she came to the bedside clock read 4:30 and she realized with a start that Mark would be wondering where on earth she was. George was sound asleep beside her, so she reached out for the phone and gently dialled her home. The phone rang for a long time until there was a click and she heard Mark's voice, husky with sleep. She imagined him lying alone in the white bedroom, the black and white bedspread rumpled, his leather slippers placed neatly on the fur rug. "Mark – I lay down on my office couch and fell asleep. Sorry."

"See you for breakfast," he mumbled.

"Go back to sleep," she said, guilty at his absolute trust.

"Bye, luv," he said.

The crisp click told her he'd hung up and she flopped back onto the pillow.

"He believed you then," said George in a voice so clear it shocked her.

Rita could barely look at him. "I feel like shit doing that to him."

"Do you love him?"

Rita felt the tears pressing at her eyes again. "I never loved him and I don't deserve him."

"Then why did you stay that time I came to London? I begged you to come with me."

"I don't know, George. I've got this stubborn streak of pride that seems bent on ruining my life."

The Pitman's Daughter

George sat up and plumped his pillows. He lay back looking at her, not saying anything. She began to feel a mild fluttering of panic as if he was about to slip away from her again.

"Just say the word, George. I'll leave him and come with you. It's you I've loved – always. Since we were bairns at Ida's shop."

George reached out and pushed back the lock of hair that had fallen across her cheek. He went to speak but she put her hand over his mouth. "Don't say it George. Don't send me away. You're in my body – my head – my dreams."

He gathered her to him gently, kissing the top of her head. "I love you so much Rita – it frightens me. I feel like it'd consume every bit of my life and at this point I'm travelling here and there at a moment's notice – we're on the brink of…"

The shrill ring of the phone broke through the quiet. George looked at Rita, his face in a panic. She nodded and he lifted the receiver. She could hear the animated voice at the other end and George's sudden attention to whatever orders were being given.

When it was over he clunked the phone down and lay back, running his fingers through his hair. "Shit – I'll have to shower quickly," he said. "Just lie back and I'll be out in a sec." He struggled out of the blankets and bent over to kiss her. "You were always my little dolly," he said, grabbing a towel and smiling back at her.

Then the shower started up and with a heaviness in her body, she gathered up her clothes, slipped them on and wrote a message on the hotel notepad. *I'll love you my whole life, Rita*, it simply said. She propped it up and then slipped out the door. It was up to him. If he wanted to find her, he would.

1984

41

Rita's car slowed to a standstill when she hit the line of cars parked nose to tail as they waited to board the BC ferry. Once an hour, on the hour, the ship crossed the Straits of Georgia from Tsawassin to Victoria carrying tourists, backpackers, visiting family members, the occasional commuter and weekend residents looking for a quiet spot far away from the daily rush of the Vancouver mainland. Rita was heading to her cottage and cursing herself for landing here at rush hour; the five o'clock ferry was the worst for crowding – especially on a Friday with all those weekenders determined to wring out every bit of enjoyment from the break. Today, the last Friday before Christmas, line-ups were worse that ever and Rita cursed herself for leaving the office so late.

The huge ship with its three red chimneys visible through the mist lay in wait beyond the line of ticket booths and offices, ready to gulp up people and cars into its hold. Rita felt a headache begin to throb at her temples and spread to the bridge of her nose. The rain was bad for her sinuses and she dreaded the thought of being turned away at the gate if the ferry was full. Besides, she was gasping for a drink – anything to loosen up the coiled springs of nerves that twisted in the back of her neck. To make things worse a child in the car in front of her had been staring right at her for the past twenty minutes. The boy, who couldn't have been more than five, pressed his face into a pink blur against the rear window and squirmed his body into the space between the window and the top of the back seat. Then he twisted his face and licked the glass with a rudely stuck-out tongue. It was almost impossible to ignore him and Rita found herself having to close her eyes. This was one of the few times when she was glad she'd never had children.

She and Mark had come to that decision without too much discussion since both were so committed to their work. Despite that, she still felt a sense of nagging guilt and incompleteness when confronted by mothers pushing strollers or fathers dealing with tired toddlers or friends whose wallets were filled with photographs of their budding young hockey player or ballet dancer or karate expert. She'd eventually convinced Mark to cut young parents from their list of friends but he hadn't wanted to.

Forty minutes later she was leaning over the rail of the ferry as it scudded through the winter waters towards Vancouver Island. On either side of the channel, cedar, spruce and pine trees appeared as ghostly frosted triangles against the slate grey sky. The bitter wind dampened her hair and slapped strands of it across her face, chilling her but reviving her senses. It had taken five gruelling years to move house four thousand miles across the Atlantic. She'd sold off the mews flat and the TV business and re-established herself with a string of video rental stores. But the house in Roker remained hers. Empty except for a weekly cleaning service who kept it spotless. She hadn't the heart to sell it.

The move had meant a welcome scaling back of activity – a time to sit back and enjoy life though Mark had relocated his interior design business in the bustling and cosmopolitan city of Vancouver. Now she and Mark had a whole week to spend together in their latest acquisition – the beach house at Rocky Point. A week together. The thought made her breathless with panic. How to fill that time? What to talk about? There'd be endless opportunities to relax, make love, walk along the beach, have drinks in front of a blazing fire and cosy candlelit dinners for two – the images were worthy of vintage soap opera scenes – but the truth was that she dreaded all of these. The truth was that she wished she could spend Christmas alone walking along the cliff tops or sorting out pebbles and driftwood on the beach.

The price of financial success had been steep. They'd simply become business partners and at thirty-seven Rita felt she had nothing to offer Mark.

Sometime during the next ten minutes, Rita reasoned to herself that if she could get plastered enough she could get through the first night with Mark who'd be waiting eagerly at the ferry terminal to take her to the beach house. The bar looked inviting – its golden light spilled out onto the deck, and she was determined to enjoy at least part of this day. Drinking alone was no problem for her. She did it all the time.

She installed herself in the lounge and sat back on a navy velvet easy chair. The circular sweep of windows let in the winter sky and the dark blue waters of the Northern Pacific. Two white tinsel Christmas trees covered in red mini-lights stood by the buffet table and the piped in sounds of *White Christmas* tinkled through the air. It calmed her and she felt faintly festive. Christmas last year had been a great success according to their inner circle of friends. Parties every night in the West Vancouver condo – the whole suite done up in white lights and ribbon-wrapped garlands. There'd been at least twelve people over for Christmas dinner and the party had gone on well into the night until two a.m., when they all trooped down to the harbour in ski jackets for a late night cruise on someone's yacht. But this year it was just going to be the two of them: Rita and Mark. Alone for the first time in God knows when. *If only the ferry could go on cruising for the whole week*, she thought, she'd be perfectly happy to celebrate with the other travellers – strangers who'd demand nothing more of her than witty conversation and a few choice jokes.

After two large gin and tonics, she loosened the top buttons of her black jacket and leaned over to pick up a newspaper from the table. It was a copy of the London Times, which wasn't really unusual since there were so many transplanted Brits on Vancouver Island. She began to flip through it while knocking back a third drink. It was then she found the article on the colliery closures in the Durham coalfield. The headline read, *Miners' Strike Tragedy* and, scanning the article she discovered two young lads had died trying to pick coal from a colliery waste heap. Her heart sank when she realized the hardship they must have been going through to resort to that.

She'd heard about the strike from her Dad when he phoned and ranted on about how the newspapers were saying Scargill and the miners were traitors. Some even claiming he'd met with Libyan leaders. And now public opinion had swung against them, the old solidarity he'd fought for had disappeared. She scanned the article and saw a small inset photograph showing a man shielding his face from the press with a rolled up newspaper and the caption underneath read, *Miners' union struggles against Thatcher who calls the miners "the enemy within" – Durham union leader, George Nelson refuses comment to press.*

That's when she began to rifle through her bag for a hanky and found instead one of the rhinestone earrings George had bought her. After all his work, he'd been branded a traitor. In her haste to take off one of the diamond studs – Mark's gift to her on her thirty-fifth – and put on the tarnished ladybird, she dropped the tiny earring on the floor. Her head whirled as she scrabbled around under the coffee table trying to find it.

"Is this what you're looking for," said a voice that seemed to come from a great distance. A young man in his mid-twenties with layered hair and a khaki trench coat, held the earring out to her. "It bounced right inside my shoe," he laughed.

Rita flopped back into the armchair exhausted. Finding out that you'd been living a lie for ten years was like being knocked over the head with a baseball bat. Dazed, she took the earring from him. "Thanks – want to join me?"

"Don't mind." He took off the trench coat and draped it over the seat. "Can't spend any more money on the pinball."

They downed the next two drinks in record time, and then moved on to shooters, laughing as they knocked back two, three or possibly four B52's. At one point in the evening they were up at a mike singing *Yesterday* together and when the ferry pulled in at the dock, she walked out arm in arm with him and almost rolled down the steps – a blubbering mess with bloodshot eyes, standing on two shaky legs to face Mark's strained and angry face.

"Couldn't wait to get loaded?" he said through thinly drawn, disapproving lips.

The first two days of the holiday were spent in stony silence. Silence was Mark's weapon of choice and he was an expert at wearing down his opposition. After two days of that treatment, Rita was usually begging for some kind of interaction – in the past the silence was broken when she agreed to make love to him. She'd realized by now that in some twisted way Mark saw this as the signal for victory – a sort of conquering of the whole body – a complete subjugation after which he was prepared to make peace.

This time was different. This time Rita welcomed the silence. She walked along the cliff tops then down along the beach for hours at a time; occasionally she stopped to read but most times just sat and gazed across the water. Heavy rains had left the grass green and lush and down below the winter surf pounded at the sandstone cliff walls. The ocean boiled and frothed around the rock mounds that lined this wilder part of the beach and she amused herself by throwing down twigs and pebbles into the waves.

It was time to end their relationship. The prospect of spending the rest of her life in this lie was impossible. Over and over she rehearsed the lines that would make for the cleanest, most bloodless break but she soon realized that she was afraid of confrontation and lacked the guts to actually face Mark to tell him. She could simply write a letter and leave, or just disappear and live like a gypsy travelling down through the U.S and Mexico, but she could never leave her parents without any word. With her head swirling from all the possibilities, she found herself jogging back and forth along the winding cliff road, putting off the time when she'd go back to the beach house with all this guilt written over her face.

When she got back after a three hour combination walk and run, she was fully prepared to watch a movie alone with only a bottle of wine for company, but as she pushed through the open door, it became clear that Mark had other plans. The dining table that looked out onto the sea was decorated with candles and poinsettias. The savoury smell of roast turkey filled the air. She stood frozen for a moment, clutching the rhinestone ladybird in her left hand. There was no sign of Mark. She crossed the living room and peeked round into the kitchen where he sat at the dinette table with his head supported on one hand, the ridiculous Tuscany apron knotted at the back of his neck. Rita's stomach lurched when she realized that pots were burning on the stove. Maybe he'd found out about the way she was feeling and couldn't take the news. For that reason she didn't know whether to comfort him or tough it out and make the break.

"I've decided," she faltered, stepping closer to him. "I've decided…."

He looked up at her and ran his fingers through the front of his hair. "Rita – It's mum – I don't know what to do – we'll have to pack up and go. Mum's had a stroke. They need us there as soon as we can catch a flight."

Rita's heart rate fell again. "I'll start packing right away."

1988
Langley Castle Hotel

42

Rita woke to the sound of a rooster crowing, its strangled cock-a-doodle doo ringing through the tail-end of her dreams. The room was quiet except for the buzzing of the fridge in the mini-bar and the faint clinking of breakfast dishes coming from downstairs.

She lay flat on her back and squeezed her eyelids together. They were puffed-up and sore like sausages. Feeling chilled and semi-conscious she sat up to see grey light streaming in through the window. *Where was she?* And then the room came into focus and she realized she was home. Really home. In a hotel room only a few miles away from where Crag Street used to be.

A small voice in her head said she should phone Mark – to see if he was all right. They'd been together for over fifteen years and she still worried about him, hoping above all else that he'd find someone – or perhaps he already had. She'd give him a few days, she decided; let him cool off and then she'd phone and say how sorry she was for all the years of neglect. There were a lot of people to say sorry to. She didn't know where to start.

Reaching out, she checked her travelling clock. It was 8:16 a.m. but *how long had she been sleeping?* The last thing she remembered clearly was when she'd sat on a pile of rubble in the middle of what used to be Crag Street. Then she had a faint memory of getting back in the taxi and crying all the way back to the hotel. She must have slept right through till the next day. Now she was starving and called room service for tea and some breakfast.

"A good breakfast'll put yer in fine fettle – *if yer all wrong it'll put yer right*," her mam always said and so, when breakfast arrived she had the girl set everything up on the table by the window; a bowl of fresh strawberries, poached eggs on whole-wheat toast, grapefruit juice and a large silver pot of tea. It was a green day outside with great view of trees and wide spans of moorland and forest. The food looked so appetizing and she tried to eat but the toast was like dry cardboard, the eggs cool and rubbery and the strawberries sour and tasteless. Tea – hot, sweet tea was all she could manage. She left the dishes outside and crawled back into bed.

Later – she didn't know how much later – the phone rang somewhere in the hotel room and she realized her cheeks were soaked with tears again. *Pick it up*, she told herself but it seemed to be ringing in the far distance. On the table, in a corner where the ceiling sloped downwards. *Ringing, ringing* but she couldn't remember what time it was. It stopped and started again and so she stumbled across the floor and picked up the receiver – her link to reality and to the present.

"Caught yer," the high-pitched voice said and all the fogginess was sucked away.

"Mam?" she said.

"Yer not lookin' after yersel – I can hear yer've caught a bit cold".

"No – no – I was just sleeping,"

"You're a sly one. Comin' up here for the grand opening and not lettin' on yer here. Olive Coombes saw yer, hinny – wandering round the ruins of Crag Street. Why are yer hiding yersel? I would've come with you."

Right then Rita wanted to bury herself in her mam's lap and cry but she still had some unfinished business to work through. "I'll come over for supper tomorrow and we'll make plans for the big day, mam. O.K?"

"Champion," she says, "I'll get a joint of beef out for yer. By, yer'll never guess, Rita. Poor old Ella Danby passed away last week. Walked out of the old folks home and got hersel' to Whittington Hill, climbed all the way up and collapsed at the top. Some folks in The Collier's Arms saw her looking across the fields and then she just toppled over. Hard to believe the meddling ard wife's finally gone."

"I can't believe her tongue's finally stopped flapping," said Rita. "Someone up in heaven's gonna get a shock when she starts up the gossiping there."

"Or she'll torment the demons in the other place," said Iris. "And you'll never guess who paid for a slap-up funeral."

"Did she have a rich cousin?" said Rita.

"George Nelson," said Iris. "He walked by the coffin as if she was his long-lost aunty."

Rita couldn't speak. She felt so fragile she would have burst into tears and then her mam would have ridden a racehorse to get there quickly and comfort her.

"Eeh – I'm sorry hinny – I shouldn't have mentioned him though he will be at the grand opening."

"I know," I said. "I've seen the guest list."

She hung up and took a miniature bottle of gin from the mini-bar, screwed the top off and drunk it down straight. "That one's for you, Ella," she said, holding the empty glass up to the light. "You were a sad, meddling old bugger but you kept the street alive." Then she devoured a fruit and nut bar, a Crunchie and a bag of crisps.

After a long, hot shower she put on her favourite black sweater and jeans, scraped her hair into a ponytail and put on her biggest pair of sunglasses.

Later she took a trip to Belton Park to see the old colliery pit wheel. Buried in the middle of an ornamental flower garden and painted high-tech blue like a plant stand for geraniums. She didn't know what to make of it. *Mark would have loved the colour, would've raved about post-industrial symbolism and the technological revolution,* but Rita hated it. Two centuries of madness and the only thing to commemorate the existence of the coalmines was a painted wheel surrounded by daisies. All the suffering forgotten. The years of crawling and digging underground, the dust-coated lungs, the wives and families at home, the falling ceilings of rock and the suffocating gas that wiped out men in a matter of seconds. Not a trace of it was left. It was all gone – just another chapter in a history book.

Next she left a bunch of yellow freesias on Maggie's grave. Maggie loved freesias. Said her idea of heaven was a bunch of yellow freesias, the colour of sunshine, set in the middle of a picnic tea spread out on a white cloth. "It would be a hot July day, with the grass blowing and all the bairns running and playing and picking buttercups. The babies were my pleasure," she said, "And when they'd gone I had nothing left. George gave me some of that happiness back so I could never hate him for leaving."

Maggie was so unselfish thought Rita. She grasped at pleasure and cherished it like a child grabs a shiny bauble, then stores it in a treasure box. Not like Rita, a greedy, withered soul hoarding her riches.

"You've become bitter and boring," Mark told her before he finally left. "You act like you've missed something and now you're making everyone pay for it." *He was dead right.*

She walked back to the rental car sick with guilt. She'd missed out on George and punished herself and everyone else for it. The worst part was the way she lied to Mark, told him she didn't want children – said their lives were too chaotic to give a child a chance of any stability. The truth was she'd always wanted George. She'd have given up the money in an instant for him. Instead she stayed with Mark out of some sense of duty and their marriage had become like another branch of the business. She'd never loved Mark but knew he'd survive without her. He'd been doing it already for the last ten years. Deep in thought, she'd lost track of time and, checking her watch realized she was late for a dinner date with a very important person.

The dining room was quiet – just a few tables filled with businessmen and the occasional well-heeled tourist anxious for a stay at a real castle. Rita felt suddenly self-conscious of her scruffy jeans as she stepped into the candlelit room, but her worries melted away when a striking woman stood up from the table in the corner and rushed forward to greet her.

"Hazel," said Rita, hugging her so hard she almost knocked her off her feet.

"I suppose you're glad to see me then," said Hazel holding her at arm's length to look at her. "You look so young you crafty bitch – what's your secret?"

Rita looked back at Hazel. With her glossy dark hair and well-tailored suit she looked every inch a confident businesswoman. "Looks like the shops are doing well then." She said, thankful she'd sold four of her shops to Hazel at such a low price; Hazel had paid them off years ago.

"Life is great," said Hazel, guiding her to the table. "And you?"

Rita sipped at her water. "Let's talk about you first. How's the family?"

"Ray is great and the kids are into the teen phase. Amy wants to be Madonna and Paul's dying to visit the USA. Life is busy but that's the way I like it."

Rita ordered a bottle of champagne. "We'll toast our friendship and the return of the prodigal daughter to the place where her heart belongs."

Hazel's eyes filled with tears as she reached her hand out to Rita. "Are you staying this time?"

"I might have to," said Rita. "No matter how far I run I can't escape the clutches of this goddamn place," she said, smiling through tears. "And the bloody people in it."

"That's true," said Hazel. "Once we get our claws into you, you're stuck with us for life."

"I visited your mam's grave," said Rita, looking down at the table-cloth.

Hazel cleared her throat. "We try to get there once a week – to keep the flowers fresh. You know me Dad's still in the asylum?"

"Do you ever see him?" asked Rita, nodding at the waiter and holding up a hand. Now was not the time to pop the cork.

"I can't bring myself to go. They tell us he's far-gone. Just sits and stares out the window. Pearl went once or twice but he didn't know her."

"There's another reason I wanted to see you first," said Rita, swallowing hard. "Your Mam asked me to tell you about something and I should have done it long ago."

Hazel held her glass out and Rita poured the champagne. The bubbles fizzed and sparkled. "You're not my real mother are you?" she said laughing.

"And what would be wrong with that you little minx?" said Rita feeling the bubbles tickle her nose. "It's something that I think will make you very happy."

"Just tell me," said Hazel, pursing her lips. "C'mon."

"I have something for you," said Rita rustling around in her purse and finding the old photograph. "This is your father."

Hazel's face suddenly drained of its colour. "I knew all along Jordy wasn't my dad. I had a gut feeling and then once when he was hitting her he said as much, but I never asked her – I was too scared."

"I should've given you this a long time ago but too many things got in the way. He was called Chuck, an American from Wisconsin – your mam told me to tell you that you were conceived in a moment of pure happiness."

Hazel smiled. "I like that, Rita – because all the others were born out of fear. It makes me feel sort of special."

"And he was a handsome lad," said Rita.

"Sometimes me mam had good taste," said Hazel. "Now fill up my glass and we'll drink to good old Chuck."

"To Chuck," they said, chinking the glasses together and drinking.

"I feel like I've been reborn," said Hazel. "I'm half American – maybe now I can change my birth certificate and take Paul over there."

Hazel's joy was infectious and Rita realized how much she'd missed her. "There's an address on the back of the photo. I'm sure you can find him. Maybe he'd be happy to see you."

"I'll take it slowly," said Hazel. "It's just enough to know about him and see his face. He was a good looker all right."

Next morning Rita woke at six-thirty still wearing her clothes from the night before. She was exhausted but light-headed – probably from the late night and the champagne. The numbers on the travelling clock glowed red in the half-light, so she stumbled out of bed and threw the curtains open. The room filled with a burst of sunlight and the deep blue sky spread out like a watercolour with mackerel clouds brushed across it. *How she'd missed it.* Her heart ached with the joy of it all. At the larks swooping down into the hedgerows, the carthorse nuzzling into a milk churn on the far side of the farmer's fence, at the row of stone cottages snaking raggedly across the top of the hill.

She pushed the window and smelled the breeze thick with the scent of lavender. *Magic.* It had to be because it made her move a chair to the wall below the window, climb up on it and slip through onto the windowsill. The field was only a few feet below her so she flopped down barefoot into the grass then ran like a madwoman, across the farmer's field and over to the hedge overlooking the valley.

The small scar on the landscape that was once Crag Street was barely visible. But this was still her world. The rows of houses waking up to the sound of the milkman, the early bus swishing down the High Street picking up the morning workers, the paper boy delivering The Echo, the newsagent setting out the Walls' ice cream sign. And then there were memories of the mines. In each front room, a miner's lamp on a fireplace, a carved pit pony on the sideboard, a plate painted with the Belton pithead, photographs of brothers, sons, fathers and grandfathers long dead, a coal shed filled with bicycles and newspapers and rusted paint tins. Now she felt like shouting out for everyone to hear, "Rita Hawkins is back home again – *and in the best of spirits."*

When she sneaked back through the front lobby of the hotel, with sodden jeans she left a trail of wet footprints in the plush carpet. The receptionist peered over the desk and adjusted her glasses.

"Jogging barefoot," Rita said. "Therapeutic for the calluses."

Later that afternoon she drove along the Roker sea front, her elbow resting on the car window frame. The benches on the promenade were empty since it was Tuesday afternoon and there were few visitors on the beach. Small whitecaps ruffled the North Sea and a red boat bobbed in the water – a single fisherman out for a late catch.

She hadn't been there in fifteen years – since she left the house on Roker Avenue. When she moved to Canada, everything was left in its familiar place but covered with white dustsheets – like a mausoleum. On visits home she always ended up checking into a hotel but today she felt the urge to drive by and see just how overgrown the garden had become or how many windows had been broken. She pulled up outside the front door. Was it just a trick of the sunlight that made the stained glass window on the front door sparkle? Even the brass doorknocker gleamed as if it had just been polished?

The rowan tree in front of the house was clipped into a perfect dome shape and the borders planted with rows of lupins, dahlias and purple pansies. At the back of the house the small oval lawn was clipped like a patch of green velvet and all over the flowerbeds a profusion of blue and white lobelia sprouted like clouds of tiny stars. She dropped to her knees and ran her hands over the flowers, remembering the afternoon of the Big Meeting when she'd run through the Durham streets with George holding her hand. The lobelias had sprouted from pots on the old sandstone balcony. She wasn't ready to go inside. It was time to see her parents and thank them for looking after the place so well.

She walked into their bungalow at half past five. Walter was watching telly and Iris scorched her fingers on the hot pan when she dropped it into the sink and ran over to hug Rita. Rita held her mother, realizing she was thinner and very light-boned and had to look up to touch Rita's face with the oven gloves still on her hands.

"Eeh, I'll ruin yer suit with these," she said, dropping her hands in confusion. "They're full of beef drippings."

"Who cares, mother," said Rita looking at her white hair. "You've lost weight since I saw you last year."

"We've been eating plenty of yoghurt and fresh fruit – after that trip to the Okanagan – eeh we loved the peaches and cherries."

"What's thoo been deein'," Walter says, taking a minute from the Sunderland – Burnley football game to peer through bi-focals at Rita,

The Pitman's Daughter

standing in front of his armchair and chewing her lip like she'd never been away.

"I've travelled four thousand miles and that's all you can say."

"We just saw yer last September – anyway Joe Barker says he's seen yer moonin' around Belton Memorial Park looking like yer've lost ten pound and found sixpence."

"It's nothing, da, I just needed time to sort some things out."

Iris stood in the background holding a tea towel, "Eeh hinny yer not well – yer need a good, strong cup of tea."

"Nowt wrong with her that a good man and a few bairns couldn't sort out," Walter said.

"It's not as simple as that, da."

"What about that – what's his name? Mark or summat – the one with the silver spoon up his arse."

"Walter leave our Rita alone now," Iris said, "yer know she'll be upset about the divorce."

"It's alright mam – we're not divorced yet, just separated."

"Mek yer mind up," Walter said, "yer are or yer aren't." His head jerked back to the television. "Why, yer bugger, a penalty – I'd like ter murder these referees."

Iris set out tea and her famous lemon slices. She had a shiny new set of English Roses china and the tablecloth was still creased from the packaging. "You're back to your old habits again, mam, shopping with a vengeance," said Rita, chewing on the buttery pastry.

"Why we don't have to worry thanks to you – eeh, I love yer suit, flower – that pale green always did look nice on yer."

"I'll take yer shopping, mam – I saw some lovely coats in Newcastle."

"Eeh yer that generous with yer money, Rita."

"Yer a canny lass, Ma," said Rita squeezing her hand, "I've missed you."

"Money can't buy everything yer na's," Walter interrupted. It was half time, so he could take a breather. "Yer far ower ard to be traipsing around the place on yer own – a woman your age."

"Give ower, Walter." Iris said. "She's got a successful career and that's something to be proud of."

"Aye but it won't keep her warm at night or be company for her when you're gone."

Rita didn't feel the urge to answer back any more. She just sat back and let her mam give him heck. They were always at each other's throats, anyway – nothing had changed. Rita suddenly realized their relationship actually thrived on the nagging and the nit-picking – the attention to the tiniest details. They even argued about what underwear she should buy him. *Maybe that's what intimacy is really about* she thought.

At that moment the front door flew open and Lenny and Bill walked in, a little balder and thicker around the waist than before, but still inseparable. Both married, they lived three doors from each other.

"How's tha deein', Sis," Lenny hugged her until her feet lifted off the ground. "There's nowt left of yer, flower."

"By yer look smashing, stranger," Bill said, kissing her on both cheeks and chucking her under the chin. "How're the Vancouver Canucks deein'." Bill had become an ice hockey fanatic since last time he visited her.

"I feel smashing and no – they haven't won the Stanley Cup yet – but it feels brilliant to be back here again. You know I never realized how much I missed the place – and you two. Come on," She led them both over to the table. "Tell me if you're the same two terrible twins."

"That's us," said Bill. "We do everything together – except getting it on with our lasses."

"Might be an idea though," said Lenny nudging Bill.

"Bloody perverts," Walter muttered. "On drugs no doubt."

"Shurrup da," Lenny turned to her as he shoved a whole lemon slice in his mouth. "Ard man's goin' senile." He winked.

"But we still put up with him – eh Da," said Bill.

Walter shuffled over to the head of the table. "Haddaway wi' yer now."

"So yer've been busy hobnobbing with all those high class business types," said Bill, draining a mug of tea "And where's what's his name – Mark?"

"We're separated now."

The Pitman's Daughter

"Bloody good job too," said Bill. "Thought his shit didn't stink, that one. Only time he came up here, I took him to the dog track – he drank wine and held a hanky to his nose – said he was allergic to animal hair or something."

Rita's Mam cooked all her old favourites. Baked ham, peasepudding, leeks, baked potatoes and all kinds of pickles.

Lenny and Bill make short work of two platefuls.

"How come yer not eating at home today?" Walter asked.

"I asked our Jinny what's for supper," Bill said, his mouth full of leeks, "and she says veggie sausages for yer diet – why I canna stand that rubbery stuff so I says I'm gannin' to me mam's house for some real food."

"Big day tomorrow, sis," Lenny winked at her.

"Yes – it'll be strange seeing all the old houses again – like they used to be."

"Irene Danby – that's Ella's cousin – her husband Tommy's, already seen it," mam said, passing her the pickled beets. "He's in construction yer know. Says it gave him a shiver when he went into Ella's old house. Says he expected the ard wife to pop out from under the table. Of course she was always hiding under there yer know from the insurance man. Never did believe in insurance that one."

"Aye, meddling old biddy," said Walter. "It's a wonder they could keep her in her coffin for fear she'd miss summat at her own funeral."

"Walter don't speak of the dead like that," Iris said as she cleared the plates.

Rita felt brave after two glasses of wine. "I hear the big union hero is performing the opening ceremony,"

"Aye – George Nelson – but he's a shadow of what he used to be," Walter said.

"What happened?"

"It's like this, our Rita – the lads in the union sold out on him."

"Da," Bill interrupted, his mouth full of chocolate éclair, "that's an old story and it's not the whole truth."

"Oh yes and how come you're sitting at home with twenty-six thousand pound in the bank and plenty of time on your hands? Both of you."

"We took the settlement Da," said Lenny, "What's the use of fighting if there's no jobs. Far ower better to tek the money and start summat else up."

"All you buggers wants hingin," Walter said, banging his fist down on the table and spilling tea on his saucer. Iris jumped up and rushed into the kitchen, returning with a wet tea towel to mop the new tablecloth.

"Yer sold your bairns' birthright." Walter continued. "After everything we fought for – all those years. He told yer to hold out but you were all far ower greedy."

"Will someone please tell me what this is all about?" said Rita.

Lenny explained. "The Coal Board offered us a buyout – we knew they were gonna close the pits – they offered us a thousand pound for every year in service – a lump sum yer na's. George Nelson wanted us to hold out – said we'd get to keep our jobs – get better wages and all, but we knew Maggie Thatcher would break us."

"And she did," said Walter, "broke a century of proud tradition. Judas's – yer sold yerself for a few pieces of silver."

"More than that Da – I'm not having my bairns see me go penniless in the dole queue," said Bill.

"So what's George doing now?" said Rita, hoping they wouldn't notice the tremor in her voice.

Walter ran a hand over his mouth. "He's a broken man – got nowt to lead any more. Does a few garden parties, writes a newsletter, teks tourists around Redhills. We sold him to the lions and he lost his faith."

"Yer Da's never got over it, have yer Walter, chuck," Mam said, hugging his shoulders.

Rita didn't feel hungry any more. Now that George didn't have a cause she wondered how he'd changed – and whether life had knocked the fight out of him too. "Did he – did he ever marry?" She tried to sound casual.

"Why?" asked Walter, "You had yer chance years ago with him and yer threw it away over that washed-out singer – what's his name?"

Iris flicked Walter's head with a tea towel. "Dinna start with that story again, Walter, it's all in our Rita's past now."

Lenny came up for air. "That bugger had a toupee and all, Carol Allen told me she'd tried to run her fingers through it when she was necking under the stairs with him. Lifted it right off his head. Oh sorry sis, did yer think you were the only one?"

"Some things never change," said Rita. "You're still picking on me."

"All right, we'll give over sis. George never married – he's been seen around with a few good lookers though," said Bill.

Rita felt a bubble of panic rising in her throat because she'd hoped he was waiting for her. Sitting in the shadows of the Light Infantry Chapel or leaning against the stone pillars of the cathedral, feelings unchanged, desire still strong. But as usual, when it came to the topic of men, she was like a child trying to read a racing form, stabbing blindly at chances and usually missing.

"You don't look too canny, Rita." said Bill, ruffling her hair.

"Nerves – that's all. I feel a bit edgy about tomorrow."

When she left the house the wind flapped the washing on the line outside, making the telephone wires dance up and down. The sun sank low in the sky. She looked across at the seafront and the grey expanse of sea. She would see him tomorrow which meant it would be impossible to sleep tonight.

43

Next day was warm and summery again when Rita drove through the gates of Wolverston Museum. She parked in the V.I.P section and walked through the old town centre with its colourful tramcars and strings of brightly coloured bunting. It was like moving backwards in time – to a time before hers. There was a neat little Victorian bandstand on a lush village green and a street of brown brick shops with the old posters plastered over their walls. She recognized the old cigarette, cough syrup and chocolate signs. A conductor in a smart navy uniform and wire-rimmed glasses welcomed tourists into the maroon and white tram with its open upper level and a brewer's dray pulled by two fine black horses *clip clopped* by.

Her feet barely touched the ground as she walked through the crowds until she stood outside the little street of houses from Crag Street. They looked so different standing in a rolling green valley instead of huddling between the grey slag heaps of the mine.

She walked along the row of clean, scrubbed houses. Each one seemed like a polished, empty shell and as she walked she tried to imagine the people who had once lived there. The children playing, neighbours gossiping, the shouting, arguing and laughing. The joy and pain of all the people who had ever passed through those doors. But she

The Pitman's Daughter

heard nothing. Strangers wandered in and out and each cramped little room was carefully replicated down to the last detail of coronation cups and framed photographs of someone else's children.

In one house false teeth soaked in a glass of water on the scullery windowsill. She laughed and remembered Nana when she got her first set of dentures and said they were like vices torturing her gums. The old lady had passed on ten years ago but Rita suddenly felt her presence now.

Tourists with cameras slung round their necks walked through familiar old rooms, laughing at the tin bath hanging on the wall – pointing at the chamber pot under the bed. She scowled at their ignorance. Didn't they know how her dad and brothers suffered to give these people electricity to run their irons and vacuum cleaners?

It was hard to step into her old house. She stood outside for a long time trying to picture how it used to be. How she used to play with her dolls in the yard. How she was afraid to go out into the street for fear of running into Carol Parker. Finally she stepped over the threshold. She barely recognized it. In her mam's kitchen a woman dressed in neat white overalls made bread, transferring the loaves calmly from oven to table. Perfect golden loaves to be put on display – sliced thinly and spread with margarine, not butter. Like an intruder in her own house, she stared at the woman. "Can I help you?" the woman asked but her voice seemed a million miles away. Rita couldn't stay here.

Hurrying outside she heard a band playing. Someone was singing *The Ash Grove How Graceful*, and she walked like a sleepwalker – eyes straight ahead, oblivious to the milling crowds, the children with bright balloons, and the tram-cars brimming with tourists. The whole place had been cleaned up, brushed down and made chocolate-box pretty. Even the pit wheels were glossy with not a scrap of coal dust on the rows of gleaming black coal tubs. She was all polished and painted too. The pitman's daughter, nicely turned out in a pale green silk dress. Hell, she could be another exhibit in the museum and she'd have a heck of a story to tell.

She wondered if George had changed much – aged, lost his hair, grown plump. "He's still gorgeous," Iris told her last night, just before

Rita left. She'd winked and said. "Hair's a little greyer – but no paunch – not like yer Dad."

Passing Ella's old house, she stopped and touched the step with the toe of her shoe. So many stories had been told here. And Maggie's house was unrecognizable with its brand new coat of red paint on the woodwork. Jordy had never lifted a finger to paint anything in all the years they'd lived there. Swarms of visitors streamed down the street towards the bandstand where the opening ceremonies were set to begin in fifteen minutes.

The sweet shop was next. She stopped and let the crowds pass by until she was alone by the stone wall bordering the front yard. The ribbon cutting could wait until she found the courage to walk inside the place they'd first met.

Not a soul was around when she climbed up onto the concrete step and looked in the window at the display of sweets, remembering Ida's pale old face. She grasped the brass door handle and let the door swing open into the dark front room separated from the back by a heavy curtain. She stepped inside and there was the samovar – smaller than she remembered. A breeze rumpled the fine lace curtains. The air was cool. On the mantelpiece a clock ticked loudly. Two armchairs stood empty by the fireplace and a row of pipes gleamed on the mantelpiece by a picture of a boy with fair hair parted to the side and wetted down. He was standing by the fence in front of the Colliers' Arms at the top of Whittington Hill. She kissed a finger and touched it to the glass, her body tingling.

Afraid to disturb the magical silence, she tiptoed to the sideboard, which was decorated with a mass of framed pictures. Many were of George. George and his mother at the seaside, George speaking at the Miners' gala, George in London in front of 10, Downing Street, George receiving a prize at school, George wearing a miner's helmet. But at the front of the display was a small black and white picture – fuzzy and slightly blurred – but unmistakeably a photo of a small girl with ringlets and a starched dress. A cut-glass goblet of blue and white lobelias sat by the side of the picture. Rita's face flushed, her heart felt a sudden rush as time seemed to shift backwards. It took a minute to register the clinking sound of flowerpots outside. She drifted towards the long striped curtain that hung in front of the garden door.

When she pushed it aside, a blaze of sunlight blinded her. Tiny dots blurred her vision. A fair-haired man in a navy suit was bending over the flowerbeds picking blooms from the carpet of blue and white lobelia. The sun warmed her body and a wide smile spread across her face when he smiled back, as if seeing her there was the most natural thing in the world.

1992

Rita took off her shoes at Roker beach and dug her bare toes into the gravelly sand. She tiptoed along the shore enjoying the bite of the seawater on her feet as the waves washed like liquid lace across her skin.

Tiny chips of coal washed onto the shore with the pebbles, shells and seaweed. Fifty, sixty, seventy years ago men and women and children used to come to the beach, not to eat ice cream and play, but to gather sea coal. They scraped up the coal into tin buckets, flour sacks or rusted wheelbarrows and took it home to keep them warm in the bitter cold winters. Others sold it to buy food.

She bent down and gathered a few pieces. They'd be beautiful for the rockery in her flower garden. She washed them until they glistened. Black, glittering carbon. It felt like a part of her – the building block of every living thing.

"We're just carbon in a different form, you know," she said, passing a piece to the fair-haired boy who paddled in the water beside her. "It took millions of prehistoric animals to make the Northumberland and Durham coalfield. All those beautiful creatures from the giant to the microscopically small, lay down to die and spread their riches into the soil. We dug it all out and burned it. It took a century and a half to get through most of the inland seams. But Dad says there are thick ribbons still lying deep under the sea that nobody can reach."

She turned and waved to George who stood on the sand, the breeze ruffling his hair. He waved back, smiling and her heart swelled with happiness. Every Sunday they brought their son to the beach to gather coal for the garden.

To put back into the earth a bit of what was taken out and give thanks for the joy and abundance they'd finally found together.

Acknowledgements

Thanks to the **Manitoba Arts Council** for their generous grants to support the development of the early drafts of this novel and to the **Manitoba Writers' Guild** which supported me in the Writers' Mentorship Program.

Thanks to Carol, Leslie, Melissa, Shirley, Felix and all the other members of the Advanced Creative Writing Program at the University of Manitoba for their enthusiastic support of the novel.

Thanks to Indigo/Chapters for their encouragement. This novel was shortlisted for the 2001 Chapters Robertson Davies First Novel in Canada Award.

About the Author

Marjorie DeLuca spent her childhood in the ancient cathedral city of Durham in North-Eastern England. She attended the University of London, became a teacher, and then immigrated to Canada where she lives with her husband and two children. She writes historical fiction as well as Young Adult Science Fiction.

For news of other books and new releases, follow Marjorie DeLuca at:
marjoriedeluca.blogspot.ca
www.facebook.com/marjoriedelucawriter

Other Books by Marjorie DeLuca

THE SAVAGE INSTINCT

Fact meets fiction in this dramatic novel set against the backdrop of real-life murderer, Mary-Ann Cotton's sensational arrest and trial.

England 1872: Clara Blackstone, a childless woman, unhinged by the mysterious events of her latest miscarriage, struggles to maintain her sanity and save her marriage when she journeys north to join her husband and make a fresh start. Her recovery is hampered by her growing interest in the disturbing and sensational trial of (real life) child murderer, Mary Ann Cotton and the increasingly cruel, controlling behaviour of her husband.

Available at Amazon.

Coming Out in October 2015

A PROPER LADY

Pygmalion meets *The Night Circus* in the story of feisty farm girl, Bonita Salt, lured by promises of fortune and transformation into the mysterious Miss Violetta de Vere's new beauty makeover business. Bonita is soon caught up in a web of deceit, fraud, immorality and murder that leads to a catastrophic event and a strange and dangerous journey to wreak vengeance and uncover the truth about her mentor.